# Whispers Through Time

## by

## Rosetta Diane Hoessli

**Whispers Through Time**

Cover Art by *Rae Monet*

The Wild Rose Press, Inc.
PO Box 708
Adams Basin, NY 14410-0708
Visit us at www.thewildrosepress.com

Publishing History
First Edition, 2021
Trade Paperback ISBN 978-1-5092-3815-6
Digital ISBN 978-1-5092-3816-3


Published in the United States of America

## Dedication

To my family, all dreamers. I love you so much.

Chapter One

A familiar pain stabbed through Sierra Masters' eyeballs. She pulled the shutters closed against the late afternoon sunlight, and once again a cloudy, pink-and-lavender aura tinted the walls of her study. Another migraine was coming on, and the meds would take at least a half hour to kick in. She padded barefoot across the cool Mexican tile and sank down on an overstuffed sofa. Closing her eyes, she prayed for relief.

Acutely aware of the new three-book contract lying near her keyboard, she pressed her fingertips against her temples and fought back tears of frustration. She'd spent every day last week staring at her blank computer screen for so long her eyes rebelled and her head exploded with pain. Without meaning to, she'd joined the throng of blocked writers and other creative misfits hiding out in the isolated, inhospitable region of the Big Bend in southwest Texas.

*Another day bites the dust. The words will never come.*

She was still embarrassed by how she'd had to beg her publisher to let her write this six-generation family saga—after all, they'd made a fortune from her work over the past three years. Still, she had to admit this contract was the best she'd ever received. But now her six-figure advance didn't seem to be working. The words wouldn't come.

1

It was all over. She'd never write again.

The cool silence within the thick adobe walls of her darkened study soothed her. Somewhere in the distance a telephone rang, but she ignored it. For one euphoric moment she drifted away from the pain. She closed her eyes, took a deep breath, and waited. It wouldn't be long now.

The soft knock on her door jarred her back to reality, and another pain stabbed through her right temple. She swore beneath her breath and covered her eyes with her forearm. "What!"

The door opened, and Lysette Kennedy, her cousin and chief assistant, peeked inside. "I'm sorry to bother you, but… Oh dear, you have another headache, don't you?"

"It's trying to go away," Sierra answered pointedly, "and it will if you leave me alone."

"Your mom called from Alpine. She says they'll stop here in the morning. Then they'll take their RV into the park to stay at the RV Village for a couple of nights. I thought you'd like to know that."

Sierra's nose went numb, a sign that the meds were finally kicking in, and she managed to nod with a little more enthusiasm. "That sounds great. I've missed them."

"Oh, and there's some guy out front who wants to see you. He says it's important."

"I didn't hear the doorbell."

"You never hear the doorbell. But he's out there."

"It's not important. Tell him I'm dead."

Lysette cleared her throat. "I don't think he's going away."

"If you tell him to go away, he'll go away."

"Oh, I don't think so. He says he's come all the way from Dallas to talk to you."

Dallas. Who did she know in Dallas? Suddenly her heart lurched. She opened one eye and peered at Lysette. "What's his name?"

"He wouldn't tell me. He just insists on seeing you. He says it's a surprise."

"What does he look like?"

Lysette answered without hesitation. "A young Robert Redford. It's uncanny."

Her mouth went dry, and she could hardly breathe. It couldn't be. He wouldn't dare. As she sat up, she waited for the pain to knife through her eyeballs again, but the headache was fading. She couldn't feel her face, but she didn't care. Anything was preferable to the torture of a migraine.

She eased herself to her feet. "I'll go outside."

"You don't want me to invite him in?"

"Absolutely not."

She made her way to the mirror hanging beside the door. The reflection looking back at her wouldn't be encouraging, especially to a male visitor. She looked like something dead.

"Should I bring y'all some tea or coffee out in the courtyard?"

"Not necessary. He won't be here long."

Sierra stood at the front door and watched as Hunter Davenport leaned against a dust-covered Jeep rental as if he had all the time in the world. He hooked his thumbs into the front pockets of his well-worn jeans, looking around with casual interest. Off to one side of the main house was an adobe guest cottage in which her caretaker, Colt Chambers, lived. Her thirty-four-foot motor home loomed beside it. Off to the other side was a flagstone verandah, outlined by a rock and cactus garden, upon which an elaborate oven-grill combination was centered. It was a perfect place to entertain, which she never did, or a spectacular spot to stargaze alone, which she did as often as she could.

He nodded, apparently unaware she was watching him.

She was trapped. If she screamed her fool head off, no one would hear her. She was a victim of her own selfish and overwhelming desire for solitude. No place else on earth offered the splendid isolation and remoteness of the Big Bend region of southwest Texas, and she, longing for solitude and privacy, had responded to its lonely call. But that might've been the biggest mistake of her life.

She threw open the screen door and stepped out onto the front porch, her hands on her hips, her eyes narrowed against the setting sun. She called out to him in an icy voice, "Hey! What do you want?"

Hunter didn't even appear startled as he turned and took a few steps toward the porch. "This ain't bad, honey," he answered in a mocking Texas twang. "You done good."

She ignored his sarcasm. "You're a long way from the main road. Are you lost?"

"Nope. I'm right where I want to be."

His phony drawl had disappeared. She stepped backward, heart thudding. She recognized that tone, even though she hadn't heard it in years. She had to come up with something that would throw him off guard so she could get back in the house and lock the door.

He walked toward her as if he had an eternity to cross the yard. She was rooted to the porch like a petrified stump, unable to take her gaze off his face. She could only pray he'd hurry and take what he'd come for.

The early evening autumn breeze tickled her cheek and seemed to whisper *don't do it...don't do it...don't do it...*

But she didn't listen. She couldn't. She did what she'd always done. She waited for him.

When he reached her, he took her in his arms and whispered her name. Her eyes filled with tears. As he cupped her face in his hands and their lips met, the heat flooding her body was so painfully familiar her legs nearly gave out. Her fingers were greedy for the feel of him; she couldn't get enough as he held her close. It had been so long.

She'd kiss him now and hold him tightly for a few moments more. Then she'd stop. She *had* to stop.

No one in the world was more dangerous to her life and her peace of mind than Hunter Davenport.

"My God, you're beautiful," he murmured. "You're still so beautiful."

She pulled away from him and gazed up into icy blue eyes, searching for the tenderness and longing he'd once felt for her. But his expression was veiled, unreadable. Like she remembered.

He was still handsome enough to make her heart stop, although he'd matured like everyone else. He'd shaved his beard, and he wore his blond hair a little shorter now, spikier, but she liked it. The cleft in his chin seemed deeper than she remembered. The faint smile lines just beginning to crinkle around his eyes made him even more attractive than the first time she'd seen him, nearly twelve years earlier.

She looked away from him, heart pounding. "You can't stay here."

"I know that. I've already got a room at the motel down the road."

"How did you find me?"

He chuckled. "I win awards for good investigative journalism. It wasn't hard. I think it took me about thirty minutes once I heard you were here."

"And where were you when you heard that?"

"Where everyone else was—sitting on the front porch of the trading post in Terlingua, drinking a beer, waiting for the sun to go down. When some lady said she heard you lived out here, everyone jumped on her like she'd just given away a nuclear code. So I knew she was talking about my antisocial Sierra Masters."

She ignored that. "Why did you come down here in the first place?"

"I'm working on a story. Discovering you is just a bonus."

She gave him a long, steady look. She didn't believe a word of it. "You told Lysette you came from Dallas to see me. You lied."

He shrugged. "It's part of my job."

"Well, you've found me, and it's been fun, and I'm sorry I won't be seeing you again." She took a step toward the door. "Be careful on your way out."

He cleared his throat. "Sierra, this isn't a social call. I'm here on business."

She cocked an eyebrow. "Ah, finally. The truth. What do you really want?"

"Have dinner with me."

"No."

He looked shocked. "Do you know how far out in the middle of nowhere you are?"

"Do you know what a stupid question that is?"

"I do. But I can't believe you would send an old friend you haven't seen in years away from your doorstep without even a square meal."

"Try me."

"Without even a glass of water?"

"You're breakin' my heart."

When he moved toward her, she raised her hands in warning and backed away. He halted.

"Sierra, I'm serious. The truth is, I've been researching a story, and I came across something that pertains to you. You have to trust me on this."

She stared at him. The word *trust* and the name *Hunter Davenport* were diametrically opposed. Still, his sober, intense expression told her this time he wasn't joking. This time he was as serious as death.

"What story?"

"Have dinner with me, and I'll tell you."

She shook her head. She'd done everything she could think of to get away from him, and yet here he was in the autumn of 2004, holding the same hypnotic power over her he'd always had. It had happened the last time she saw him, about three years ago, and the time two years before that. Something between them just sparked and crackled and had to be unhealthy.

She took a deep breath. "I don't want to see you again. It took me a long time to put my life back together, and I don't want you in it now. If you've ever felt anything for me, please go."

He was silent for so long she began to think he

7

wasn't going to answer her at all. His gaze was fixed on the Chisos Mountains far in the distance, the peaks of which blazed crimson and deep purple in the setting sun. The bleak expression that fled across his face seemed to match the darkening evening shadows moving over the desert floor, but she was determined not to give in. He had to leave.

"Have dinner with me tonight," he said finally. "I'll tell you what I came to tell you, and then you'll never have to see me again. I swear it on anything you want."

She searched his face, but nothing in his veiled expression gave him away. She surrendered. "We'll eat here. Come back at seven."

"I saw a steakhouse near the motel—"

"That's The Oven. It gets so loud I wouldn't be able to hear anything you say. We'll eat here, or we won't eat at all."

He gave a mock salute and winked at her, once more all charm and business. "Hey, you're the boss," he said with a grin. "I'll see you at seven."

Chapter Two

Sierra stepped out of the shower and wrapped her slender body in a fluffy white towel, then stood before a floor-length mirror and squinted to see her reflection through the steam. At least she looked rosy now and not like warmed-over death.

Hunter had often said she was beautiful, but she'd never quite believed him—perhaps because it wasn't important to her. Her father had reminded her many times her looks would fade someday, and she'd better have something more reliable to fall back on, like talent, intellect, or a decent sense of humor. She'd taken his advice to heart. If she was attractive, that was fine, but it didn't have much to do with who she was.

Besides, down in this part of the world, she lived and looked like the locals. The easy lifestyle appealed to her. She used moisturizer and lip balm instead of cosmetics. She parted her silky, blue-black hair in the middle and let it hang loose down her back, almost to her waist. Five feet tall and a little shy of a hundred pounds, she wore shorts, sneakers, and faded T-shirts almost year-round. Only when the desert evenings grew cold did she throw on her boots, blue jeans, and hoodies. She owned just three dresses and two business suits. They hung, lost and forlorn, in the back of her closet.

She was thirty years old now, but she thought she

still looked pretty good: wholesome, strong, and healthy. She was full lipped with an olive complexion, but her favorite feature had always been her eyes— slanted and penetrating with long, thick lashes, an unusual shade of light brown speckled with topaz gold. No one else in her family had eyes like hers, so that unique feature had always appealed to her. Yesterday she'd noted a couple of faint lines at the outside corners. She was getting some character in her face, and she liked that.

*Besides, Hunter thought you were beautiful this afternoon, and that was with a migraine.*

She caught her breath. It was happening again. For far too long she'd seen herself through Hunter's eyes instead of her own. She'd lost her true identity in her desire for him and his approval. And for far too long he'd been the most important part of her life.

*Of course, you were eighteen at the time, and everyone knows how silly eighteen can be. Well, truth be told, eighteen, nineteen, twenty…*

Lysette's voice came from the master suite. "Sierra, are you decent? I have the jeans and sweater you were looking for this morning. You want to wear them tonight?"

"Hold up a minute!" Sierra toweled herself dry, slathered moisturizer over her body, and slipped into a white terry-cloth bathrobe. She opened the door. "Thanks, sweetie. Where did you find them? I looked everywhere."

Lysette tossed her the missing outfit. "Everywhere but in the laundry room, which is where most logical people would look first." She entered the spacious bathroom and walked toward the fire blazing in a small fireplace beside a circular tub, her hands outstretched. After a few minutes, she pointed to a large picture window that opened onto a private courtyard, framing a towering mountain range beyond. "Look at those stars. It's going to be a cold one tonight. September's kind of early, don't you think?"

"This isn't the Texas hill country, sweetie. This is the desert. It can freeze any time it wants to."

"That's right. I keep forgetting. Oh, Conchita asked me to tell you she's fixed a chicken fajita and guacamole salad for tonight, mixed fruit for dessert, and raspberry iced tea. She also has some chardonnay on ice. You want anything else?"

"No, that'll be fine. I don't want her to go to a lot of trouble. He won't be here long."

"That's what I told her. How's your headache? You look a little flushed."

"My headache's gone. It's just steamy in here."

Lysette sat on the edge of the tub. Sierra pulled on faded blue jeans and a white turtleneck sweater, then twisted her long hair into a casual knot at the top of her head and clasped it with a claw-like barrette. Applying clear gloss on her lips and mascara on her lashes, she met her cousin's eyes in the mirror. Lysette gave a faint but knowing grin.

"What's so funny?" Sierra snapped, dropping the cosmetics in a drawer. "Have I sprouted two heads or something?"

Her grin broadened. "I've been down here with you for six months, and I've never seen you use one iota of makeup. For anyone. Who *is* this guy?"

Sierra was silent for a moment, unsure about whether or not to confide in her cousin. After all, they hadn't been that close until Lysette had moved down to help out. Finally, she decided it couldn't hurt. After all, she didn't have to tell her *everything*.

"His name is Hunter Davenport. We met in 1986 when I was eighteen." She hoped she sounded more casual than she felt. "I met him at a horse refuge near my dad's ranch in Bandera. I was writing one of my very first articles for a small magazine about abandoned and abused horses, and he came in with a film crew that day. They were putting together an exposé about wild horses being slaughtered out west, and the owner of this sanctuary was one of his sources."

She paused, brushing a bit of blush on her high cheekbones. "I found out later he was an investigative journalist on his way up, even though he was only twenty-four. But he got to name the stories he wanted to do, control his projects, and travel all over the world. I wanted that kind of independence. Anyway, I thought he was the most handsome thing I'd ever seen in my life. He was my first real mentor—among other things."

Her voice trailed away, and she studied her reflection in the mirror with a frown. Maybe she should wear a long turquoise pendent necklace with this simple turtleneck. She looked kind of plain and frumpy.

"Well, go on," Lysette prodded. "What happened?"

Sierra shrugged. "Nothing. We had a thing for nearly four years, but when I was twenty-two and ready to graduate from college, we went our separate ways. We both knew it would never work. I was obsessed with writing, and he lived out of a suitcase. He moved on, and so did I."

Their relationship sounded so simple when she recited the facts like that.

Lysette cocked her head to one side and ran her fingers through short, sandy-blonde curls. "Have you seen him since the split?"

"A couple of times. Nothing serious."

Suddenly, Lysette stood up. "I think I heard the doorbell. Don't worry. You look gorgeous."

After giving Sierra's shoulder an encouraging pat, she walked to the bathroom door and turned around. "Just remember who you are now—a successful woman in charge of your own life. But, in case you need saving, I'll be in my room."

Sierra nodded and gave a tentative smile, still staring at her reflection in the mirror. To her, the woman gazing back looked uncertain and almost unbearably young.

If she wasn't careful, history would repeat itself.

\*\*\*\*

Sierra and Hunter sat across from one another at a long mesquite wood table in the dining room. Flames crackled in the large pueblo-style fireplace, bathing the swirled adobe walls in warm red-and-yellow light. Navajo baskets decorated the walls, handwoven Southwestern rugs were scattered across Mexican-tiled floors, and french doors opened onto a small grassy yard sealed off by a privacy fence. The spectacular view of the mountains visible beyond the enclosure was Sierra's favorite.

Yet, even though the atmosphere was warm and welcoming, they ate in silence.

Her apprehensive gaze moved toward his briefcase on a small table nearby, but she didn't ask about it. Instead, as she sipped her chardonnay, she admired how the firelight danced across his face, illuminating the deep cleft in his chin and emphasizing the hollows beneath his cheekbones. Time and experience seemed to have removed all youthful softness from his features, replacing it with a hardened maturity she found even more attractive.

She was determined to find out why he was here and move him on his way as quickly as possible, so she couldn't dwell on how handsome he was. It was far too dangerous to her peace of mind.

He pushed his plate away. "That's the best salad I've ever had in my life. Did you make it?"

"You know better than that. I don't do kitchens."

"Still?"

"Still. Conchita Salazar de Leon is my cook and housekeeper. She does kitchens better than anyone I know."

"Does she want to get married?" Hunter asked hopefully.

"Sorry. She's already married to a huge Mexican *vaquero* named Esteban."

He sighed in mock disappointment. "Well, I guess that's that." He changed the subject. "Do you have horses? I didn't see a stable anywhere."

"I used to, but they're too high-maintenance. I ride when I visit my parents." She gripped her hands together so tightly her knuckles were white, but she couldn't relax. This strained conversation terrified her. Even the wine didn't help.

But he seemed undisturbed. "I'd love to see your folks. Does your dad still dabble in politics?"

"He does. And he's even more conservative now than when you knew him."

"Impossible. Last time we got into it, he made

Richard Nixon look like a left-wing radical."

Her fond chuckle was reminiscent. "You two used to fight about politics all the time. He called you a 'pinko commie,' and you called him a 'racist pig.' Yet you loved each other in spite of it."

"You're right. We did."

"Now he's involved in the fight against gun control, like all the ranchers in Texas."

He snapped his fingers. "That's what I'm missing. No animal heads on your walls. You don't hunt down here?"

"Everyone hunts, but I hunt at the Super S up in Alpine. Or, rather, my assistant Lysette does—with a carpool that goes up there every couple of weeks or so. It's the highlight of her social life, bless her heart."

He chuckled. "What do you do for fun the rest of the time?"

"We watch the cactus grow, what else?"

"Is that big motor home out there yours?"

She had a hard time keeping up with his rapid change of subjects, but she did her best. "Yes. I hate to fly, so whenever I have to tour or go off to research, that's how we travel. My caretaker, Colt Chambers, does the driving. He calls her *Roberta*, but I don't know why. I store her up in Alpine, but Colt's working on her right now, so she's here."

His voice was gruff. "And where does *he* live?"

"In that adobe guest house near the courtyard."

"Is he a cowboy?"

She shrugged. "Colt is like most everyone else down here—he keeps to himself. Sometimes he disappears for weeks, but it's okay. He's terrific at what he does. He can fix anything, and I need that. I can't change a light bulb without blowing something up."

"I know."

Her cheeks grew warm, and she looked away in embarrassment. "You remember that about me, do you?"

"You'd be surprised what I remember about you."

She fidgeted in her chair and stared at a colorful Mexican bowl set at the end of the dining table. She couldn't think of a thing to say.

He didn't seem to notice her discomfort. "So you have a cook, a housekeeper, an assistant, and a caretaker. Must be nice. I haul my own equipment, and I'm lucky to stay in a Motel 6."

"I've had a lot of Motel 6 days," she reminded him. "I've earned this. I've worked hard for it."

"I know how hard you work. I lived with you, remember?"

Now she stared down at her hands, still clenched into tight fists in her lap. *How could I forget? Those were the happiest, most miserable years of my life.*

"Well, with all these people to do things for you," he continued, "what do *you* do?"

She drained the last of her chardonnay. "You make me sound like a spoiled brat," she muttered. "I used to write, but now I'm thinking about returning to college to be a brain surgeon. It has to be easier."

"What's the problem?"

"I don't want to talk about it." She reached for the ice bucket near her plate. "More wine?"

"That's your third glass," he warned with a grin. "You'd better watch out."

For a fleeting moment she remembered the pain medication she'd taken earlier for her headache. It lasted for twelve hours, and she wasn't supposed to drink when she took it, but she put that minor detail out of her mind. She was a big girl. She could take care of herself.

"Don't worry about me. Do you want one or not?"

"No, thanks." He winked at her. "I guess I'd better talk to you before it's too late, huh?"

She poured herself another glass and shoved the bottle back into the bucket. "I guess you'd better."

"Okay, hear me out. You're not going to understand why I'm telling you this, but there's a reason, I promise. Can you hang with me?"

She squinted as she tried to focus on his face, then gave up and took a desperate gulp of chardonnay. "I'll do my best."

Chapter Three

Hunter glanced quickly at Sierra, a little concerned by the high color in her cheeks and her obvious nervousness as she poured herself another glass of wine. He needed her full attention, and he wasn't sure he was going to be able to keep it for long. She'd never been the world's greatest drinker.

He cleared his throat and asked, "Have you ever heard of the Pine Ridge Indian Reservation in South Dakota?"

She frowned. "I don't think so."

"Don't feel bad—most people haven't. But Pine Ridge has quite a history, and I thought you might be aware of it since you write historical novels."

"I don't write about cowboys and Indians. My primary interest is the American Revolution."

He recognized the irritation in her voice and backed away. "Fair enough. Do you know anything about the Black Hills or the Badlands of South Dakota?"

She shook her head. "Sorry."

*Damn.* He pushed his chair away from the table and stood up, then strode across the dining room, picked up his briefcase, and carried it back. He opened it, pulled a single photograph out of an interior compartment, and pushed it toward her. For the first time in years, he was nervous.

He sat back down. "What do you know about American Indians?"

She was silent a moment, then offered, "I saw *Dances with Wolves* three times. Does that count?"

He shook his head. "No. Take a look at these pictures, would you?"

As she peered at the aging black-and-white photograph he'd pushed across the table, Hunter tried to be patient. He'd viewed these photos so many times he'd recognize them in his sleep. In this one, a handsome, dark-haired Indian man wearing braids and a wide beaded choker spoke into a microphone. Another man whose long dark hair was held back by a leather, silver-studded headband stood beside him, his pockmarked face intent. Behind them were scruffy Indian children and a single teenaged boy holding up a rifle. Written in scrawling penmanship at the bottom of the photograph was *Taking on the Feds, March 3, 1973*.

She looked at him, clearly puzzled. "Who are they?"

"They're leaders of an organization known as the American Indian Movement or AIM. This was taken during what's known as the Occupation of Wounded Knee, 1973. Do you know anything about it?"

"No."

"How about the movie *Thunderheart*? Have you seen that?"

"No."

He held out his empty wine glass, more nervous than ever. "May I have another one? I'm having a little trouble here."

"I'm sorry." She passed him the bottle. "I'll try harder."

He sympathized with her confusion. He'd felt the same way in the beginning. After he'd filled his glass, he started over. "I saw *Thunderheart* not long ago, and it was a terrific movie. It was set on a fictional Indian reservation located in the heart of the Badlands of South Dakota. It woke me up to the reality of what it means to be an American Indian in this country…at least, in some places."

"Okay…" Her voice trailed away.

"Well, you know me—I had to start researching. I learned that back in the 1970s, a corrupt tribal chairman named Dickie Wilson ran the Pine Ridge Indian Reservation, and that's what *Thunderheart* was really about. Wilson had his own gang of thugs, called GOONs, which stood for Guardians of the Oglala Nation—"

"Wait a minute. What's Oglala, and why did they need guardians?"

"The Oglalas are one of seven bands of Lakota Sioux," he answered patiently. "The Pine Ridge Sioux Indians call themselves the Oglala Lakota."

She squinted at him. "Oh dear…"

"Come on, hang with me. Dickie Wilson and his GOONs joined forces with the FBI and the federal government. Most of the federal money that was supposed to go to the Lakota people went to Wilson's family and buddies instead. He turned nepotism into an art form while his people starved to death."

"Oh Lord, you're not going to go off on one of those bleeding-heart tangents, are you?" She looked at her nearly empty wine glass anxiously. "Because I took some pain meds this afternoon, and I may not be able to stay with you. What you're telling me is fascinating, but—"

"Sierra, please focus," he interrupted sternly. "Racism against Indians was terrible in South Dakota back then, and it got bloody both on and off the reservation. By the mid-1960s, Indians began to realize it was going to be open season on them again, like it had been a hundred years earlier. So, led by a man named Dennis Banks, they began to organize all over the country, and they called themselves the American Indian Movement."

"Like the guys in this picture?"

"That's right."

"Hunter, I'm trying to follow this," she blurted, "but I just don't see what it has to do with me."

He sighed. He'd known this was going to happen. It was too much information, too fast, too soon. "I'm sorry. I knew you wouldn't, but I wanted to give you some background. It's complicated."

She stood up. "Then let's go to my office, okay? I need coffee. Maybe that'll help."

****

As Sierra made her way down the narrow hall toward her study, Hunter walked close behind her. As always, his presence had a strange effect on her heartbeat, but this time it was something more. She sensed *his* anxiety, which was so uncharacteristic she had to fight panic.

Reaching the study, she opened the door and flipped on the overhead light, then gestured toward an antique oak table with four chairs placed between two large windows. "Sit over there. I'll be right back."

She headed for a small pantry located beside floor-to-ceiling bookshelves. This area provided an efficient little kitchenette—in case she could write again and needed to work around the clock. She flipped on the coffeemaker, which was always ready for a spontaneous call to duty.

"Do you still take your coffee black?" she called.

"I sure do. I can't believe you remember."

"Don't flatter yourself. I never forget anything."

As she waited for the coffee to finish percolating, she heard him open his briefcase in the study and shuffle through papers. She swallowed in apprehension.

His voice floated to her from the sitting area. "You know, I remember how much you always wanted an office like this. How did you end up down here?"

With a faint, reminiscent smile, she poured the coffee, carried it to the table, and placed a cup in front of him. She sat across from him and took a few sips of the steaming liquid before she answered.

"It was an accident. When my first novel, *Regina*, hit the stands a few years ago and went so big, so fast, I needed to get away from everything. I rented a little motor home for a couple of weeks and headed out I-10 toward New Mexico. But the scenery south of the freeway was so gorgeous I just had to see it, so I ended up down here in Old Terlingua. I couldn't resist it. The residents are eccentric, and the town is haunted. I had to stay."

He nodded but said nothing. He drummed his fingers on the table.

She waited until the silence threatened to explode. Finally, in a low voice, she said, "Whatever it is, you can tell me. I'm a big girl. I can take it."

He drew in a deep breath, then opened a large manila envelope and removed several photographs. He looked directly at her. "Sierra, what do you know about your parents?"

"I assume you have a good reason for asking such an idiotic question."

"I do." He shuffled through the photographs and put them into some kind of order. "Come sit by me. I won't bite."

Her curiosity got the better of her, and she moved around the table to sit beside him. The photo he pushed toward her depicted a slight incline in the middle of a flat prairie, at the top of which was an old cemetery. In front of the cemetery was an arched entrance with a single cross in the center. It looked familiar, but she wasn't sure why. The date at the bottom of this photograph read *March 5, 1973*, a couple of days after the first picture had been taken, and the photo was labeled simply *The Knee* in that same scrawling handwriting.

"This is the Wounded Knee Memorial," he explained. He pointed to a long and narrow stretch of ground beyond the arched entrance, outlined by rocks and bricks. "This is a mass grave for more than three hundred Indian men, women, and children massacred by the 7th Cavalry in December, 1890." He moved another photo toward her. "Now this was the church in Wounded Knee, in front of the cemetery. See, it's got the same date, March 5, 1973."

Then, without another word, he handed her a fourth photograph entitled *Trading Post at Wounded Knee*. A young woman stood beside what appeared to be a store, a camera slung over her shoulder. Her waist-length blonde hair was parted down the middle, and she wore snug hip-hugger jeans with psychedelic-patterned patches on the knees.

She frowned. "Wait a minute…is that my mother?"

He nodded, passing her a fifth picture. "And this is your father. Both photos are dated March 11, 1973."

She shook her head. "I don't get this. I knew my folks got married in January 1973, but I've never heard they left Texas, not even once. But here they are together, up in some old cemetery in South Dakota." She gave a rueful chuckle. "It's kind of funny. We never think of our folks as having a life before we were born, but mine must have."

Hunter seemed to have no intention of becoming philosophical; his face was grave as he handed her another photograph. "Now look at this one."

Her parents, long-haired and almost unrecognizable in their hippie attire, stood arm in arm, sandwiched in with several unsmiling, long-haired Indians holding shotguns and hunting rifles, probably AIM members, most of whom were wearing headbands and jean jackets. This photo was dated *March 12, 1973.*

Her ears began to ring. She swallowed hard. "I don't understand."

"Well, here's the historical chronology. On February 27, 1973, AIM members and their supporters rebelled against the corrupt tribal government on the Pine Ridge Indian Reservation. They took over and occupied Wounded Knee, which is sacred ground for them because of the 1890 massacre. For seventy-one days they stood against Dickie Wilson, his GOONs, and the United States military. I don't know how your parents came to be there, Sierra, but they had to be supporting the Indians in this protest. I admire them for that. I would've been there, too—if I'd been out of preschool."

But she was still a little miffed. "Wow. You never really know anybody, do you? My dad has called you a 'pinko commie' for years, yet here he was back in the day, fighting against the federal government with a bunch of pissed-off Indians. And God alone knows what my mother was doing."

He didn't respond. He was silent for so long she couldn't stand it anymore.

"What in the world is it?"

He took a deep breath, released it in a gusty sigh. "Sierra, I need you to understand something. I'm showing you this because I think you have a right to know who you are, not because I want to stir up trouble in your family."

The ringing in her ears grew louder.

His voice was low. "When's your birthday again?"

"You know when my birthday is. March 28, 1974."

He passed the last photograph to her. She stared at it, but she couldn't take it in. It made no sense.

The photo showed an exquisite and very pregnant American Indian girl, no more than fourteen or fifteen years old, standing between a stone-faced elderly woman and an expressionless younger one. Beside the older woman was an attractive White couple, looking so traditional and middle class that, at first, she didn't recognize them.

And then she did.

They were her parents.

Smiling and holding hands, Noah and Alexa Masters no longer wore patched bell-bottom jeans, and they seemed to be good friends with these three unknown Indian women. But none of that mattered. All that mattered to Sierra was the handwriting at the bottom of the photograph.

*March 23, 1974, Rapid City, South Dakota.*

A year *after* the Occupation at Wounded Knee had ended.

Five days *before* Sierra was born.

But that didn't make sense. That couldn't be right.

*Alexa Masters wasn't pregnant.*

And then, finally, she knew why Hunter had come.

She stood so abruptly her chair toppled over. Tears streaked down her cheeks as the full import of the photograph sank in. "Get out."

"Sierra, wait a minute—"

"Get. Out."

He stacked the photographs and opened his briefcase. He looked miserable.

She struggled for control; she couldn't breathe. At last, she managed, "Can you leave those pictures here?"

"No, I'm sorry. They're originals, and they aren't mine. I have to return them."

"Who do they belong to?"

"No one you know."

Her lips tightened. "Can I make copies? My parents are coming tomorrow, and I want them to see these pictures."

"No."

"Why on earth not?"

"They're part of my story. They're from a source, and I don't share sources—with anyone. But I'll come tomorrow and show them to your folks if you want."

Suddenly her legs gave out, and she sat down on the floor, hard, right next to her overturned chair. She buried her face in her hands and rocked back and forth, trying to make sense of everything...*anything.*

The blinding, throbbing pain behind her eyes returned.

He knelt beside her, but he didn't touch her. "It's all right, Sierra. This doesn't change who you are."

"Don't be insane. That little Indian girl must be my mother. My *mother.*"

"She probably is. So what?"

"*So what?* My parents have lied to me for thirty years! Do you know how that feels?"

"No. I don't."

She shook her head and covered her face with her hands once again. "Please go," she whispered. "Please. Just go."

## Chapter Four

*A young Indian girl runs down a deserted highway that snakes ribbon-like through hellish and unfamiliar terrain scarred by deep gullies and buttes as high as towers, like castles made of rock. A full moon fills the starless sky; an eerie wind howls through the night, whipping through her long hair, lashing at her cheeks and bare legs, stealing her breath.*

*A truck follows her down the highway. The driver is drunk and White and leans out the window—calling her name, laughing. The young Indian girl falls to her knees on the side of the road and cries out in pain. Blood trickles down her legs, but she gets back up and runs again. The truck stays behind her, comes alongside, drops back...the truck teases her, tortures her...*

*The young Indian girl knows what's going to happen. She knows she can't win...*

Sierra jerked awake and lay very still in her bed, her heart thudding in her throat. The moonlight streamed into her bedroom, helping her to get her bearings as she struggled to catch her breath. She'd never had such a dream—a dream so real it was like she was running *inside* the young girl, feeling her terror, smelling her fear, even *hearing* the silence in a place she'd never been before. She was afraid to close her eyes again, but she had to. She was so tired...

*A young Indian woman screams in a bed with no sheets. She raises herself to her elbows and pushes hard against another crushing wave of pain. She falls back against the pillow, exhausted. Water gushes, and blood explodes from her body. There's so much agony, so much...so much. The young Indian woman closes her eyes and drifts away, floating into a starless sky that blankets the deep gullies and tower-like rocks.*

*It's time. She's going home.*

*Then the sky opens like a wide tipi, and an old man with long silver hair moves toward her, his arms outstretched, welcoming her into a spirit world she never thought to see. His smile is tender as he tells her not to be afraid. They are waiting for her.*

*The young Indian woman's face is familiar and radiant as she enters the old man's embrace. The pain disappears, and joy overwhelms her.*

*She's free at last.*

Sierra sat straight up in bed, panting as if she'd just run a marathon. Tears streamed down her cheeks, and her heart thundered. She felt bereft and heartsick, like she'd lost someone she loved with all her heart and not just the unknown phantom figure in a dream. Finally, afraid to return to sleep, she threw back her blankets and slipped into her bathrobe.

She padded barefoot into the shadowy kitchen and prepared a cup of hot tea. Her hands shook, and her heart was still pounding, but at least now she knew where she was. She was in the real world, she hadn't had any babies, and she wasn't dead.

Yawning, she leaned against the kitchen counter and gazed out the window into the darkness beyond. Just a few miles down the road, Hunter was sleeping like an innocent in some lumpy motel bed, unaware of the havoc he'd just wreaked onto her life.

*How typical...*

Even before she finished that thought, she knew she was being unfair. He'd tried to leave, but she wouldn't allow it. If she'd let him go, taking those horrible pictures with him, she'd be sound asleep now instead of staring out a window at three o'clock in the morning.

But, no, she'd needed to keep him here with her tonight, for just a few minutes more, no matter what. She remembered the taste of his lips against hers, the feather-softness of his touch against her body, the heat of her hunger for him. Whether she wanted to admit it or not, she would've done anything to keep him from walking away from her tonight. Even if it meant she destroyed her own world.

Which she had.

And that wasn't his fault.

\*\*\*\*

The next morning, Sierra didn't recognize herself in the bathroom mirror. She was ashen with dark shadows ringing her eyes, but at least her headache was gone. She yawned and leaned forward to look at her reflection more closely.

Even though everything she thought she knew about her life and her place in it had changed, she was still herself. But now those slanted, gold-speckled brown eyes told a different story. Her cheekbones seemed higher and more prominent, her lips fuller, the bridge of her nose straighter. She brushed her waist-length hair with angry strokes.

Then, out of pure frustration, she parted her hair

right down the middle and plaited it into long, thick braids, wishing she had a silver-studded headband like that fierce Indian in the photograph. All she had was a white terry-cloth sweatband she always wore when she went jogging, but she hoped it made her point.

She jerked her cosmetic drawer open and grabbed the sweatband. As she pulled it down on her forehead, just above her eyebrows, her hands shook like she'd just come off a three-day drunk. She stepped back.

Her reflection was that of a stranger.

She moved away from the mirror and wriggled into a pair of snug jeans. After she had pulled an oversized University of Texas sweatshirt over her head and jammed her feet into scuffed-up cowboy boots, she left the bathroom and slammed the door closed behind her.

It was all Hunter's fault. Her compassion and understanding of earlier had disappeared with the night, and all that was left now was irritation. All he had to do was walk into a room, and her entire world exploded. He had to have known this bit of news wasn't something she was going to take in stride. He wasn't stupid.

He knew what he was doing. He always did.

She flung open her bedroom door and stared at Lysette, who stood in the hallway, her hand poised to knock.

"Oh, hey, your folks are here. Good Lord, girl, you look terrible."

"Thank you."

"What's the matter?"

"Nothing. I'm fine."

Lysette turned away. "Your folks are in the dining room."

She seized her cousin's arm. "Wait, don't go yet. I'm sorry, sweetie. I need you to do something for me."

Lysette turned back, her lovely face troubled and confused. "Name it."

Sierra took a deep breath. The last thing she wanted to do was bring Hunter back into her world, but she had no choice. She needed him. She couldn't do this alone. "Please call the Big Bend Motel and ask for Hunter Davenport's room. I was too upset to get his cell number last night. Ask him to bring the photographs here right away. He'll know what you mean. And tell him I need him to stay. He'll understand that, too."

"Not a problem."

"One more thing, sweetie. Once he gets here, please bring him to my folks and me—and you stay, too. This concerns you as well."

As Sierra entered the dining room, her hair hanging in two long braids over her shoulders and the white sweatband around her forehead, she met her parents without a greeting. When the blood drained from her mother's face and her father swore beneath his breath, she was perversely satisfied.

Hunter arrived not long after, and it was clear he hadn't slept much, either. That pleased her because she didn't want to be in this alone. He'd been comforting and sympathetic last night like a real friend, and she prayed he would be the same today. This confrontation was going to be difficult for everyone, and she needed someone in the room to be calm, controlled, focused. It wouldn't be her.

She hugged her parents, but she knew by their stiff embraces they were waiting, too. Mama and Daddy sat next to one another, as if arming themselves for the confrontation they knew was coming, and she sat across from them, not wanting to miss a single expression on their faces. Hunter sat beside her, that horrible briefcase next to his chair, while Lysette moved to the very end of the table. The tension was suffocating.

For a long, choking moment, no one said anything, but she never took her outraged glare from her mother's face. She refused to be intimidated by either of her parents—they were the ones who had some explaining to do.

Once everyone had their coffee in front of them, Mama spoke in a calm voice. "I never noticed how much like your mother you look, angel. How did you find out?"

She couldn't answer right away. Instead of responding, she looked at her mother's face and wondered why she'd never noticed how unalike they were. Mama's eyes were cornflower blue, her hair was as blonde as spun gold, and her beautiful, unlined complexion was as pale as porcelain. No, she and her mother looked nothing alike.

"I told her," Hunter answered finally.

Now Daddy erupted, his Texas drawl even more pronounced than usual. "Why, you lousy sunuva—"

"Noah, you're not helping matters, my love," Mama interrupted with a chuckle. "We've always known this might happen. Now it has, that's all. Now we deal with it."

"Hunter, will you show them the photos, please?" Sierra asked. "And explain how you got them. I was so shocked last night I didn't even think to ask."

He opened his briefcase, removed the large envelope from a front pocket, and pushed it toward

33

Mama. She stared at it for a long, silent moment, like she feared a rattlesnake might slither out before she could open it. She shook the photos onto the table, then fanned them out in front of her and gazed at them for a long time.

At last, she looked straight at him. "Where did you get these?"

"It's complicated, Mrs. Masters."

"I'm not a stupid woman. I can probably keep up."

He pushed his chair away from the table, leaned back, and stretched his long legs out in front of him. "Well, the truth is I was researching the Pine Ridge Indian Reservation online because of a movie I'd seen, and I came across a fascinating family that lives there. They want to bring what they call 'the old ways' back to their land. They decided to begin raising buffalo on their ranch, not only for food but also for ceremony. They're doing this in hopes the people will return to good health—physically, spiritually, and emotionally."

Mama's eyes widened. "Are you talking about Nathan Winterhawk and his family? Are they still there?"

He cocked an eyebrow. "Yes, ma'am. Do you know them?"

Mama's response to his question was so matter-of-fact that, for the first time in her life, Sierra felt isolated from both her parents. The very thought seemed ridiculous to her, but she felt as if they had no right to this experience if they weren't going to tell her about it.

"Of course we do. We met him at Wounded Knee. He's brilliant. I loved listening to him. I knew his wife, Melanie, too. I was scared to death of her, but I loved her. How is this a good story for you?"

"It'll make a great documentary. PBS, National Geographic, and a few private corporations are interested. Our working title is *The Return of the Buffalo Culture*."

Hunter glanced at Sierra's father as if waiting for a snide remark from the conservative rancher, but it didn't come. "Nathan and I started corresponding through emails and phone calls," he continued after a moment. "Then a few months ago, I went to Pine Ridge to meet him. Those photos are Nathan's."

"Did you meet Melanie?" Mama asked.

"No, I'm sorry to say."

"If you're going to do an in-depth documentary, you must talk to her."

"Stop interrupting the man, Lexy," Daddy growled. "I want to know about these pictures."

Sierra began to feel detached from the conversation, as if her parents didn't know—or care—that she was still in the room. They might've been two strangers sharing a story that probably wouldn't be interesting in the long run.

But Hunter seemed very interested. He nodded. "During our initial meeting, Nathan showed me lots of photographs. Several of them were of people involved in the Occupation of Wounded Knee, 1973. When I saw the picture of both of you with the pregnant Indian girl, I realized you couldn't possibly be Sierra's birth parents."

For the first time Mama showed irritation. "And you felt compelled to tell my daughter about this…why?"

"I'm sorry, Mrs. Masters. The last thing I wanted to do was hurt your family—"

Daddy laughed out loud, a humorless, grating sound that was almost painful to hear. "Good Lord, boy! Did you think that if you waltzed back into my daughter's life after all these years and turned it upside down, there wouldn't be any fallout?"

"No, sir, of course not. But I believed Sierra deserved to know about her heritage and who she is."

Mama took her husband's hand. "Hunter's right, darling." She paused, shuffling through the photographs. "Deep in my heart I've always known this would happen."

As a tiny smile played across Mama's face, Sierra suddenly felt embarrassed, as if she were intruding on personal moments and private memories of a secret time in her mother's life.

Mama placed the pictures on the table and looked at Sierra, her eyes soft with love. "I hope you can forgive us, angel. So often I thought to tell you the truth, but then I remembered how it all came about and changed my mind. Besides, you were our daughter, no one else's, and I didn't want you to be confused. If I did the wrong thing, I'm sorry."

Sierra's throat swelled with tears, and she was unable to speak. She felt abandoned, angry, overwhelmed. Everything she'd taken for granted in her life—her birthright, her ancestral line, even the long and illustrious history of her family—no longer had anything to do with her. For some reason, that realization made her feel invisible, like she didn't even exist.

"May I see those pictures again?" she whispered.

Mama pushed the photographs across the table, and Sierra began to look at them more carefully. When she reached the picture of her parents, the young, pregnant Indian girl, and her two female companions, she stared at it in silence for a long time, then asked, "Who are these women, Mama?"

Mama's reminiscent smile was tender. "This lovely young girl is your birth mother, Pauline Kills Quick. The lady in the nurse's uniform is her aunt, Julia Farewell, a dear friend of mine while we were up there. The old woman is Pauline's grandmother, Madonna Kills Quick."

Sierra gazed down at the photograph and looked at each woman closely. The girl was little more than a child, with the youthful curve of cheek and fullness of lips, but her breasts were large, and her protruding belly looked as if she might give birth at any moment. Her thick, lustrous, blue-black hair was brushed to one side and cascaded over her shoulder down to her waist in the same way Sierra often wore her own. Her eyes, beautiful and wide and dark, looked frightened...and ashamed.

*This child is my mother.*

The woman wearing the nurse's uniform was attractive, professional, contemporary—and probably not as old as she looked. But the elderly woman was another story altogether.

This woman's stiff posture and clenched fists belied the lack of emotion on her face; her fury was obvious. She definitely wasn't modern. She wore a wide bone choker around her fleshy neck. Her silver-streaked hair was parted down the middle and plaited into a single braid. Her body was shapeless and heavy in a faded, loose-fitting dress. Tossed over her shoulders was a ragged sweater.

And then, at last, the truth and all its ramifications sank in.

In a part of the country Sierra had never seen lived an American Indian family that hadn't wanted her…or maybe they had. If circumstances had been different, she might've been raised in poverty on a reservation with none of the opportunities she'd always taken for granted.

No matter how she looked at it, her life would've been different if Noah and Alexa Masters hadn't entered it.

As she met her mother's loving gaze, all her anger and confusion melted away. No matter how it had come about, she owed them far more than gratitude. She owed them her love, acceptance, loyalty, and trust. She reached across the table for her mother's hand and fought tears.

"It's all right, Mama. I know whatever you did, you did for me. So I want to know what happened. Tell me everything."

Chapter Five

As Sierra squeezed her mother's hand in encouragement and prepared to listen, Mama took a sip of now-tepid coffee and began her story.

"You probably don't remember your grandparents—my folks—very well, but they loved you so much." Glancing at Hunter, she added, "They died together in a car accident when Sierra was four years old.

"By the time I was twelve, I knew I wanted to be a journalist. By the time I graduated from high school in 1970, I was already publishing articles, mostly for liberal causes, in small newspapers and magazines."

"You were a writer?" Sierra blurted. "I never knew that."

Mama smiled and winked at her. "There are a lot of things about me you probably don't know. Anyway, at the beginning of 1973, I told my parents I wanted to see the west coast before the whole hippie thing was over. They weren't happy, of course, but I was nearly twenty years old. I left in early March and headed for San Francisco because that's where the action was.

"Outside of Kerrville, I saw this skinny, nerdy-looking guy hitchhiking, and I felt sorry for him because it was cold—at least for Texas. When he got in my car, I asked him where he was heading, and he said, 'I'm trying to get up to South Dakota. The Indians are on the warpath.' I'll never forget that."

Daddy grinned; his earlier anger seemed to have vanished. When it came time to tell a good story, he was always ready. "I hadn't been on the road but two hours when she stopped. Talk about luck. I didn't care if she was dangerous. All I cared about was the heater in her car."

Mama chuckled. "Anyway, when I asked him what warpath he was talking about, he told me that he was a journalist for an underground publication called *Revolutionary World*, and he was going to the Pine Ridge Indian Reservation to report on the violence there. Well, I was embarrassed to admit I hadn't heard about any violence, so I asked him—"

Daddy interrupted, "Everyone was watching it on television. These radical Indians had taken over a sacred historical spot and were holding off the entire United States government, but your mother didn't know a thing about it. I didn't think anyone should be that politically ignorant, so I told her all about Wounded Knee—the original massacre in 1890, which she already knew a little about, and the occupation going on now because reservation leaders were so corrupt. I felt she needed to be enlightened. Besides," he finished with a lecherous grin, "I thought she was hot."

Blushing, Mama punched him. "Anyway, I decided Indians on the warpath were probably more interesting than drugged-up hippies in San Francisco, so we turned around and headed for South Dakota. I was looking for adventure and maybe a good story. I had a feeling that this skinny dork was going to provide it."

Sierra stared at her father, incredulous. The idea he'd ever been a "skinny dork" who once wrote articles for far-left magazines was more than she could believe. Sierra felt like she was stuck in the Twilight Zone.

When Hunter nudged her, she guessed he was thinking the same thing.

Once more, Daddy picked up the narrative. "We drove through some of the most beautiful country I've ever seen in my life. That is, until we hit the border of Pine Ridge. That's where the state highway stopped, and you could tell this upcoming stretch of land didn't mean anything to anybody. As we drove onto the reservation, we passed broken-down trailers and houses made from old signs and garbage. I'd never seen anything like the poverty in that place."

"You look like you were old friends with these AIM people," Sierra said thoughtfully. "How did you get in? How did all of that happen?"

"As luck would have it," Mama answered, "we rolled into town the morning of March ninth, which happened to be the day *before* the federal government announced that they were taking down all the roadblocks leading into Wounded Knee. On March tenth, once all the roadblocks were down, people poured out of the compound—I guess to get home to their families for a while—so that's when we went in. We used your father's press credentials, both our cameras, and my gift of gab. Other people came in with us, but most of them were Indians from different parts of the country and a few anti-war Vietnam vets. There were other White people besides us who cared about the protest and got it, but not many."

Sierra couldn't quite understand one thing. "You said you hadn't even heard of it, so how could you care so much?"

Mama chuckled. "Your father had more than a thousand miles to teach me, so by the time we got to Pine Ridge, I was practically an expert on Indian sovereignty over the Black Hills, which was what the soul of the occupation was about. We joined them without a second thought."

"How long did you stay in the compound?"

"Long enough for me to get a super-good story," Daddy replied. "I was able to see with my own eyes what was happening on the reservation and what the Indians were fighting for. On March twelfth, when the feds announced that they couldn't ensure the safety of any press or media, our new friends told us we'd better leave for our own protection. So we snuck out late that night through the same woods that other people were sneaking in from. By then the feds had put their roadblocks back up, they were armed to the teeth, and Wilson's men were running wild all over the reservation. It was pretty clear there was no way the Indians could win.

"The next day your mother and I left the motel and moved to Hot Springs, about an hour from the reservation. We rented a crummy apartment in an old house, and I started writing."

Lysette spoke up. "So when—and how—did it end?"

"A man from North Carolina named Frank Clearwater—I think he was Cherokee—was shot through the back of the head in April and died several days later," Mama said. "Then another one of the AIM members, a very sweet young man named Buddy Lamont, was shot and killed by a federal sniper, and a federal agent was shot and paralyzed. Finally, on May fourth, the White House promised the Indians they'd examine 'the problems concerning the 1868 treaty.' I knew it was a lie, but that's what the elders wanted to hear. On May ninth, after seventy-one days, the occupation officially ended."

"And the Reign of Terror began in earnest," Daddy added.

Sierra's heart skittered. "The Reign of Terror?"

Mama massaged her temples wearily and sighed. "The Reign of Terror was a period between 1973 and 1976. Most Lakota recall that time as a battle between what they call the 'Traditional Indians' and the federal government, which was secretly helping Dickie Wilson and his GOONs and using them for cover.

"After the occupation ended, the FBI instigated a 'divide and conquer' policy inside AIM, a ploy they often used against groups they labeled as threats. That was so sad because the government placed AIM in a position where it could no longer defend the community because it was so busy trying to defend itself. AIM lost its momentum, if not its mission."

Daddy picked up the narrative, his voice gruff. "The feds turned Wilson's men loose on the Traditional Indians of Pine Ridge so people lived in terror all over the reservation. They burned down houses, destroyed sweat lodges, and residents who were suspected AIM members or sympathizers were murdered in cold blood. More than seventy people died during that period. There were 'suicides' where folks shot themselves in the back of the head or ran over themselves with their own cars. Most of those murders weren't even investigated, much less solved."

Sierra didn't know what to say. She couldn't

believe the federal government would ever commit such violence against its own people or that she'd never heard anything about it.

"It was a war zone," Mama added softly. "It was horrible, terrifying…" Her voice died away. Reaching across the table, she laced her fingers with Sierra's.

Sierra met her mother's gaze and squeezed her hand in encouragement. "It's all right, Mama. Go on."

Mama swallowed hard. "By the end of 1973, your father and I were living in Hot Springs, trying to document everything we saw on the reservation without being caught. My parents helped support us, so Noah was able to keep writing. They sent care packages of medicines, food, and clothing for us to smuggle onto the reservation. I worked in a small bookstore in town to help out.

"One day I met a lovely Lakota woman named Julia Farewell. We became good friends, and she told me she worked at the Indian Hospital in Rapid City as a nurse's aide. I learned she had relatives—many of them AIM members—who lived in Wanblee, a tiny village on the reservation that had been shot up by Wilson's men not long before I met her. She was terrified for their safety. But, even worse, her young niece, Pauline Kills Quick, had been raped by a wealthy White rancher with powerful connections in the state government—and now she was expecting a baby. She was only fourteen years old."

Sierra closed her eyes. Once again, those dream-like images floated through her mind. As clearly as if she'd been thrown back into those desolate Badlands with the castle-high rocks, she watched the young Indian girl running to escape the drunken White man in a pickup truck, stumbling, falling, bleeding…hearing his laughter…

"Angel, what is it? Are you all right?"

Sierra nodded. "I'm fine, Mama. Please go on."

Placing a comforting hand on his wife's arm, Daddy cleared his throat. A muscle in his jaw worked as he fought obvious anger, but he managed to continue. "Julia never would tell us who did it. She said it didn't matter. He was White, Pauline was a full-blood Lakota, and that was the end of it.

"One night, not long after we found out about Pauline's pregnancy, Julia woke us up banging on our door, screaming and babbling like a crazy woman. She'd been beat to a bloody pulp. Someone had grabbed her outside of the Texaco on the reservation, took her into the Badlands, beat the crap out of her, and threw her out of the car. A decent White guy picked her up. I guess he lived in or near Hot Springs, and that's how she ended up at our apartment."

Mama glanced at his crimson face and patted his hand. "That night we learned Julia was an AIM member herself, and she'd been working with some colleagues to document what they believed were Wilson's embezzlement of federal funds. Julia said she didn't know who beat her up, but she wasn't surprised. He was just sending her a message.

"But I've never seen anyone so terrified. She begged us to come to a motel she was staying at in Rapid City because Pauline's baby was due any day, and all Pauline could talk about was getting it off the reservation. Pauline's grandmother was staying with them to help out, but she wanted to get back home. Julia didn't know anyone who could take the baby, but she knew they had to get it out of South Dakota. She said there were too many people in her family who were AIM members, AIM sympathizers, or just Traditional Indians who wanted to go back to the old ways. The whole reservation was about to explode, and it was no place for a baby…"

Mama's voice trailed away, and for a moment she seemed lost, almost confused. But the moment didn't last. She finished quietly, "Sierra, it was easy for us to decide to take you. I'd been told when I was very young my chances of having children were slim—not impossible, but slim—and I couldn't think of anything I wanted to do more than to help a friend and save a baby's life. So I called my folks and told them what we wanted to do. They agreed right away."

Sierra's grip on her mother's hand tightened; her eyes filled with tears. She knew this story already. She'd seen it, felt it. She'd lived it. Once more she envisioned the young girl straining to give birth on the mattress with no sheets. Once more she watched the old Indian man hold out his arms to embrace her in the clouds high above the Badlands.

"Did Pauline Kills Quick die in childbirth?" she asked, her voice shaky.

Mama looked surprised. "Well, to tell the truth, I don't know. When you were two days old, Julia brought you to us. She had a birth certificate with your given name on it she had somehow managed to wrangle from the Indian Hospital, and she told us to leave the state. She didn't give any details, and we didn't ask." A fleeting expression of sadness stole across her face. "I don't know what happened to any of them."

Suddenly Sierra was nearly overcome by a sense of

loss and longing so great she could hardly breathe. She was grateful when Lysette broke the silence.

"Has my mother always known this story, Aunt Lexy?"

"Of course. She's my sister. Everyone in the family knows about it, but it's never mattered. Sierra was our little girl, and we all agreed we were going to protect her. Any time someone questioned her appearance—her black hair and olive complexion, especially—we just said she looked like Noah's Italian side of the family."

"And you never saw my mother again?" Sierra asked.

Mama shook her head. "We only met her one time, when that picture was taken, and she was so grateful to us for giving you a home it broke my heart. I couldn't imagine the pain of giving up a child, and I knew she had to love you beyond anything."

"What was my given name?"

"Julia told us they'd named you Madonna after the Holy Mother and after Pauline's grandmother—your great-grandmother, Madonna Kills Quick. Indian names are very fluid—they used to change them all the time— so I didn't feel bad about changing yours. Your father and I named you Sierra after the Sierra Nevada Mountains, but not for any particular reason. I just loved the sound of it."

"Madonna," Sierra mused. "How pretty…"

"It is, isn't it? Anyway, when I asked Julia about Pauline and how she was doing, she just shook her head, and I knew she wasn't going to tell us anything. We left that night and went back to Noah's family's ranch in Bandera. We joined the establishment, raised you as best we could, and hoped none of this would come up again."

"Other than my birth certificate, there's no paperwork…?"

Mama shook her head.

Sierra jumped when Hunter cleared his throat. She'd forgotten he was there.

"You've not heard from anyone since then?"

"No, but we never expected to," Daddy answered. "They wanted us to keep Sierra safe, and we've tried to do that. We've followed events on the reservation for years and tried to help the tribe financially as we could, but it's been hard—being so far away. We haven't regretted anything except we couldn't teach Sierra about her heritage, culture, or history. We felt we had no right to do that. We're White, and she's Indian. We might even be the enemy as far as they're concerned."

"I know you have tons of questions, sweetheart," Mama cut in quickly, "so please feel free to ask them."

But now only one question mattered to Sierra. She met her mother's steady gaze head-on. "It's not really important," she began, a little embarrassed, "but considering what wild revolutionaries you were in your day…maybe you could tell me this. Are you actually married…or not?"

The room exploded in relieved laughter.

Mama smiled. "Yes, my love. We married on April 20, 1974, in my parents' living room with only our families present, and you were christened the same night. Our minister had marched on Selma with Martin Luther King back in the day, so he was thrilled to be a part of our little ceremony. It was kind of like the closing paragraph in a long saga." She winked at Sierra, then changed the subject with a glance at Hunter. "If I wrote Nathan Winterhawk a letter, could you send it to him when you return his photographs?"

"Well, I won't send it to him, but I'll be glad to take it with me. I'm going back up to South Dakota in a few days."

"I'm jealous," Mama murmured.

"You and Mr. Masters are welcome to join me—"

Daddy pushed his chair away from the table and stood up, his face as dark as a thundercloud. He leaned over the table so he was eye to eye with Hunter. Somehow nothing was as intimidating as an Italian man the size of Noah Masters making his point.

"Don't go getting the wrong idea about this afternoon," he said, his voice dangerously soft. "Just because you and I seem to be on the same side of this issue doesn't make us warriors in the same revolution. I know who you are. If you can put together a documentary that'll show the truth about Nathan Winterhawk and Pine Ridge, good for you. But you'll do it without our help."

Hunter didn't respond but turned toward Sierra as if her father had never spoken. "How about you, Sierra? You want to come and see if we can find your family?"

"No." The last thing she wanted was to go anywhere with Hunter Davenport, especially to a place as godforsaken and violent as this Pine Ridge Indian Reservation seemed to be. "I have a contract. I have to work."

Mama spoke up then, putting a placating hand on her husband's arm. "Sit down, Noah. You're making me nervous. Angel, if you don't want to go to South Dakota, that's fine. But don't stay here on account of us. I'll be happy to give you all the information I can remember. I'd never blame you for looking. I understand."

"What would you do, Mama?" she whispered. "If you were me, would you go?"

Mama was silent for quite a while, thinking. When she spoke, her answer was clear and definitive. "Honestly? Wild horses couldn't stop me."

Chapter Six

For the first time, Hunter allowed himself to hope Sierra might accompany him to South Dakota...or at least meet him there. Even though he was happy with his life as it was, he couldn't think of anyone whose company he would enjoy more.

"Excuse me," Lysette said quickly, "I think I hear the doorbell. I'll be right back."

As she hurried from the dining area, Noah frowned. "That's disturbing. I didn't hear anything."

"You're not going deaf, Daddy. I never hear it. She always does."

Lysette returned to the dining room. "Colt and Skye are here. She's back from Oklahoma—"

"We're right here," a deep voice said from beyond the dining room entrance. A sunburned and weather-beaten yet handsome face with piercing green eyes peered around the doorway. "I thought that was your motor home out there, Mr. Masters. I just wanted to pop in and say howdy."

"Colt Chambers! How the hell are ya?" Noah jumped to his feet, and the two men shook hands vigorously, like they were pumping water in unison. "It's been a long time. Last time we visited, I think you were out in the desert somewhere."

"Well, I'm sorry I missed you, sir."

Colt removed his Stetson and ran his fingers

51

through dark, wavy hair. His forehead was two-toned, half white, half mahogany. Probably, Hunter guessed, because folks down here were never in the sun without a hat.

Colt smiled at Sierra. "Howdy do, Miss Masters."

"Hi. How are you?"

"I'm good. Listen, I brought someone special to see you. She was going to leave, but I told her you'd never forgive me if I let her go."

Sierra squealed with delight and rushed around the dining table with her hands outstretched. One of the most exotic-looking women Hunter had ever seen entered the dining room and engulfed Sierra in a bear hug.

Finally, stepping back, she looked at Hunter with interest. "And you are?"

Sierra blushed. "I'm sorry. I was so excited I forgot my manners. Hunter, this is my best friend, Skye Morning Sun Parker. We just call her Sunshine around here."

He cocked an eyebrow. "Morning Sun?"

"Half Comanche."

"She's a well-known artist and wildlife photographer," Sierra interjected. "Skye, this is Hunter Davenport, an old friend from my college days. He makes documentaries. You guys have a lot in common."

Hunter agreed with that. Skye Parker had to be close to six feet tall, and her prematurely silver hair glistened like liquid starlight as it tumbled down her back past her waist. He had to fight a desire to start taking photographs right away.

Instead, he gave her a killer crooked smile that

women almost always responded to and made a mental note to add her name to his rolodex. *You never know when you're going to need a resource like an Indian-artist-wildlife photographer.*

Aloud he said, "It's a real pleasure to meet you, Miss Parker."

"*Sunshine*, please. I'm glad to meet you, too."

"Gosh, it's good to see you!" Sierra burst out. "We've all missed you so much. Would you guys like some coffee?"

"None for me, thanks," Colt answered quickly. "I gotta get to the auto parts store up in Alpine before it closes. Seems my thermostat's on the blink." He walked toward Hunter and held out his hand. "Howdy. Looks like we're not gonna get a formal introduction. Name's Colt Chambers."

Hunter grinned as they shook hands. "Hunter Davenport. Sierra tells me you fix everything around here."

"Well, I try to keep up with it. It ain't easy sometimes."

Hunter nodded and dropped his hand to his side. He didn't know what role Colt Chambers played in Sierra's life, and he didn't like not knowing. After all, this guy was handsome, rugged, confident, and could take care of himself. Hunter didn't like being in the dark about his competition—whether it was film or women.

As the silence grew uncomfortable, Chambers cleared his throat and turned back to Sierra. "I'm heading out now. You need me to get anything while I'm up there?"

"No, thanks. We're fine."

"All right. I'll bring you the receipts tomorrow, Miss Lysette." Colt offered his hand again to Noah as he prepared to leave. "See you next time, Mr. Masters. I haven't forgotten that beer you promised me."

"You bet. I look forward to it."

"Can I ride with you, Colt?" Skye asked. "I need to get some art supplies up there."

"Sure thing. I'd like the company."

Alexa got to her feet. "Daddy and I have to leave, too, sweetheart. We need to get the coach checked in at the RV Village before it gets much later. Hunter, it was very good to see you again."

"The pleasure's all mine."

Noah moved closer to Sierra. Looking down at her, he said in a low voice, "You let us know what you want us to do, baby, and we'll do it. Your mama's right—as usual. I was a horse's butt, and I'm sorry." He tilted her chin so he could drop a light kiss on the tip of her nose. "You're all grown up now, and you don't need me running interference for you anymore." He turned to Hunter and held out his hand. "If Sierra goes to South Dakota with you, Davenport, I'm counting on you to take care of her."

Hunter was shocked at the older man's unexpected overture, but he managed a nod and gripped Noah's hand in both of his. "I will, sir. I swear it."

\*\*\*\*

Once everyone had gone, Sierra watched nervously as Hunter opened his briefcase, placed the now-familiar envelope back into the top pocket, and closed the lid with an air of finality. He locked it and gave her an apologetic smile. "It looks like I've done all the damage I can do here."

"Well, give it a minute. I'm sure you can come up with something else."

"I'm sorry."

"That's all that matters, isn't it?"

He stared at her and didn't answer. She had to look away from the intensity in his gaze. She was being hateful and rude, she knew that, but she couldn't help it. She was too afraid of him and his effect on her to behave any other way.

She began clearing coffee cups and saucers from the table. "If you'll excuse me, I really need to get back to work this afternoon, not that it'll do any good. My brain is too jumbled to think straight, but I have to try."

"Then go for a ride with me," he urged. "That always did you a world of good, and I don't know what to see down here. I'd love it if you'd show me around."

*Oh no*, she thought frantically, *oh no*. She shook her head and headed for the kitchen, carrying cups and saucers. Close behind her, he pushed the door open and followed her into one of the most inviting rooms in the house. It was also the room with which she was least familiar.

Without waiting for instructions, he opened the dishwasher and began filling it. "Are you going to take that drive with me?"

Hot tears of frustration filled her eyes. She wanted nothing more than to be alone with him, and nothing she wanted less, either. She shook her head and pushed through the swinging kitchen door back into the dining area. "No, I'm sorry. I just don't have time."

His fingers closed over her shoulders, stopping her in mid-stride. He turned her to face him and lifted her chin so she was forced to meet his eyes. "Sierra, wait a minute. I know what you think, but I'm not playing games with you. You've been through a lot in the last two days, and I caused that. I want to help, that's all."

*You've been through a lot in the last two days.*

That was a fact, but she couldn't trust him. Still, she had no choice. She had to talk to someone, or she'd explode.

And then she recognized the truth. She didn't want to be alone.

She backed away from him. "I'm only going with you for medicinal purposes."

He grinned. "I understand."

She removed the sweatband from around her forehead and unplaited her braids, then shook her hair loose and pushed it away from her face. "We'll take my Jeep—it's always ready to go. I'll get a couple of gallons of water and let Lysette know I'm leaving."

"I'll meet you outside."

"Sounds good. I won't be but a minute."

Hunter was waiting for her in the front passenger seat of her four-wheel-drive Jeep when she opened the door and climbed in beside him. She backed out of the courtyard and drove through the opened gates toward a narrow dirt road that would lead them to the main highway.

"Have you decided where we're going?" he asked, putting on his sunglasses and pulling a baseball cap down low on his forehead. He leaned back in his seat and yawned.

She nodded and glanced at her watch. "I think I'll take you on one of my favorite drives. We have plenty of time. Do you ever hike anymore?"

"Only when I can't find an elevator."

"I used to feel that way—until I moved here. Now I hike whenever I can."

She left her property and turned east, heading toward the entrance to Big Bend National Park. About a fifteen-mile stretch of road, it was one of her favorite drives because it was so deceptively subtle in its beauty. For long expanses of the Chihuahua Desert, nothing grew on either side of the highway except patches of creosote bush or withered cactus attempting to survive in a water-starved wasteland dotted by abandoned residences and empty storefronts. But then, without warning, immense boulders and craggy overhangs and yawning rock canyons appeared.

She never tired of this short trip. As usual, and as she had expected, the stresses of the last two days seemed to seep out of her body, and her head cleared. No pharmaceutical company had yet invented a muscle relaxant or tranquilizer that could begin to compete with this drive.

She turned into the park entrance and stopped beside the welcome gate. A middle-aged ranger stepped to the Jeep as she let down her window.

"Howdy do, Miss Masters," he said, touching his hat. "You're looking mighty fine this afternoon. Are you hiking today?"

"Not today, Pete. I'm just taking my friend down into the Chisos Basin."

"Great day for it. Enjoy." The ranger waved them through.

"He knows you by name," Hunter said, obviously impressed.

"I know most of the park rangers because I try to hike at least twice a week." She chuckled. "This is also where I come when I can't write. I guess I'll be out here a lot."

She slowed her speed to less than the mandatory forty-five mph; anything could leap, dash, or slither over the road in front of her. Besides, the landscape gradually changed as she drove the several miles toward her turnoff, and she wanted to take it in.

"This is just weird," he said in a hushed voice. "It's like being on the moon."

"That's one of the things I love about this place. Only about three hundred thousand people visit each year, and most of them come during the Terlingua Chili Cook-Off in November. Other than that, it's just too hard to get to—thank God."

As she neared the Chisos Mountains Basin Junction, the desert floor yielded to tall stalks of ocotillo cactus, grouped bunches of prickly pear, and the occasional petrified tree lifting its fossilized branches toward the sky. Gargantuan volcanic boulders seemed to have erupted from beneath the earth in some kind of ancient and agonized contraction, then exploded and tumbled all around one another into mammoth-sized piles of granite and limestone.

She turned and slowly followed the winding road down into the giant bowl-shaped valley of the basin. As the sun disappeared behind the towering volcanic pinnacles of the Chisos Mountains, the ocotillo cactus and creosote bushes surrendered to tall, cool pines that seemed to grow right out of rock. Finally, she spotted one of her favorite scenic lookout points and pulled over.

"Be careful when you get out," she said softly. "The ground is fragile."

Sierra joined Hunter on his side of the Jeep and leaned against the door. She looked out over the valley, enjoying the cool mountain breeze that brushed against her cheeks. As always, the unceasing wind moaned and whispered through the cracks and crevices of sky-touching rock formations millions of years old.

She'd never visited anywhere else in the world that made her feel so insignificant or her problems so small. As always, in response to this breathtaking beauty, a lump formed in her throat, and her eyes filled. In an instinctive habit she should've forgotten long ago, she took Hunter's hand—then tried to drop it as soon as she realized what she'd done. When his fingers laced between hers and she struggled to pull away, he wouldn't allow it.

"Don't," he said quietly. "I have a confession to make."

She caught her breath. She didn't want to hear his confession right now; she couldn't think. Her response to his touch was as unnerving as it had always been. Even though he'd mopped the floor with her heart years earlier, at this moment she wanted to pretend it had never happened.

She wanted to pretend he cared about her.

"I told you I came down here to do a story," he said in a low voice, "but I lied. I came alone. There's no story. I just wanted to see you. When Nathan Winterhawk showed me those pictures, I really was shocked. But honestly, all I saw was an excuse to see you again."

She gazed down into a secluded little campground nestled at the bottom of the basin. Her heart slammed in her throat. "Why didn't you tell me that in the first place?"

"You probably would've had that Chambers guy blow my head off."

"Would you blame me?"

"Yes. You and I both know what happened."

She glanced up at him. He thought he knew the truth—that their breakup had been a mutual decision—but he was wrong. She'd set him free because he'd have resented her for the rest of his life if she hadn't. It was as simple as that.

He cleared his throat. This was a subject that obviously made him uncomfortable. "Listen, I know this is probably a stupid question, but is there somewhere to eat around here? I'm starving."

She breathed a silent sigh of relief. An emotional conversation, during the few times they'd ever had one, always left him hungry. His appetite had given her one more reprieve.

"We can go on to the Chisos Restaurant. Their Mexican food is pretty good, and the view from the top of this basin is one you have to see to believe."

She walked back around the Jeep and climbed into the driver's seat. Once he was situated next to her, she gave him a broad wink. "After we eat, we'll visit the gift shop, and I'll let you buy me something."

Chapter Seven

Hunter closed his menu and settled back in his chair, waiting for Sierra to finish ordering.

"I'd like a chef salad with low-fat Italian dressing on the side and some hot tea with honey, please," she was saying, handing the waiter her menu. "It's getting chilly outside."

"And I'll try your Mexican plate," Hunter said. "Oh, and a Corona beer."

"Yes, sir. Can I get you or the lady anything else?"

"I think that'll do it. Thanks."

She leaned back in her chair and gave a long, contented sigh. "Isn't this gorgeous? I just love this place."

He nodded as he looked around the restaurant. Almost entirely glassed-in, it afforded diners a breathtaking view of the desert and the mountains from every conceivable angle. Even if the food was lousy, people would pay a fortune to eat in a place like this—if they knew it was here. But what he enjoyed most was sitting at a dining table with Sierra Masters, as he had done so many times before, and not feeling any compulsion to speak. Their silence was companionable, easy. She didn't have to flirt; he didn't have to impress. It just didn't get any better than that.

She glanced at her watch. "My goodness, it's nearly four o'clock. No wonder you're hungry."

"I'm always hungry. But since you don't cook, I figure this is probably my dinner. I'd better make the best of it."

"There's a little restaurant next to your motel that's open pretty late if you need it. Their breakfast is terrific, and they serve it all day."

"That's good to know."

The waiter arrived with several plates on a portable tray and began placing them on the table. "Here you are, folks. Can I get you anything else?"

"We're fine, thanks. This looks great. Sierra, are you all right?"

She was staring at her huge chef salad with a dismayed expression on her face.

He grinned. "You still hate to eat in front of people. Do you want me to cut up your lettuce?"

"Be quiet."

"Just fix your salad. A tomato isn't going to fly across the room and land in someone else's plate. That can only happen once in a lifetime."

She glared at him. "I'm a big girl now, Hunter, so leave me alone. This salad is just bigger than I thought it'd be."

He nodded, buttering a warm tortilla as he remembered how she'd always hated to eat in front of people she didn't know. He knew these little details about her, and she knew these little quirks about him, and he relished that about their history together. He'd never shared such intimacy with any other woman.

Her voice interrupted his reverie. "You know, I'm at a decided disadvantage here."

"I told you I'd cut up your lettuce."

"No, seriously. I just realized I don't know

anything about you anymore."

"What do you want to know?"

"Well, where do you live now? How are your folks? Did you ever get married?"

He chuckled and held up his hand. "My folks are fine. They sold their home in Houston, bought a huge motor coach, and they travel the country. When they start feeling like they need to settle down, they volunteer to host at some national park for a while and stay there until they're ready to move on."

"Wanderlust," she muttered, stirring honey into her hot tea. "It's in your DNA."

"It is. As for me, I mostly use a film crew out of Dallas, and I live wherever I land. But, just in case I get tired of it, I own a little place on the beach in Rockport."

"That sounds nice."

He gave a wry smile. "It is, but it can also be pretty lonely. Oh, and no. I never got married. You're the closest I ever came. I never found time, I guess."

*And I never found a woman who could compare with a tiny spitfire I once knew from Bandera, Texas...*

Blushing, she changed the subject. "Hunter...can we find out if Pauline Kills Quick is still alive?"

Amused, he paused, his fork halfway to his lips. "I'm already on it."

She choked on an onion and took a hasty gulp of tea. "Why? What if I didn't ask you to look for her?"

He grinned. "I'm not doing it for you. I'm doing it for me."

"But you didn't say anything about it this morning. You just sat there."

"I'm an investigative journalist, remember? It's my

job to accumulate sources, verify them, and then see how many angles there might be in one story." He took a bite of tamale and savored it before he finished, "When I saw her picture, I asked Nathan who she was. I didn't tell him why I wanted to know, of course, but I knew you'd eventually ask me to find her."

"Did he know anything?"

"He said he didn't, but the detective I've hired is a full-blood Lakota—"

She stared at him in amazement. "You've hired a detective?"

"Of course. How else could I find her? His name is Byron Little Hand. He works out of Rapid City, even though he lives on the Pine Ridge Reservation, and they tell me he's older than God, which could help. I'll meet him when I get back up to Dakota."

"Why didn't you just ask Nathan Winterhawk what he knew about her? Wouldn't that have been easier?"

He didn't answer right away. Even though they'd lived together and planned to marry, he'd never told Sierra much about how he worked. It'd been the one portion of his life he always kept to himself.

*That's probably part of what went wrong.*

Maybe he could change that now. At least, a little. "Well," he began, "I always try to keep my stories separate. See, I don't think that Pauline Kills Quick has anything to do with Nathan Winterhawk or his story, and his story is what I'm being paid to do. On the other hand, Nathan Winterhawk could well be part of yours. I knew you'd want to find out about your family, so I just thought I'd help you out if I could."

She cocked an eyebrow. "So how much of Pauline's personal story did you already know before you located me?"

"What do you mean?"

"My mother said that Pauline Kills Quick was raped by an important White man. Did you know that before today?"

"No."

"You have no idea who that man is?"

"No."

"Did you know that Mom's friend, Julia Farewell, was an AIM member investigating Dickie Wilson?"

His response was immediate. "Yes, Nathan told me that. She was a good friend of his and Melanie's."

"Is she still living?"

"No."

She looked like he'd just slugged her. "Oh God...really?"

"I'm sorry."

"It's all right. I don't know why—"

He wanted to reach for her hand and tell her that at some point in her life this was all going to make sense, but he didn't move. He kept his voice matter-of-fact. "She was your blood. She seems to have meant a lot to your parents. It's a shock."

She dashed a tear off her cheek. "Why didn't you tell my folks she died?"

He hesitated. "There are just some things you develop an instinct about," he answered finally, "and I didn't think it was a good time to tell them. They'd already been through enough. I also didn't think I should be the one to do it." He shook his head. "I don't know. Maybe I was wrong—"

"No, you were right. My mother cared about her. I'll tell her later." She paused. "Do you know how she died?"

He worded his answer cautiously. "They found her body dumped out in the Badlands around the end of 1974. She'd been beaten, but that wasn't in the report. The report said she was an alcoholic who got drunk and staggered out in front of a car in the Badlands. She died instantly. But Nathan insists that Julia Farewell didn't drink. He believes she was murdered somewhere else and her body was dumped out there. They never really looked into it—which wasn't unusual if it involved the death of an AIM member or a Traditional Indian. Especially back in those days."

Sierra paled and pushed her plate away. "Who's *they*?"

"The FBI. In fact, they released a list back in 2000 of fifty-seven reservation murders that happened during the Reign of Terror and their so-called solutions. It's online now. Julia's name is on it. The solutions they offer for most of the cases are ridiculous. I think they just dreamed up explanations so they could close the cases quickly."

He spooned some guacamole onto a flour tortilla and rolled it into a cone, then held it in the air without taking a bite. "The craziest part of it all is the FBI blames most of the reservation murders at that time on the leaders of AIM."

"AIM? That doesn't make any sense. Why would...what did you call them? Traditional Indians? Why would Traditional Indians go around killing other Traditional Indians? They were on the same side, weren't they?"

"Don't ask me. Listen, I'm not saying that AIM was perfect or that it didn't have violent people in it. It did and still does. Some folks believe they've done more harm than good to Indian people—it depends on who you talk to. But the bottom line is this. Part of the FBI's job back in the '70s was to dismantle groups like AIM, the Black Panthers, various anti-war organizations…and they did that quite effectively. AIM is little more than a community organization now. They're certainly no threat to anyone."

"You'd better be careful what you say, Hunter. You sound a little crazy."

He shrugged, unconcerned. "I can't help that. I know if a White person was hurt or killed back in those days, the FBI was all over it. If an Indian was killed, it didn't matter—and lots of Indians were. I'm telling you the facts."

"Would you tell me something else?"

"Shoot."

"I thought Indians preferred to be called Native Americans, but you call them Indians. Why is that?"

"That's a good question. Most of the older or more traditional Indians I know prefer to be called Indians, American Indians, or even Indigenous People. Younger Indians and most Whites use the term Native Americans. Twenty years from now, it'll probably be something else."

"I know, but—"

He interrupted with a grin and changed the subject. "Listen, Sierra, your mom wants you to go to South Dakota."

She nodded.

"Am I the only reason you don't want to go?"

She gazed out the window. "I told you. I have to work."

He recognized the expression on her face and immediately understood.

*She's got the block...the bane of every writer's existence.*

"You've mentioned that a dozen times," he said aloud. "What're you trying to work on? I don't think I've ever seen you with writer's block."

"Well, I have it now. I can't string four words together."

"Maybe you need a break." He took a bite of his guacamole. "Come on, talk to me. Your work may be different from mine, but the creative process is the same."

She looked at him skeptically. "It's no big deal. I wanted to write a three-book family saga based on my father's ranching history. I begged my agent, my editor, and everyone else I could think of to get me this contract. But then, when my publisher finally approved it, I got a migraine, and it won't go away."

"Maybe you're thinking about the wrong family," he suggested, "or the wrong time period or maybe...the wrong location."

"What do you mean?"

"Well, when things don't gel right, the problem is often pretty simple. Maybe it's a point-of-view issue or a single line of dialogue that's out of whack. Like, you're thinking about setting your saga in Texas where the history is terrific, but maybe your story about a ranching family has been done so often you can't find the unique peg you're looking for."

"Oh, I don't know. I don't think so. My father's family history is fascinating—"

He held up his hand and raised his eyebrows in

feigned innocence. "But what if you have a family in South Dakota whose history is even more remarkable than your father's? You could be related to…Lord knows…I don't know…anybody."

She sighed. "You don't give up, do you?"

"Never. Not if I believe in something."

"Why do you care? Why is this so important to you?"

"I don't know," he answered slowly, "but I told you—I live by my gut, and my gut tells me you should go to South Dakota."

"Maybe I will. Someday."

No point in discussing it further. She could be as stubborn as hell, and he didn't want her to dig her heels in so hard he'd never be able to reason with her. It had to be her decision.

"I'm not going to say another word about it. I have to go back to Dallas early in the morning, but I'm leaving for Pine Ridge in a few days. I'll give you my cell number, and you call me if you change your mind."

"I can't go." She dropped her napkin over her remaining salad and pushed away from the table. "Come on. We need to get out of these mountains before it's too dark to leave."

Chapter Eight

A flaming Big Bend sunset had burst across the deep purple sky in streaks of hot pink and crimson as Sierra pulled into the courtyard of her property. Off to her left, in front of the adobe guest house, was her motor home, hood up and engine running. Deep in conversation with Skye Parker, Colt Chambers stood beside it, leaning on a metal cane he sometimes used when an aching right knee bothered him. Looking up at her arrival, they both waved in welcome.

She flipped off the ignition, dropped the keys into her purse, and glanced over at Hunter. He had been quiet on the drive home, as if he were a thousand miles away, but she understood and respected his silence. It seemed to be a universal emotional response to a day spent in this awe-inspiring part of Texas.

"Would you like to come in?"

When he didn't answer, she was terrified. When he left tonight, she wouldn't see him again. It would be over...finished. When she looked at it that way, she couldn't breathe.

He turned slightly in his seat. His gaze caressed her face, as if he wanted to commit her features to memory. The seconds inched by; the silence was heavy. In desperation, she looked away.

"Would you like to come in?" she repeated.

"No, thanks. I have to get up early, and Dallas is a

long way off."

His refusal affected her like a slap in the face. She shrugged and opened her door. "Suit yourself. After you get your stuff, please lock up."

"Sure. Sierra, wait a minute. I had a terrific time today. Thanks."

She softened. "You're welcome. I enjoyed it, too."

"Please think about South Dakota. Your blood is up there—in more ways than one. You can't ignore that."

She looked at him for a long moment before she climbed out of the Jeep and walked toward the house, a painful lump in her throat. She kept her eyes straight ahead—the last thing she wanted him to see was her looking back at him. When she reached the front door, Hunter started his engine and pulled out of the courtyard. Her eyes began to burn.

Skye's fingers closed over her shoulder. "Hey, wait up. Where's the fire?"

Sierra shook her head, pushed the front door open, stepped into the wide foyer, and took a deep breath. She tried to compose herself before she turned to her friend and gave her a quick hug. "I'm surprised to see you and Colt back already."

Skye gave a breathless laugh. "Well, you know how he drives. Like a bat out of hell, in mountains or on flat land, rain or shine—he doesn't care. He's an adrenalin junkie. My heart's still in my throat."

Sierra dropped her purse on a small mesquite table at the end of the foyer. "Well, it's not like you don't know he drives like that."

Skye frowned but changed the subject. "By the way, your friend out there gave me his cell number for you. He said not to lose it because Pine Ridge is waiting, and you're going to change your mind."

She shook her head.

"Is he talking about the Pine Ridge Indian Reservation?"

She gulped. He'd said he was going to drop the entire subject, but she should've known better. Just because *he* wasn't going to talk about it anymore didn't mean he was going to leave it alone.

*I don't give up if I believe in something.*

She knew how true that was. Over the years, she'd watched in amazement as he went after the stories he'd wanted to work on but no one wanted to finance. She'd seen him badger and harass people for interviews or photographs until they surrendered out of pure exhaustion, and he'd always come up with his funding. Now, if she wasn't careful, she was going to be one of those people.

Well, why not? Maybe he was right when he said she'd left her blood in South Dakota in more ways than one, and maybe finding that blood *was* important.

Skye's voice came from behind her. "Do you want to talk about it, sweet pea?"

Her first instinct was to refuse; she never confided in anyone. Then, just as quickly, she knew what a terrible mistake that would be. Skye was part Comanche—she'd understand in a way no one else could.

"Yes," she answered, "I think I do."

\*\*\*\*

"Wow." Skye sat back in her chair, playing with a wine goblet filled with chardonnay, and stared at Sierra. "I don't know what to say."

"Well, say *something*."

"Are you okay?"

"I don't know, Sunshine. Are you familiar with any of that American Indian Movement stuff?"

"We cut our teeth on it. My uncle was an AIM member and went up to Pine Ridge during the Occupation of Wounded Knee to help out."

"No kidding!"

Skye chuckled. "No kidding." Then she grew serious and leaned forward. "How do you feel about this? Some people choose to ignore their Indian blood. Others get all obsessive about it. Where do you stand?"

Sierra thought for a moment. She looked the same, but she felt like a stranger to herself. She no longer knew who she was.

"I don't stand anywhere as far as that goes. The Indian part of it doesn't mean anything to me. It could be Mongolian for all I care. All that matters to me is I'm not who I thought I was. My parents aren't my parents, and my life isn't my life—"

"Wrong. Absolutely wrong."

Sierra fought a grin. "Why?"

"Look, sweet pea, your parents will always be your parents, and no one can take away your life unless you want to give it up. Your mother understands that. That's why she doesn't care if you go to South Dakota. She knows in your heart you're always going to come back to her. And Hunter has done you a huge favor. He's added another element to your life. I'm amazed that you, as a writer, aren't just flipping with curiosity."

Sierra sipped her wine as she studied her best friend. "Well," she admitted grudgingly, "Hunter does have a detective searching for Pauline Kills Quick."

"That's your birth mother, right?"

"Yes."

"Don't you want to meet her?"

"No. I don't know. Maybe."

Skye was silent for a while, then drained the last of her wine and announced, "Well, I do. I'll let you know what she's like."

"Excuse me?"

"I've always wanted to go to South Dakota. I've just never gotten up that far."

Sierra's eyes narrowed. "Have you lost your mind?"

"No, but I'm pretty sure you have. The Sierra I know would leave in the morning. But since you've lost all creative curiosity, I'm going to take my camera and go to South Dakota with your friend Hunter Davenport. What do you think about that?"

Before she could even formulate an answer, Colt Chambers limped into the dining room, leaning on his cane.

"I rang the doorbell, but I guess you didn't hear it."

"I never hear it. Come on in."

"Thanks. I just wanted to let you know we gotta get new tires on *Roberta*. The tread's pretty lousy." Colt pulled out a chair beside Skye and sat down with a weary sigh. "We can't take any more trips 'til that's taken care of."

"Sure," she agreed. "Get them."

"I need to tune her up, too, and—"

Skye snapped her fingers and smacked the tabletop so hard her wine glass rattled. Her dark eyes danced with excitement. "Oh. My. God. I'm so brilliant I scare myself."

Sierra, still a little perturbed with her friend's lack of empathy, ignored her. "Do whatever you need to do, Colt. You know that. Can I get you a beer or something?"

"No, thanks, I'm good. What's your brilliant idea now, Sunshine?"

She focused her full attention on Sierra. "Colt will drive us to South Dakota," she announced.

Sierra gave her a blank stare. "Now I'm sure you're crazy."

"No, it's perfect. You said Hunter was leaving in a few days, right?"

"Yes."

Skye turned to Colt. "How soon can you get *Roberta* ready to go to South Dakota?"

"By morning if I have to. What's in South Dakota?"

Skye didn't answer. She stared hard at Sierra.

"Family," Sierra muttered when the silence became uncomfortable. "On the Pine Ridge Indian Reservation."

He lifted one eyebrow. "And this Hunter guy wants you to go with him?"

She nodded. "He's working on a story up there."

He pushed his chair back and stood up. "Well, you gals work out the details. I can see we're leaving. Seems I gotta get *Roberta* set to travel."

****

Once she'd made the decision to go to South Dakota, Sierra called Hunter on his cell phone to give him what she considered her momentous news, but he seemed unsurprised—and underwhelmed.

"Good," he said. "I'm glad you came to your

senses. I'll be staying in a cabin at the Wiconi Campground near Interior, in the Badlands, so call me when you get into South Dakota. When do you think you'll be there?"

"In about a week. We're leaving the day after tomorrow."

"Okay, good. Here's their number in case our cells don't work. They'll get a message to me. They know who I am." After giving her the information he seemed to think was important, including his email address, he added, "Is there anything else?"

His distant tone threw her for a loop. "Do you mind that Skye and Colt are coming with me? I thought—"

"Why should I care about that?"

"You sound so…funny."

"I'm editing film right now." His voice was a little warmer when he added, "Be safe. I'm glad you're coming. If you don't mind, email me your itinerary so I know where you're at, and call me when you get in."

The phone clicked in her ear, and that was the end of it.

When she remembered the last moments of their day together and now his aloof attitude on the telephone, she could see how he wanted it to be. He was making it easy for her not to become involved with him again, and that was a good thing.

When Mama and Daddy stopped in to say good-bye on their way back to their ranch, Mama handed Sierra an envelope with the words *Nathan Winterhawk* scrawled across the front.

"When you meet Nathan, sweetheart, please give him this note from me. I was going to give it to Hunter, but when you decided to go yourself…well, this is much better."

"Of course."

"And I appreciate you telling us about Julia. I was sad to hear it, but I'm not surprised. She was on a mission." Mama sighed. "Angel, once you figure out your final itinerary, send it to me, will you? I want to follow along with you. My favorite place in the whole world is South Dakota."

"I promise."

She fought tears. She'd been an independent traveler for several years, but now, somehow, she knew this time would be different.

This time, her journey would change her life.

Chapter Nine

Bathed in early morning sunshine, the vast plains of southern South Dakota seemed endless, battle-scarred by centuries of ceaseless wind and cutting rain. Deep canyons and high buttes, created by millions of years of erosion, shaped some of the most godforsaken landscape Sierra had ever seen.

Yet the farther north Colt drove, the more colorful the countryside became, with fields of jade green, topaz gold, and tiger's-eye brown spreading away from both sides of the highway like soft velvet blankets. An occasional tree sported leaves that appeared to be changing color, one leaf at a time, so the foliage gradually progressed into a blazing kaleidoscope of cherry red, burnt orange, and rusty gold. Small herds of Angus cattle ranged closer and closer to the road, indicative of human habitation somewhere, yet she couldn't figure out where.

The countryside was magnificent, but the condition of the state's official welcome sign threw her. Written at the bottom of a white metal picture of four presidential heads carved into famous Mount Rushmore were the words *Great Faces, Great Places.* In near-perfect straight lines across the foreheads and down the noses were bullet holes.

Shifting her position in the booth, Sierra pointed to the sign as they passed. "I've never seen anything like that. What's that about?"

Skye grinned. "Well, it could be one of two things. Either it's some redneck using that sign for target practice, or it's an Indian who doesn't appreciate those four White faces staring out at what used to be—and still should be—Indian land."

"I don't understand."

Setting her camera on the table and handing her a glass of orange juice, Skye slid into the booth across from her and gazed out the window, a pensive expression on her face.

"It's simple," she said finally. "Mount Rushmore is located in the heart of the Black Hills, which are sacred to all the Plains Indians. They call them *Paha Sapa*, which means *the heart of everything that is*."

"Why are they sacred?"

"The Plains Indians believe them to be the center of the universe where *Wakan-Tanka*, the Great Spirit or the Great Mystery, lives."

"What does that have to do with Mount Rushmore?"

Skye shrugged. "Mount Rushmore is the White man's monument to American leaders who stole Indian land after signing treaties guaranteeing they wouldn't, and those faces are carved on hallowed land where *Wakan-Tanka* lives. The desecration continues today. So my guess is that those bullet holes are a political statement."

For the first time, Sierra glimpsed the pain that might have filled Skye's spirit for as long as they'd known one another. She didn't know what to say. She felt as guilty about the role her unknown White ancestors played in this violent history as if she'd participated in it herself.

Skye gave a quick grin. "Don't go beating yourself up, sweet pea. You never even heard of the Black Hills until a little while ago. I know lots of Indians blame everything on White folks, but I'm not one of them. If you have a great-grandpa that carved out a homestead in the Black Hills, that's his load to carry, not yours. You don't need to haul the cross for everyone. There's plenty of blame to go around."

Suddenly Colt pulled over, came to a halt, and opened his door. "Y'all need to get out and stretch your legs for a minute. I'm hearing a noise I don't like."

When Skye frowned, Sierra gave her a reassuring smile. "Come on, it'll be all right. Colt can fix anything."

With Skye right behind her, she stepped outside and took a deep breath of crisp morning air. She walked away from the motor home toward a barbed-wire fence that kept the cattle away from the road.

Deciding to check in with her parents, she flipped open her cell phone and punched in Mama's number. When it went straight to voice mail, she left a message and shoved the phone into the back pocket of her jeans. Mama was always so busy on the ranch, but Sierra would've loved to share this moment with her.

She leaned against a fence post and looked up into a cobalt-blue sky dotted with cottony white clouds that looked soft and pure enough to sleep in. The isolated beauty of this place soothed her in the same way the Big Bend region always did, and she was grateful for that. She had to call Hunter and set up a meeting place for later today. She punched in his cell phone number, hoping against hope he wouldn't answer and she could just leave a message, but she wasn't that lucky.

His deep voice sent a familiar shiver down her spine. "Hello?"

"Hunter? It's Sierra. Are you busy?"

"Not at all. I was thinking about you. Where are you?"

"I think I just saw a sign that said we're a few miles from a town called Presho."

"Well, that's not too far. Are you coming in today?"

"We are, and I'd like to stay at your campground. Can you make a reservation for us?"

"Sure, not that I need to. We just have three other motor homes here. My assistant and I are the only ones in a cabin, and he's leaving for Rapid City in a few minutes. He's flying back to Dallas from there."

"Is it hard to find?"

"No, but it can be sort of intimidating getting here. Come to think of it, there's an interesting truck stop/restaurant/museum/cheesy souvenir place near the Kadoka exit. Take that exit and then call me. I'll direct you to the truck stop and meet you there. We can grab a snack, and you guys can follow me back to the campground."

"Oh, I'm sure that's not necessary," she protested. "That's way too much trouble. Colt can find anything."

He chuckled. "Well, even though you're coming in the easiest way, you still don't want to get lost and be looking for this place after dark. I mean, in the Badlands, dark means *real* dark."

"You're the expert. Have you met with Byron Little Hand yet?"

She wanted to meet this old man who was going to

help her find her birth mother, but she was afraid to meet him as well. The young girl she'd seen in her dream wasn't young anymore, and Sierra was possibly the last person in the world she'd want to meet. In fact, Sierra might even be a secret she'd kept from everyone. Sierra wouldn't blame her if she had. A baby that was the product of a rape wouldn't be her most cherished memory.

He interrupted her thoughts. "No, I haven't. I talked to his secretary earlier, and she said Byron had to go out of town suddenly. She didn't tell me where, but she promised he'd call me the minute he got back."

She tried to conceal her disappointment—and relief. "Okay. Listen, I've got to go now. I'll call you when we leave the highway."

"Fine. I've got so much to tell you. We're going to have a great time."

She backed away from the fervor in his words. His enthusiasm was dangerous to her heart. "Sure," she responded, her voice as casual as she could make it. "We can talk about it later. Skye's planning steaks for tonight. She's a wonderful cook. You'll join us, right?"

"That sounds terrific." After a long pause, Hunter added, "I'm looking forward to seeing you, Sierra."

Her heart stopped. She recognized that caressing, velvet tone in his words. Once she had lived for it, but not now. Not anymore.

She tried to sound distant and unmoved. "I'll see you later."

She closed her cell phone, swallowed hard, and blinked back tears. Even if she couldn't manage to keep anything else of value in the course of this journey, she had to keep her dignity. It was all she had.

She frowned. The atmosphere had somehow changed, but she couldn't tell how. She looked around, confused. Moments before, the breeze had been light and chilly. Now the air felt thick and mysterious, as if it were filled with hidden secrets. A feeling of all-enveloping insignificance descended on her, suffocating her with a sense of loneliness and isolation. For a moment she thought about how silent it was out here on these prairies and how lonesome the early pioneers must have been.

No.

Like down in Big Bend, the silence was deceptive. These plains weren't silent. If she held her breath, she could hear the noises of rustling insects and scuttling prairie dogs and even, somewhere nearby, the whooshing murmur of a stream.

That was strange. She saw nothing that heralded the presence of running water. Then she heard laughter in the distance, wafting through the silence like a party in a town a hundred miles away.

Suddenly, without warning, she found herself seated cross-legged on a riverbank, viewing a vast camp of tipi circles nestled deep in a fog-enshrouded valley across the water. The air was thick and damp and icy cold. Small fires flickered within the tipis, like orange-and-red lightning bugs. She smelled the acrid odor of nearby horses and heard slow, steady, throbbing drumbeats from somewhere in the camp, far beyond her vision.

Somehow, and she didn't know how, she *knew* this was a Lakota winter camp from an earlier generation, and this flowing water she sat beside was somewhere on the White River.

"Sierra!"

Something, someone, grabbed her shoulders and shook her so hard she bit her tongue. Tasting blood, she stared at a wide-eyed woman who seemed a stranger for a long moment. She began to return to herself. The woman was Skye, and they stood together beside the barbed-wire fence.

She looked out across the plains where just moments before there had been an Indian camp and throbbing drums and laughing children, and now...

Now there was nothing.

"Are you all right, sweet pea?"

She closed her eyes, took a deep breath, and nodded. "I thought I saw something, that's all. It's nothing. I'm fine."

Skye smiled. "You probably ought to get used to it."

"Why?"

Now Skye met her gaze and held it before she spoke. She felt as if Skye needed to tell her something important, but she couldn't read what it was.

"I'm Indian," Skye stated after a moment, as if that explained everything. "We live with one foot in the spirit world. My culture doesn't try to explain it. It just is. On the other hand, White culture traps you into believing that only what you see, touch, taste, hear, and smell is real. That's arrogant and sad. Keep your mind—and your heart—open."

Sierra was silent. She didn't know what to say. She only knew she didn't want any part of a spirit world.

When Colt joined them, she was grateful for the interruption.

"Where'd you say we're meeting Hunter?" he

asked.

"We're supposed to let him know when we take the exit to Kadoka. There's a truck stop nearby he wants to take a closer look at. He said he'd meet us there."

"Call him now, okay?" Colt sounded frazzled. "I need to get *Roberta* to water."

\*\*\*\*

Sierra gazed at her reflection in the full-length mirror next to the bed and glanced at Skye who leaned against the doorway, watching her with an inquiring expression on her face. She looked away, embarrassed by the amusement she read in Skye's eyes. Hunter's deep voice and Colt's answering laughter from outside the motor home sent a nervous shiver down her spine.

"You look beautiful," Skye said in admiration. "I don't know what it is about this guy, but he certainly brings out the best in you."

Sierra shook her head and turned her attention back to the mirror, brushing her waist-length black hair over her shoulder with strong, sure strokes. *No, that's the one thing Hunter Davenport doesn't do. He doesn't bring out the best in anyone.*

As she made certain the center part in her hair was perfectly straight, she wished her color wasn't so high and her gold-flecked brown eyes weren't so bright. She looked like she had a fever, but she couldn't do anything about it now. She dabbed a bit of pastel peach gloss over her lips, brushed blush on each cheekbone, then dropped the small containers in a drawer. Her mouth was so dry she couldn't even swallow.

"Hey, Sierra! You in here?"

"Shoot," she muttered, taking one last glance at her reflection. "Here goes nothing." She looked like a schoolgirl in her snug, black jeans and red-and-black flannel shirt, but she didn't have time to change. She tossed her hair back and tilted her chin in defiant bravado as she made her way to the doorway. "Coming!"

And then there he was. He stood in the kitchen area and blocked her path so completely she was forced to stop and wait for him to move. He didn't. He ran his slow, admiring gaze over her, from her head to her feet, and she couldn't look away. As he gave the leisurely, crooked grin that had never failed to stop her heart, she fought the urge to touch the deep cleft in his chin. No matter how much time passed, she could hardly resist him.

But then, when he held out his hand in an odd, professional gesture, she was disarmed and responded without thinking. She watched her fingers disappear in his grip.

"Welcome to South Dakota," he said in that deep, velvety voice. "I thought you'd never get here."

Chapter Ten

Hunter had called it right. The old truck stop was nothing more than a cheesy souvenir place. He knew Sierra wondered why he'd want to take a closer look at it, but he wasn't free to tell her. As always, his job sealed his lips.

In a remembered habit, he pressed his hand against the small of her back as he guided her across the parking lot, passing an eighteen-wheeler from Minnesota, a caravan of Harley Davidson motorcycles, and three gas pumps with no prices listed. A hand-painted sign above the door read *Turner's Truck Stop Open 24 Hours*. He held the door open and followed close behind her as they entered a dim, rather grungy convenience store.

Many of the shelves were practically empty, although someone had managed to stock a long glassed-in refrigerator with beer, wine, and sodas. Exhausted-looking, leather-clad bikers stood in a straggly line beside a row of half-filled coffee pots. The poorly maintained store looked like most of the others he'd seen in this rural part of the state.

He cupped his hand around her elbow. "Come on. We need to get a table."

"Colt wants to get something for the motor home—it's making a noise he doesn't like. He and Skye can join us when he's found it. After we eat, let's take a look at this museum."

"Are you sure? These old places sort of creep me out."

She paled, and an inexplicable, almost panicked expression fled across her face, but Hunter couldn't read it. As far as he could tell, she had nothing to be afraid of.

But she sure as heck was afraid of something.

"Hey, are you all right? I was just kidding—I'd love to see this museum."

She gave a shaky laugh. "I'm fine. I'm just hungry."

"Well, let's eat, then."

When they reached the restaurant entrance, a short, wiry man barred the doorway. Hunter didn't miss the way his squinty eyes raked up and down Sierra's body, and his lip curled as if he had a nasty taste in his mouth.

"Sorry, folks. We're closing up in a few minutes. I'm afraid we can't serve you."

Hunter glanced at his watch. "It's only four o'clock. Why can't you serve us?"

"The law says I don't have to serve Injuns. So I'm not serving her."

Sierra gasped and took a step backward. Hunter gripped her shoulders to steady her. This kind of racism wasn't unusual in South Dakota—he'd seen it before. But he'd never personally known anyone on the receiving end of it, as she was now.

His anger began to simmer. "Excuse me?"

"I said, I don't have to serve Injuns—"

Just then a silver-haired gentleman in an expensive western suit joined them. He dropped his hand on the proprietor's shoulder. "What's going on here, Turner?

Why won't you let these people in?"

"Sir?" The color drained from the little man's face. "You know these folks, sir?"

"No, but I know this woman is no Indian. This is Sierra Masters. She's a famous writer. I saw her on *Oprah* not long ago. Am I right, Miss Masters?"

When she managed to nod, her body tensed in front of Hunter. He looked at the older man more closely.

He looked familiar, but Hunter couldn't figure out where he'd seen him before. He'd trained himself to remember faces, dates, and names, but this man had somehow managed to escape through the trapdoor of Hunter's memory.

No matter. He'd remember if he needed to.

Turner's shaky voice interrupted his thoughts. "I-I'm sorry, sir. I didn't know. Please forgive me, Miss Masters. Can I seat you and your friend with Mr. O'Neill? I'd be more than happy to do that."

Hunter's eyes narrowed. O'Neill had put himself in the same bigoted category as Turner when he'd said, "This woman is no Indian," yet he instinctively knew the men were in two different leagues.

O'Neill oozed power. Turner cringed in the face of it.

When Sierra responded in a saccharine-sweet voice, Hunter realized in amusement that she'd found her strength and self-respect. When she tilted her head from her position in front of him, he knew she'd lifted her chin in stubborn defiance, an expression he'd seen many times in the past. The little man didn't stand a chance.

This was the Sierra he remembered.

"I'm sure Mr. O'Neill will understand when I say

I'd rather eat dirt in the parking lot than spend another second in this place."

Hunter noted with interest that now the man was nearly apoplectic, babbling in his panic. "Oh, please, Miss Masters. Please don't leave. I didn't know who you were."

The handsome stranger took that opportunity to move between Sierra and Turner, an apologetic smile on his face, and introduced himself.

"I'm Logan O'Neill," he said as if they should recognize his name, "and I own a large ranch near Hot Springs. Please, I'm terribly sorry for this misunderstanding. It would mean a lot to me if you would let me buy you lunch."

Sierra said nothing, letting the silence stretch, but Hunter wondered what a wealthy man like Logan O'Neill was doing in a trashy dump like this. Why would he just show up and introduce himself to Sierra? And how did he know this Sloan Turner so well?

Whatever the story was, O'Neill was clearly the boss. The terrified proprietor was visibly shaking.

"Please, Miss Masters," O'Neill repeated, "won't you and your friend join me? And don't be too hard on old Sloan here. He's an idiot."

She placed a hand on Turner's arm, oozing sympathy. "If I were you, I'd be careful who I insult these days. Some powerful Indians run around up here, and most of them would love to mop the floor with your head. You should remember that."

Turner nodded, hard.

Hunter choked on laughter. For all his blustering racism, the man was nothing more than a bully and a coward.

Now she turned her attention to the rancher. "As for joining you for lunch, sir, I'm flattered you're a fan of my work. But I won't go inside this restaurant or give this man a dime. On the other hand, I'm very interested in this museum. Perhaps you wouldn't mind showing us around?"

O'Neill looked pleased. "It would be my honor, Miss Masters."

"Good. I have friends in the store as well. Can they join us?"

Turner's oily face went white. "You can't go in there, ma'am! The museum is closed. I have stuff I need to get categorized."

O'Neill lost his temper. "Oh, for God's sake, Turner, don't be ridiculous. You heard the lady. Go unlock the door."

\*\*\*\*

Sloan Turner entered the dark, silent museum ahead of the group and flipped on four switches beside the door. What appeared to be several rooms, each one connected to the next in a straight line, were illuminated in an ugly yellow glare that reminded Sierra of the bug lights Colt set up in campsites. Glass display cases marred by fingerprints were placed in the center of each room, rickety dust-caked shelves lined walls streaked by peeling green paint, and dilapidated books and posters were stacked in the corners. The air was stifling, as musty as the smell of death.

Skye stopped at the door. "I'll wait out here." Her voice sounded tight, strangled, like she couldn't catch her breath.

"I'll stay with her," Colt announced. "Call if you need me."

Sierra scarcely heard the conversation as she entered the room, Hunter following close behind her. Their voices seemed to be coming from inside her head instead of outside of it. Her legs shook, and her heart pounded. She couldn't get air. Something invisible threatened here, something not at peace, something cold and inhibiting and dangerous. Trying to isolate the source of this unrest, she allowed her gaze to wander slowly around this first room.

Finally, her fingers laced tightly behind her back, she walked to a large display case and glanced through the glass at mundane items typically found in small museums. She saw nearly illegible correspondence dated from the early 1900s, torn envelopes bearing postage stamps she didn't recognize, and faded photographs of miners, soldiers, lawmen, gamblers, saloonkeepers, and ladies of the night. Hidden in a dark corner was a case of dusty six-ounce Coca Cola bottles that had never been opened.

Nothing seemed unusual, yet she kept her hands locked behind her back as the sense of oppression deepened. But she still couldn't isolate the source.

She remembered reading an article about a family in Utah that had been arrested for digging up valuable Indian artifacts they'd discovered concealed in an old burial ground on their land and selling them on the black market. This slimy character looked capable of that.

"Where do you get your...items, Mr. Turner?" she asked, trying to keep her voice casual. She brushed past him as she hurried into the next room. "You have some very interesting things here."

"Do you think so, ma'am? I get my stuff from

estate sales all over the Midwest, and lots of folks just give it to me when they clean out their attics or basements because they don't want to bother with it. Fact is some people even hand over entire family collections."

"My, that's generous of them. They just hand them over?"

"Why don't you just hand this stuff over to the Smithsonian or something?" Hunter asked bluntly from his protective post close behind her. "I'm sure they'd love to have it."

"Nope," Turner answered. "I've called them, but they're not interested. Besides, they want everything for free, and I don't give anything away. So I just keep on collecting. Sometimes my wife picks junk up at garage sales, and it turns out to have lots of historical value."

Sierra cocked an eyebrow but said nothing. She had yet to see anything that had "lots of historical value," but that didn't mean it wasn't here. She glanced without interest at a black velvet portrait of Elvis hanging next to an eleven-by-fourteen photograph of some oily, round-faced politician, then came to a quick halt before a painting so old she wouldn't have been surprised if its colors vanished right before her eyes.

It was a fascinating portrait of a remote time and place. In the distance, beneath a glaring sun and cloudless sky, was a rather dilapidated ranch house with a corral off to one side. A family stood in the forefront. An older man, obviously the patriarch, leaned against a young buffalo, his arm draped around its neck. Beside him was a thin, sour-faced woman who looked like she wanted to be anywhere but where she was. Three uncomfortable young boys, dark hair slicked back and stair-stepped in age, stood nearby.

The portrait wasn't well done—the artist possessed little more than mediocre talent—but the scene still managed to draw in her rapt attention.

"I'm a collector from way back, and I donated this, Miss Masters," Logan O'Neill said from close behind her. "The painting itself isn't very good, but it tells an interesting story."

He made her skin crawl. She moved away from him. "What story is that?"

"This was my grandfather, Paul Scott O'Neill. He joined a group of gold prospectors when he was just fifteen and came to the Dakota Territory from St. Louis, Missouri, in 1875. The unhappy woman with him, Sarah Chamberlain, was my grandmother. Grand-Pop was an Indian fighter and a buffalo hunter in his heyday. He was nearly a hundred years old when he died." O'Neill pointed to one of the young boys in the portrait. "This was my father, Christian. The other two boys are my uncles Wayne and Jonathon. They died rather young, but my father didn't pass away until he was eighty-six years old."

"I'm sorry," she replied automatically. Why was he telling her this?

"Oh, he had a great run. He was a successful civil rights attorney in Rapid City, and I followed in his footsteps, although most of my work was in legal services on the Rosebud Reservation down by the Pine Ridge. Anyway, later on he became a senator, a well-known conservationist—specifically of bison—and finally the owner of three huge ranches, all of which are still working today. My wife, Valentina, and I live on the Bison Head Ranch about twenty miles southeast of

Hot Springs."

For the first time in several weeks, her writer's imagination raced so fast it was all she could do to keep up. *An innocent young boy joins a group of scruffy old gold miners and becomes an infamous character like Wild Bill Hickok and begins a line of successful politicians and ranchers with a woman who clearly detests him...*

Now *there* was a family saga she could sink her teeth into.

Aloud she said only, "You must be very proud of him."

"I sure am. The whole O'Neill family story is fascinating. In fact, since you're so interested in American history, I'd love for you to come out to our ranch while you're here and let me show you the real thing."

Sierra's smile was faintly superior. "I grew up on a ranch in Texas, Mr. O'Neill. The Triple M, to be exact. I think I know the real thing."

On the other hand, what was it Hunter had said?

*Maybe you're thinking about the wrong family, or the wrong time period, or maybe even the wrong location...*

She changed her mind. "Mr. O'Neill, we're all staying at the Wiconi Campground near Interior in the Badlands. Is that too inconvenient for a visit out your way?"

O'Neill pulled his wallet from the back pocket of his gray slacks and removed an ornate business card. "Not at all. Here's my cell phone number and anything else you might need to reach me. Call me when you're ready. We'd love to have you."

She took his card. She didn't like or trust him at all, but she wasn't an idiot. She had no intention of ignoring this opportunity. "Thank you so much, Mr. O'Neill. I'll be in touch."

"Will you be visiting the Pine Ridge Indian Reservation?"

"I hope so. There's a lot I'd like to see there."

O'Neill looked doubtful. "Be careful. Pine Ridge is dangerous, and the residents don't like Whites. Have a full tank of gas and bring snacks. You won't find much in the way of fuel or food there."

Sierra felt Hunter's barely contained rage and didn't understand it, but she had to get him away from O'Neill before something happened that had no chance of ending well. She smiled at the rancher. "Thank you. We'll keep that in mind."

She walked away from the men and made her way back to the entrance. As she walked, she felt Hunter's ever-protective presence close behind her.

*What in the world is wrong with him?*

Hunter's cell phone rang, breaking the tension in the room, and she was thankful for it. She walked away from them all—through those ugly rooms, past Skye and Colt still standing at the entrance—and out into the parking lot. With pleasure, she inhaled the cool autumn breeze.

Unlike the dank, musty air inside the museum, it was crisp and clean and pure.

She'd never been so glad to get away from a man and out of a building in her life.

Chapter Eleven

Hunter joined Sierra in the parking lot. "That was Nathan Winterhawk on the phone. He's waiting for me at my cabin. Will you ride with me? I'd like to talk to you."

Sierra was still intent on trying to get away from the museum, so his words only half registered. "Who?"

He raised his eyebrows in amusement. "Nathan Winterhawk. The reason I came here, remember? And you, too."

Her cheeks grew warm. "Of course. I have a letter for him from my mother."

"Well, like I said, he's waiting for us." Then he repeated, "Will you ride with me? I'd like to talk to you."

She hesitated a moment. "Okay. Let me tell Colt and Skye."

"I already did. They're going to follow us." He opened the door of a beat-up four-wheel-drive Jeep that looked like it might have been an old WWII army reject. "She doesn't look like much, but she'll get us where we need to go."

Sierra climbed into the coffee-stained cloth passenger seat and clasped the seat belt across her abdomen. "Are you sure?"

"I rented her in Rapid City, and she hasn't let me down yet." He climbed into the Jeep, strapped himself in, and turned on the ignition, then gazed at her for a long, silent moment and smiled. "Tired?"

"Some."

He pulled out of the parking lot and returned to the main highway, heading west. "Take a nap if you want. You have a little time."

"I thought you wanted to talk to me."

"It's okay. It can wait."

As the conversation died away, she gazed at golden prairies flying past her window and wondered how the Whites and Indians had ever managed to run into each other out here in the first place. Other than the occasional few head of cattle grazing nearby or a single prairie dog standing upright, nose twitching, these endless plains were boring and empty. Every mile or so an enormous billboard appeared on the side of the highway, advertising free ice water at a drugstore in some town called Wall, but otherwise, apparently, South Dakota couldn't claim much of importance.

Hunter slowed and exited the highway onto a two-lane road heading south. Far in the distance emerged the jagged outline of what might have been a mountain range but probably wasn't. Still, excited because *something* promised to break the monotony of these prairies, she pointed to it and bounced in her seat. "What's that?"

"That, my pet," he answered with a chuckle, "is the beginning of the Badlands National Park. We're only about thirty minutes from your new home."

As she looked out the window, she caught her breath in wonder. All the photographs she had seen of this region fell far short of its true magnificence. As the shimmering and luxurious grasslands fell away, peaks and valleys and gullies and buttes of a thousand different colors began to band together for what seemed to be hundreds of miles to form another world, an ethereal moonscape more mystical than anything she'd ever seen before. As the afternoon shadows crept up the sides of saw-toothed ridges and red rock formations, the towering summits and plunging ravines changed shape and texture right before her eyes.

She felt an overpowering urge to get out of the Jeep. "Please stop. Just for a minute."

Without argument, he pulled onto the shoulder. Colt drove right in behind them and parked. She hardly noticed as she opened the Jeep door, stepped outside, and gazed down into a cavernous basin surrounded on all sides by rust-colored buttes and silver-topped mesas.

As she stood there, drinking in the splendid isolation, she realized she wasn't isolated at all but stood in the middle of a deathly silent Indian camp. Even though it was freezing cold, no fires flickered within warm tipis. These tipis were ragged and torn. Scarecrow-thin people walked by her, so close she could've touched them, so close she could smell the odors of sickness and filthy clothing, but no one looked her way. Somewhere in the distance but at the edges of the camp came the long, haunting wail of a tortured woman, a woman beyond heartbreak.

"Are you all right?"

Hunter's concerned voice shattered the stillness, and aching sadness overwhelmed her as the camp dissipated into a dark and murky fog. As soon as the sunlight returned, she took a ragged breath and reached for his hand.

He intertwined his fingers with hers; his touch was

99

comforting. "Let's get back in the car," he said gently. "Colt is watching you like a hawk, and I think Skye's going to get out."

"Stop her," she whispered, holding on to his hand with a death grip. "Please stop her."

He put his arm around her and guided her to the Jeep, waving reassuringly at the motor home. Helping her into her seat, he said in a low voice, "Come on, baby girl. Talk to me. What's going on?"

The familiar endearment brought tears to her eyes, and she caught her breath. She'd never felt so alone in her life. Once, she couldn't have kept so powerful a secret from him—she'd told him *everything*. Once, his touch would've opened the floodgates to her emotions, and she would've blanketed herself in his arms, seeking encouragement and refuge. But not now. She couldn't trust him now.

Now she was losing her mind.

"I'm fine," she whispered as she managed to pull her hand away from the warmth of his grasp. She linked her fingers together tightly in her lap and stared straight ahead, blind to the brutal splendor of the landscape. "You said you wanted to talk to me. Let's talk."

"It can wait."

She leaned against her window and closed her eyes. She didn't care whether they talked or not. She needed to get away and back home to Texas. Something told her she was in a dangerous place; she wasn't welcome here...

"Wake up, Sierra. We're at your campsite."

Startled, she sat upright and rubbed her eyes. Somehow, she'd fallen asleep and missed the last several miles to the campground, but the catnap had helped. She felt a little more in control than before. Suddenly she remembered her mother's note for Nathan Winterhawk. She needed to give it to him as soon as she could, or she'd forget she even had it.

She glanced over at Hunter and yawned. "Please bring Nathan when you come for dinner tonight. We'll eat about six."

"Are you sure?"

"Of course. Skye's a wonderful cook, and she loves to feed people. She'll have more than enough."

"To tell you the truth, that would be great," Hunter answered, clearly relieved. "I still can't cook worth a damn. Can we bring anything?"

"Not a thing. Just yourselves."

"I think we can manage that. We'll see you about six, then. Now let's get you guys settled in."

****

Sierra loved the campsite Colt selected for them. Secluded and romantic, the area opened up to reveal a magnificent view of the tall, pink-and-red rock pinnacles and silver granite bluffs located not a mile away. A full moon shimmering over that region would be amazing. This spectacular scene would also be perfect for her early-morning cup of coffee, which was vitally important to her work. Her favorite time was that quiet period before her busy day began.

Skye joined her at a concrete picnic table in the center of the campsite and handed her a glass of iced tea. "Cooking dinner is going to be great out here. All this rugged isolation brings out the Comanche in me."

"I can understand that. This campground is set up to encourage that feeling, isn't it?"

Because the cabins, tent area, and motor home slots

were all set somewhat away from the busier center of the campground where the store, swimming pool, and playground were located, patrons could easily imagine they were alone in the Badlands. She felt a little chill and looked up at the sky. It was cloudless, the soft pastels of that time right before sunset, empty of anything that might warn about a possible cold snap, but she felt chilled nonetheless. The short nap she managed to take before dinner hadn't helped her feel any more rested.

"Hello, Sierra."

She jumped, startled. She was always a terrible hostess—which was why she tried to never have company. "I'm sorry. I didn't hear you come in. Good evening."

Hunter gave her a puzzled look but said nothing and put a comforting arm around her shoulders. She was grateful for his silence. He moved her toward a dark-skinned stranger standing just inside their campsite.

"Sierra, this is my good friend Nathan Winterhawk. Nathan, this is Sierra Masters."

Sierra didn't know what she'd expected, but it wasn't this Nathan Winterhawk. This man was lean and sinewy, and his ready grin exposed a crooked front tooth. Although he was supposed to have once been a militant Indian, he looked like an ordinary rancher to her, even with the beautiful bone-and-brass choker around his neck and the long, black braid hanging halfway down his back. Like most other ranchers, his jeans were faded, and his battered cowboy hat looked like it had been stomped on by an angry bull. Although deep laugh lines surrounded his dark eyes and gray dotted his heavy brows, his lips were a little pouty, like a child's. She couldn't begin to ascertain his true age.

She offered him her hand. "I'm glad to meet you," she said with a shy smile. "I've heard so much about you."

His grin disappeared, and he didn't take her hand right away. He just looked at her, eyes narrowed, his gaze so probing it went far beyond simple curiosity. Yet when his fingers did touch hers, she felt a jolt of recognition that made no sense at all. She'd never seen this man before in her life.

But she knew him, and he knew her.

At that moment, she and Nathan Winterhawk might have been the only two people in the world. All sound receded into the background: tinkling ice cubes and soft music, Skye and Colt's friendly argument about the correct way to grill a perfect steak, a neighbor's barked commands to a disobedient dog.

Sierra gestured to the picnic table. "Please, sit down. I'm glad you could join us."

He didn't move.

Hunter cleared his throat and introduced Nathan to Colt and Skye. Watching them, she jammed her hands into the front pockets of her fleece-lined jacket and touched the letter her mother had written. As a nippy autumn wind blew her long hair around her face, she shivered and yearned to go back inside the motor home where it was warm. But her feet were rooted to the ground.

Hunter had claimed this man and his family were doing all they could to bring the old ways back to the reservation. Her imagination had conjured up the image of an angry warrior like Crazy Horse or Red Cloud, but not this mild-mannered rancher. While this man was intense and strong, he wasn't threatening.

Finished with the introductions and quiet chitchat, Nathan Winterhawk turned away from Skye and Colt, his gaze once more seeking Sierra. He found her, and she couldn't look away. Her heart pounded, and her throat went dry. She'd never felt the pull of a magnetic force so powerful she couldn't resist it, but she felt it now.

Then, without any warning at all, she heard her mother's voice.

*We met him at Wounded Knee. He's brilliant. I loved listening to him.*

The memory calmed her, and her heartbeat slowed to a more normal rhythm. Whatever this was about, it was meant to happen.

She pulled the letter from her jacket pocket and handed it to him. "This is for you. It's from my mother."

He didn't even look surprised. He just nodded and ripped open the envelope. "Do you mind if I read it now?"

"Please do."

He sat down at the picnic table and began to read. Every once in a while, he stopped long enough to fix that penetrating stare on Sierra's face, as if he could see into her soul, but then returned to the letter without a word. Feeling like she was intruding on his privacy, she grew so uncomfortable she turned her back on him and gazed out toward the Badlands now swathed in deepening evening shadows.

Out there was land no one could thrive on, which was the main reason the government had given it to the

Indians in the first place. Yet the Lakota had managed to survive on it for more than one hundred and fifty years in spite of everything that had been thrown at them. Out there was land that told the story of a remarkable people, holding within silent tombs of granite and clay the bones and artifacts of ancient history.

And, out there on that land, something was calling to her, but she didn't know who or what it was, friend or enemy. She only knew she had to respond.

"Miss Masters?"

The sound of Nathan's deep voice behind her, then the feel of his hands on her shoulders as he turned her around to face him, left her weak with fear—but that didn't make any sense. She had no reason to be afraid of him.

"Yes, sir?" Her voice was hoarse. She cleared her throat and tried again. "Yes, sir?"

He dropped his hands to his sides and took a step backward. "Why are you here? What do you think we can do for you?"

Colt's voice exploded through the tension. "Hey, wait just a damn minute! Who the hell do you think you are—"

She held up her hand and gave a fierce shake of her head, not taking her gaze from Nathan's face. She wasn't a confrontational person, but she had to make him understand she wasn't a threat to him or anyone else.

"May I read my mother's letter, Mr. Winterhawk? I haven't read it. It wasn't addressed to me."

He handed it over without a word. She took it from him, removed it from the envelope, and turned her back on him. Her hands shook as she began to read.

*Dear Nathan,*

*Before I begin, please let me tell you I pray you and your family are all well.*

*Your colleague, Hunter Davenport, is a friend of our family and informs us you're working with him on an important documentary. We're all very glad to hear it. Hunter has also agreed to introduce you to our adopted daughter, Sierra Elyse Masters. If you're reading this letter, you've met her by now.*

*Sierra is actually the child of little Pauline Kills Quick—whom you may or may not have known. We legally adopted Sierra right after her birth in Rapid City on March 28, 1974, at the pleading of Pauline and her auntie Julia Farewell, whom I understand is no longer living. Sierra's given name was Madonna Kills Quick after her great-grandmother. We have no idea who Sierra's father was, except he was a very powerful White man who raped Pauline when she was just fourteen and got away with it. That, of course, isn't surprising—especially during that time.*

*We've had no contact with any of these people since we took Sierra from Rapid City and returned to Texas. I've always felt terrible about leaving you and Melanie without even a good-bye, but you know how dangerous everything was. We needed to get Pauline's baby off the reservation, and the fewer people that knew we had her, the better. For everyone's safety, we've stayed away and out of contact.*

*Sierra found out about her birth not long ago when Hunter showed her some photographs of us at Wounded Knee in 1973. As you can imagine, she's pretty confused and shocked right now.*

*Please be kind to her, Nathan. This isn't her fault, and she's just looking for answers. As a Lakota Sioux, you know how important heritage and family is. I'm trusting you will help her find this part of hers.*

*Hunter will give you our phone numbers, email addresses, and home address in case you want to get in touch with us for any reason. We've thought of you so often over the years but realized it was best we not contact you. However, we'd love to hear from you, so please don't hesitate…*

*Give my love to Melanie. I've missed her.*

Mama had signed the letter with the swirls and flourishes of her familiar signature. Homesickness washed over Sierra. She'd never felt so alone.

After a long silence, she walked to Colt, who still stood beside the grill with his fists clenched, and handed him her mother's letter.

"Please read this," she said in a low voice. "You need to understand what's happening here. Nathan Winterhawk isn't my enemy, Colt. He's not yours, either."

Colt shook his head. "I don't need—"

"I want you to," she interrupted, touching his arm. "Please. It's important to me."

Colt subsided and began to read. Once he had finished, he folded the pages and handed them back to Sierra. He looked a little pale and perplexed but summed up his feelings in just three words. "I'll be damned."

She smiled at him and walked back to Nathan, her heart pounding in her throat. "May I tell you something?"

He shrugged. The man wasn't big on words, Sierra

thought, but neither was she. Yet this time she had no choice; she couldn't write her feelings. This time she had to speak, straight from her heart.

"I want to bring this right out into the open, Mr. Winterhawk," she said in a calm voice that gave no hint of how nervous she was. "I think I understand how you feel. You look at me, and you see a White woman. You're right. My parents are White, and they will always be my parents. They gave me a wonderful life, and I wouldn't change a thing about it. I have no desire to be anyone other than who I am.

"All I know about Indians comes from my friend Skye here—she's part Comanche—and the movie *Dances with Wolves*, which I saw three times. As pathetic as that sounds, it's the truth. I honestly don't know much more than that.

"But what I *do* know is you have no reason to trust me. I know White people have always lied to you, stolen your land, and ripped you off your reservation in some sick attempt to turn you into something you're not. I know White people are trying to steal your culture and your spirituality even today—maybe because they don't have any of their own. But please understand this—I'm not trying to steal anything from you. I'm an American capitalist, and very proud of it.

"I just have relatives here—or I think I do—and I'd like to know them. I'd like to know if they're alive. I'd like to know if they're all right. I'd feel that way no matter what ethnicity they are. You don't have to trust me right now. I understand. All I ask is you don't judge me because I consider myself a White woman. If you can do that, Mr. Winterhawk, I promise I won't judge you because you're an Indian."

When amused respect danced across Nathan's weathered face, Sierra's legs went weak with relief. In some way she didn't quite understand, she'd cleared a dangerous impasse and come out, victorious, on the other side.

He tilted her chin and gazed deep into her eyes. "My spirit recognized you as soon as I saw you, and yours recognized me. I'm sure your parents thought they were doing the right thing when they took you off the reservation. It's happened often over the years, and I don't judge them. I'm just happy you're back."

He spoke in a sort of clipped cadence, with little inflection in his words. She suspected English wasn't his first language, but he didn't speak with that ridiculous, stilted "Indian talk" she'd always heard in the movies. He stroked her hair away from her face as if she were a child at his knee instead of a full-grown woman, and the deep sorrow in his expression was almost unbearable.

"You're welcome here, Madonna Kills Quick," he finished with a gentle smile. "Like so many of us...you've been gone far too long."

Chapter Twelve

Hunter was glad to see Nathan so relaxed. He was an intense man with a lot on his mind, so this evening was a great idea.

Nathan leaned back in a camp chair outside of Sierra's motor home, an expression of blissful satisfaction on his face, and patted his now somewhat distended belly. His dark eyes twinkled as he grinned up at Skye. "I'd have married me a Comanche woman if I knew you were such good cooks."

Skye twinkled back. "My grandma taught me. She was Irish."

He roared with laughter. Then, wiping his eyes, he sputtered, "Well, whoever taught you, they knew what they were doing. Thanks for inviting me. I didn't realize I was so hungry."

"The more the merrier, Mr. Winterhawk," Skye answered, blushing. She began clearing the table. "I love to feed hungry folks."

"*Nathan*, Miss Skye. Call me *Nathan*."

When Sierra arose to help, Skye waved her off. "Go visit. It's getting cold outside. Colt here's a real man. He'll give me a hand."

"Slave driver," Colt muttered.

Sierra smiled and opened the door to the motor home. "Thanks, guys. Hunter, would you and Mr. Winterhawk like some hot tea?"

Nathan gave a broad grin. "If you don't stop calling me *Mr.* Winterhawk, I'm leaving right now. You're insulting me."

"Oh, I'm sorry... I didn't realize..."

Hunter laughed out loud. "He's kidding, silly. We'd love some."

Hunter followed Nathan inside and was grateful for its warmth. Watching her as she took three coffee mugs out of a cabinet above the stove and removed tea bags from a canister on the counter, he stifled a grin at how ill at ease she still seemed in a kitchen, even after all these years.

"This is a real nice place," Nathan observed as he removed his windbreaker and handed it to Hunter. "A house on wheels."

She smiled. "Thank you. We enjoy it."

When the tea had finished brewing and she'd served her guests, she slid into the booth beside Hunter and propped her chin on her hand. She said nothing—a little trick to getting the other guy to say more than he intended. It was a ploy Hunter had taught her himself. The silence stretched.

"How are your parents?" Nathan finally asked, dropping a sugar cube into his tea. "I've thought of them a lot over the years."

"They're fine, thank you."

"What does your father do now?"

"He and my mother run the family cattle ranch in Texas, the Triple M outside of the little town of Bandera. A couple of years ago, they made it into a guest ranch. It keeps them busy."

"Cowboys and Indians, huh? I like that idea—as long as you let the Indians win every now and again."

Hunter could see from her uncertain smile she wasn't sure if Nathan was serious or not.

"Do you have children?" she asked finally.

His eyes lit up. "I have three sons and two grandchildren. My oldest, Eli, works with me."

"I'll be sure to tell Mama. She'll be glad to hear about them."

"Do you have any brothers or sisters?"

She shook her head. "No, I'm sorry to say. I was it."

This time the conversation died abruptly, and no one seemed willing to voice the question hanging over the room like a dark cloud.

Hunter decided to cut to the chase. "Nathan, did you know Pauline Kills Quick?"

After what seemed an eternity of silence, Nathan looked directly at Sierra. "Yes, I knew little Pauline. Everyone did."

"What can you tell us about her?"

Nathan's face clouded. "She was a special little girl, beautiful and smart. Her mother, Angel, died in childbirth, so Angel's sister, Julia Farewell, and Grandma Madonna mostly raised her. They were very traditional, but Pauline's father, Arlin Black Thunder, wasn't at all. He's a Sicangu Lakota, and his family lives in the town of St. Paul on the Rosebud Reservation. That's right next to Pine Ridge. He wanted to be whiter than the White man, and he turned his back on everyone.

"One day he drove past Grandma Madonna's house and saw Pauline playing out in the yard. She was only about seven years old. He just grabbed her up and took her straight to the Indian boarding school at St. Paul

Mission there on the Rosebud. I heard later that Grandma Madonna sang her death song right there in the front yard. There was nothing anyone could do about it. Anyway, Pauline did okay in the school, and I guess she liked it well enough. I never heard that she didn't.

"I was older than she was, and I moved to California in 1968 when I was sixteen, so I didn't know much about her. But I do know she lived at the boarding school nearly all the time, and then she babysat for a White family during holidays, so she didn't have much contact with anyone. I think that's the way her father wanted it, but I heard it broke her Grandma Madonna's heart. Arlin Black Thunder doesn't have much to do with Traditional Indians even now."

"Do you know anything about his family?" Hunter asked curiously.

"Well, I know that *his* father, Joseph Black Thunder, had a nice little farm near the town of Mission on the Rosebud. When Arlin was about ten, the government sent him to an Indian school up in Minnesota, and Joseph died not long after. I don't know what happened to the farm, but Arlin didn't come back to the reservation for a long time. I heard the Indian school turned him into a real hang-around-the-fort Injun, but I don't really know. I've only seen him a couple of times in my life."

Sierra frowned. "What's a hang-around-the-fort Injun?"

Nathan grinned. "Well, back in the day, reservation Indians who squealed on other reservation Indians were called hang-around-the-fort Injuns. They got special treatment from the government—land and commodities, stuff like that—for being such good Indians. I don't know if that really fits Arlin Black Thunder, but he's done pretty well by White standards. He's been on the Rosebud Tribal Council, and last I heard he volunteered at the Rosebud Chamber of Commerce. He lives in a nice house and drives a nice car. I don't know anything else about him."

Hunter understood. Traditional Indians, especially militants, had little use for Indians who had successfully adapted to the White culture.

Nathan changed the subject quickly. "Anyway, let me get back to little Pauline. It's getting late. I didn't like California, so when I headed back to Pine Ridge in the early '70s, I was part of that whole Red Power Movement, an AIM member, and mad as hell. There was a lot of trouble brewing, and I didn't have time to worry about Pauline or anyone else. Melanie and I were married in 1972, and then in '73 us Indians took over the Knee. When the occupation ended, many of us had to run like hell to stay ahead of the feds. We did that for quite a while. When I finally came back to the rez to stay, I found out little Pauline had disappeared in late '73, and no one seemed to know where she was. She was only fourteen."

Hunter was perplexed. "How does a girl so young just disappear like that?"

"Back then it wasn't all that unusual. People disappeared all the time. Anyway, toward the end of 1974, her auntie Julia Farewell was run over and her body dumped on Whisper Butte out in the Badlands. Melanie told me later everyone knew it was because she was an AIM member snooping around into Dickie

Wilson's financial affairs. Anyway, when Julia's body was identified, Madonna Kills Quick—your great-grandmother, Sierra—went sort of crazy. She left her husband and moved out into the Badlands right afterward. Melanie is the only one who sees her now."

Sierra's eyes widened. "My great-grandmother is still living? I assumed she was dead."

"Oh no, she's definitely not dead. Your great-grandfather died not long after she left him, but Grandma Madonna is still very much alive. She *is* old, though, and she doesn't like anybody except Melanie, who was a good friend of Julia's. So Melanie goes out to see to her once or twice a month. Some say she's crazy, but Mel swears she's not."

"Madonna doesn't have any actual relatives who would check on her?"

"In her heart Melanie *is* related. *Mitakuye Oyasin.*" Nathan grinned. "It means *we are all related.* We Lakota take that pretty seriously. We end every prayer that way, like 'Amen.' It actually means we're related to everything in the universe, not just to each other, but we still have to be careful who we fall in love with—if you get my meaning."

He winked at her. "But here's a little trivia that might interest you. The Kills Quick name came from your great-great-great-grandfather, Kills Buffalo Quick. When the White men began carving out land allotments in the 1880s, they shortened the name to Kills Quick."

"Kills Buffalo Quick..." she mused. "I like that. Was your name always Winterhawk?"

"No. My father's grandfather was called Red Hawk Soars in Winter. But the Indian agent that registered him on the Pine Ridge Reservation shortened it to

Winterhawk."

"Well, I like it. *Winterhawk* would sound good in a book title."

His eyes narrowed. "Would it? I never thought about it. You're not going to write a book, are you?"

"I don't know, Nathan. I'm a writer. It's what I do."

"Well, that just shows how White you really are." His smile took the sting out of his words. "Lakota history, *all* Indian history for that matter, is oral. We never wrote anything down. At least, not like you do. I have a friend named Byron Little Hand who can recite you fifteen generations back in his family. One of these days you'll be able to do that, too."

"Byron Little Hand?" She looked at Hunter. "Isn't he the private detective you hired to help find Pauline?"

"Yes. I hoped we could meet with him tomorrow, but he's out of town."

"Little Hand is a good man," Nathan said with a nod. "If anyone can find Pauline, he can."

She returned her attention to Nathan. "What was my grandfather's name again? The hang-around-the-fort-Indian guy?"

"Arlin Black Thunder. Like I said, we don't have anything to do with him, but he's still here...hanging around."

For a moment, Hunter almost felt sorry for this confused, misplaced Arlin Black Thunder who hadn't done anything except try to survive in a White world he'd never asked for. Hunter, had he been an Indian, would've probably done the same thing.

He decided to change the subject to one a little safer. "Excuse me, Nathan. You said earlier that

Pauline babysat for a White family. Do you know who that was?"

"No, but it wouldn't be hard to find out. There aren't too many secrets on the rez—even old secrets. And that wouldn't have been a secret, anyway."

Hunter snapped his fingers. "Listen, Nathan, speaking of White people... I need your help with something. I meant to tell Sierra this afternoon, but I forgot."

"Sure, if I can."

"Actually...what I need you to do is back me up. I need her to understand that Logan O'Neill is a very dangerous man."

"Logan O'Neill?" Nathan all but spat the name, and his lip curled in distaste. "Sierra, how do you know him?"

"I don't. We just met today."

"And you told him you'd visit his ranch," Hunter said. "That's not safe. I don't want you to do it."

"You don't want me to do it? Really?"

Nathan cleared his throat. "Sierra, you don't know anything about him. Whatever you consider yourself, the truth is you're Indian, and you can't trust him. Period."

"But he doesn't know that. I'm a writer interested in his story, that's all."

Hunter snorted. "The O'Neill family is very powerful here. More powerful than you can imagine. They do what they want, and no one stops them. You're no match for him."

"And none of that matters. He's only interested in me because he thinks I'm some kind of a celebrity."

Nathan cocked his head to one side, and a look of

amusement crossed his weathered face. "I don't think you're going to talk her out of anything, Hunter," he said finally. "My wife is just like her. So just do the best you can to keep her out of trouble."

She tossed Hunter an icy look of triumph. "I'll be careful, I promise."

Nathan looked doubtful as he glanced at Hunter. "Anything else?"

"Just one more thing. Alexa Masters said Pauline was raped by a very powerful White man, but nobody would say who it was. Do you know anything about that?"

"No, I wasn't here. But I'm not surprised. Those were brutal times. Back then people on the reservation, especially traditional people, just tried to survive. People disappeared all the time—sometimes on purpose, sometimes not. Now we're fighting to rediscover and reunite our *tiyospayes*. It's a matter of life and death to this reservation—in fact, to American Indians everywhere."

"*Tiyospaye?*" Sierra repeated, frowning.

"*Tiyospaye* is the Lakota word for our extended family. In the Lakota tradition, everyone in a family— mother, father, grandparents, aunties, uncles, cousins, children—everyone lived together and took care of everyone else. The *tiyospaye* was the most important aspect of Lakota society until the White man came in and destroyed it. Not only did he exterminate our culture, our spirituality, and our language, but he also broke up our families with land allotments. That diluted our strength as effectively as his slaughter of the buffalo herds and the massacre of our women and children." Nathan gave a wry, apologetic grin. "Sierra, I know that this sounds like a classroom lesson, and I'm sorry, but what I'm saying actually concerns you."

"Me? How?"

"You're a part of somebody's *tiyospaye*, Madonna Kills Quick. Out there, somewhere, somebody's been looking for you. You're the missing piece of somebody's heart, somebody's family, a puzzle part so important the puzzle will never make any sense without you. There are many families like that on this reservation because they were shattered just as your family was."

Hunter couldn't even imagine the myriad of emotions that had to be racing through Sierra. She'd come here to find her birth mother, that's all. He was sure she'd never considered someone here might actually want to find her.

Nathan slid out of the booth and stood up with a grin. "Speaking of broken *tiyospayes*... I'm sorry to leave like this, but I need to go before my wife throws me out of mine. I'm supposed to pick her up from her sister's house in Wanblee tonight, and I'm already late. Melanie may be little, but she can kick my butt."

As Hunter and Sierra followed Nathan to the front door, Hunter decided to jump right in while she was still speaking to him. He was amazed at how nervous he was—like a high school kid with a crush. "Can I pick you up in the morning? I'd like to take you to the Wounded Knee Memorial."

"Well, I'm pretty tired..."

Determined, he forged ahead. "Come on, Sierra. I'll pick you up about ten. If I didn't have some film to edit first, we'd leave a lot earlier. It takes forever to get anywhere around here."

119

She gave him a suspicious glance. "What about Colt and Skye?"

"They're more than welcome, of course. We'll all fit in the Jeep."

"Listen," Nathan cut in with a grin, "why don't you all join us for a gathering the day after tomorrow at Red Tail Park near my home? Hunter knows the way."

"A gathering?" she asked.

"We're all getting together for games, dancing, horseback riding, races...and lots of food. Most of the rez will be there."

She frowned. "Are you sure it will be all right with...well, with everyone?"

"Of course." He patted her shoulder in reassurance. "I won't tell anyone who you are until you're ready. My friends know Hunter's filming with me, so we'll just say you're all friends of his from Texas."

She nodded. "I appreciate that. We'd love to come. What time should we be there?"

"Whenever you want. Once you've been out here a while, you'll find we Indians don't put much stock in time."

Chapter Thirteen

The next morning, Sierra closed the motor home door behind her and prayed she wasn't making a huge mistake by going with Hunter alone into the Badlands. She'd tried to come up with an excuse he'd believe, but she knew better. No matter what she said, he'd never buy it. So here she was.

"Is it just the two of us?" he asked as they walked together to his Jeep, now dirtier than it had been the night before. "I thought you wanted Skye and Colt to come along."

She shrugged and climbed into the passenger seat. "They're tired, and Skye has an upset stomach. Colt wanted to stay with her. I think they've got a thing going."

"Well, that's too bad. They would've had a good time. Buckle up." He slammed her door shut, then joined her in the Jeep and buckled his own seat belt. "All set? Do you have your camera?"

"Check." She glanced around the Jeep. "I don't see any of your equipment. You're not working today?"

"Nope." He backed out of the drive and headed toward the campground entrance. "I worked this morning. Today is all yours."

She gazed out her window as he drove away from what she thought was probably the only semblance of civilization she'd see all day. She was accustomed to heading out into the boonies, but these boonies were different from any she'd ever seen before.

These were *real* boonies, and she needed to put her guard back up—fast. He doubtless thought he was going to spend the day sweet-talking an old flame who was still into him, but that just wasn't going to happen.

She'd determined that this morning as she was getting dressed. Even though she was going to be alone with him in the middle of the Badlands, she had no intention of looking good while she was out there.

As a means of protection, she'd tied her hair up into a casual ponytail, slathered moisturizer over her face, and rubbed lip balm into her lips. Dark sunglasses covered her eyes. She wore comfortable jeans, a pair of unattractive but excellent hiking boots that made her feet look too big for her body, and a baggy red sweatshirt over a lightweight blouse so she could layer down if necessary. The afternoon sun could easily burn off the early-morning chill.

After slowing for a fork in the road, he headed south on a fairly smooth highway and glanced over at her. "I've read all your books, Sierra. You're a wonderful writer."

"Thank you."

Why did he make her so nervous? Why was it so difficult for them to talk? Once, there hadn't been enough hours in the day—or night, for that matter—for them to say everything they had to say to one another. Now, all she wanted was to...well, she didn't know what she wanted now. And that was the problem.

"Have you ever thought about writing the script for a documentary?"

"No."

"Why not?"

She was silent as she tried to decide how honest she should be. If she told him the truth, he'd laugh out loud. If she told him a lie, he'd see right through it.

When she reached a decision and spoke, she hated how tentative she sounded. "I'm not like you. I don't know how I feel about much of anything. I don't have the nerve to put myself out there like that."

She waited for his derisive laughter, but it didn't come. Instead, he ran his fingers through his hair in a gesture of frustration she recognized but had long forgotten.

"I can't tell if you're serious or not."

"I'm serious. But don't get a big head about it. It's just not what I'm good at."

"You mean you're better at lying than expressing facts."

An angry retort arose to her lips, but she glanced at him before she spoke and saw the teasing grin on his face. She chuckled nervously. He didn't know how close to the truth he'd come.

"I guess you could say that," she said after a moment. "That is, if you consider a historical novel based on well-researched fact a lie."

"Touché. I guess I walked into that one."

"You did."

He laughed and slowed the Jeep so he could turn off the well-maintained highway onto a pothole-dotted road. As they wound their way through the rugged terrain, bouncing and jostling enough to jar their teeth loose, memories washed over Sierra, memories she hadn't recalled in years. The long Sunday afternoon drives she and Hunter had taken deep into the lush

Rosetta Diane Hoessli

Texas hill country had always been like this for her—quiet and sleepy as she got lost in her own thoughts, never feeling the need to break the silence with meaningless chatter. They were together, and nothing else mattered.

Now the immense isolation of this vivid landscape magnified the silence in the Jeep—the companionable, unstrained silence she remembered so well—and she was bathed in a once-familiar sense of serenity and calm.

His voice broke the stillness. "I need to talk to you about Logan O'Neill."

The serenity disappeared. "Why? He's just an old man. I appreciate you wanting to protect me, but I think you're overreacting."

"I'm not protecting *you*. There's just something about O'Neill I don't like. So even if you won't be careful of him for your own sake, I'd appreciate it if you'd be careful of him for mine."

"You're just here to do a film on Nathan Winterhawk's attempts to bring back the old ways to the reservation, right? Why would O'Neill care about that? Besides, he wasn't interested in you at all yesterday. He was interested in me."

He shrugged. "I don't think so. He's interested in a lot more than just you. Be careful. He's dangerous."

She subsided. Hunter Davenport was a lot of things, but he'd never steered her wrong. If he said something was dangerous, she had no doubt it was.

"All right," she agreed. "I'll be careful—and I won't go anywhere near him without you."

"Thanks."

The conversation died. As she wracked her brain to

find a safer subject to discuss, a thick, black cloud seemed to pass over the sun and enveloped the craggy landscape in darkness. An unpaved road appeared out of nowhere, and a pickup truck crossed in front of them. She heard the drunken laughter of the driver as he leaned out of the window.

A young Indian girl stumbled alongside the truck. Her breathless and terrified sobs carried across the wind.

Then, as quickly as it had appeared, the road and the truck vanished.

The man vanished.

The young girl vanished.

Heart pounding, Sierra glanced at Hunter to be certain he was still driving and everything remained the same. He drummed his fingertips against the steering wheel like he always did when he was thinking. His face remained unchanged.

He hadn't seen a thing.

****

Something was going on with her, that was for sure, but Hunter didn't know what it was. Once, he could've asked her and she would've told him, but not anymore. She'd changed so much over the years. For the most part he liked the changes, but her refusal or inability to confide in him now was one change he didn't like at all. A blind man could see she needed help, but it seemed that he, Hunter Davenport, was the one person she'd never ask.

Now she stared straight ahead, white-faced and tense in direct contrast to her earlier relaxed demeanor. He had to bring her back to a comfortable place, and he had to do it fast.

"Are you familiar with the history of Wounded Knee?"

"Not much. I remember there was a battle there or something—"

"Not a battle," he interrupted firmly, "a massacre. Back in the late 1800s, a Paiute religious leader named Wovoka convinced the Indians—mainly Lakota, Arapahoe, and Cheyenne—that he'd seen a dance in a dream. He called it the Ghost Dance and promised the Indians that if they learned it and danced it religiously, it would bring back the buffalo and make the White people disappear. They even wore shirts called Ghost Shirts that were supposed to make them bulletproof. Even Sitting Bull believed it, or they thought he did."

"How sad."

He nodded. "It is, but these people were desperate. They were starving on reservations, unable to hunt, practice their own traditions, or care for their families. The Whites had emasculated warriors, turned nomads into farmers, and destroyed a way of life that had been theirs for centuries. They were desperate prisoners, so the Ghost Dance was the lifeline they grabbed on to.

"But the Ghost Dance Movement scared the White settlers to death. So they got the Indians all worked up and then reported to the government they were on the warpath. This forced the feds as well as the governor of South Dakota to send in troops in 1890, which was what brought on the massacre at Wounded Knee. Chief Big Foot was actually bringing his starving people to the Pine Ridge Reservation to surrender and had set up camp down by Wounded Knee Creek. The village was attacked by the 7th Cavalry in the early morning, and many of them were slaughtered."

He could see she was doing everything in her power not to cry, but he wasn't sure why. He wished he could help, but he couldn't. He had to wait until she finally confided in him, and he had no idea when—or if—that would happen.

He took one more stab at it. "Are you all right, Sierra?"

"Why wouldn't I be?"

He shrugged. "I don't know. I'm just asking."

"It's a sad story, that's all."

And then suddenly, for some reason, he recalled the day before when she'd asked him to pull over and let her out of the Jeep. As he watched her from the driver's seat, he'd known something unusual was happening, but he had no idea what it was.

Now he took a chance and desperately plucked a bizarre notion right out of the air. "I read on the internet where someone called South Dakota 'a thin place.' Do you know what that means?"

She shook her head.

"Well, this lady said some places on this planet have only a thin veil separating the known world from the spirit world, and Pine Ridge Indian Reservation is one of them. I thought you might want to know that."

"Why?"

He answered with a teasing chuckle, "Hey, it's okay. If you don't want to tell me, I understand. But we're not far from the Wounded Knee Memorial. There's something wrong with you if you don't see ghosts there."

"I'm not seeing ghosts," she muttered. "I don't believe in ghosts."

He slowed the Jeep as he turned off the rutted road

onto one that promised to be even more jarring, and stopped. He reached for her hand. "I don't know what's going on with you, but I do know it's nothing to be ashamed of. People see things out here all the time. Don't be afraid of it."

She jerked her hand from his and glared at him defiantly. "I don't know what you're talking about." Then she added in a whisper, "I'm not afraid."

He said nothing.

When she looked at him again, as if she wanted to determine whether she could trust him or not, he was as intrigued by the flecks of topaz in her dark eyes as he'd always been. He could lose himself in those eyes, and he had…many times. Those eyes, slanted and unfathomable, had always been his downfall.

She broke the silence. "What about you? Do you see things out here?"

"No, that's a gift I don't have. But I keep hoping."

She continued to gaze at him. Hunter held his breath as he waited for her to talk to him. He knew that look. She was trying to make a decision.

"Are you teasing me?" she whispered finally.

He released his breath in a gusty sigh and shook his head. "No, I mean it. It's a gift I'd love to have."

She lightly touched the deep cleft in his chin in a familiar gesture of affection he'd almost forgotten. When she blushed and looked away, he knew she'd never intended to touch him. He took her hand once more and pressed his lips against the soft, warm flesh of her palm before gently placing it back in her lap.

"Remember, Sierra, I'm in your corner. When you're ready to talk, I'll listen."

Chapter Fourteen

When Hunter parked in an open area near the Wounded Knee Memorial, Sierra was struck by the heavy sadness in the air. And as he helped her from the Jeep, she knew from the sober expression on his face he felt it, too.

This land was so much more than just another dusty historical site, lost and forgotten out on the plains. Here, a people had been betrayed and slaughtered by a country that had seen them not as human beings, but as impediments to progress. This truly was sacred ground. *A thin place*, Hunter had called it, and for the first time she understood why.

As crazy as it seemed, she was certain all she had to do was take a single step in any direction and she could move through a delicate but invisible veil of time straight into the past.

"Don't take your camera with you," Hunter advised, closing the Jeep door. "I have dozens of photos of this place, and you're welcome to any of them." He took her hand and pointed toward a fork in the road out in front of them. "That's the Wounded Knee Valley," he told her softly. "Right down there behind the tree ridge is the Wounded Knee Creek and the dry ravine where the original slaughter happened. Up that hill behind us is the old cemetery. Nearly three hundred Indians are buried in a mass grave up there—buried by soldiers who left them out in the freezing snow for several days before finally returning to drop them into a ditch."

She couldn't speak. Speech seemed a sacrilege.

As they walked toward the cemetery, she counted only three other vehicles in the unpaved parking area, and two of them were small tour buses from the nearby town of Custer. A little group of sightseers passed various headstones as they followed their tour leader, a pale and balding man who often gestured toward Wounded Knee Creek as he spoke.

A washed-out green sign described the history of this area, and a metal sheet bearing the word *Massacre* covered what Sierra assumed had been the word *Battle*. To her, this was a prime example of how the Lakota had begun to reclaim their history.

They halted at the entrance to the cemetery. Enclosed within a chain-link fence was a long, rectangular piece of ground bordered by a brick-and-concrete walkway. A tall but unimposing stone obelisk stood nearby as a desolate memorial to an episode in history that few cared to remember.

This was the mass grave Hunter had spoken of.

Clearly, the cemetery was personal to the Lakota. Here, straggly weeds grew tall around headstones, markers, and wooden crosses. Colorful fabric pouches tied with string were attached up and down the fencing and fluttered in the afternoon breeze. Only the faded artificial flowers stuck atop a few isolated gravesites seemed lonely and forgotten.

She pushed open the fence gate and made her way to the monument.

Etched on the stone was a long list of Indian

names: *Chief Big Foot, White American, Pretty Hawk, Spotted Thunder*, and many more. At its base were sticks of sage and braided sweetgrass, perhaps left as gifts. Without thinking, she reached out and touched the monument.

She heard the soft, plaintive cry of an infant. It came from a distance, little more than a whisper on the wind. Puzzled, she looked around the old cemetery. It was quiet, deserted except for the small tour group. No young children, no babies…

Nathan Winterhawk's voice broke the stillness. "Good morning, my friends. I thought I might find you here."

Sierra frowned, confused. Where had he come from?

"Hi," Hunter responded. "This is a surprise."

"I stopped in to do a little cleanup. I live nearby, and people may come here tomorrow during the gathering. I wanted to be sure it looks nice." He touched Sierra's shoulder. "I'm glad you're here. Follow me. I want to show you something."

Nathan walked back through the gate and away from the fenced-in memorial toward a few isolated headstones at the rear of the old cemetery. She walked behind him, trying not to step on any other graves. When he stopped and pointed at a flat marker on the ground, she read the inscription. Her eyes blurred with tears.

*Julia Kills Quick Farewell, 1944-1974.*

"This is Pauline's auntie I told you about last night," Nathan said softly. "Your mother's good friend. She was murdered during the Reign of Terror."

Sierra glanced at him. "Why do you say she was

murdered? Hunter said the FBI claimed she was drunk and got run over. He says they called it an accident."

"No way. Number one, Julia was beaten by someone and left at your parents' apartment not long before her death, so we know someone was after her. Number two, Julia was a nurse's aide in the Indian Hospital up in Rapid City, and she didn't drink. Number three, she always wore a medicine bag around her neck that had been in her family for generations. But when her body was returned to her mother, the medicine bag was gone. No, she was murdered by one of Dickie Wilson's GOONs to keep her from finding out any more about his financial dealings."

She frowned. "Surely a missing medicine bag doesn't prove anything. Maybe someone at the morgue took it. Lots of people steal Indian stuff."

Nodding, he cupped his hand around her elbow and escorted her away from the gravesite. "You're probably right. Now listen, I would like it very much if you two would join Melanie and me for supper tonight. Our sons and their wives and kids live with us right now, but they won't be home tonight. Tonight, we're alone."

She remembered her mother's description of Nathan's wife, Melanie, and shivered.

*I was scared to death of her, but I loved her…*

Nathan seemed to read her mind. "Don't worry. No one's going to hold it against you that you don't know our culture, especially not Melanie."

"Please don't tell her who I am, okay?"

His roadmap of a face grew completely serious. "I promised you I wouldn't tell, and I won't. You'll tell her when you're ready."

\*\*\*\*

As Hunter drove toward the Winterhawk home, Sierra's gaze swept the horizon. She expected to see hundreds of painted warriors on horseback line the hills as they had in dozens of old Hollywood westerns, but the landscape remained empty and remote. Still, she had the unmistakable sense they weren't alone. The atmosphere felt heavy and teeming with invisible souls yearning for an opportunity to tell stories never voiced before.

The sky had darkened during their visit to the old cemetery, and Sierra glanced over at Hunter curiously. "What time is it?"

"Nearly six."

"It looks a lot later than that. How far are we from Nathan's house?"

"Just a few miles."

She leaned her head against the window and closed her eyes. Even though the potholes in the road all but jarred her teeth loose, she needed to rest.

One enormous raindrop splattered against the windshield; thunder rumbled in the distance. She caught her breath, and her eyes popped open. Purple and pea-green thunderheads churned across the sky.

His voice was soothing. "Don't worry. We'll head straight for Nathan's house and get there before the storm hits. Buckle up."

Lightning shot straight down to the earth; explosive claps of thunder reverberated like an orchestrated percussion concert. She stifled a shriek. She'd never been afraid of thunderstorms before—in fact, she'd always enjoyed them—but now, now she was frightened to her core.

He frowned as he pulled onto the road, but he said

nothing. Even though she knew what he was thinking, she had no answers. Back in the days when they couldn't bear to be apart, they'd taken long, leisurely walks in the rain and made love on a fake fur bedspread when the downpours grew too violent to enjoy outside. The ferocity of the storms had fueled their passion.

She had to stop remembering. It wasn't safe.

He leaned his elbows against the steering wheel and peered at the road in front of them. Sheets of rain made visibility almost impossible, but he didn't seem bothered at all. He seemed to be enjoying the potential dangers inherent in such a fierce storm.

"We're almost there." He pointed straight ahead. "It's that little place at the bottom of the hill."

She nodded, but she couldn't see a house or a hill. What she saw was a white buffalo calf standing in the middle of the road. "Watch out!"

And then it was gone.

He muttered an expletive as the Jeep hit a deep pothole in the unpaved road and splattered mud like a tidal wave around them. She held her breath as he fought to keep the old vehicle on the road.

"I'm…sorry. I thought I saw something…"

He shot her a strange look and turned onto a wide drive that had been created by tire tracks. Nathan's battered truck was parked next to an old mobile home that had seen better days, but the area around it was neat and clean.

"Here we are. Home sweet home. Are you okay?"

The vision of the young buffalo remained in her brain, but she managed a nod.

"Come on now. It's over."

"Wait. Just give me a minute."

"Sierra, you'd better get used to these storms. They happen all the time."

She fixed a smile on her face, climbed out of the mud-covered Jeep, and followed him to the front door of the mobile home. A grinning Nathan immediately opened it and ushered them into a small living room. He closed the door behind them.

"Get in here, you two! *Wakinyan*...I'm sorry. The Thunder Beings have been busy tonight. Did you get caught in that little storm?"

Hunter nodded. "We did."

"Well, we're in a bad drought right now, so we'll take what we can get. We'll go to the kitchen in a minute, and Melanie will fix you some tea."

As Nathan busied himself making his guests comfortable, Sierra looked around the room. Nathan had said that his sons and their families lived here with them, but now she was sure she'd misunderstood. Nine people couldn't possibly live in such a small trailer.

Still, thank God, it was a normal room...quiet, calm. No buffalo here, no bones, no blood. Native flute music played softly in the background, a magnificent handmade quilt with a red-and-orange starburst in the center hung on the wall above a small beige sofa, and a superb collection of colorful Indian pottery was arranged on shelves scattered around the room. An unfamiliar mouthwatering aroma wafted from the kitchen, reminding Sierra she hadn't eaten in several hours.

She breathed a sigh of relief as the image of the white buffalo calf began to fade.

When Nathan called Melanie's name, the woman who emerged from the tiny kitchen was nothing like

Sierra had pictured her. Based on her mother's description, she'd envisioned someone big-boned and humorless, sort of like a medicine woman from an old Hollywood western.

But Melanie Winterhawk was no taller than Sierra with an infectious smile that seemed to light up the entire room. Her exquisite features were childlike and small, except for enormous dark eyes. Glossy black hair without a visible strand of silver hung straight to her waist.

Melanie shoved a dishrag into a deep pocket on the front of her apron and held out both her hands in welcome. "Hello, Hunter. It's so nice to see you again."

As he took her hands and kissed her offered cheek, Melanie's penetrating gaze found Sierra's face and remained there. Finally, after what seemed an eternity, she disengaged herself from Hunter's grasp and moved toward Sierra, her head cocked to one side.

"So you're Noah and Lexy's Sierra," she said softly. Her voice was throaty and low, as if she'd just awakened from a long nap. It was perhaps the most sensual sound Sierra had ever heard. "You're welcome here."

Sierra's eyes filled with tears of pure gratitude.

Chapter Fifteen

Melanie took Sierra in her arms and held her close.

"I'm sorry," Sierra managed at last, sniffling and embarrassed as she pulled away. "I don't know what's wrong with me. This isn't like me at all."

"Don't be silly. You've been to Wounded Knee. Most people with a heart and a conscience get pretty emotional after that."

Sierra nodded and didn't answer. Melanie didn't know the half of it—at least, she didn't think she did.

"Come with me." Melanie tucked her hand cozily in the crook of Sierra's arm and pulled her toward the kitchen. "You can help me chop vegetables. I went to Rapid to pick them up this morning, and I don't want them to go bad."

"You go on," Nathan agreed. "I want to talk to Hunter about an idea I have for our documentary. Don't work too hard, ladies."

Melanie snorted. "Huh! You're sounding more like a bossy White man every day, Nathan Winterhawk. I don't like that one bit."

Nathan winked at his wife and said, "See what happens when a man's been married to the same woman for more than thirty years? His life is no longer his own. Lakota society was once matriarchal, you know, so if Mama's not happy, nobody's happy."

"That's White man's society, too, my friend,"

Hunter responded with a wry grin. "I guess we're all in heap big trouble, huh?"

Melanie tossed her head with a smile. "Come on, Sierra. I'd much rather talk with you in my kitchen than listen to these crazy men. They're not allowed in there."

Sierra followed Melanie into the kitchen and stood, uncertain, beside the door.

"Come sit down. Don't worry about chopping vegetables—I was just trying to get you all to myself. I'll make us some hot tea. You look a little frazzled."

Sierra sat at a long table placed flush against a wall in the kitchen, painfully aware of her red sweatshirt, faded blue jeans, and oversized hiking boots. She'd concentrated so hard on not being attractive to Hunter that she hadn't thought about how she'd look to anyone else. Now if she could've dropped through the faded linoleum floor and died of embarrassment, she would've been happy.

Melanie pushed a cup of hot tea in front of her, moved some large food containers to the other end of the table, and sat down. She propped her chin on both hands and fixed her amused gaze on Sierra once again. "Don't worry, you're beautiful. I just meant you seem tired, that's all. Relax."

"Thank you." Sierra sipped her tea. The warmth and fragrance were soothing, the flavor unfamiliar. "Is this some special tea you've made from herbs native to this area? I love this aroma."

Melanie's eyes twinkled, and a deep dimple appeared in her left cheek when she smiled. "Well, I guess you could say that. It's Earl Grey from Rapid City."

Sierra burst out laughing. "I walked right into that

one, didn't I? I'm sorry. That was stupid."

"Not at all. We have elders on the rez who know how to use every plant imaginable for food, medicine, even cleaning stuff. I'm just not one of them."

"I hear that. Especially the food part. I'm allergic to cooking."

Melanie looked astonished. "Really? I love to cook. Like for this gathering tomorrow—I've been cooking all week. It's mostly the elders who help me."

"Skye is the only person I know who loves to cook. Thank God. We'd starve to death on this trip if not for her."

"Skye?"

"My best friend. She's part Comanche and a very well-known wildlife photographer in Texas. She and my friend Colt are back at the campground battling a stomach bug or something."

Melanie shook her head and looked embarrassed. "Oh, I'm really sorry."

"No, it's okay. I think it's just a twenty-four-hour thing—"

"No. I mean, here I've been rambling on about elders and cooking, and I didn't even ask about your parents..." Melanie's husky voice trailed away, and her face softened with what appeared to be a sweet memory. "I've thought of them both so often, especially Lexy. She was such a special spirit. We all loved her. And Noah as well, of course, although he could be a little intimidating."

*Lexy.* No one called Alexa Masters Lexy except her family and most intimate friends. Sierra thought it strange that Melanie and Mama had been close enough for her to use this pet name. That was one detail her mother hadn't mentioned. There were probably others.

But Sierra said only, "My dad can still scare the heck out of anyone he wants to." She paused. "Can I ask you a question?"

"Sure."

"What did Nathan tell you about me?"

Melanie looked puzzled. "Not much. Just that you're Noah and Alexa Masters' daughter, a writer, and a friend of Hunter's. He said you learned your parents had been up here during the Knee and you were curious about it, so you came for a visit. Why do you ask?"

"I just wondered."

Melanie's smile was gentle. "Nathan didn't tell me everything, did he?"

"What do you mean?"

"I mean, Noah and Alexa aren't your real parents, are they? You're Indian. Where do you get your blood?"

"I don't understand."

Melanie's eyes were dark pools of compassion. "I don't know why you don't want to say it, sweetheart, but it's obvious. What nation are you?"

She was right. It didn't make any sense not to admit it.

"My birth mother was Pauline Kills Quick. I just found out my parents adopted me and got me off this reservation when I was a few days old."

Her mouth dropped. She sat back in her chair and gaped at Sierra. "Well, good grief," she said finally. "I didn't see that coming."

"Neither did I, but it's true. Hunter found some pictures that Nathan had and brought them to me. I always thought my looks came from my father's Italian side of the family, and no one told me otherwise. I don't guess they ever would have, either, if Hunter hadn't shown me the photos."

Melanie chuckled. "Italian? Please. Not one person in South Dakota would believe that."

"I guess in my part of Texas, no one really cares."

"Well, they care here." Melanie shook her head. "Pauline Kills Quick," she mused after a moment. "Grandma Madonna's granddaughter. I haven't heard that name in years."

Sierra's heart skipped a beat. "Did you know her?"

"No, not really. I knew her auntie Julia pretty well because we were both AIM members, but Pauline was too young. She was at a boarding school most of the time. And then one day she just disappeared. I never thought anything about it."

Sierra said nothing.

The silence stretched on until Melanie cleared her throat. "What is it?"

"You never heard Pauline was raped by a White man...or that she got pregnant?"

Melanie shook her head. "I know that sounds terrible, but those days were so...difficult. We lived in a war zone. Armed patrols everywhere, people shot and stabbed or just disappeared, never to be heard from again. White men raped young Indian girls all the time. It's not much different now." She paused, reached across the table for Sierra's hand, and cradled it in Melanie's own. "I'm glad Pauline got off the reservation and you had a good home. Your parents are the best. The absolute best. But the greatest news is you've found your way back to us."

"Thank you," Sierra whispered.

141

"The truth is I owe your mother my life. She told you about that, didn't she?"

"About what?"

A faraway look appeared in Melanie's dark eyes, and when she began her story, Sierra couldn't believe her ears. These were her parents, yet she didn't know them. But as Melanie became more involved in the narrative, Sierra began to see them for who they really were—passionately committed people willing to risk everything for a cause they believed in.

"When the occupation was over," Melanie said quietly, "everyone scattered. Lexy and Noah had already moved into a little apartment in Hot Springs, and Noah was writing his heart out about the problems on Pine Ridge. Lexy became very close friends with Julia Farewell, who was also a good friend of mine. I remember, too, she had so much respect for Madonna Kills Quick."

"Why?"

Melanie grinned. "Grandma Madonna is an icon to Traditional Indians. She was one of the main Lakota elders to encourage members of the American Indian Movement to come to the rez in the first place. Then, as violence escalated and it was obvious tribal chairman Dickie Wilson wasn't going to let up, Grandma Madonna was one of the women who suggested everyone go to Wounded Knee and occupy it until the feds gave in. She'd lost ancestors in the original Wounded Knee massacre, so she had a personal reason for wanting the tribe to take a stand there. I heard Grandma Madonna actually told a meeting of the elders, 'We want an independent sovereign Oglala Sioux nation. We don't want no part of the government, tribal or BIA. We want our old 1868 Treaty back.' Talk about guts. Anyway, Lexy just loved that story."

Sierra was startled. "Are you telling me a little old lady actually started the Occupation of Wounded Knee? Where were all those terrifying Sioux warriors?"

"Well, she wasn't that old back then, and there was nothing *little* about her. Sioux society has always been matriarchal, and Grandma Madonna was highly respected by the entire tribe. She was one of the women who actually contacted AIM in the very beginning and got them to come to Pine Ridge. For the most part, the men—including so-called AIM warriors—were *shamed* into standing up to Dickie Wilson."

Sierra couldn't believe it.

*My great-grandmother was a warrior in her own right...and some of my ancestors were killed at the massacre of Wounded Knee.*

Skye had been spot-on. Sierra's history suddenly seemed so much *larger* than before.

Melanie sipped her tea. "Anyway, Nathan and I had only been married a little while when the Occupation of Wounded Knee started. Lexy and I became good friends during that time, and we stayed in touch even after everything was over. But when the occupation ended on May 9, 1973, Nathan was forced to run. He hid somewhere up in Montana. Other AIM members scattered all over the country. A few even managed to get into Canada.

"Meanwhile, my sister, her little boy, and I all lived together in a small house in Wanblee. We knew the feds were watching us because of Nathan, but we were also being watched by Dickie Wilson's GOONs because our entire family was active in the American

Indian Movement. Consequently, since someone was always watching, there was no way Nathan and I could get together."

Melanie paused and looked at Sierra with a fondly reminiscent smile. "I don't know if you realize what a romantic your mother was, but she really was a Romeo-and-Juliet kind of gal. So one night your mother called me. She said she'd heard from Nathan and he was out of his mind, needing to see me. She said he'd begged her to help him find a way to be with me."

Sierra grinned, remembering all the times Alexa had helped her and Hunter get together when Noah hadn't wholeheartedly approved. "My father always teases her about what a romantic she is."

"Oh, Noah isn't any better," Melanie retorted with a grin. "When Lexy finally went to him to ask for his help in setting up a rendezvous for Nathan and me, Noah was in the thick of it. They managed to sneak me out of my house and take me over to a crummy motel in Wyoming, where Nathan and I managed to be together for an entire weekend. We were all scared to death Nathan would be busted and hauled off to jail, or the GOONs would hurt me to make me talk, but we didn't care. We had to be together, and we were willing to risk everything to do it. What meant the most to us, though, was that Lexy and Noah were willing to risk everything, too."

Sierra heard a discreet cough in the doorway.

"Are you telling our love story?" Nathan asked.

"I am. Why don't you and Hunter come in and sit down? She has a right to know how wonderful her parents are."

"Of course she does." Nathan and Hunter pulled

out chairs and sat at the table. "Go on."

"I got pregnant with my first son that weekend," Melanie continued with a soft smile, "and I was very happy, even though Nathan was nowhere around, and I couldn't contact him at all. The political heat was intense on the rez, but Lexy and Noah still managed to go back and forth between Hot Springs and Pine Ridge. Lexy's folks had sent food and medical supplies to the Knee while it was going on, and they continued to send whatever they could after it was over. Even baby stuff for my upcoming delivery."

"Was it dangerous for Mama and Daddy to bring stuff here?"

"Well, there were roadblocks set up all over the rez, and they were stopped and searched all the time, but I don't think anyone ever seriously tried to keep them out—probably because they were White. They were able to help a lot of families during those days, and everyone loved them."

To Sierra's surprise, Melanie's voice trailed away, and her eyes suddenly welled with tears. Nathan reached for her hand and said something so softly to her that Sierra couldn't hear his words. Melanie nodded and swallowed hard, but a few moments passed before she could continue.

"In February 1974, not long before my baby was due, my sister, Priscilla, was shot and killed by a sniper as she was leaving an AIM meeting over in Kyle. Then, just four days after that, Priscilla's little boy, Leonard, accidentally killed himself when he was playing with a loaded pistol I kept to protect the family. It was all my fault, and I fell into a horrible depression. Everyone wanted me to get in touch with Nathan, but I couldn't do that. I knew he would come back to take care of me and the feds would get him, and then I would lose him, too. So everyone left me alone, which was all I wanted.

"But Lexy couldn't bear the idea of me being alone out there, so she left Noah in their apartment and came to stay with me. She knew GOONs and feds were watching the house. After all, *someone* had obviously gotten me pregnant, and they were waiting for Nathan to show up. But those creeps didn't scare Lexy. In fact, they just made her mad. She'd go outside and wave at them—usually with her middle finger—but other times she'd actually take them sandwiches. The chances she took scared me to death."

This feisty woman Melanie was talking about was totally unfamiliar to Sierra. Her mama was no risk-taker, and she'd never seen her buck authority. Waving her middle finger at armed men? How in the world had her mother managed to hide this part of her personality so completely?

Sierra tried to conceal her shock. "Then what happened?"

"Well, Lexy was planning to take me up to the Indian Hospital in Rapid when I went into labor. It's a couple of hours away, so we just figured we'd head up when I had my first contraction. No worries, you know? First babies always take longer, right?

"But, as luck would have it, one of South Dakota's nasty blizzards hit in the middle of the night on February 24, 1974. There was no power, no heat, no phone lines, nothing but wind, sleet, snow, and temps falling well below zero…"

When her voice trailed away, Nathan picked up the story. "Melanie went into labor in the middle of that storm, of course, and, as Lexy explained later, there was nothing she could do but deliver that baby boy. It was a hard, long birth, but everything came out fine. Melanie has always said Lexy saved her life that night, and our son Eli has always wanted to meet her. Maybe now we can make that happen."

Sierra sat at the kitchen table, trying to assimilate this story into what she'd always thought was true about her mother and father, but she couldn't do it. Her parents, these brave and committed people, were strangers to her.

"How come you didn't know my parents left South Dakota with a baby, Melanie?" she asked.

"One day they were just gone." She managed a small smile. "But we never forgot them, and I always felt they'd gotten out safely. They weren't Indians. They could go where they wanted."

When she gave a wide yawn and rubbed her eyes, Sierra quickly got to her feet. "I'm sorry we took so much of your time. We should probably head home."

"Oh no, that's all right. Nathan said you were joining us for a light supper—"

"Maybe another time. I'm really tired."

Melanie's relief was obvious. "Of course. You should get off these roads before it gets too late, anyway. We'll see you tomorrow?"

"Absolutely. Is there anything we can bring?"

"Just yourselves—and your friends. There will be lots of people there."

"Thank you." Then she added shyly, "I'm really looking forward to it."

And when Melanie enveloped her in a warm hug, Sierra was surprised to find she truly was.

Chapter Sixteen

Sierra was grateful when the next morning arrived with a crisp autumn breeze and brilliant sunshine, a perfect day for a cookout and horseback riding. Hunter pulled into a parking area near a large hand-painted sign that read *Red Tail Park—Call Nathan Winterhawk if you have any problems.*

She pointed at it with a giggle. "Now that's the way to handle complaints. Don't leave your number."

"No number needed," he told her with a grin. "Everyone knows Nathan Winterhawk. Let's roll. We're late."

"Well, if you'd asked for directions..."

Her voice faded off—she was teasing. As soon as they'd left the main highway, they hadn't seen a soul anywhere. They might've been driving on top of the moon. And she learned maps weren't all that helpful, either. She felt fortunate they'd found this place before Christmas.

When she stepped out of the Jeep, she heard the rhythmic thuds of drumming—as strong as a heartbeat—from somewhere in the park, the high-pitched voices of several singers, and the laughter of young children playing nearby. This seemed to be much more than a simple family cookout.

She took in the awe-inspiring landscape surrounding the park. Rolling hills covered with tall prairie grasses stretched before her as far as she could see, and a small herd of bison grazed across the endless terrain. The strange rock spires and sandstone pinnacles that made up the Badlands seemed tossed about as if God Himself had dropped them there and forgotten them. Trees already shedding leaves in preparation for winter clustered around the park. She clipped a leather fanny pack around her waist and walked to the back of the Jeep to join Hunter, who was digging around in a large canvas bag.

"Can I help you with anything?"

"No, thanks, I'm good. I'm just bringing one small camera—if I can find it. Could you put these batteries in your pack?"

She nodded and tucked them into a side pocket.

He zipped his bag shut. "Did you reach your mom this morning? I forgot to remind you."

"Yeah, I did, for a minute. But the service was terrible. I did manage to tell her about Nathan and Melanie, though."

"Good. Was she excited?"

"I have no idea."

He chuckled and announced to no one in particular, "I'm hungry. Is anyone else starving?"

For the first time, Sierra noticed mouthwatering aromas floating through the gentle prairie wind, reminding her she hadn't eaten any breakfast. "Something smells delicious. What is it?"

Skye chuckled behind them. "My culinary Indian nose tells me it's fry bread, and I'm following it—"

"Well, here you are. I was ready to send out a search party."

Before anyone could respond, Nathan Winterhawk

pumped Hunter's hand, enveloped Sierra in an enthusiastic embrace that left her breathless, and gave Skye a broad wink. "Hello, Great Comanche Cooker Woman—and Mr. Colt. It's good to see you both. Welcome to our gathering."

Sierra returned his hug. "We got lost." She moved away from him and tried to tuck her now-mussed hair back into its sophisticated french braid. "I'm sorry we're late."

"I told you, Indian time is whenever you get here. We're just glad you found us. Come on and get some food."

"We brought a big bowl of Skye's wonderful potato salad. I know it's not traditional, but—"

"Great Comanche Cooker Woman made it," Nathan interrupted with a grin, "so I know it's delicious. We'll give it to Melanie—if I ever see her again." He looked around the crowded grounds for a moment, then gave a broad smile and pointed. "There she is, over by the fry bread."

Hunter chuckled. "Let's go say 'howdy,' Sierra. You can give Melanie the potato salad."

"Okay. We'll catch you later, Nathan."

"Good. Oh, listen…my sons are riding with some friends in a couple of hours, and I thought you might want to join them. I've got a small pinto I think you'd like, Sierra, and horses for the rest of you, too. Would you like to ride?"

She didn't even have to think about it. "That'd be wonderful. Thank you."

She loved to ride, and something about this rugged country ordered everyone out of their vehicles. Anything easier than riding a horse or hiking was a sacrilege. She'd been so hopeful that she wore a loose pullover sweater, jeans, and cowboy boots...just in case.

The riding she'd done in Texas, even those long trail rides through the Big Bend region, might be a cake walk compared to the kind of riding she could do today. The Lakota were horse people from eons ago, and she was light years away from that part of herself. But she was eager to try.

"All right," Nathan was saying, "I'll let you know when they're leaving. You go on and find Melanie. She'll show you around."

Red Tail Park seemed much more accommodating than many community parks Sierra had seen across the United States. This one boasted a wooden corral for horses, a circular dance arena with a branch-covered arbor where the musicians sat during powwows, and a large open-air pavilion for group gatherings. Like most other parks, a basketball court was nearby, as well as an area reserved for tent camping. Today, near the arbor, tipis stood in a circle around what appeared to have been a large campfire the night before, lending a days-gone-by ambiance to the gathering.

"A group of Cheyenne brought them in yesterday," a throaty voice said in Sierra's ear. "And they had quite a celebration last night—you should've been here. Hello, Hunter, Sierra."

Sierra would have recognized that sexy voice anywhere. She handed the bowl of potato salad to Skye and turned to give Melanie a hug. "I slept like a baby last night. No partying for me. Here, let me introduce my friends. This is Skye Morning Sun Parker—we call her Sunshine back home—and Colton Chambers. He was nice enough to drive us all the way from Big Bend to South Dakota. Y'all, this is Nathan's wife, Melanie Winterhawk."

"Glad to meet you, ma'am," Colt said, coloring beet red.

In almost comical contrast to Colt's painful shyness, Skye was unrestrained. "I'm so glad to meet you, Melanie."

Sierra stifled a giggle as Melanie's gaze traveled up, up, and up some more to finally fix itself on Skye's face. She knew how Melanie felt—like an ant meeting an animated giraffe for the first time—but that never bothered Skye. She was who she was, one of the main reasons Sierra loved her so much.

Melanie's fingers disappeared into Skye's hands. "Nathan told me what a wonderful cook you are, but he never said you were so tall."

"Almost six feet. They tell me my Comanche great-great-grandfather was six-four. I guess I get it from him."

"Well…wow. Is that bowl for us?"

"It is," Sierra answered. "It's Skye's potato salad. There's nothing better in this world than Skye's potato salad."

"Let's go put it out, then. We have a lot of hungry Indians here today."

****

Nathan's voice came over a loudspeaker as he welcomed the crowd in the Lakota language before he began speaking English. Sierra finished piling her paper plate with food, some items familiar and some not, and carried it to a wooden picnic table nearby. She sat down, waving for her friends to join her.

As she waited, she looked around. The men, most of whom were large and long-haired, wore rolled-up bandannas for headbands and T-shirts bannered with menacing slogans, like *FBI—Full Blooded Indian* and *Illegal Immigration Started in 1492*, while the women seemed less daunting in their jeans, sneakers, and sweatshirts.

As she analyzed people in the crowd, she filed mental pictures of those who interested her. Someone here might make a great character later.

And that was when she saw him—the most mesmerizing specimen of manhood she'd ever seen in her life. Lounging against a large cottonwood tree near several long tables loaded with food, he stood well over six feet tall—muscular, lean, and mahogany brown. His long hair, parted in the middle and held back by a braided leather headband, flowed loose to his waist like liquid ebony. His black leather vest was dotted with various Indian symbols, slogans, and American Indian Movement patches. He wore a wide turquoise-and-bone choker around his neck.

Hunter glanced over his shoulder to see who she was looking at and turned back to her. "I see you still have a soft spot for the bad boys," he said quietly, amusement dancing in his eyes. "That's Eli Winterhawk, Nathan's oldest son—the one your mom delivered. He's the baddest Indian on the reservation, but I guess his angry activism is part of his DNA. You want to meet him?"

"Later maybe."

Nathan appeared at Sierra's side, an apologetic grin on his face. "I'm sorry that took so long. Did you get enough to eat?"

"Yes, and it was wonderful. I'm stuffed."

"I'm glad," Nathan answered with a grin. "Sierra, here comes my son, Eli. Let me introduce you."

She stood up and waited as Eli Winterhawk made his way to her table. When he finally reached them, he stood silently, an inscrutable expression on his face.

Nathan squeezed her shoulder. "Sierra, this is my eldest son, Eli. Eli, this is Sierra Masters from Texas. She's a writer. You remember Hunter, of course. And these folks bringing up the rear are Skye and Colt, also from Texas."

Eli nodded to everyone, offered his hand to no one, and never took his snapping black gaze from Sierra's face.

Her heart hammered in her chest, but she was determined not to let him see how unnerved she was. "I'm very glad to meet you."

He nodded again but said nothing.

Slow anger began to simmer. She'd created leading characters like Eli Winterhawk in her books, but she'd never actually met one: strong, silent, brooding. Her female characters had gone all weak in the knees, but she was no female character. She was flesh and blood—and so was he. He was no better than her, no matter what he thought.

She looked directly at Nathan. "Does your son speak English?"

He rolled his eyes. "Yes. And I taught him better manners. I apologize."

"Apology accepted. Parents can't be held responsible for the behavior of their children forever." She gave him a sweet smile and turned her attention back to Eli. "Have I offended you in some way, Mr.

Winterhawk?"

The sunlight captured shimmering, blue-black highlights in his hair as he shook his head. He smiled, but it didn't quite reach his eyes. "No, I'm sorry. I've been very rude. I've just been trying to figure out where I've seen you."

She shrugged. That was the oldest line in the book, and apparently even Indians born and raised on a reservation weren't above using it. "I have no idea, Mr. Winterhawk. I'm quite positive I've never seen you."

"Hello, Nathan. I've been looking all over for you. Hey, Eli. Is this gathering private, or can I join you?"

"Gideon! What a pleasure." As Nathan shook hands enthusiastically with the newcomer, he introduced him to the group. "This is Gideon O'Neill. He's an anthropologist and one of the best friends the Lakota has. It makes me happy to see you. It's been ages."

"I've been down in Lincoln working with the Nebraska State Historical Society for several weeks, but I couldn't miss this gathering. How are you?"

Sierra's mind was racing. How could this White guy be one of the best friends the Lakota had? And why was Eli Winterhawk pounding his back like a long-lost brother? That was crazy. Eli Winterhawk obviously didn't like anybody.

Especially not an *O'Neill*.

Sierra tried to remember what it was Hunter had said about the O'Neill family.

*They're very powerful in South Dakota. They do what they want, and no one stops them.*

Now she was more confused than ever. "Excuse me, Gideon," she interrupted, "but I have to ask. Are you any relation to Logan O'Neill?"

He turned crimson beneath his shaggy blond hair, and his bright blue eyes actually looked pained. He managed a small grin. "Jeez, I can't get away from that mistake of birth no matter what I do. He's my father, Miss Masters, but please don't hold that against me. We haven't spoken in years."

She was surprised. "I'm sorry. I shouldn't have asked—"

Gideon laughed out loud, a gradual rumbling sound that seemed to come from somewhere near the soles of his feet. "It's okay. I'm used to it."

Skye spoke up. "We met your father just a few days ago at some icky truck stop on Highway 90."

He nodded. "That would be Sloan Turner's place. I hope they weren't too rude to you, Miss Masters."

"Please call me Sierra. Why would they be rude to me?"

"Well, you're an Indian, aren't you? My father hates Indians."

She stared at him, unable to believe how matter-of-factly he'd said, "You're an Indian." Was it that obvious? She shook her head. "Your father was very nice to me."

"You were lucky. He must've had a reason."

*Of course he did*, she thought, embarrassed at how self-important she'd felt at the time. Hunter had spotted the man's insincerity right away, but she hadn't. Aloud, she added, "Turner, on the other hand, was horrible."

"That's just Turner. He's always horrible. Our families go back a long way, but he's from very bad blood."

"Well, your father talked him into showing us his

museum."

"That must've been a thrill. What'd you think of it?"

"It gave me the creeps."

"Me, too," Gideon admitted. "I went once, a long time ago, and I'll never go back." He turned to Nathan. "I hear you're all going riding. May I join you?"

Nathan shook his head. "I'm not going today. I have to help get ready for the dancing. But my young friends here are. You can ride with them if you want."

Gideon gave a warm smile, displaying the most perfect teeth Sierra had ever seen. "That'd be great. Eli, are you coming, too?"

The heat rose to her cheeks as that black gaze fell on her again.

"Well, if our...Indian...princess here is going, I don't think I have much choice."

Chapter Seventeen

When Sierra and Hunter walked toward the horse corral where Nathan had asked them to meet him, Hunter's hand rested against the back of her neck in an affectionate gesture she'd almost forgotten. Her first instinct was to move away from him, but that warm hand against her skin was comforting—and painfully familiar.

She glanced up at him from beneath her long lashes and allowed her gaze to rest on his face a moment longer than she should've. He seemed so much more handsome than before. It wasn't because his looks were so altered, but because his heart had somehow changed. He'd softened and mellowed over the years; the tenderness in his touch was different. Once she'd longed for him because their physical chemistry was so explosive and refused to be denied, but now he was even more irresistible—if that was possible. Now he was a man, in every sense of that word.

He stopped and gazed down at her. His eyes seemed softer, darker blue than usual. "What is it?"

She looked away from him. He could still play her. She still forgot every warning and ignored every alarm when she was with him. And this had all happened without her even knowing it, without him even trying.

"Shoot," he muttered, "here comes Eli. Listen, don't let him get to you. He's been involved in radical causes since the early 1990s. That's just who he is. If there's a fight, Eli's in the thick of it. He can't help it."

She interrupted his lecture with a grin. "Don't worry about me, Hunter. I can take care of myself."

He cocked an eyebrow with amusement but stepped away when Eli reached them, as if he didn't want to crowd her space. She recognized the gesture and appreciated it.

Eli cleared his throat. "May I speak to you…alone?"

"Whatever you have to say to me, you can say in front of Hunter."

He nodded slowly. "You're right. I owe you both an apology. I was rude to you back there, and I'm sorry."

She stared at him. This was the last thing she'd expected to hear from Eli Winterhawk. A few seconds passed before she granted him a warm smile. "Please don't worry about it. It's okay."

"It's just that you do look so familiar—" His voice trailed off, his face darkened, and he muttered an expletive under his breath.

She followed his gaze toward a well-dressed man heading in their direction, carrying an expensive Stetson hat in his hand. "Who's that?"

Eli's lip curled, like he had a bad taste in his mouth. "Scum named Breeden Jones."

She wondered why Eli's face had turned into a Badlands thundercloud. The man looked nice enough to her. "Who's Breeden Jones?"

"He used to be one of my father's best friends."

Breeden Jones joined them with his hand outstretched. "Hello, Eli. It's been a long time."

He stared at the man's hand without answering, then shook it once and wiped his palm against his jeans. "Not long enough. What're you doing here?"

As Jones appeared to be weighing his response, Sierra took the rather uncomfortable moment of silence to study him. Tanned and slightly built, with dirty-blond hair and green eyes, he might've been able to pass for White in a state less bigoted against natives than South Dakota—but his wide nose, high cheekbones, and full lips proclaimed his Indian heritage.

Finally, Jones answered with an unusual accent she was unable to identify. "I heard through the grapevine your friends were going to be here today, and I wanted to meet them." He turned to Hunter with his hand outstretched in welcome. "Breeden Jones."

His gaze slid to Sierra's face and remained there longer than she liked. A nervous shiver raced down her spine. For some reason she felt there might be more to him than met the eye.

But Hunter didn't seem to have any problem with this man. He shook Breeden's hand warmly. "Good to meet you."

"Likewise. Are you enjoying your visit with us?"

"We are, thanks."

Eli didn't join the conversation. His eyes and voice remained icy cold as he returned to Breeden Jones' original statement. "What grapevine?"

"Some folks on the council were talking yesterday about your friends being here." He looked at Sierra again and smiled. A front gold tooth flashed. "There aren't many secrets on the rez. You're Sierra Masters, aren't you? The writer?"

She nodded.

"Well, I work for the Bureau of Indian Affairs, and most of my job has to do with land management around the reservation. But I also try to bring publicity and new business to Pine Ridge. I just wanted to welcome you and let you know that I'll be available to help you in any way I can. All you have to do is ask."

She smiled. "Thank you."

But Sierra's thoughts belied her warm words. Breeden Jones didn't work too hard—the reservation hadn't seen any serious new business since before the massacre at Wounded Knee. Yet his own clothing—creased black jeans, black leather vest over an Indian-print western shirt, tan Stetson, expensive boots, gold tooth—either the BIA paid well or business kickbacks were healthy. Whatever it was, Breeden Jones clearly did all right somewhere.

Eli broke the silence. "You got anything else to say?"

"No."

"Good. You'd better go before my dad sees you."

Jones shrugged and touched the brim of his Stetson. "Glad to have met you all."

"You, too," Hunter said.

Sierra nodded and smiled. As she watched him stride away, she shook her head. Back in Bandera, the ranch hands would've run him out of town for walking with such a cocky, arrogant swagger and dressing up like a drugstore cowboy. But here he seemed to be respected, if not liked.

Nathan's amazed voice broke into Sierra's reverie. She hadn't heard him join the group.

"Is that who I think it is?"

"Breeden Jones," Eli answered with a nod. "When was the last time you talked to him?"

"About thirty years ago. I'd be happy to go another thirty years."

"That's what I thought. I got rid of him as quick as I could."

"Thank you, son."

"I understand why you don't care for him, Eli," Hunter said soberly, "but remember, we might need his help at some point."

"How could he help us?"

"I don't know that he can. I've just learned over the years not to burn any bridges until you're sure you're never going to cross them again. Oh, by the way, Byron Little Hand's secretary called me this morning and said he'd be back by this evening. If he has any information, he'll come here."

Sierra's heart gave a nervous flutter. "You mean information about Pauline?"

"Maybe," Nathan answered vaguely. "Come on, you guys. Skye, Colt, and Gideon are waiting with your ponies. If the Creator is with us, we'll all get some answers very soon."

\*\*\*\*

Horses always tested a new rider if for no other reason than to check out their boundaries, but the little pinto mare didn't do that. From the moment Sierra settled into the saddle and clicked her tongue against her teeth to ease her out of the corral, horse and rider moved as if they'd been riding together their entire lives. Hunter rode beside her on a big gray-and-white dappled stallion that seemed determined to dump him at the earliest opportunity, and Eli rode ahead of them on a spectacular palomino. As Gideon, Skye, and Colt brought up the rear on what appeared to be matching chestnut geldings, their laughter and low voices floated into the wind.

The plains, broken by rolling hills and ridges of pine trees, stretched for what seemed miles ahead of them. Only afternoon shadows moved across the land, transforming colors and deceiving Sierra's vision as earth and sky seemed to come alive. A cool autumn breeze whispered against her face as two red-tailed hawks swoop-dived overhead in a cackling game of tag against a cloudless sky.

"Where are we going, Eli?"

He turned in his saddle and grinned. It was a great smile, crinkling his eyes and creating dimples in both his cheeks deep enough to swim in. Suddenly he seemed far more approachable. "Would it really help if I told you?"

"Oh, give me a name, any name. I wouldn't know the difference."

"I thought we'd head down to Wounded Knee Creek. It's not too far, and it's a good ride."

"See how easy that was? Thank you. I feel much better now."

As the group rode over a gentle incline and down toward a cluster of cottonwood trees, heading for a flat, open space of land Eli promised them was beside Wounded Knee Creek, the tall prairie grasses were dry and brittle, thirsting for rain. Pausing for a moment to look out over a ribbon-like stream she could barely see in the distance, Sierra couldn't help but be amazed a little nothing of a creek could be of such monumental historical importance.

As they neared the water, she sensed death in the air. She heard it on the wind, even felt it as the hair on her arms stood straight up. The heat of frenzied killing had left its bloody imprint in this ground more than a hundred years ago. It still remained.

*Such a lonely place. Such a terrible place to die.*

The mare's agitation broke her concentration. The pinto didn't want to move any closer to the creek, nor did anyone behind her. She tossed her head, pawed at the ground, snorted, and whinnied as Sierra urged her forward.

Finally, Sierra took pity on her, pulled in the reins, and leaned over to murmur in the frightened animal's ear. "Trust me, baby, nothing's going to hurt you…"

Gideon O'Neill spoke behind her. "Do you want to go down there? I'll hold her if you do."

She flashed a teasing grin over her shoulder. "You don't want to come with me?"

"Not a chance. I've been down there a million times. It's not my favorite place."

"I can believe that." She slipped from her saddle, led the pinto back to Gideon, and handed the reins up to him. "I won't be long. I just want to see it up close."

The others eased their horses up to a cottonwood tree, slid from their own saddles, and tied their reins to low-hanging branches.

"I'm coming with you," Skye announced in a voice that told Sierra she wouldn't tolerate any argument. "You don't mind, do you?"

"Of course not. Do you want to come, Colt?"

He shook his head and turned away, fiddling with his saddle.

"How about you, Eli? Hunter?"

When neither man answered, Sierra shrugged and headed down the hill, shivering from a biting chill in the air she hadn't noticed before. It cut through her sweater as if she weren't even wearing one. "Come on, Skye. It's getting cold out here."

"We could come later..." Skye's voice trailed away.

"No. Stay up here if you want. I'll be back."

Sierra headed toward a shallow drop-off that led to a wide opening on the bank of Wounded Knee Creek. She *knew* it was there; her feet had a mind all their own. All she could do was follow them wherever they intended to take her. A tinny humming in her ears was distant but distinct and irritating, like a fly buzzing around her head. She was dimly aware of Skye moving behind her, but her stomach was beginning to churn, and she didn't want to look over her shoulder. She needed to keep moving.

Her throat swelled with tears. She tried to choke them back, but she couldn't. She was blinded by them as she stepped off a jutting dirt ledge and down into that wide, open area beside the creek, then stood still and listened to the silence. She wasn't sure why she needed to be in this place, but she knew she'd been led there by some unseen force and was determined to remain until she understood.

A procession of Indians on horseback, enshrouded in a pale blue fog, appeared on the other side of the creek and headed through a crooked row of cottonwood trees. One warrior, half his face painted black, led a riderless pony transporting a large bundle wrapped in a buffalo robe. The group was silent, their heads bowed in obvious mourning.

And then unfamiliar words came out of nowhere and wafted across the wind.

*Tasunke Witko...Tasunke Witko...*

The procession vanished.

And then, off to her right in a wider part of the creek, an assembly of horses stood knee-deep in the water. Even though the temperature was dropping fast and a biting wind whipped past her head, freezing her ears and chilling her neck, the horses remained in the water and drank deeply, as if they'd been traveling hard. Her stomach lurched and growled and rumbled. Her legs grew weak, and her hands began to tremble.

She was starving. She shook with exhaustion and cold. She stood in snow.

Across the creek, silent children, their big eyes purple shadowed with hunger and exhaustion, played between tipis placed in small family circles, smoke wafting from the openings at the top. She longed to join them and ask them who they were, but her feet were frozen, stuck to the ground. All she could do was stand in the snow and watch.

Her breath looked like gusts of steam in the darkening shadows of this arctic evening, and her eyelashes crusted over with ice. She'd never been so cold in her life, but the bedraggled, starving people in this tribe moved through the camp with purpose as they stopped to speak with one another, punctuating their conversation with an occasional burst of laughter.

Regardless of their hunger, in spite of the cold, these were a loving and affectionate people. Desperate, she longed to join them. She wanted to tease with them and participate in their banter. She loved the sound of their laughter. The bittersweet aroma of wood smoke and burning sage tickled her nostrils and aggravated her hunger, but she yearned to hold her freezing hands near a fire and curl her chilled body into a buffalo robe. When drumbeats pounded in the distance, accompanied by high-pitched singing, her heart ached and throbbed in response.

These were her people. Perhaps somewhere in this camp were members of her family. She had to warn them. She had to tell them they couldn't stay here. She had to move her feet, lift them out of the snow, run across the creek, and let the people know.

But she was so tired, so cold, so hungry…

"Sierra! Sierra, stop! Sierra, please!"

She struggled against powerful arms holding her close and screamed in pointless, silent rage. They had to let her go, had to… Couldn't they see what was going to happen? Why wouldn't they let her go?

The arms tightened around her. God, he was strong! The voices sounded dim, distant, like they were floating through a thick, syrupy fog, voices she couldn't recognize.

Who was holding her? He was so strong she couldn't move, but he was warm, and she was so cold.

The voices were much clearer now. The fog was lifting. She pounded against her captor's arm, whimpering like a helpless child as tears streamed down her cheeks. When his grip finally relaxed, she stepped away from him, turned around, and looked straight into Hunter's troubled blue eyes.

Her legs buckled and gave out. She floated up into the wind. Two red-tailed hawks led the way.

Chapter Eighteen

Hunter tried to find a comfortable place against the trunk of a cottonwood tree without disturbing Sierra. With her head resting on his shoulder, the sweet familiarity of her body against his was so poignant he could hardly bear it. The fragrance of her freshly washed hair and the delicate softness of her cheek brought waves of the past crashing over him once more.

*This is all my fault.*

Why had he talked her into coming? She could've gone the rest of her life without knowing any of this, without experiencing whatever she was experiencing now. She'd created a life perfect for her. Maybe that was what he'd wanted to destroy—a perfect life with no room for him in it.

*Selfish bastard.*

He couldn't even remember what had been so important at the time—except he would've moved mountains to have her with him again. Nothing else had mattered.

And what had he been prepared to give her in return?

*Nothing.*

Skye squatted beside him and stroked a strand of Sierra's hair away from her face. "You know, I had more to do with making her come here than you did."

"I'm sure that isn't true."

"No, it is. So don't blame yourself."

"I'm not blaming myself. I never blame myself. It's a waste of time."

She shrugged. "Have it your way. But I told her I'd come to South Dakota with you if she didn't. I knew she'd never let that happen."

"That wouldn't have mattered to her. We've been apart for a long time."

She chuckled. "I didn't mean that, silly. I just meant she's too adventurous to miss a trip like this. She hadn't thought it through until I more or less dared her to go. I knew she'd bite."

He said nothing. Maybe she was right. All he'd done was offer Sierra a challenge, to come to South Dakota and find her birth mother. She'd made the decision. He instantly felt better, just as he always did when he talked himself out of taking responsibility for something he'd done.

He glanced at Skye. "May I ask you a question?"

"Sure."

"What's going on with Sierra?"

Skye sat on the ground across from him and fiddled with a long strand of silver-white hair that had come loose from her braid. She tucked it behind her ear and took a deep breath.

"I think she's seeing things out here. She acted strange in Nebraska, before we met you at the truck stop. I tried to tell her not to be afraid, but she changed the subject. Whatever it is, she doesn't want to talk about it."

He nodded. "I know. I've seen it, too—when we first entered the Badlands. I just wondered if you had a clue—"

"No." Her answer was abrupt as she got to her feet. She wiped her dusty palms against her jeans, glancing down at Sierra. "Gideon and Eli have gone back to the park to get Nathan. They shouldn't be long."

"Where's Colt? Why didn't he go with them?"

"He's with the horses. Besides, he'd never leave her."

Hunter gave a crooked grin. "I thought that might be the deal."

She chuckled. "No, it's nothing like that. He feels like he owes everything to her, but there's nothing...romantic...there. He thinks she's way out of his league."

"She is. She's way out of mine, too."

Sierra cleared her throat and eased her way into a sitting position. "It sounds like I'm going to be pretty lonely, huh? I mean, since I'm out of everybody's league and all..."

Hunter chuckled uncomfortably. He couldn't even remember what else she might have overheard, but he was sure it was more than she should have. "How are you? Are you better now?"

"I think so, thanks."

A cloud of dust in the distance heralded the imminent arrival of Hunter's battered Jeep, so Skye held her hand down to Sierra. As they helped her to her feet, Hunter was bone-deep grateful she couldn't see his face and the embarrassment that had to be written all over it.

****

Ribbons of scarlet, gold, and deep purple were splattered across the sky like an artist's palette; wispy cotton-like clouds played among the rich colors. It was a glorious sunset, unlike any Sierra had ever seen before. When she felt the warmth and strength of Hunter's body behind her, gratitude flooded her.

Without even thinking, she turned to him, and her tears began to flow once more. Hunter picked her up and cradled her against him; she wrapped her arms around his neck and rested her head on his shoulder.

"Let's go home, baby," he whispered.

Her heart leapt at the once-familiar term of endearment as he carried her to the Jeep. She was aware of Eli giving orders and people mounting horses, and somewhere nearby she heard Nathan's voice and Gideon's rich laughter. But nothing seemed to register except the warmth of Hunter's neck against her forehead and the softness of his hair as it curled against her fingers.

Although she was exhausted, she couldn't remember another time when it had felt so *right* to be in his arms. She didn't want anyone else to take care of her, reassure her, hold her. Once, Hunter Davenport had been all she needed, but she'd believed she'd moved on. Now, as he gently placed her in the front seat of the Jeep, she realized she hadn't.

Nathan spoke from the back seat, his voice deep with concern. "Are you all right, little one?"

Nodding, she managed to fasten her seat belt. "I'm okay." She leaned her head back and closed her eyes. "Can they get the horses back without any problem?"

"Sure. There's plenty of help."

"I'm so sorry about this, Nathan."

"Don't be silly. Just rest."

She heard Hunter close the Jeep door, start the motor, and pull out onto the unpaved road, but she felt as if she were floating above her own body. When Nathan moved closer to the front seat and spoke to Hunter in a low voice, she thought she might be dreaming.

"Don't worry too much about this, my friend. Everyone who visits Wounded Knee Creek has some kind of experience—"

Hunter interrupted, his voice trembling with anger. "This wasn't an *experience*. It was more than that. I don't know what it was, but I sure as hell don't like it."

She yawned and patted his knee. "Calm down. I'm all right."

Nathan cleared his throat nervously. "I'm going to tell you something that might help."

She turned in her seat so she could hear him more clearly. She needed all the help she could get.

"Your great-grandmother, Madonna Kills Quick, had strong medicine herself, ever since she was little. She could tell people when they were going to get sick and what they should do when they did. Sometimes all she had to do was touch something, and she could tell you all about it. She had dreams...but she wasn't what you White folks call a 'psychic.' My mother used to say that most of the time Grandma Madonna just wasn't part of this world and we had to respect her for the power she had."

Hunter snorted in disbelief. "Are you saying this is somehow...hereditary?"

It sounded crazy, but Sierra didn't care. Nathan's words meant she wasn't alone.

"I don't know anything about heredity," he answered. "I just know that Grandma Madonna was the same way. Now, living out in the Badlands the way she does, hardly anyone ever sees her anymore. I doubt if too many people even remember her."

"What about my grandmother or my mother?" Sierra asked. "Did they—?"

"I told you the other night that your grandmother, Angel, died having Pauline, and no one's seen Pauline in years. So I don't know about them."

Her mind jumped to the obvious question, but Hunter asked it before she could speak.

"But Madonna Kills Quick might know, right?"

Sierra held her breath.

Nathan's response was quick and firm. "You can't go out there."

"Why not?" Hunter asked.

"I told you. No one goes to see her but Melanie."

Sierra's voice was equally firm—and determined. "But that doesn't mean *nobody* can, right? Just that nobody does."

Nathan sighed. "I'll talk to Melanie about it, okay? Later. Right now, you might want to meet someone who's waiting back at the park to talk to you."

"Who?"

"Byron Little Hand is here."

She caught her breath. For the first time since she left Texas, she realized how much she longed to meet her mother...and how afraid she was her mother wouldn't want to meet her. "Does he want to talk to me?"

"I don't know. I guess we'll see soon enough."

Hunter pulled into the parking area beside the Red Tail Park, turned off the ignition, and stepped out of the vehicle. Nathan climbed out of the back seat and met Hunter at the front of the Jeep. Sierra watched as he gripped Hunter's arm, talking rapidly about something clearly quite important. Hunter nodded and patted Nathan's shoulder, then gestured toward Sierra. Nathan glanced back at her, a worried frown on his wrinkled brow, and gave a brief wave before he strode toward the park. Hunter came around and opened Sierra's door.

"What on earth was that all about?" She took his hand as she climbed out of the Jeep. "Is everything okay?"

"Yeah, it's fine."

She tucked a stray lock of hair behind her ear and looked up at him, worried. "Do I look as terrible as I feel?"

Smiling, he shook his head. "No, you look beautiful." Suddenly he gave a long, low whistle. "Here comes Nathan—and would you look at the size of that Indian."

Her jaw dropped. Nathan didn't even reach the man's shoulder. As they drew closer, she was reminded of the character actor, Will Sampson, who'd portrayed the enormous Indian mental patient in *One Flew Over the Cuckoo's Nest*—except this man was about a century older.

"My sweet Lord," she murmured, taking an involuntary step closer to Hunter.

"Mr. Davenport?" the man rumbled, holding his bear-paw-sized hand out even before he reached them. "I'm Byron Little Hand. I'm happy you're here. I'm sorry we couldn't meet when you arrived. Something came up, and I had to take care of it."

"That's all right, sir."

As Hunter's hand disappeared into Byron's grasp, Sierra had to choke back a giggle. Hunter was a big man and could be intimidating if he wanted, but Byron Little Hand, for all his obvious years, was overwhelming. His snow-white hair was plaited with leather strips into two long braids that hung over his broad shoulders almost to his waist, but he was straight and slender and powerfully built. She couldn't determine his age.

"Mr. Little Hand, I'd like you to meet Sierra Masters." Hunter withdrew his hand from Byron's grip and flexed his fingers behind his back.

Byron Little Hand had to bend down to get a better look at her, but Sierra managed to meet his gaze head-on. She wasn't usually conscious of how petite she was—her mother had raised her not to see herself that way—but Byron Little Hand made it impossible for her not to be aware. Yet, as soon as she looked into his eyes, the fear left her. She felt cloaked in serenity and stillness.

"So…this is our Miss Sierra."

Gripped with shyness, she managed a nod.

Byron reached down for her hand and held it in both of his. "It makes me so happy that you're here."

She lifted her gaze. "Mr. Little Hand, please. Please, did you find—?"

"We'll talk tomorrow," he said firmly. "Hunter, are you still at the Wiconi Campground?"

"Yes, sir. We're all there."

"Wonderful. How about if I come to your cabin about eleven in the morning?"

"Perfect. I look forward to seeing you."

Byron Little Hand turned his attention back to Sierra and smiled, the sweetest smile she had ever seen. "Get a good night's sleep. We have a lot to talk about."

Her heart caught in her throat. "Thank you, sir. I will."

Nathan spoke up for the first time. "Sierra…would you like to join us for the dancing? It's going to start in a few minutes."

She yawned. "Thank you, no. I'm exhausted. I've had an…emotional day. I need to go home now."

"Of course, I understand."

She gave him a hug, offered her hand to Byron. "It's been a real pleasure meeting you, Mr. Little Hand. We'll see you tomorrow."

Chapter Nineteen

Hunter pulled into Sierra's parking slot and turned off the ignition. "Sierra, will you stay out here with me for a minute? I need to talk to you about something important."

She yawned and feigned more exhaustion than she actually felt. "Are you sure it can't wait?"

Skye chuckled. "That's our cue to leave, Colt. Thanks for the day, Hunter. We had a wonderful time."

"I'm glad you could come."

When they were alone, Hunter reached across Sierra to open the door. "Walk with me."

"It's cold outside." The excuse was weak, but it was all she could think of.

"I'll get you a jacket out of the back. Please."

She shrugged and stepped out of the Jeep. The night air was chilly, but not freezing cold like she'd experienced this afternoon. She forced that memory from her mind. She had to stay alert. Being alone with Hunter like this was too dangerous.

"Here you go." He draped a heavy windbreaker over her shoulders and took her hand. "Come on," he repeated, "walk with me."

"It's too dark."

"Sierra Masters, are you afraid of me?"

"Don't be ridiculous."

"Good. Then walk with me."

Inside, someone turned on flickering lights that outlined the motor home awning and lit up the patio. Lacing his fingers with hers, he pulled her hand close to his body so she had no choice but to walk away from the campsite with him.

He turned her toward him and tilted her chin so he gazed down into her eyes. His voice was soft, tender. "There was a time, Sierra, when you could tell me anything. You told me *everything*. Now something's going on with you, and you're trying to handle it all by yourself, but you can't. And you don't need to."

"It's nothing."

"I'm not letting you off that easy. What happened out there today?"

She shook her head again, trying to pull away, but his fingers tightened on her chin.

"See? This is what I mean. I'm not going to hurt you. I'd never hurt you—and I don't think I ever have. Your pride, maybe, but not you, not your heart—"

She jerked away from him and marched back to the campsite. What was he talking about, he'd never hurt her? Had he lost his memory? Had he managed to convince himself over time that their breakup was a mutual decision?

*Well, why wouldn't he? You never told him otherwise. You never told him the truth. Not about anything that mattered.*

She sat down at the picnic table and watched him walk toward her, slowly, as if to give her time to collect her thoughts. In many respects, he knew her so well. He was right about that. But he was wrong if he thought she'd always told him everything. She'd kept one monumental secret from him, one he could never find out. No one knew the truth, and it had to stay that way.

She had to fight him now. She had to remain immune to his tenderness and charm as she had managed to do for so long. She had to.

If she didn't, she would break his heart.

He sat down beside her and took her hand. His touch sent a shiver up her arm, but she didn't move. She gave away too much every time she let him know how he made her feel. She had to stay cool and composed—not just for her, but for him.

When he finally spoke, his voice was gruff. "Tell me something. I don't think I've ever asked. Is there anyone special in your life now?"

"No."

"Why not?"

"Same reason as always. I don't have time."

*Or the heart...or the stamina...or the will...or the desire...*

"Is that the only reason?"

"That's it."

She could tell he didn't believe her, but she didn't care as long as he changed the subject.

He didn't. "Does that include me?"

Her heart stopped for a moment, and she realized she was holding her breath. She released it carefully. "Does what include you?"

Suddenly he gripped her shoulders and turned her to face him. The flickering lights accentuated the intensity in his eyes and the tension around his mouth. She'd gone as far as she could.

"Don't play games with me. We've come too far together for that. I've always told you the truth, and I'm going to tell you the truth now—"

She panicked and pressed her fingers against his lips. "Hunter, don't."

His smile was slow and crooked as he moved her fingers away and kissed the palm of her hand. "I have to. I'm thirty-five years old, and I know what I want. I want you. I need you with me. I always have. I always will."

She couldn't speak, couldn't move, couldn't even breathe. Once, she would've given everything she owned, sacrificed every goal she ever had, to hear those words. When she thought she lost him, her world had shattered like glass, and she feared she'd lost her own soul, her own identity. Now he was saying what she'd yearned to hear for so long...

And now, when he took her in his arms and kissed her, it was as if he'd never left her, had never broken her heart, had never taken away her reason for living. Now, as his lips moved tenderly against hers, his hands cradled her face in the way that had always turned her insides into liquid fire. A familiar rush of heat surged through her so every part of her body blazed and throbbed with desire.

But he didn't say, "I love you..." She jerked away from him and took refuge in anger. It was all she had. "No! You destroyed me years ago, and it's taken me all this time to—"

"How did I destroy you? You're the one who broke it off, not me."

Tears filled her eyes, spilled over. "You and I have been playing at this 'mutual agreement' thing ever since we split up, but here's the truth. After we'd set a wedding date and everyone knew we were getting married, you still grabbed that assignment in South

Africa and ran like the wind. I know I told you I didn't want to marry you, but it was a lie. I *had* to say that. It was the only way I could hold on to my dignity. But if you'd come back and asked me again, probably as recently as yesterday, I would've done it. I would've given up everything I worked for, and I would've done it."

He stared at her in disbelief. "My God, you can't blame me for that! If I'd stayed and you'd married me, you wouldn't be who you are today. I knew you had way too much talent to be stuck in the kitchen, waiting on some guy who couldn't live the way you wanted to—"

"And you had way too much talent to be stuck with some little woman that wanted you to be with her instead of off in South Africa or some such place! Let's don't get into this again, Hunter. It doesn't matter anymore. I just wanted you to know the truth—why it hurts too much to be around you. You haven't changed, and you never will. I understand that. I accept it. Listen, our story is always going to have the same ending. Just let it go."

He frowned. "Let it go?"

"Yes."

"Okay, but this is your choice, not mine. Just remember this—I've wanted you since the first moment I laid eyes on you, and nothing you do or say is ever going to change that. You don't need to be afraid of me. Nothing else matters to me as long as you understand that."

She looked away from him. She wanted him to leave; she had to be alone. If he didn't, she was going to give in and tell him the truth. And if she did that, he would disappear in a flash…just like he had before.

"I understand," she whispered.

"Okay. I'm sorry I was so honest, and I'm sorry I kissed you." He stood up and took his jacket from her shoulders. "I swear it won't happen again."

\*\*\*\*

Panting and drenched in perspiration, Sierra sat straight up in her bed. For a split second she wasn't sure where she was, but she got her bearings as soon as she realized the moonlight was streaming in through the window. The dream about the young girl had come again, but this time she thought she knew why.

Byron Little Hand would arrive in a few hours, and he had news.

She crawled out of bed, slipped into a warm robe and fuzzy slippers, and made her way to the kitchen. A cup of hot tea would help.

"What are you doing up?"

Skye's voice startled her so badly she swallowed a shriek. "My God, you scared me to death!"

Skye chuckled and flipped on a wall lamp next to the kitchen table. "Sorry. Can't you sleep, either?"

She rubbed her eyes, yawned, and slid onto a bench across the kitchen table from Skye. She shook her head.

"Want some tea?"

"Yes, thanks." She nodded toward Colt, who was sleeping soundly on the sofa in the living area, and chuckled. "That man can sleep anywhere—and through anything."

"Even on top of a horse in a thunderstorm, or so he says." Skye poured a cup of tea and set it in front of Sierra, then joined her at the table. "Why can't you sleep?"

"Lots on my mind, that's all."

"That 'lots on your mind' wouldn't have a name, would it—like…Hunter Davenport?"

"Well, it has a name, but it's not Hunter. Actually, I'm thinking about Byron Little Hand and what he's going to tell me about my birth mother. He may have found her. I don't know." She yawned and sipped her tea. "This is really good, Sunshine. Thank you."

"Sure. Who's Byron Little Hand, and why would he have found your birth mother?"

Sierra rubbed her eyes; a fog seemed to have settled over them. "Oh, that's right. You weren't there when we met him. He's a full-blood Lakota private investigator Hunter hired to find Pauline, and he also seems to be working on something with Nathan. Anyway, he's meeting Hunter at eleven this morning, and I guess they're coming over here. He said he had stuff to tell me. I had a horrible nightmare that woke me up, one I had back when Hunter first told me about my birth mother. So…I can't sleep."

"What was your nightmare?"

She shook her head and took another sip of tea. "I don't want to talk about it."

Skye ran her fingers through her hair and shook it back out of her face in a warning of frustration that Sierra had seen many times, but the gesture was usually accompanied by a grin. This time it wasn't. This time Skye rested her elbows on the table and leaned forward, her eyes narrowed.

"If you don't want to tell me about your nightmare, that's fine. But I'm still going to stick my nose in where it doesn't belong because it's late, I'm not on your payroll, and I can. I know what I'm talking about, sweet pea. Hunter Davenport adores you, and you're wild about him. Neither of you can hide it. I don't know your story, but whatever it is, it's in the past. Don't waste any more time. Fix whatever's wrong between you and keep it right."

Sierra shook her head. "You don't understand," she whispered. "I can't do that. I can't let him back into my life. My heart couldn't take it."

"Sweet pea, listen to me—"

Colt sat up in his bed and rubbed his hair until it stood straight up in little spikes all over his head. "She said she didn't want to talk about it, Sunshine, so drop it. Please go back to bed so I can get some sleep, okay?"

Sierra stood up instantly, grateful for the interruption, but she touched Skye's hand in an attempt to let her know she wasn't angry. "I just wanted to thank you for taking care of me today," she said softly. "It meant more to me than I can say—just knowing you were there."

Skye's dark eyes softened, and her slow smile was maternal. "I'll always be here, sweet pea. Don't you ever worry about that."

\*\*\*\*

Voices and laughter from the kitchen told Sierra that Byron Little Hand and Hunter had arrived, so she finished applying cover-up to the purple circles beneath her eyes, added some blush and lip gloss, and caught her hair back in a ponytail low on her neck.

Hunter's deep voice responded to something Skye had said, and her heart skipped a beat at the sound of it. She had to block out the memory of last night—his words, that kiss. Today was a new day, and she had a feeling it was going to be an eventful one. She had to remain focused.

She opened the bedroom door and stepped into the kitchen. "Good morning, y'all." Her voice was too bright, too forced. She had to tone it down. "How are you, Mr. Little Hand?"

Byron waved from his place at the kitchen table. He reminded Sierra of an elephant at a tea party, and she had to choke back a giggle. In the background she heard bacon sizzling and coffee percolating as Skye issued orders to Colt while he tried to set the table, but every sound seemed muffled. All her senses were focused on Hunter.

He leaned against the wall beside the front door, one long leg crossed over the other, looking casually handsome in black jeans and a turquoise western shirt that accentuated his icy blue eyes. But those remarkable eyes were dark-shadowed and red-rimmed, like he hadn't slept, either.

"Nathan and Melanie will be here in just a minute, Miss Sierra," Byron said suddenly. "Do you mind?"

"Of course not. We have plenty—"

Before she could finish her sentence, someone gave a sharp rap on the door. Hunter leaned over to let them in.

She planted a smile on her face and walked toward her guests, hands outstretched, hoping she looked like a warm, welcoming hostess instead of a babbling idiot. "Melanie…Nathan…how good to see you again. Is Eli with you? Are you guys hungry?"

"No, he and Gideon had something else to do." Nathan patted his belly in anticipation. "Is Great Comanche Cooker Woman fixing breakfast?"

Skye turned around from the stove and gave a solemn bow. "She is. Breakfast tacos Texas-style, your royal Indian-ness. Are you interested?"

"If you're cooking it, he's interested," Melanie replied with a grin, "and so am I. I haven't heard anything since the gathering except how great your potato salad was—and I agree. You wouldn't happen to have a recipe floating around anywhere, would you?"

"In my head, along with a bunch of other junk, but I'll be happy to give it to you. I'm glad you liked it."

As the laughter and bantering went on, breakfast came together, and the atmosphere was that of old friends enjoying one another's company. Grateful they didn't seem to need her, Sierra moved to an out-of-the-way corner between the kitchen and her bedroom and watched Hunter. She drank in his presence, absorbed every detail of him, because before long she wouldn't have him at all. No one in the world was like him; no one was as perfect for her.

As if he felt her gaze on him, he looked straight at her, unsmiling and intense. She didn't look away. That moment hung in the balance, stretched for eons, seemed to last a lifetime.

Skye's voice broke through. "Are you joining us, Sierra, or are you just going to sleep standing up? Come on, sweet pea. Sit down and have a cup of coffee."

Sierra held Hunter's gaze for a few seconds more, then turned away.

Once breakfast was finished and Melanie had dried the last of the dishes, Byron spoke with quaint formality and leaned back in his chair. "That was wonderful, Miss Skye. I don't think I've ever tasted anything so good."

"You're very welcome. Would you like more coffee?"

"Yes, thank you."

When he turned to Sierra, who was wiping her lips with a napkin and wondering how she could stand this suspense for five more minutes, he touched her cheek in a paternal gesture that didn't make much sense to her. But when she met his dark eyes, she understood.

She reached for his hand. "It's all right. Did you not find her, or did she not want to speak with you, or does she not want to meet me?"

The room grew quiet with unspoken tension, but Sierra was calm. If her birth mother didn't want to see her, that was all right. Her true parents were Noah and Alexa Masters, and they couldn't have raised her with more love if they'd given her life themselves.

Byron squeezed her hand and shook his head. "I'll have your answer in a couple of days, Miss Sierra. I'm close. I can feel it."

"But you have no answer now?"

"Not from Pauline." He looked at her more intently. "But I feel you've gotten answers on your own…from somewhere. What's happened?"

Chapter Twenty

The room was so still a rubber band hitting the floor would have sounded like a pistol shot. Sierra had to tell everyone here what had been happening to her—they'd understand in a way no one else could. At least Skye, Nathan, and Melanie would.

Her heart pounded. "I can be honest with all of you, can't I? And you'll keep what I say between us?"

Colt moved toward the door. "Maybe I should leave…"

She stopped him cold. "Stay. Please."

He flushed but didn't argue and sat back down on the couch. After she was sure she had everyone's attention, she looked at Hunter and spoke straight to him.

"The night you first told me about Pauline, you showed me the photos and told me about the Wounded Knee Occupation. After you left, I had a dream where a young Indian girl was running through the Badlands, chased by a drunken White man in a pickup truck. I saw how he tortured and played with her, how she fell down and pleaded with him not to hurt her. I knew what was going to happen—what *did* happen. The next day my mother told us Pauline had been raped by an important White man and became pregnant, and Julia Farewell wanted her off the reservation before I could be born. Do you remember that?"

He nodded.

She cleared her throat nervously. "Well, I wasn't surprised to hear it because I'd seen it all in my dream the night before. Then, when you and I went to visit Nathan and Melanie, I saw the truck from my dream being driven by the same drunk White man, chasing that same young girl...but then everything disappeared. The man, the truck, the young girl...just vanished. Then last night I dreamed it again. I'm beginning to think it's a recurring dream that won't stop until I find out who that man was—or is."

Nathan leaned forward. "But when you were out in the Badlands with Hunter, you *saw* the truck...like in a vision?"

"I know it sounds nuts, but—"

Skye interrupted. "That was the nightmare you had last night?"

"Yes, but it's more real than that." She closed her eyes as she attempted to explain. "It's like I'm *there*, like I'm *inside* of her. Everything around me disappears, and all my senses become extra-sharp...focused. It's crazy, but it's real. I'm sure of it. I know what I'm seeing happened at some point, and for some reason I'm seeing it now."

"It's not crazy, sweet pea. Unusual, maybe, but not crazy."

Sierra managed to give her a quick grateful smile before she turned back to Byron. "Mr. Little Hand, I have wonderful parents, and I love them very much. I don't want to hurt Pauline or upset her life in any way, so if you never find her, that's all right. After all, I'm the product of a terrible trauma I'm sure she wants to forget. I just want to be sure she doesn't need anything.

I want to know she's well now…and happy."

He nodded. "I understand."

She shocked herself with her next words; she hadn't planned them. "In fact, if you should find her and you think she shouldn't know I'm looking for her, just drop it, okay? I'll leave that decision up to you."

Byron Little Hand gazed at her for a long time before he nodded again, his sympathetic smile showing a touch of new respect. "I'll remember that."

Hunter spoke up. "So *that's* what you saw when we were on our way to Nathan's house. A drunk White guy in a truck chasing a young girl. Is that what you wouldn't tell me?"

Sierra's cheeks went warm, and she refused to answer. He'd been with her on other occasions when she'd "seen" something odd, but maybe she could throw him off the trail by ignoring his question. Hunter was an investigative reporter, a believer in facts. He wasn't going to buy this.

She was wrong.

Hunter looked at Nathan. "You said that Pauline had spent a lot of time with a White family when she was away at the boarding school. You said you didn't know who that family was. Are you sure about that?"

"Yes."

"And you, Melanie?"

"Absolutely, but Grandma Madonna might know. I'm going out there this afternoon to deliver some supplies to her. I could ask her."

Sierra began to tremble. "Do you think she'd tell you?"

"Nope," Nathan stated. "Trust me. You don't want to ask Madonna Kills Quick about that time. Everybody knows she lost her mind back then. And I mean that for real."

She ignored him. "Could I go with you, Melanie?"

"Absolutely not." Then Melanie's eyes widened. "Oh my Lord, wait a minute! Of course…"

Nathan's objection was firm. "Don't even think about it, Melanie."

"My love, I appreciate that you want to protect me, but I think Grandma Madonna is still alive because she's waiting to see Pauline again. But if she can't see Pauline, finding Sierra would still be a blessing, I'm sure. Besides, Sierra *needs* to know her, Nathan. I think they share the power, and Grandma Madonna can teach her how to use it."

Sierra caught her breath, shocked. "Wait a minute. *The power?* What power? You said she healed people and stuff. I can't do that. I don't think I even believe in that."

Now Skye interrupted in a low voice. "It doesn't matter what you believe in, sweet pea. What matters is what happens to you…and you haven't told us everything, have you?"

Sierra looked away, embarrassed.

But Skye persisted. "You saw something when we were down in Nebraska, didn't you? And I saw you get out of Hunter's car the day we got here and just stand looking out over the Badlands for the longest time. What were you watching then? And whatever happened yesterday down by Wounded Knee Creek goes without saying, huh?"

Sierra managed to give a small, self-mocking chuckle. "There's just something in my brain that's going a little…haywire, that's all. I could even have a tumor, you know."

Melanie shook her head. "I doubt that. What we have here is a culture clash."

"A what?"

"A culture clash. White culture gives experiences like yours a physical explanation: a tumor, a stomach virus, drugs... But American Indian culture, at least traditional culture, accepts it because it just *is*. Crazy Horse himself was said to be a mystic. Anyway, we believe the spirits bring the power to special people, and people who are gifted with the power are revered and highly respected. We never laugh at them."

"Look here," Byron interjected suddenly. "How many Indians are in this room?"

"Five," Sierra answered, then added with a grin, "counting me."

He nodded. "And two token White guys. You're never going to have a better opportunity to have these dreams analyzed than right now. You might as well tell us about them."

She yearned to drop through the floor. "It'll take too long. You don't want to hear—"

Nathan leaned forward and held up his hand. "Us old Indians love stories. Byron's right. Tell us."

\*\*\*\*

Hunter listened to Sierra's detailed description of her dreams and so-called visions in amazement, committing them to memory as accurately as he could. He knew Sierra Masters as well as he knew himself, or at least he thought he did, and she wasn't making this up. This was happening to her—and she had to be terrified.

The Sierra he remembered, while as idealistic as all

young people, was more likely to quote her conservative parents than to question their beliefs. The Sierra he remembered didn't know anything about Indians—their history, poverty, spirituality, or their present state of affairs. If she'd been well versed in any of this, he might've been able to chalk up her current experiences to previous in-depth knowledge, but he knew better. She didn't understand what she was seeing or why she was seeing it.

Yet he was positive it was happening.

He looked around the room and waited for someone to speak.

The man who broke the silence was Colt Chambers. His gravelly voice commanded everyone's attention.

"I was born and raised in Quanah up in the Texas Panhandle," he began with that slow drawl. "One of my father's best friends was a Kiowa elder from Oklahoma named Frank Blue Bear. Anyway, I was a bull rider, and one day I rode a badass bull in Amarillo. He slammed me into a gate so hard I broke my right leg in four places, and I knew my rodeo days were done. I went nuts...all disabled athletes go nuts. But Frank Blue Bear saved my life.

"He took me out of rehab and up to some friends of his in Muskogee. It was like a little Indian village— Kiowa, Cherokee, Choctaw, Comanche, even a few Cheyenne—and they took me in. They became like family. I'm not going to say any more about that, but I'll tell you this—Frank Blue Bear had strong medicine, the strongest anyone ever saw, and it went back several generations. I saw it with my own eyes. I felt it. It gave me my life back." Colt paused as he looked around the room, then seemed to come to a decision. "If Sierra's seeing things out here, there's a reason. For everybody's good, we need to find out—or figure out—what it is. And that's all I have to say about that."

Hunter stifled a grin. He didn't know how many times he'd heard Nathan Winterhawk or other Indian leaders end a proclamation that way, *that's all I have to say about that.* It seemed to go back to the days of medicine men and warriors.

But Colt Chambers was no Crazy Horse. He was just a cowboy…and he had a point.

Hunter ran through Sierra's recited list of dreams and visions.

A terrified young girl stumbling through the Badlands, chased by a drunken White man driving a pickup truck.

An ancient Indian man in the sky, holding the clouds apart as if to welcome a young woman who was screaming in the pain of childbirth on the earth's floor far beneath him.

A normal Lakota Indian village camped beside a babbling creek, fires flickering, children laughing, the music of drums and singing.

A camp of starving Indians out in the Badlands, silent as ghosts moving between ragged tipis.

A white buffalo calf standing on the road to Nathan's house…visible one moment, gone the next.

A procession of grieving Indians leading a pony that bore an unwieldy bundle covered by a buffalo robe toward the cottonwoods down by Wounded Knee Creek.

And finally…walking among the Indians camped near the creek bed…feeling the freezing cold, weak with hunger and exhaustion, desperate to tell others what was going to happen to them, unable to warn them to run.

That one was far more than a dream. It went beyond a vision. Hunter's memory of the expression of terror on her face was so vivid it made him sick to his stomach.

Once again, he castigated himself for showing her those photos in the first place. He should have left everything well enough alone. But no. What he wanted was all that mattered. He hadn't cared that Sierra's life would be turned upside down. This was all his fault.

Melanie's amazed voice broke into his thoughts. "You never let on, Sierra. The night I met you...you didn't say a word."

"Well, I had to act normal, didn't I? I didn't want you to think I was crazy."

Byron Little Hand waved his arm in warning. "Ladies, let's don't get off the subject, okay? Colt here is right. These visions and dreams of Miss Sierra's are important. They may be warning her about something. That's what we need to focus on."

The room was silent.

Finally, Sierra spoke. "You're so big on family, Nathan. Why don't you think it's safe for me to see my great-grandmother?"

"It just isn't."

"Nathan, if you tell me not to go with Melanie, I won't go. But I'd so appreciate it if you could trust me enough to tell me why not."

He answered her with his gaze fixed on Hunter. "Number one, trust has nothing to do with it." He glanced at his wife and gave a rueful grin. "And it has nothing to do with protecting you, Melanie. I'm worried about Grandma Madonna herself."

"You're not making any sense, my love. Grandma Madonna's lived out there alone for years, and no one's ever bothered her. Why would she need protecting now?"

"Because she's been out of sight, out of mind. Everyone knows you visit her, and they don't pay attention. But if you take Sierra out there with you, the people will notice, and they'll talk. Remember, they don't know who Sierra is."

Hunter appreciated the humor and warmth of the Lakota people, but they were like the residents of any small town. They knew each other's business and didn't hesitate to comment on it.

"Excuse me, you guys," he interjected. "I have an idea."

"What?" Nathan asked, clearly eager to avoid a fight with his wife.

"Well, maybe Melanie should go alone to see Madonna today like she always does and tell her Sierra is here. That would put the ball in Madonna's court, and Madonna can decide for herself if she wants to see her. I'm sure she will, but she *is* very old. You don't want her to have a stroke or something. This would give her some warning." He paused, added, "Of course, you should do what you want. It was just an idea."

"And it's a good one," Byron said hastily. "I like it. What do you think, Melanie?"

She looked disappointed, but after a moment she nodded. "Well, I hate to admit it, but I think you're right."

Surprised, Hunter shot her a look of gratitude

before he added, "I know Sierra, and I know whatever you tell her is going to be safe with her. In fact, she may actually be able to help."

"How?" Sierra asked.

"People know you. They know your work. Look at Logan O'Neill and the way he acted around you. Look at Breeden Jones. He all but kissed your feet. That tells me you might be able to go where no one else in this group can, including me. I don't like it, but there it is."

Nathan glanced at Byron Little Hand. "What do you think?"

Little Hand shrugged his massive shoulders. "It's up to you. I don't have a problem with it as long as you don't think she'll be in any danger."

"I can't promise that."

Sierra cleared her throat. "Look, I'm sitting right here, guys, so you don't need to talk over me. My safety is my problem, not yours. If you think I can help in some way, just lay it out there."

Nathan seemed lost in thought for several moments, but when he reached his decision, he was firm and emphatic, leaving no room for argument. "Hunter's right. Sierra's new to the people, but she's one of us. My spirit recognized her right off. Her parents were among the strongest gifts the Creator ever gave to the people during the bad times. Sierra wants to find Pauline Kills Quick and heal her *tiyospaye*. She needs to do that. I believe her dreams and visions will help her even more than we can, but perhaps she can help us at the same time. So we will work together. That is all I have to say about that."

Chapter Twenty-One

Sierra leaned back in her chair and waited patiently as Nathan gave a reminiscent smile. Like most older people, he seemed to spend part of his time in the past, but she didn't mind. His wisdom was worth waiting for.

"Before I start, you have to promise you'll be patient, okay? White folks are always in a hurry. But to Indians, time flows in an endless circle. So just listen to me, and I'll do my best to have this finished by Christmas."

"Of course," Sierra answered with a grin. "Take your time."

"Thank you. First, I'm a Traditional Indian in that I love our culture and spirituality, and I want to see those beautiful old ways return to my people. On the other hand, I'm not crazy. I know we can't hunt the buffalo as they thunder across the freeways—saying there were enough buffalo left to hunt. I understand we have to live in a White man's world to a certain degree, or we can't live at all. That's why a few of us have tried over the last several years to establish business plans that would allow us to make a living, but we've tried to do it so it doesn't compromise our spiritual or cultural beliefs."

When Nathan paused to take a sip of his coffee, Byron Little Hand stepped in. "Even though the days of the Reign of Terror are behind us, the old ones—like your great-grandmother, Miss Sierra—have long memories. They're afraid to share stories about our culture, heroes, and long-past history with the children and teenagers who desperately need to hear them. But because of their fear, our culture is dying, and we Indian people don't know who we are anymore. I'm not sure it matters how much money we make. I often tell Nathan that the *heart* of a people is who they are, not your almighty dollar."

Sierra squirmed. "It isn't *my* almighty dollar—"

Grinning, Nathan held up two fingers in the famous 1960s peace sign. "Ignore him, Sierra. He was a militant AIM member back in the day. He spent two years in a Nebraska federal prison after the Occupation of Wounded Knee because he wouldn't give the feds the information they wanted. He was a hero around here, but I think he just wanted some free food and a roof over his head. They kicked him out when they couldn't find a bed big enough for him to fit in."

She managed a smile, but Byron's words still stung.

Nathan gave her a worried look. "Am I taking too long?"

"Of course not."

"Anyway, rez land is so checkerboarded that it took me almost twenty years to put together more than fifteen hundred acres of Winterhawk property—"

Perplexed, Sierra interrupted, "Wait a minute. What're you talking about? What's *checkerboarded*?"

"Well, back in 1887, when the Indian Wars were supposedly over and we were herded onto reservations, the Dawes Act was passed. It's complicated, but the government allotted pieces of land to every tribal member—every man, woman, and child. Each plot ranged from forty to three hundred and forty acres or so, depending on the age and gender of each tribal member, and each plot has been passed down in that family from generation to generation. This may sound fair to the White folks, but it didn't work for us. The Lakota didn't understand the concept of land ownership. Many still don't. There's not even a word for it in our language. Chief Crazy Horse said it best when he said, 'One does not sell the earth upon which the people walk.'

"The pieces of land were selected by the government with no rhyme or reason, so people ended up owning land in little squares all over the reservation, away from other family members. Like I told you the other night, this helped destroy our *tiyospayes*, which I believe was their ultimate goal. Plus, the land was put into a trust and is managed by the federal government to this very day, so Indian landowners have practically no say about what happens to their property. Lots of Indians don't know where it is, who lives on it, or that they even own it.

"Anyway, the Winterhawk clan is huge, and it goes back a long way. Some of our family's land was down by Wounded Knee, some of it was up by Porcupine, some near Kyle…it was all over the place. It had also been leased out many, many times through the years, so we had to locate all those people. It was a nightmare. If you look at a map of allotted land on all thirty-five hundred square miles of the Pine Ridge Reservation, it looks like a checkerboard. That's where the term came from.

"The feds then said that once all the land

allotments on the reservation were given to eligible tribal members, the government could buy up whatever was left over and sell it to White homesteaders. By the time it was all said and done, sixty million acres of Indian land was either ceded outright or sold to White settlers and corporations. *Sixty...million...acres!* They called this surplus land, but there's nothing surplus about it. It's all Indian land promised to us by treaty 'for as long as the grass grows and the rivers run.' Some of it was part of our hunting grounds, some of it our sacred lands, but the White folks took it from us with a stroke of the pen, without firing a shot. Chief Red Cloud summed it up perfectly when he said, 'They made us many promises, more than I can remember, but they never kept but one; they promised to take our land, and they took it.' "

When Nathan paused for breath, Hunter picked up the narrative. "Today, almost sixty percent of the lands allotted to Lakota families back in 1887 are being leased out by the Bureau of Indian Affairs to White ranchers for an average of three dollars and fifty cents per acre. Lakota landowners receive about fifty cents per acre on average—if they get anything at all. White ranchers who lease all that land from the BIA are counting on the unfairness of the system to make it as hard as possible for the Indians to get their land back. Most Indians won't even try, but Nathan refused to give up. He was able to do it with the help of an amazing organization based out of Colorado. That was the original reason I wanted to film this documentary."

"You guys," Melanie interrupted with a soft chuckle, "Sierra's eyes are glassy. Tell her what all this has to do with her."

Sierra smiled, but in truth she was fuming. It was one thing to beat a nation in a fair-and-square battle, but nothing was fair-and-square about this. This was robbery, pure and simple.

Nathan gave an apologetic grin. "Anyway, in order to begin to rebuild my *tiyospaye*, we had to *find* our land, which, like I said, was all over the reservation. Then we started trading it with other families closer to us who wanted to rebuild their *tiyospayes* as well, until the Winterhawks were pretty well consolidated. It was like putting a puzzle back together. It took a long time, and we spent a lot of money. We still don't have all of it, but we had to start somewhere. Once we had put together our first five hundred acres and moved my sons and their families back onto our property so we could all work together, we watched our *tiyospaye* come back to life. And I began to feel like a true Lakota.

"After we all sat down and discussed what we wanted to do next, we decided to establish a bison ranch. We named it The Buffalo Spirit Ranch. We started it with four head of bison donated by a White rancher in Colorado named Conrad Parker, and began working on our business plan, which was a nightmare. Finally, rather than trying to track down owners of fractionated land and spend years bickering between families, we decided to lease another five hundred acres of tribal land adjacent to our Wounded Knee property." Nathan paused. "But so far we haven't been able to do that because someone doesn't want us to lease it."

Sierra frowned. "Do you know who that is?"

"I have no idea, but we can't get approval through the BIA, and the system is so tangled with bureaucratic red tape and tribal politics it's almost impossible to get through it all. If someone wants to keep that land out of our hands, they could probably do it forever. But we'll figure it out. We still have a couple of options open to us. We have to do this. Our goals are too important not to."

"What goals?"

"The Lakota were caretakers of the buffalo and the plains, and that's the attitude we want to bring back to the reservation. We want to promote this healthy meat because so many of our people don't eat right. Bison is low-fat and low-cholesterol, very important tools in healing the heart disease and diabetes in our population. Because the buffalo took such good care of us in the past, now we want to take care of them. We'll harvest our bison in a good way, giving thanks in ceremony out in the field and always treating them with respect. We hope this will encourage our people to return to self-reliance and connect once again with the Buffalo Culture. It would also allow us to teach our children the old ways of the Lakota and the earth—the prayers, ceremonies, language, and songs. It will bring us back to our core."

It sounded like a perfect plan to Sierra, but apparently someone didn't think so. "So who wouldn't want this to be successful?" she wondered aloud. "It sounds like a win-win to me."

Now Colt spoke up in his matter-of-fact Texas drawl. "Maybe it doesn't have anything to do with that. Maybe someone just doesn't want a lot of attention focused on this reservation."

"Well, that could be true, I guess," Nathan admitted. "Pine Ridge is the second-largest rez in this

203

country, but few people know about it. That's how Dickie Wilson managed to get away with everything he did back in the '70s."

Colt turned to Sierra. "You just came up here to find your birth mom, right?"

"Right."

"And that's how Byron Little Hand got involved."

"I guess so."

Byron cleared his throat. "Well…not entirely."

When everyone looked at him expectantly, Byron seemed a little uncomfortable.

"Earlier this month, I was trying to help Nathan figure out who was behind the big holdup. The BIA said they needed more paperwork, which we knew they didn't need, and we didn't have it, anyway. We knew that was pretty much our last shot. We were trying to decide what to do, and Nathan told me about the documentary he wanted to do with Hunter. I thought it might be a good idea to shine a light on the political crap happening on this reservation.

"But when you called me, Hunter, and told me you were looking for Pauline Kills Quick because you thought you knew her daughter, I didn't connect the two projects. To be honest, that's an old story in Indian country, babies taken from families and turned over to White people so the babies grow up with no idea who they really are. If you have no history, no culture…you have no baby Indian." He glanced at Sierra. "In other words, even though I agreed to help Hunter, you and Pauline Kills Quick weren't on the top of my list at that minute."

"I understand."

"So at first I didn't think much about Pauline Kills

Quick. But then a couple of days went by, and the name started bothering me. You know...like I'd heard it somewhere before. I'm almost seventy years old, so my memory isn't what it used to be. I thought it might be because everyone knows Madonna Kills Quick, and the Kills Quick name goes way back...but then I knew that wasn't it. I'm famous for knowing the family trees of just about everyone on this reservation. I hardly ever forget a name. Finally, I realized it was the name Pauline Kills Quick itself that bothered me."

Byron clamped his lips shut as if he were never going to speak again. The silence stretched until Sierra thought she would explode.

"I figured it out a few days ago."

Silence again.

At last, Byron continued. "I realized I'd heard her name when I was arrested down in Gordon, Nebraska, not long after the Knee occupation was over. That was sometime in July 1973. Anyway, there were some rednecks in the holding cell next to me, and they were laughing about a little Indian girl that 'got hers' from some high-powered White guy out in the Badlands. Seems no one ever pressed any charges that stuck, even though he seemed to make a habit of getting little girls from the Indian boarding schools around South Dakota. They were laughing about one up in Sisseton and another one over in Marty—"

"One what," Hunter growled, "a little girl or a boarding school?"

"Both."

"What do you mean—getting little girls?" Sierra asked nervously.

"I don't know for sure, but I think they were

talking how the rich or powerful White men could go into an Indian boarding school and get what they wanted. A babysitter, a housekeeper…you know, anything. Because they were White and had a lot of pull, no one even asked. That was back in the day. It's a little better now, but not much. At least not in South Dakota. Out here, racism against American Indians is still rampant.

"Anyway, the other night I sat straight up in bed because it came to me—the young girl that they were laughing about was named Pauline Kills Quick, and she'd lived at the St. Paul Indian School on the Rosebud."

"So you believe she *was* raped out in the Badlands," Sierra whispered.

Byron nodded.

She could hardly breathe. "Like I dreamed…"

"It would seem so, yes."

"Who was the man?" Hunter interrupted.

Byron looked embarrassed. "Well, I tried to get that information from those rednecks in the jail, but my powers of persuasion were limited."

"By what?"

"By the fact I got so mad about this little girl I went crazy, and one of the guards coldcocked me. I'm a pretty big guy, so someone clobbered me good. When I came to, I was in solitary, and I didn't see anyone for three days. By the time I did, I had more important things to deal with—like trying to stay out of prison, which I didn't. So I forgot all about Pauline Kills Quick until you brought up her name these thirty years later."

"How can we find out who this man is?" Skye asked.

"I'm already on it," Byron answered. "This is what I've done so far."

Sierra leaned forward and focused her intense gaze on his face.

"I have a good friend who was a counselor at the St. Paul Indian School on the Rosebud back in the 1960s and '70s. It was run by Jesuit priests for years, but in 1974 it was turned back to the tribe. My friend's name is Cecilia Long Soldier, and she's retired now, but she still knows a lot of people around the state who work, or used to work, in Indian education. I called Cecilia as soon as I remembered about little Pauline Kills Quick and asked if she could check the old files about what might've happened. I hope to hear something from her soon."

Sierra relaxed in her chair. "Thank you, Mr. Little Hand. I appreciate anything you can do."

"Of course."

"If your friend finds something, do you think she'll feel free to tell you?"

"I think so. I'm sorry I don't have any information for you yet."

She gave him a wan smile. "Well, it's a little more than we had, so it's all good. May I ask you something else?"

"Of course."

"When we first met, you said you were sorry we couldn't meet earlier because you had to leave Rapid City on short notice. Did you go somewhere that had to do with Pauline?"

"No," he answered without hesitation. "I went to Fort Collins, in Colorado, to see our rancher friend, Conrad Parker. He had a very important Indian artifact he wanted to show me. Since I'm not a recognized expert, I took Gideon O'Neill with me in case the artifact proved to be valuable."

"Is Parker a collector?" Hunter asked.

"No, but he has a lady friend who's in charge of Native American exhibits at a western art museum there in Fort Collins. While she was organizing an exhibit that had been donated to the museum for the next several months, she came across something she believed didn't belong in a personal collection. But she wasn't sure it was authentic, so she asked Conrad to bring in someone even more expert than she was if he could, so he invited me—and I brought Gideon along as an extra pair of eyeballs. We didn't get to meet the lady, but we did see the artifact. Gideon got pretty excited and left right away because he needed to meet with someone on the rez about it. I couldn't get home until later last night."

"What was the item?" Skye asked curiously.

"I'm sorry. I'm not at liberty to say yet." Byron paused and leaned forward in barely concealed excitement. "But I will tell you this—Conrad's lady friend was right. Gideon says it's an item that no one should own."

Chapter Twenty-Two

Sitting on a concrete bench at the picnic table outside the motor home, Hunter watched Melanie pull away from the campsite in Nathan's old pickup truck. Although he should've been thinking about organizing his documentary, his mind was fixed instead on alleged rapes Byron Little Hand claimed had occurred more than thirty years earlier—the rapes of young, defenseless Indian girls by powerful White men who knew how to use the system.

A soft voice broke into his reverie. "What're you thinking about?"

"Nothing special."

Sierra sat across the table from him and pushed her sunglasses to the top of her head. Her blue-black hair cascaded over her shoulders, and the gold flecks in her dark eyes flickered like topaz. She gave him a shy smile. "Can I talk to you a minute?"

Protective armor clamped over his heart. "Sure."

She bit her bottom lip in a gesture so vulnerable it seemed almost sensual. "I just wanted to say…I'm sorry. About last night. I was…tired and upset. I said things I didn't mean."

He gazed out at the rolling grasslands beyond her right shoulder and shrugged. "We both did. It's all right."

"Are you sure?"

"It's not a problem. Forget it."

She cocked her head to one side and asked hesitantly, "So...we're good, then?"

Nodding, he scooted off the concrete bench and stood up. He needed to get as far away from her as he could, and he needed to do it very soon. "Where are Nathan and Byron?"

"They'll be outside in a minute. Colt wanted to talk to them."

"Well, tell them I had to leave, would you? There's something I've got to do."

"No, wait. Please. Sit down."

"I said—"

"Hunter, please."

He sighed and sat back down. He couldn't let her know how much power she had over him, so he had to act as if being near her didn't bother him. Not an easy feat but one he could accomplish.

He yawned. "What's on your mind?"

She looked a little embarrassed but determined. She plowed forward. "Do you think any of this has to do with Sloan Turner, that slimy scumbag who owns the truck stop? He has lots of stuff in there."

"Any of what?"

"You know. The artifact the lady found."

"Why would Turner have anything to do with it? You saw his place. It's full of garbage."

"Yeah, but there's something in that museum. I could feel it—"

He leaned forward earnestly. "Sierra, drop this. We're not Lakota, and we can't get involved if we're not invited. Remember, the Pine Ridge Indian Reservation is sovereign land. It might as well be a foreign country. We can't go into a foreign country and start nosing around where we don't belong. We have to remember who we are."

"I know that, but Turner's place isn't on the rez. Besides, you're here to film a documentary. The people know you're out here nosing around. It's what you're supposed to do."

"We still have to be careful. Especially you. You're an Apple—red on the outside, white on the inside. You're a guest here. You haven't been invited anywhere."

"Wrong," Nathan announced, pushing open the screen door. He stepped out of the motor home, followed by Colt, Byron, and finally Skye, who was hastily re-plaiting one of her waist-length silver braids. Nathan walked to the head of the picnic table and gazed at both Hunter and Sierra, his weather-beaten face serious. "I'm inviting you. No, scratch that. I'm ordering."

Hunter grinned. "What about our safety? I seem to remember you saying something about that."

Nathan's sober expression didn't change. "I did. But Colt here says that neither one of you worry too much about safety, so I guess I shouldn't, either."

"Colt?" Hunter frowned. "He doesn't know me."

"No, he doesn't," Nathan agreed, "but I do. So I've made an executive decision. We need your help."

"What can we do?" Sierra asked immediately.

"Well, a while back, Gideon got word from a friend of his in the National Park Service that they'd been tipped off about someone who was trying to sell a Sioux scalp shirt, an old medicine bundle, and a buffalo horn headdress online. The seller claimed these items were authentic and could be documented."

"Is that illegal?" Sierra asked.

Byron leaned against the motor home and crossed one long leg over the other. "It depends. Back in the early '90s, the Native American Graves Protection and Repatriation Act was passed. NAGPRA says that all federal agencies and institutions that receive federal funding—like museums and such—have to return Indian stuff to the tribes or lineal descendant. But that law doesn't have real teeth. The key is in the term 'federal funding.' If someone finds that kind of stuff on private property or even on state or leased lands, nothing much will happen. But if you're caught trafficking in it, you can get a pretty stiff fine. Of course, you have to get caught, and you have to find someone who cares enough to follow it through."

"What kind of Indian stuff?"

Byron gave a bitter smile. "Oh, you know. Unimportant stuff like human remains, sacred objects, items used in burials. For example, if authorities can prove the medicine bundle was part of an actual burial, it would be illegal. If they can't prove it, the bundle would be up for grabs. Still, what matters is these items were important enough to alert the tipster, and he asked the authorities to check them out."

"Do you know who the tipster was?"

"No. He was anonymous, which isn't unusual. Anyway, Gideon's friend in the park service set up a sting and went undercover as a collector, at first just out of curiosity. He contacted the seller, asking for verification of authenticity, which the seller had…or appeared to have. Then Gideon's friend brought in his wife to seal the deal, and they made a viable offer a couple of weeks ago as part of the sting, which is still going on. I understand even the FBI is involved now, so something might come of it. But that's not what's important. What's important is who the seller was."

Hunter cleared his throat. "Let me guess. Sloan Turner, right?"

"How'd you know?" Nathan asked.

"I didn't. Sierra and I were just talking about him."

Nathan nodded. "Well, when you said that Logan O'Neill was at the truck stop when you met Sierra there, bossing Turner around and acting like he owned the place, our interest went up several notches. That's why we asked you to do that little private investigation."

Sierra frowned. "What private investigation?"

Hunter felt a twinge of guilt because he hadn't confided in her earlier. "After I saw how scared Turner was of O'Neill, I thought since O'Neill had been an important attorney back in his day—according to him, anyway—he might just be holding something over Turner's head. I investigated a case several years ago in Dallas where an attorney did that to several of his former clients. Anyway, I did a little research, and I found out he'd managed to get an attempted rape charge against Turner dropped back in the 1980s—a charge I'm willing to bet Turner's own wife doesn't know about."

"So you think O'Neill might be blackmailing Turner in some way?" she asked.

"Maybe."

Now she gave all her attention to Nathan. "So how can we help?"

He appeared to struggle for a moment with the

decision to take her into his confidence, but his voice was resolute when he finally answered. "The collection that Gideon and Byron went to check out in Fort Collins is owned by Logan O'Neill."

Hunter's mouth dropped. "Well, I'll be damned."

"How can we help?" Sierra repeated.

Nathan looked relieved. "Two ways. One, he wants to impress you—so let him think he has. Second, you have visions, and most of them seem to be in the Wounded Knee area. We don't know why that would be, but I have a feeling of my own that O'Neill could be connected. I'm hoping you can help us figure out how."

She shook her head. "I'm sorry, but that's impossible. You guys don't trust us enough to tell us everything you know. So I'd be going in blind—and that's where the real danger is."

Hunter glanced at her in admiration and said nothing. She had this.

"What do you mean?" Nathan asked.

She lifted her chin in that gesture of determination Hunter recognized. He stifled a grin.

"You won't even tell me what the artifact is, Nathan. Don't you think I at least need to know that?"

Byron Little Hand stepped away from the motor home and sat down beside her on the concrete bench. When he spoke, his voice was so low Hunter had to lean in closer to hear him.

"Okay, I guess I can tell you. The lady found an authentic Ghost Shirt wadded up and stuffed like trash into the bottom of one of the boxes she was unloading. The only one I've ever seen is one a Scottish delegation returned to us from their little museum in Scotland back in 1999, but Gideon assures me this one is real, too. He also assures me it's part of his father's collection. He recognized it because of a bloodstain on the side. He remembers it from when he was a boy."

She frowned. "A Ghost Shirt? Like the Ghost Dancers wore? Weren't they supposed to be magic or something?"

Byron nodded.

Hunter was baffled. "How the hell would something that historically significant get shoved in a box? Was it listed on O'Neill's item manifest?"

Byron shook his head. "No. Conrad said it was stuffed into the bottom of the box like someone added it at the last minute."

"Do you know if Gideon told his friend?" Hunter persisted. "The park service guy involved in the sting?"

"I don't know," Byron answered. "Gideon took the shirt with him when he left Conrad's place, and I'm sure he went straight to the authorities with it as soon as he got home."

Hunter couldn't believe his ears. "You trusted Gideon enough to let him take it? O'Neill's own son?"

Nathan held up his hand. "You don't know Gideon. We do. You can ask him what he did with it when we see him." He turned his intense gaze onto Sierra. "That vision you had yesterday down by the creek...would you tell us about it again?"

She shook her head.

Nathan reached across the table and took her hand. "Please, it can't hurt you now, and it might help us. Listen, I believe that visions are messages. Please. Try to tell us again—every detail you can remember."

Hunter had no choice but to sit across from her and watch her battle a million emotions at once, but he had to do it. He couldn't take her in his arms. He couldn't comfort her. This was her war, and it was one she had to fight alone. When she took a deep breath and began to speak, her pleading eyes met his. He gave her an encouraging smile and reached for her hand. Her icy fingers gripped his as she recalled her vision in a halting, shaky voice.

"It started with a procession of Indians who seemed to be mourning, but that was more a feeling I had than actual knowledge. And they disappeared almost instantly…"

By the time she'd come to the close of her story, she seemed much stronger, more determined than ever to make sense out of it. "I heard the words *Tasunke Witko* over and over again, like a whisper through time, floating over the wind. I think the words were Lakota, but I'm not sure.

"I wanted to warn everyone they had to move away from that area. I wanted to tell them they needed to go somewhere else so they could continue playing their games and laughing together. I wanted them to know their world was going to end, but I couldn't move. I couldn't talk. They couldn't see me…"

Her voice trailed away.

Hunter got to his feet and walked around the table without even thinking, stopped behind her to rest his hands on her shoulders. He'd promised to watch her back, and that's what he intended to do. He stroked her hair, giving her time to pull herself together, and looked at Nathan with determination. "She's had enough for today."

Nathan met Hunter's gaze head-on. "You don't understand the significance of this."

"No. I don't."

"Sierra, look at me," Nathan said gently.

She wiped the tears from her cheeks and obeyed.

"Do you know who *Tasunke Witko* was?"

She shook her head.

"Have you ever heard those words anywhere before?"

"I don't think so."

"*Tasunke Witko* is the Lakota name for Crazy Horse. More literally it means His Horse Is Crazy. I believe your vision is from Chief Crazy Horse himself. This is what I believe."

Her fingers curled around Hunter's hand still resting on her shoulder. "But Crazy Horse was murdered twenty years before the massacre at Wounded Knee. What message would he be trying to send me?"

"I don't know, but we have to follow where he leads. I think the answer might be down by the creek."

"Nathan, I don't believe in ghosts."

He smiled. "You don't, but we Indians believe in spirits. Everything in nature has a spirit, and we respect that. We have no fear of them. You shouldn't, either."

She said nothing, but her expression was skeptical.

"Eli and Gideon are waiting for us down by the Wounded Knee ravine, and we need to go," Nathan said after a moment. "Will you be all right here, Sierra?"

She stood up. "I'm going, too. May I ride with you, Hunter?"

Hunter remembered the last time they'd been to the creek and struggled in vain to come up with a reason to keep her from returning. He didn't much believe in visions being floated in front of normal people by spirits that just couldn't die, but he did believe in whatever was happening to Sierra. He'd seen it himself.

And the embarrassing truth was he didn't want to see it again.

But it wasn't up to him.

"Are you sure you want to go back down there?"

Her voice was patient, as if she were talking to a backward child. "Hunter, if there's something down at that creek, I might see it. I can't help anyone if I'm sitting here."

He touched her cheek with all the tenderness he felt inside—before he remembered he wasn't supposed to. An almost indescribable sorrow crept through him.

He was going to miss her even more than he'd realized.

Chapter Twenty-Three

"Just follow me," Byron said as he walked toward a primer-gray pickup truck that looked like it had been put together with the body parts of several vehicles and held together by paper clips and bailing wire. "It'll take a couple of hours to get down there, so enjoy yourselves."

Sierra opened the Jeep door and dropped a tote bag on the backseat. Climbing inside with no help from Hunter, she placed her purse on the floorboard and fastened her seat belt. When Hunter sat beside her and started the engine, his face was grim and dark. Her heart sank.

This was going to be a long ride.

"Do you have hiking shoes in that bag?" he asked.

"I have everything in that bag."

"Where are Skye and Colt heading off to?"

"Up to some tourist-trap place...in Wall, I think she said."

"I'm surprised they didn't want to join us."

She looked at him, cocked an eyebrow, and smiled. "Are you really?"

"I was being sarcastic."

"Oh." She sighed and gazed out the window. He wasn't going to make this easy. "Well, Skye said she wanted to visit some Wounded Knee museum in Wall."

"I've been there. It's interesting."

The conversation fizzled and died. Frustrated, she stared out the window and wished she was anywhere but locked in a Jeep with a man who didn't want to be with her.

As he drove south on a well-paved federal highway, following a safe distance behind Byron's old truck as it periodically belched out a poisonous cloud of gray-black smoke, she glanced at him. She knew that look. She'd hurt him so much the night before she'd never be able to apologize enough. He was done, and she couldn't blame him. At the same time, she'd had to protect herself. She was sure, once this journey was finished, he'd disappear back into his life like he'd done before and forget about her.

The problem was, she didn't know when this journey would be finished—and the silence was breaking her heart.

She grabbed at the first subject she thought of. "Hunter, what was that man's name we met at the gathering? The man Eli didn't like?"

"Breeden Jones?"

"That's it. Breeden Jones. Do you know anything about him?"

"A little. I found out he and Nathan grew up together, but their families were polar opposites. Jones' parents were alcoholics and nontraditional. They were both dead by the time Nathan and Jones left the rez and went to San Francisco. When Nathan came back a few years later, he was an AIM member, and he tried to be everything that entailed. But when Jones came back not long after Nathan did, he went the other way. He joined Dickie Wilson's GOONs and even participated in firebombing a house that belonged to one of Nathan's relatives in Wanblee. Thank God, no one was home at the time, but that was the end of their friendship. They've been on opposite sides ever since."

"He firebombed a house? He doesn't look the type. Did he know it belonged to someone in Nathan's family?"

"I'm sure he did."

"That's incredible. And Nathan didn't kill him?"

Hunter cocked an eyebrow and looked at her. "It appears not."

Her face grew hot with embarrassment, but she forged ahead. "Well, I was just thinking. What if he has something to do with Nathan not being able to get any action out of the BIA? After all, he said he worked in land management."

"Why would he care?"

"I don't know. He just seemed pretty...sleazy to me."

He drummed his fingertips against the steering wheel. "I don't think he'd try to keep Nathan from starting a bison ranch, and I don't think he'd care if Nathan became successful. They're both Indians, after all."

He came to a halt at a stop sign, then turned right onto a BIA highway that seemed somewhat smooth and was all but engulfed in black smoke erupting from the tailpipe of Byron's truck. He shook his head and slowed the Jeep to a crawl to put more distance between them. "We're going to be asphyxiated before we get there."

She didn't answer and turned her attention to the sepia-toned landscape gliding by her window. For the first time she noticed they were taking an unfamiliar, roller-coaster-like southern route through dipping and rolling hills covered by tall buffalo grass. Outcroppings of enormous boulders, shaped like ragged mounds of oatmeal cookie dough, seemed to have been dropped by the Hand of God on prairie lands and hillsides. Cattle grazed near glittering tank ponds, and thick patches of cottonwood trees lined the tops of sloping ravines. The difference between these soft hills and meadows and the stark isolation of the rugged Badlands was like the difference between a Technicolor daydream and a black-and-white nightmare. She was mesmerized.

Hunter broke the silence. "This is BIA Highway 2, also known as Big Foot Trail. It's the trail Big Foot and his band took down to Wounded Knee Creek. If you keep your eyes peeled, you might see buffalo and kids on painted ponies—always a treat. Nathan sponsors a lot of horseback rides on this trail for the youngsters."

"I'd love to see that," she murmured.

Her gaze swept the vast panorama as she imagined a long line of Indians riding horses along the ridges, some of them dressed in full regalia on painted ponies. What a vision that would be.

She began to comprehend and appreciate the importance of Nathan's dream. *Bringing back the old ways* wasn't about living in the past or denying the painful reality of the present. It was about returning a people to a value system that had once been as much a part of them as their heartbeats—the Buffalo Culture. It was a culture in which they were all related and responsible for one another as well as the earth they lived upon, a culture that had once brought them pride, self-reliance, and the pure joy of living.

This was the meaning of Nathan's vision for the future of his people, and for the first time she understood.

"Hunter."

He looked over at her and cocked a questioning eyebrow.

"Who's writing the script for your documentary?"

"I guess I am. Why?"

For one fleeting moment she panicked, caught in the realization she'd have to work closely with him, but she ignored it and pushed ahead. Hunter couldn't touch the perspective she would bring to this documentary, and she could hardly contain her excitement. Even more thrilling was her fervent desire to write again.

"I want to help."

His fingers tightened on the steering wheel, and he didn't answer right away. When he did, he spoke with no emotion at all. He didn't even glance at her. "I don't think so."

Her heart caught in her throat. This was it, then. She'd played all her cards last night, and she hadn't played them well. He'd opened himself up to her in a way he'd seldom done before, and she'd slammed the door in his face. Hunter Davenport wasn't a fool. He wouldn't put himself in a position to be hurt again, and she couldn't blame him. No one knew more about self-protection than she did.

How could she have spoken with so much arrogance? *Our story is always going to have the same ending, so let it go...*

But *she* couldn't let it go, even though he clearly intended to try. She wanted him as much as she ever had. She always would. That would never change.

She stared out her window. Why had she ever thought she could do this? She hadn't been with him for

223

even a week, and already she was sick with confusion. Already her body ached because he was so close and she couldn't touch him.

She took a deep breath. "You're right. I'm sorry. I wasn't thinking."

He shrugged as if he didn't care whether she'd been thinking or not and slowed to a halt at another stop sign, then took a left on a nice state road heading south toward a town called Porcupine. Sierra recognized it as the home of one of AIM's most famous activists, Russell Means, and managed a small smile. Means was famous for being pretty prickly himself.

*Bad joke, Sierra. You know you're in sorry shape when you start telling yourself bad jokes.*

"Are we almost there?" she asked. Her voice sounded desperate to her ears.

"Yeah, we're not far."

She lapsed into silence once more, but this time it wasn't uncomfortable. She wasn't frightened. This time it felt more like a soft blanket of serenity had settled around her, enveloping her in what seemed like a different season, or a different place or time. She knew it was a harbinger of something more to come. She didn't move, tried not to breathe or blink. She just waited.

When she saw the man dressed in old priest's garb standing in the middle of the road, she wasn't surprised. Her voice was calm. "Please slow down."

He took his foot off the accelerator.

As the Jeep drew closer to the priest, she could see he was quite young and wore a long black robe from a much earlier time. An ornate crucifix dangled from a rope tied around his waist, and he held large black rosary beads in hands that were folded in prayer. Although she wasn't Catholic, she knew without a doubt he was a Jesuit priest, perhaps sent to the reservation to Christianize the Indians at least a century before.

And then he was gone.

She closed her eyes.

"Are you all right?"

She nodded, opening her eyes to gaze around the grassy prairies and rolling hills. The landscape was beautiful—but empty of humanity. "How far are we from the creek?"

"We just drove through Porcupine. A few miles more."

"Good."

She slipped into silence and closed her eyes again. Why would a priest show himself to her? She wasn't Catholic, she wasn't from this place, and she didn't believe in ghosts. He was part of a bigger picture, she was sure, but she didn't know what that picture could be.

"Your vision is from Chief Crazy Horse," Nathan had said about her earlier experience at Wounded Knee Creek, but she didn't understand that, either.

"There's Eli," Hunter said with relief, "and that's Gideon with him, waving his arms around like a lunatic."

Her eyes flew open, and she leaned forward. Off to her right and high on a hill was the arched entranceway to the old cemetery, dozens of colorful prayer ties attached to the bowed chain-link fence blowing in the afternoon breeze. Waving, Eli and Gideon stood several hundred feet off to her left alongside a two-rutted road that ran parallel to a line of cottonwood trees. Behind those trees was the deep and grassy ravine beyond which snaked the Wounded Knee Creek.

Farther down the road a black, late-model Cadillac Escalade was parked.

*That luxury SUV is no rez bomb.*

Sierra caught her breath in recognition as a tall, older man made his way through the tree column and strode toward the road, snapping photos. Byron whipped his smoke-belching pickup truck in behind the Escalade and slammed on his brakes in a spray of dirt and rocks. He leaped out with Nathan close behind him.

"That's Logan O'Neill," she told Hunter as she opened her own door and grinned when she heard him mutter an expletive under his breath. Her grin widened as Hunter and Eli joined Nathan and Byron beside the Escalade. She walked toward them, but Gideon remained rooted to his spot on the side of the road. He turned his back on his father.

*Oh dear, this isn't going to end well...*

"How are you, Mr. Winterhawk?" O'Neill asked, tucking his camera into his jacket pocket and offering his hand.

Nathan stepped backward. "What are you doing here?"

O'Neill shrugged. "Well, the truth is I've heard this land is for sale, and I'm looking into buying it." He waved his arm toward the old cemetery. "It's not like any of you people take care of this place. If I bought it, I'd turn it into a real memorial to the Battle at Wounded Knee. We might all make some money. How are you, Miss Masters?"

She stared at him, dumbfounded. "You can't be

serious."

"I am." He jutted his chin in the direction of his son. "What's he doing here? Looking for something old and rotten to exhume?"

"That's more your line of work, isn't it?" Hunter muttered.

O'Neill ignored him and turned his attention to Sierra. "I'm glad I stumbled across you today. I wanted to invite you out to my ranch tomorrow, but I couldn't remember where you were staying. My wife hasn't been well, and she'd be thrilled to meet you. Also, I'd love to show you around. What do you say?"

"Sierra, that's not a good—" Hunter began, but she curled her fingers around his arm and shook her head.

"I'd love to come out tomorrow," she told O'Neill with a smile, "but only if you have time to show me your wonderful historical collection. I'd love to see it."

"It'd be an honor." O'Neill glanced at Nathan. "Give her directions to the Bison Head, will you? I'm too busy. I'll see you about two, Miss Masters."

She fumed at the way he expected everyone to follow his orders without question, but kept her opinion to herself. Her smile widened. "I look forward to it."

Once O'Neill had pulled away in his big, black Escalade, she turned to Nathan with a frown. "Is that true? Is this land for sale?"

"He's lying," Eli stated. "The man who owns this land—only about forty acres or so—has been talking about selling it ever since the Occupation of Wounded Knee, but it won't happen. O'Neill was working on something, but no one's selling anything. I would've heard about it."

At that moment, Gideon joined the group, a look of

227

disgust on his ruddy face. "I'm sorry about that."

"Just a minute," Nathan interrupted. "Sierra, you're not planning on going out there tomorrow, are you?"

She looked at him in surprise. "Of course I am. Who else can get in there to see what he's collected? He's easy to play, you guys. I'll be fine."

Hunter's expression was determined as he shook his head. "I'm going with you."

"Not necessary—"

"It certainly is necessary," Nathan interrupted. "Come on, let's take a walk."

But Sierra couldn't move. Her feet were rooted to the ground, and her eyes were glued to a shadowy figure near the line of cottonwood trees that shielded the wide ravine from view. She caught her breath.

The priest had returned.

But, this time, he held his arms out to her, palms up, in a pleading gesture for her to come to him. She obeyed without thinking, without fear. Beyond him she heard a cacophony of voices and whispers and moans floating on the wind, all embracing a different time and space.

And then, out of the confusion, came a low mournful sob that seemed to arise from the depths of another world. *Tasunke Witko…Tasunke Witko…*

The priest headed toward the wide ravine that should have protected the village of starved Indians camped at Wounded Knee Creek more than one hundred years earlier—but hadn't.

She followed him. She had no choice.

Chapter Twenty-Four

The blizzard had passed, but now the air was thick, the sky overcast, and a bone-chilling wind whipped across the prairie. Sierra's brows and lashes were crusted with ice, and her face burned with cold as she bounced on a high bench seat in a wagon pulled by two miserable horses. Her wide-brimmed sunbonnet was lightweight and useless, and her long skirts and petticoats did little to protect her from the cold. Holding on to the seat with a death grip, she ducked her head away from the wind, grateful for the young priest who sat beside her, gripping the reins in his gloved hands. He was a slight man, but his black woolen coat was bulky and helped to shield her from the wind.

"Whoa!" The priest pulled the reins toward his body, and the horses halted, lowering their heads against the treacherous chill. He jumped down from the bench seat and walked around the wagon to Sierra's side; snow and ice crunched beneath his shoes. He wore a black robe under his long coat. He offered his hand up to her and helped her out.

Sierra stood beside the wagon and looked around in disbelief. Her mind recoiled from the truth as she tried to make sense of what she saw.

She was in a nightmare where pools of blood were frozen solid. Clumps of brush and grass peeked through snow. Ice-crusted bodies were scattered as far as the eye could see. Stiff. Grotesque. What appeared to be small mounds of clothing were tossed carelessly in the snow, but Sierra knew what they were.

Children.

Babies.

Tipis were burned out. Fire-blackened rocks stood stark against dirty snow.

Men wore wide-brimmed hats and carried notebooks as they stepped around dead warriors, old men, young women, grandmothers. They talked, laughed, picked up items on the ground, and shoved them into deep pockets.

White men.

As soldiers and civilians dug a deep trench, they leaned on shovels to rest, smoke, laugh among each other. No sorrow here. No mourning. No remorse.

But the priest was on his knees, encircled by the dead. He rocked back and forth, cried, prayed. He held a worn Bible and black rosary beads. His black coat and black hat completed a figure of darkness that somehow felt evil, even demonic. No light surrounded him, no purity.

The priest ripped the large, ornate crucifix from around his waist and threw it hard in the direction of the creek. It disappeared into the brush and grass. His face was filled with rage and agony and shame.

Sierra stumbled over a large solid object and looked down to see an old man with a white scarf wrapped around his head. His face was skeletal, and his thin arms were raised in entreaty; his clothing was too large. Not far from him was a dead elder, and someone had posed a rifle next to his frozen body.

The old man removed the white scarf, smiled, and

arose to his feet. He motioned for her to follow him.

This was old Chief Big Foot, the leader of this bedraggled band of Sioux turning themselves in to the White world in hopes they could survive. Sierra didn't hesitate to follow close behind him, but he no longer seemed old and ill. He moved like a young man in his prime—agile and spirited. He disappeared into a mist arising from a line of cottonwood trees.

A low-pitched sobbing moan drifted through the icy afternoon air like a wandering phantom searching for its lost spirit. Sierra began to tremble, not from fear but from a mysterious cold that reached out to her from beneath the snow and ice. It swirled around her, imploring, pleading with her from beyond the killing fields.

Abruptly, she stood next to a soldier and observed his face as he kicked a woman's frozen body into the trench they'd dug. He was young and seemed familiar. He reminded her of someone. He leered down at the woman as she dropped with a thud into the ditch. Sierra knew what he was thinking. He enjoyed this project, this extermination of a people. He was proud of his work here this day. He'd repeat his handiwork in a heartbeat.

The man turned away and reached for the arm of another soldier who held a folded shirt in his hands. It was Sloan Turner. They spoke, but Sierra couldn't hear them. The man reached into his coat pocket and pulled out a blood-encrusted strip of long black hair, gave it to the soldier, and took the shirt in exchange. They laughed together.

It was a Ghost Shirt, and the side was stained with blood.

A whisper floated across the wind. *Good trade…*

The Ghost Shirt slowly faded, dissolved, then transformed into a white buffalo calf that joined a young boy who appeared from nowhere, wearing short pants and large shoes. Sierra followed without effort as the boy and calf glided together beyond the tall, stripped tipi poles; they floated down into the deep ravine and closer to the creek. The incessant moaning shadowed her, but now it was tinged with panic as it escalated into a long, grief-stricken wail. More voices joined the fray, as if time was running out.

A wagon piled high with frozen bodies lumbered past them, accompanied by a civilian burial team as it headed toward the freshly dug trench, but the boy child paid it no mind. He and the white buffalo calf moved down the center of the deep ravine toward Wounded Knee Creek.

Sierra glanced at the top of the hill in front of them. A line of soldiers leaned on rifles and lounged on horseback. Without looking, she knew more soldiers stood on the hilltop behind them. These were the soldiers who picked off desperate and panicked Indians as they ran for cover down into the ravine—the same Indians now frozen and grotesque and contorted among rocks and mounds of blood-splattered snow.

So many women.

So many children.

Sierra heard death songs drifting through the wind, many different death songs.

The young boy tugged on her hand, and Sierra looked down at him. He was too thin, and his hair was chopped short, and his eyes were wide with terror. The front of his shirt was covered in blood. He held a large crucifix in his hand, dropped it into the snow. The low moan intensified in the wind, and Sierra understood she had to follow him.

Now the jumble of groans and voices gave way to the harsh discord of pain-wracked death songs and exploding rifle fire and wagons rolling over snow and ice and frozen bodies. The white buffalo calf moved ahead of them, now carrying a baby girl on its back, and a diamond-white light seemed to burst from its thick winter coat, illuminating the prairies as dusk settled in. Beyond the radiance a single voice whispered encouragement, offering hope.

*Keep going...keep going...*

The white buffalo calf passed a modern Indian man who stood at an easel, painting a row of cottonwood trees. He was oblivious to the chaos all around him, focused instead on the blood-splotched canvas in front of him. Sierra moved past him without another look.

It was night now, and the cold was unbearable, but still Sierra stayed with the young boy. He staggered, holding his belly, but he didn't whimper in pain. He made no sound at all. Then, not far in the distance, a frame building appeared, perhaps a church, and candlelight flickered beyond a single window. The priest stood in the doorway, his hands folded in prayer. There was no sign of his crucifix.

Weak, the boy tugged on her fingers.

*Keep going...keep going...*

Sierra was inside the church, and the boy lay on the hay-covered dirt floor near a wall decorated with Christmas garland. Above the altar she read a hand-printed sign that said, *Peace on Earth and Good Will to Men*. An Indian doctor leaned over the boy, stroked his hair away from his eyes. The doctor straightened, turned, and looked at Sierra. As tears streamed down his cheeks, he seemed to recognize her. His face was suffused with rage.

She heard his thoughts as if he'd spoken aloud.

*One of our own, Joseph Black Thunder. Black Rolling Thunder has sacrificed his son for nothing...for nothing...*

Sierra watched the white buffalo calf, now bathed in dazzling light, as it entered the church and lowered its thick-coated body into a bowing position before the altar. The baby girl rolled off its back and crumpled into a lifeless heap on the floor.

\*\*\*\*

Hunter sat on the ground, his back propped against the trunk of a pine tree, and glared up at the concerned faces gazing down at Sierra. She lay with her head in his lap, so still he couldn't tell if she was even breathing. Her hair obscured her face, but he made no attempt to smooth it back. She remained unconscious, but he knew she'd return to them. She deserved these last few moments of privacy.

He'd never seen so much terror and hopelessness on anyone's face in his life—it would haunt him forever. Her nausea was real, her tears and sobs were real, and the words she had spoken—both Lakota and English—were very, very real. Wherever she had gone was the closest place to hell he ever wanted to witness.

What had happened out there wouldn't happen again, not if he had anything to say about it—even if he had to put her on a plane himself and send her home.

Stiff with determination and beyond anger, he glared up at Nathan. "We're done here. She came to this place to find her mother, and that's all." He shifted his furious gaze to Byron. "I hired you to do that for her. If you can't do it, tell me now. If you've got a lead and it's a good one, I want to know about it. If you don't, she's leaving."

Byron nodded. "I understand."

Eli's voice was soothing. "She's not a child, Hunter—"

"Shut up. This is none of your business. I know her better than anyone here, and she'll do anything to help you. If she thinks she has a gift you need, she'll use it. But I promised her father I'd take good care of her, and I haven't done that, so I'm starting right now. She's my responsibility, and I'm finished with all this."

"Something tells me she's not going to appreciate you—"

"I said, shut up."

Nathan placed a calming hand on Eli's shoulder and squeezed. "It's all right, son. Hunter's right. This is dangerous business, especially since we don't know where this power comes from. Byron, have you told them everything you know?"

"Of course. Like Hunter said, he's paying me. I'll tell him everything I know as soon as I know it. I'm waiting for a call from Cecilia Long Soldier to see if she can tell me anything about Sierra's mother from school records. I'm sorry, but that's it."

"Sierra's mother?" Gideon asked. "Who's her mother?"

Hunter glanced at him and made an instant decision. "That's private, Gideon."

Sierra shifted in Hunter's lap and moaned. Hunter looked down at the luxuriant blue-black hair covering her face and shook his head. Eli was right. She wouldn't appreciate his protection. She'd see it as a sign he didn't trust her to take care of herself.

He looked up at Eli and managed an apologetic grin. "Hey, man, I'm sorry. I hate to see her this way, but I had no right to take it out on you. That was stupid."

Nathan squatted down beside him. "No, it wasn't. She's your woman. You love her. You want to take care of her. It's natural. But you must remember that sometimes the Creator asks us to do difficult things. We have to trust he'll give us the tools we need to do them."

*She's your woman.*

Everything Nathan said after that one statement floated away as if he hadn't spoken at all.

Embarrassed, Hunter forced a chuckle. "She's nobody's woman. Especially not mine."

"No? I'm sorry. I just assumed—"

"You assumed wrong. She's her own person, and that's why I had no right to say that."

"You love her," Nathan repeated. "When a man loves a woman, it's his nature to want to take care of her—whether she's her own person or not."

*You love her.*

Well, of course he loved her. He had history with her, after all. He'd once been prepared to offer her the rest of his life. But he'd come to his senses just as soon as she'd come to hers, and that had finished that. He loved her now because he'd always loved her, he couldn't remember a time when he hadn't loved her, but he didn't love her the way Nathan meant.

At least, he didn't think he did... No, of course he

didn't. That time was long gone, and he had no desire to go back there. That was a place too agonizing to recall for even one second. He'd put it out of his mind years earlier and covered the pain with his work, and that's what he'd continue to do. Their relationship had been much too intense back in the day. He'd often consoled himself with the knowledge that a fire burning as hot as theirs had no choice but to burn itself out.

No, he wasn't going back there.

"Help me move her so I can stand up, will you? My legs are asleep."

He felt Nathan's speculative gaze on him as he helped ease Sierra out of Hunter's lap and placed a rolled-up jacket beneath her head, but Hunter ignored the look and got to his feet. If Nathan was just voicing what everyone else thought—that he was in love with Sierra Masters—he had to be much more careful in the future. After all, she'd made her feelings about him very clear.

"We're always going to have the same ending, Hunter," she'd told him, "so just let it go."

He fully intended to honor her request, even if it killed him. And, he thought without humor, it just might.

\*\*\*\*

The voices came from a great distance, and Sierra didn't know who they belonged to or what they were saying. She was exhausted, unable to focus. She opened her eyes and met Hunter's gaze as he stood over her. Shifting her weight, she realized someone's jacket had been bunched into a pillow beneath her head. She raised herself to a sitting position and leaned against the tree trunk.

She'd never been so tired.

Hunter held his hand down to her. "Can you get up?"

She shook her head. "Not yet. Give me a minute. I'll be all right."

She couldn't square her peaceful surroundings with the nightmare she'd just lived through. No more tranquil place existed in the world than this spot nestled among rolling hills, tall buffalo grass, and rich green pine trees bending toward the earth after years of battling the constant prairie wind.

*Just like the Indians themselves. They bend, but they don't break.*

And then a single word began to crystallize in her brain. *Crucifix.* It didn't make much sense to her, but she knew that was the word. *Crucifix.* An angry priest had thrown his crucifix in the direction of Wounded Knee Creek.

She looked up at Gideon. "Did you guys take a walk?"

He shook his head. "Not yet. We couldn't get you...well, you wouldn't...oh, hell. We stayed with you."

She closed her eyes in humiliation. Gideon O'Neill didn't know anything about her, so she could just imagine what he was thinking now. *This woman is freaking crazy...*

She looked up at him. "I'm sorry, Gideon. I'm not a lunatic. The truth is I'm pretty grounded."

Gideon reached down and patted her shoulder. "Don't worry about it. Nathan explained it to me, but I'd already pretty much figured it out. I've seen it before."

Her heart skipped. "Really? When? Where?"

"Not important. What do you remember?"

She leaned her head back against the tree trunk, closed her eyes, and gripped her hands together in her lap. "I saw a young priest. He was on his knees, surrounded by the dead in the aftermath of the massacre at Wounded Knee. He was crying, and he jerked a large crucifix off his waist and threw it hard in the direction of the creek."

Byron squatted down in front of her. "Was your whole vision about the aftermath of Wounded Knee?"

She yawned, still unable to shake that soul-stealing fatigue. "Yes, I think so."

"Do you remember anything else?"

Hunter's irritated voice broke through her exhaustion. "Can't this wait?"

She waved him off. "I need to remember this. It's important."

He knelt down beside Byron and took her hands in his. "Sierra, please—"

She met his gaze, marveling at how his turquoise shirt brought out the deep ice-blue color of his eyes, and wondered why he looked so concerned. Almost afraid. What was he afraid of? Hunter Davenport was never afraid.

She squeezed his hands and looked at Byron. He'd called himself "the resident genealogist" earlier and said he seldom forgot a name, so maybe he could help her now.

"Byron, does the name Black Rolling Thunder mean anything to you?"

Chapter Twenty-Five

Byron frowned and rubbed his chin. His gaze slid to Nathan, then back to Sierra. "It might," he said after a long moment. "How did you hear it?"

She stopped, bewildered. She wasn't sure. She fought to remember. When it finally came to her, it was crystal clear. "Well...I *think* it must be a name. If it is, he had a son called Joseph Black Thunder. Would that make sense?"

"It might," Byron repeated. "Talk to me."

She hesitated and rubbed her eyes. Everything around her was blurred.

"There was a little boy," she said after a moment. "He was injured, badly injured. He took me down into the ravine where many Indians were running and falling. Then we were in a church where other wounded Indians were. An Indian doctor was there, and he looked right at me. I heard his thoughts like he was talking to me, and he thought *one of our own, Joseph Black Thunder. Black Rolling Thunder has sacrificed his son for nothing.* That's what I heard him think."

Byron looked perplexed. "So the little boy who took you to the church, perhaps like a spirit guide...that was Joseph Black Thunder?"

She ducked her head, humiliated. "Oh dear. I don't know. I just know that's what the doctor said. I mean, that's what he thought."

"Good Lord," Byron whispered.

She closed her eyes, mortified. She sounded insane. "I'm so sorry—"

"I can't believe it."

"Neither can I."

Silence stretched. Nathan finally broke it. "Do you remember when I told you the other night about Arlin Black Thunder, your grandfather?"

"The man you called a hang-around-the-fort Indian?"

Nathan nodded, shamefaced.

Byron grinned at his friend. "Don't feel bad. Everyone calls him that." Then he sobered and turned his attention to Sierra. "But the truth is your grandfather, Arlin Black Thunder, comes from strong blood. Joseph Black Thunder was Arlin's father, your great-grandfather."

She was confused. "You mean, Joseph Black Thunder didn't die in the little church?"

"No. Joseph's father was Black Rolling Thunder—your great-great-grandfather. Black Rolling Thunder was a highly respected warrior and hunter. He was a close friend to Crazy Horse and rode with him at the Battle of the Little Big Horn. Legend even has it that Black Rolling Thunder accompanied Crazy Horse's family to bury him in a secret place somewhere, but no one really knows where that is. Some say they buried him near the Wounded Knee Creek, others say out in the Badlands, still others claim he's hidden high in the Black Hills. But no one knows for sure.

"Anyway, after Crazy Horse was murdered by his own people when he surrendered at Fort Robinson in 1877, Black Rolling Thunder married a Cheyenne woman named Little Hawk. She gave birth to Joseph Black Thunder, and several years later they had a little girl. They sent Joseph to the Indian school at the St. Paul Mission—he was one of the first three boys to go there from the reservation. Black Rolling Thunder was determined for Joseph to learn to live in the White man's world in a way that Black Rolling Thunder knew he never could."

She caught her breath as she recalled the lifeless child lying across the back of the white buffalo calf. "A little girl?" she whispered.

Byron nodded. "She died at Wounded Knee. I think that Black Rolling Thunder, his brother Grey Wolf, and his wife, Little Hawk, who was pregnant, died there, too. I'd have to check that out, but I'm almost positive."

"Thank you," she said softly. "There's one more thing that might mean something to you guys. Especially you, Gideon."

"What's that?"

"On this killing field—I can't think of it as a battlefield—I saw Sloan Turner with a soldier near a trench they were digging. Turner gave a bloody Ghost Shirt to the soldier, who gave Turner a black-haired scalp in exchange. Byron said you recognized a Ghost Shirt you saw recently as one that had been part of your father's collection. So I wanted you to know."

He nodded. "Thank you. The truth is that makes sense."

"It does?"

"Yes. I remember my father telling stories when I was little about how his grand-pop came with Turner's grandfather from St. Louis to hunt for gold up in the

Black Hills. Like I told you before, our families go back a long way. So the Wounded Knee massacre site could actually be where their collecting together began. I don't think my dad ever said, and I never thought of it before now."

Hunter broke in. "What did you do with that Ghost Shirt, Gideon? Byron said you brought it back from Fort Collins with you."

"I gave it to my contact this morning. He was pretty excited."

"And it doesn't matter to you that it might bring down your father?"

Gideon's face tightened. "Nothing would make me happier than to bring down my father."

Hunter looked skeptical, but he said nothing and turned back to Sierra. "We need to get ahold of O'Neill and reschedule with him. You're white as a ghost."

"I'm fine. I have to go. It's important."

"Damn it, it's not important." He dropped her hands and stood up. "You've got to stop this. Your parents would never forgive me—"

Gideon interrupted in disbelief, "You can't go to see my father."

She was disgusted with them both. "Excuse me, I can take care of myself."

Gideon cleared his throat. "Sierra, you don't know my father. He's dangerous. He's nearly killed my mother. You have no idea what he's capable of."

"What do you mean, he's nearly killed your mother?" Hunter demanded.

"Well…let's just say it's not a figure of speech."

Nathan gripped Gideon's arm. "She'll be fine if she can rest. Hunter, why don't you drive on to Hot Springs tonight instead of going back up to Interior? That's a million miles out of your way, and you'd have to get up very early to be at O'Neill's by two o'clock tomorrow. Hot Springs is about an hour from here, maybe a little more, and it's about thirty minutes from there to the Bison Head Ranch."

Sierra recognized the intelligence of that suggestion right away. She had a change of clothes and everything else she needed in her bag in the back of the Jeep, so she couldn't think of a reason not to do it. She could eat, shower, and go to bed. That would be a dream come true.

She softened. "Thank you, Gideon. But Hunter's going with me, so I'll be fine." She turned her attention back to Hunter. "Can we go to Hot Springs tonight? Please?"

A veil dropped over his face. "Sure," he said with a nonchalant shrug, "why not?"

\*\*\*\*

"Thank you for standing up for me back there, Hunter. I appreciate it."

He took a right onto Highway 18, which ran east to west across the reservation. He glanced at Sierra in amazement. "Are you being sarcastic?"

She chuckled. "Nope. I mean it."

"Okay, then. You're welcome." He switched on the heater in the Jeep, surprised at how chilly the late afternoon air had become. "Are you warm enough?"

She nodded as she tucked a travel pillow into the small of her back, then rested her head against the window and closed her eyes. He looked at her, concerned. She was still too pale, and this fatigue was unnatural for her.

"Are you hungry?" he asked.

"A little."

"Well, we might find something in Pine Ridge Village, but I'd rather wait until we get to Hot Springs if you can handle it. There's a little Italian place there I like. I have some snacks in the back if you want something to tide you over."

She yawned. "I can wait, thanks. Italian sounds perfect. I'd give my life for a glass of wine."

"I imagine you would. Oh, you should try to touch base with Skye when we get there. Your cell service will be better once we get off the reservation."

She sighed and nodded. He glanced at her again, still worried. Seeming to feel his eyes on her, she turned her head to meet his gaze with a sleepy smile.

He looked away and focused on the highway. It seemed to stretch out forever in front of him, flat and straight without another car for miles. Glancing at her again, he was glad to see she appeared to be absorbed in watching the passing scenery. This expanse of land had always seemed rather boring and nondescript to him, but he wasn't sure she'd view it that way. After all, if she looked out at rolling hills covered with tall buffalo grass, clumps of pine trees, and random groups of multihued boulders, was that all she'd see? Or would she be observing and experiencing something more, something that had existed out there a hundred years earlier?

He didn't know the answer to that, but the question itself was a little disconcerting. And the truth was this silence between them was killing him. Once, they would've had the most interesting conversations about what this new phenomenon in her life meant, but not now. Now he couldn't even broach the subject.

Two red-tailed hawks seemed to appear out of nowhere, perhaps from behind the clouds. They swooped down, hovering in front of the Jeep for several miles. He chuckled aloud when he realized they were playing a bird version of tag with his vehicle and the wind.

"Hunter, does the hawk have any special meaning to the Lakota?" she asked suddenly.

"Everything has a special meaning to the Lakota, but I think the hawk as a spirit guide signifies fortitude and swift action. Why?"

She shrugged. "I just wondered." Then she asked, her voice tentative, "Do you see them?"

"The hawks?"

She nodded.

"Yes, of course. Why wouldn't I? They're right in front of us."

She nodded again, relief written all over her face. Relief...and loneliness.

Wretched loneliness.

His fingers tightened on the steering wheel. Why wouldn't she feel that way? Here she was, out in the middle of nowhere with people she didn't know, experiencing something so phenomenal and terrifying she couldn't even put it into words—and she couldn't share it with anyone.

*This is my fault.*

He'd turned his back on her because she told him the truth about where he stood with her, which she had every right to do...and she'd stepped on his almighty ego.

*That was her big crime. Really, Davenport, could*

*you be any more selfish than that?*

He loosened his death grip on the steering wheel and sighed. "I'm sorry, Sierra. I'm so sorry."

"Why?"

He gave a sheepish chuckle. "You used to tell me how self-centered I am, and you're right. I've been looking at this whole thing like it's all about me, but it isn't. I dragged you out here just because I wanted to see you again. Those pictures, this trip, finding your mother...those were all excuses, and I never stopped to think how much your whole life was going to change. And now here you are, going through something I can't begin to understand, and I'm acting like...well, I don't know what. But I do know it's not good, and I'm sorry."

*But I'm still not going to give my heart to you.*

She was silent for so long he began to fear she'd never speak again. When he peeked at her from the corner of his eye, a single tear rolled down her cheek and just about broke him.

*Oh dear God, now what have I done?*

Tears, especially hers, had always destroyed him, but these tears...well, he wasn't even sure he could handle it. Without thinking, he reached over the console and touched her hand.

She linked her fingers with his and took a deep breath. "Thank you," she whispered. "Oh my God...thank you."

\*\*\*\*

"Look at the buffalo!" Sierra pointed at a large herd of bison making their way across the wide expanse of prairie land toward a gentle incline lined by a row of cottonwoods. She gave a little bounce and leaned forward in excitement. "Oh, they're magnificent, aren't they? Who do they belong to?"

"I think those belong to the tribe."

"Well, they're gorgeous. And look way up there on that hill...that line of ponies and riders. Oh...how beautiful! It's like something right out of a movie."

"I hoped you might get to see that." He grinned and changed the subject. "Listen, I've been thinking about your offer to help with the documentary. I'd love for you to work with me on the script. I just had a crazy moment back there, and I'm sorry about that, too."

She gave him a dazzling smile and clasped her hands together in childlike enthusiasm, hardly able to contain her excitement. "I'm so glad. I think I could bring something to it that would be unique, maybe even unheard of—"

He burst out laughing. "Yeah, I think you could."

She wrinkled her nose at him and didn't answer.

What had appeared to be wild and free beauty beyond description just a few miles back she now recognized as an illusion. Now, as they sped down the highway, she saw an occasional mobile home with boarded windows, tarp-covered roofs, and doors hanging off hinges. Rusted and wrecked cars were abandoned in yards like discarded aluminum cans. Appearing at the end of a potholed street off the main thoroughfare was a small neighborhood of identical homes a few yards apart, and a pack of feral dogs prowled around a dumpster overflowing with trash.

When the speed limit dropped and she noticed a tall, blue water tower labeled with the words *Pine Ridge*, she decided they must've entered the main metropolitan area on the reservation.

This poverty was inescapable and undeniable, but it didn't fill her with pity the way it would've just weeks earlier. Her research had listed harsh statistics that created a nightmare picture. Youngsters committed suicide in alarming numbers. Elderly people froze and starved to death during treacherous South Dakota winters. Child abuse cases were increasing so fast officials couldn't keep up. Few families on the reservation were untouched by alcoholism or drug abuse, and the number of Indians in prison was mind-boggling.

Yet, because of her relationship with Byron Little Hand and the Winterhawk family, she now recognized many of these people saw themselves as far more than their lack of material possessions. They claimed a powerful heritage that was becoming the envy of the world—a heritage she shared with them. They were survivors who managed to laugh at their circumstances. They enjoyed a genealogical memory that could go back several hundred years, called up stories that justified who they were, and claimed a spiritual compass that enabled them to rise above everything the US government had thrown at them.

Suddenly she had an idea. "Tell me something, Hunter."

"Sure…if I can."

"If I were to set up a foundation on this reservation to help bring businesses here, or to help people who really needed it, or to establish scholarships for students on the reservation, how would I do it? Who would I talk to?"

"Are you serious?"

"Yes, but I want to do it the right way. I don't want

anyone to know I'm behind it because people will just think I'm another White person with a guilty conscience throwing money around. And I'm not. I want the money to go where it needs to go, and I don't want it lining the tribal council's pockets, either." Her enthusiasm increased as she warmed to her idea. "If we started a program where we got the elders to come in to share what they know, like other schools use senior citizens as mentors, we might help bring the language back to the people. I read somewhere many old folks are still afraid to speak it, so most youngsters don't even know it. I'd love to establish programs that would teach the kids their culture and encourage them to participate in it. So how would I do that?"

"Wow. That's a little ambitious, isn't it?"

She glanced at him in irritation. "Listen, I've invested my money well. Don't you think this is a good idea?"

He chuckled, nodded, and reached for her hand. "Yes, ma'am, I do. I've never heard a better one. Now be quiet and let me think."

Chapter Twenty-Six

Hot Springs was a quaint small town, but it was the most populated area she'd seen since arriving in South Dakota. Many of the older buildings were constructed of red sandstone and had a late-Victorian ambiance to them, but Sierra didn't much care for that architectural era. It felt snooty and cold to her, as if the town founders had been more focused on impressing visitors than expressing their individuality.

Dusk was falling, bathing the small town in the soft, mellow pastel colors of a beautiful South Dakota sunset.

Hunter turned on his headlights and glanced at her. "Do you want to find a motel first and clean up, or are you all right to eat?"

"I'm starving. Can we eat now?"

"Sounds good to me."

He turned onto a side street that ran beside a meandering creek lined with picnic tables. He drove a couple of blocks and slowed in front of an old house that had a sign labeled *Luigi's* flickering above a large bay window. He pulled into the parking lot and stopped right at the front door. No other vehicles were around.

"It looks like it's just us tonight," he commented as he opened his door and stepped out.

As she watched him walk around the Jeep, her breath caught in her throat. How ridiculous was it for her to feast her eyes on him as if she were starving and he was her last meal? Yet that was how she felt, and she couldn't do anything about it.

When he opened her door and offered his hand to help her out, she looked at him in sudden nervousness. "What if they don't serve Indians?"

"They do. I've been here before."

She gulped and took his hand, afraid of the humiliation she'd feel if they ordered her to leave. She was too exhausted to fight back.

He tucked her hand into the crook of his arm and patted it. "Come on, baby girl. You're safe with me."

*Baby girl...* Her heart gave an extra thud. Another of those priceless endearments she'd thought she'd never hear again.

"I hope you like this place," he said as he pushed the door open and guided her inside. "They turned the bottom floor of this house into a restaurant a long time ago. I found it the last time I was up here. I loved their pasta so much I think I gained twenty pounds."

As she looked around the restaurant, waiting for her eyes to adjust to the dim illumination coming from old-fashioned lanterns set in the center of each table, a faint image niggled at the back of her memory, but she couldn't place it. After a moment she realized the restaurant reminded her of an Italian bistro in Austin she and Hunter had often frequented back in the early days of their relationship.

"Good evening, folks. May I seat you?"

Sierra gazed in admiration at a stunning Indian girl standing before them with two menus in her hand.

"Thank you," Hunter answered.

She gave him a shy smile. "As you can see, the

place is yours for now. Is there a special table you'd prefer?"

"How about somewhere in the next dining room?" he suggested.

"Of course. Right this way, please."

Following the hostess, he placed his hand against the small of Sierra's back as he guided her toward a small table set in a softly lit corner. He pulled out her chair and helped her into it as if she were a priceless piece of china.

Their hostess handed him the menus, a look of approval in her dark eyes. "Your server will be right with you, sir."

"Thank you," he said once more, winking at Sierra as he handed her a menu.

The girl's old-fashioned demeanor fit right in with Hunter's own impeccable manners, which she'd always enjoyed and nearly forgotten. In fact, she'd never been with anyone since who knew more about how to treat a lady than Hunter Davenport did.

A forgotten art, but one she had every intention of enjoying now.

She smiled. "Since you've eaten here before, what do you suggest?"

"Do you still love lasagna?"

"I do."

"Luigi's has the best lasagna I've ever tasted…especially with a sweet moscato wine. You'll love it. Their salad and garlic bread are to die for."

"Thank you. That sounds wonderful. Do you mind if I go to the ladies' room for a moment and try to freshen up? I didn't know you were going to take me to such a neat little place."

"Of course not." He stood up immediately, helped her from her chair, and handed her the handbag she'd placed on the floor beside her. "Take your time."

"I'll be right back."

As she made her way toward the ladies' room, she was aware of his gaze on her. What was he thinking about? Was he as wrapped up in old memories as she was? She felt nostalgic and on the verge of tears, but that was because she was exhausted, hungry, and the intimate atmosphere of this sweet restaurant brought back a flood of recollections she'd long forgotten.

Hunter, on the other hand, just seemed pleased to have a pretty girl serve him a luscious dinner in a place he liked to visit.

Entering the ladies' room, she sighed. No matter how hard she tried, she'd never be that uncomplicated.

She took a critical look at herself in the mirror. She looked like death—pale and stringy-haired with purple shadows surrounding her bloodshot eyes. No wonder Hunter had been so worried about her. Now that she saw herself, she was worried, too.

As she rummaged through her pocketbook in search of her cosmetic bag, her fingers touched her cell phone and reminded her of his suggestion that she check in with Skye. After she located the small sequined bag that held a few cosmetic necessities and splashed cold water on her face, she dialed Skye's number and prayed she'd have service for at least the next five minutes.

Skye's voice was anxious when she answered, "Hello? Is that you, Sierra?"

"It's me." She patted her face dry with a paper towel, pulled a small hairbrush from her purse, and attempted to unsnarl her tangled hair. She grimaced with pain. "Ouch."

"What's wrong?"

"Nothing, Sunshine. I'm fine."

"Your mom's been trying to reach you all day."

She stopped brushing and frowned. "Really? My phone hasn't rung at all. Is everything all right?"

"Fine. She just misses you."

Sierra chuckled and shoved the brush back into her purse. "I know. I miss her, too. Did you and Colt have fun in Wall?"

"Typical tourist trap, but the museum was fascinating. You should go."

"I will." Skye's voice was fading, and her words were beginning to break up, so Sierra knew the connection would be cut off before long. "I can hardly hear you, Sunshine. Is there anything else?"

"Byron called a few minutes ago and said he heard from that school lady he told you about. He also wanted to be sure you were still going to O'Neill's tomorrow."

She muttered an expletive. "Yes, we are. Will you call my mom back—or try to—and tell her I'm fine? And let Byron know that everything's still a go for tomorrow afternoon."

"You're not going to that horrible man's ranch. You can't—"

"Sunshine, you're breaking up. Listen, I'm sorry. I have to go."

She closed her cell phone with a mischievous grin and shoved it back in her purse. Bad service sometimes paid off.

By the time she returned to the table, steaming garlic bread, a glass of wine, and an Italian salad had been served.

Hunter helped her into her chair and sat back down with an admiring smile on his face. "You look much better," he said, his eyes twinkling. "Amazing what a little mascara can do, huh?"

She grinned. That had been her standard response whenever he complimented her, and then he'd always told her she was a natural beauty, and then she'd told him…

She slammed the door on the memories. Even though he'd apologized earlier and they seemed to have reached some sort of uneasy truce for the time being, she still had to keep a firm grip on her emotions. The last thing she wanted to do was take a trip down memory lane.

She sipped her wine, placed a napkin in her lap, and removed a slice of hot garlic bread from the basket. She dipped it into a small bowl of melted herb-flavored olive oil and butter. Taking a small bite, she savored the taste.

"Good?" Hunter asked.

"Delicious. I didn't know I was so hungry."

He pushed his empty salad bowl off to the side and leaned back in his chair. "Well, I knew I was. I'm a growing boy, and I haven't eaten since this morning."

She chuckled and dove into her salad. His appetite had always amazed her because he could eat whatever he wanted every thirty minutes in a twenty-four-hour period and never gain an ounce. She'd often warned him he wouldn't be able to do that forever, but so far, he was making a liar out of her. He could still do it with no problem.

She finished her salad, pushed her bowl away, and

dabbed at her lips with her napkin. "I managed to reach Skye. She said that Byron called earlier."

"Yeah?"

She smoothed the napkin back in her lap. "He wanted her to tell me that the school lady called him."

"Cecilia Long Soldier?"

"I believe so. He also wanted to be sure we were still going to O'Neill's tomorrow. I don't know why that matters so much."

"Why didn't he call you?"

She shrugged. "He couldn't reach me or you. My mom couldn't, either."

"Shoot," he muttered. "Is everything okay at home?"

"Everything's fine. You know my mom. She just misses me."

"Was there anything else?"

"I don't know. We lost our connection."

Before he could respond, steaming dinner plates containing mouthwatering lasagna arrived on a portable serving table. The waitress, a beautiful Indian girl who bore a striking resemblance to the hostess, served them and clasped her hands together.

Sierra took a bite of lasagna and rolled her eyes in pure delight. "Oh my God, this is fantastic. Thank you so much."

"Can I get you anything else?"

"No, thank you," Hunter answered with a smile. "This looks—and smells—wonderful."

"I hope you like it. I'll be back to check on you in a few minutes."

"Thanks."

As that familiar, uncomfortable silence enveloped

them, Sierra tried to concentrate on eating without dropping her food in her lap. She'd never been able to eat in front of him without feeling awkward.

He interrupted her thoughts. "If I ask you a question, do you promise not to get mad?"

"Of course not. You know I never miss an opportunity to get mad."

"Well, I thought I'd check in case you've changed over the last decade or so."

She laid down her fork. "Okay, I give up. What's your question?"

"What do you expect to find at O'Neill's place that's so important?"

She didn't answer right away. She didn't know. She just had a feeling. "I have to go, that's all."

"Well, I thought I'd ask in case there's something you want me to do."

She cocked her head to one side, studying him. They'd once worked together like a well-oiled machine in which they were the two major components. If one of them malfunctioned, the other could take up the slack. Could they still do that now?

She yawned. "Hunter, would you do me a favor…at least for tonight?"

"Sure. What is it?"

"Let's don't talk about Indians or O'Neill or visions…or anything else like that, okay?"

He finished the last of his lasagna and took a slice of still-warm garlic bread from the basket. He sipped the remainder of his wine before he finally nodded. "I agree. We'll get a room, and then we'll take a walk around town."

She stared at him. "One room?"

"Or two." He winked at her. "That's up to you."

She thought quickly. She was a big girl, for crying out loud, and she knew how to handle Hunter Davenport. She'd done it before, and she could do it now.

"One room, two beds," she stated.

He gave her that slow, crooked grin and patted her hand. "Of course. That's what I meant."

Chapter Twenty-Seven

Their motel was small and timeworn but immaculate and decorated with simple rustic charm that fit its name, The Moving West Inn. Sierra loved it on sight because it reminded her of the old auto courts her father used to drag the family to stay in up on old Route 66 out of Amarillo when she was a kid.

Hunter climbed back into the Jeep and drove to a secluded, covered parking place next to a room at the rear of the motel. He parked the Jeep and turned off the engine. "Here we are, my princess. Bail out."

He grabbed their two large gym bags from the back of the Jeep and let himself into the room, Sierra following close on his heels. She flicked on an overhead light, closed the door, and looked around.

This room was so sweet she was afraid she'd awaken in the morning to find the ever-macho Hunter wearing a tutu and a pair of ballet slippers, but she loved it. A small dressing table next to the bathroom sink was encircled by a white lace skirt, and an antique rose-colored lamp with a frothy pink lampshade was on a table beside an oak rocking chair, illuminating a cozy reading area. On a bureau near the door was a television that had seen better days, but beside it was a modern coffeemaker and two mugs encased in bubble wrap. Between the two queen beds was a single oak table containing a telephone, a notebook, a remote control, and an old Bible. At the foot of each bed was a matching pink-and-white quilt. This was no cookie-cutter motel room.

But Hunter looked around with such dismay that Sierra burst into laughter.

He sighed. "You like this, right?"

She couldn't help it. She giggled.

"Well, if Mama's happy, everybody's happy. But I'm going to need a shot of testosterone in the morning."

"I was just thinking that. Listen, what time is it?"

"A little after seven."

"Is there a place where I can buy a decent shirt to wear tomorrow?"

"I saw a western store when we drove into town. We could check that out."

"Thanks." She shoved their overnight bags inside a tiny closet and grabbed her purse.

On their way back to the city limits, they stumbled into the historical district of Hot Springs. Old but elegant two-story sandstone buildings housed art galleries and antique shops, and charming streetlights illuminated the area. On her side of the wide street, Sierra spotted a small clothing store with a rustic sign over the door that read *White Buffalo Apparel*. It was still open.

"Hey, let's try this one. I like its name."

He whipped the Jeep into a parking space in front of the store. "Go on in. I'm going to try to make a phone call."

"Byron?"

"Yeah."

She nodded and stepped out of the Jeep. The night

air had taken on a definite chill in less than an hour, and she hurried into the store. Once inside, she stood in the doorway and looked around, trying to get her bearings. Well lit, it was a two-story building with rock walls and dark wood stairs, and every corner seemed crammed with merchandise.

When Sierra realized everything in the shop was on sale, she began plowing through shirts, jeans, sweaters, and sweatshirts with a vengeance. She was so intent on her task Hunter's voice behind her almost sent her through the roof.

"They have an art gallery upstairs. I'm going to check it out."

"Did you reach Byron?"

"I left a message. You're not going to try all that on, are you?"

"Of course not. They'll fit. Besides, the prices are so crazy good that I'll find someone to give them to if they don't. I'll meet you upstairs when I'm finished."

As she watched Hunter head with dogged determination for the staircase, she couldn't help but grin. He'd always been allergic to shopping, calling himself a "get in and get out man." She'd never even allowed him to go to the grocery store with her. Apparently, that quirk hadn't changed over the years, either.

By the time she was ready to check out, she'd selected two dressy white blouses, three pairs of jeans, one pair of slacks, six T-shirts, and even a khaki skirt with a matching blazer. As she waited for the saleswoman to run her credit card, she admired some gorgeous Indian pottery pieces in a large, locked glass case behind the cash register.

"Excuse me, ma'am? Where do you get your Native American items?"

She smiled as she returned Sierra's credit card and began folding her purchases. "Mostly from the reservations," she answered. "Do you like them?"

"I do. They're spectacular. Does the money go to the artists?"

"Every penny. We're happy to give the Indians a place to show their work." She handed three large sacks to Sierra and gestured toward the second floor. "You should go upstairs and check out the art. Everything up there is marked down. You might find something sensational."

"Thank you, I will. May I leave my bags with you?"

"Of course. And be careful on those stairs. They're very old."

"Thank you so much."

As she made her way up the stairs, the creaking and moaning of aged wood sounded as if it was going to give way at any moment, but she made it to the top without incident. She stood on the landing and looked around for Hunter, finally spotting him in a far corner examining a painting she couldn't see. As she walked toward him, she admired oil paintings, charcoal etchings, watercolors, and pencil drawings of South Dakota landscape, reservation life, even Native spirituality—all exquisitely framed and illuminated by modern recessed lighting. This tiny art gallery was one of the loveliest she'd ever seen.

When she reached Hunter and touched his arm, he grabbed her hand and moved away from the painting he'd been studying with such interest.

His voice was brusque. "It's getting late. We should go."

But she didn't move. She couldn't.

In the painting, an ancient Lakota medicine man floated above a tipi in the sky, his arms outstretched in welcome to a young woman lying on a blanket far below him, her hands uplifted in prayer. Her belly protruded in pregnancy; her face was a study in anguish. Off to one side, just below a dark thundercloud, was a warrior astride a splendid stallion painted for war. Off to the other side, just beneath a setting sun, was a white buffalo calf.

And then she saw the artist's name and the numbers *2002* written near the bottom of the oil painting. She frowned, leaned closer, began to tremble. She could hardly breathe.

"This medicine man, this young girl, this tipi... Hunter, this was the dream I had when you first told me about my mother."

He squeezed her hand.

"And look. Look who painted it."

He nodded.

Tears filled her eyes. This painting was a lonely man's secret longing, a dream he couldn't share with anyone. The artist was a hang-around-the-fort Indian no one respected.

The artist was her own grandfather, Arlin Black Thunder.

\*\*\*\*

Clad in an oversized faded nightshirt with Winnie the Pooh blazoned across the front, gray thermal leggings, and a pair of yellow slipper socks, Sierra sipped chardonnay from a paper cup and stared at the painting propped against her headboard. Hunter sang off-key in the shower just as he always had, but this time she wasn't paying attention.

Something about this painting bothered her, but she didn't know what it was.

She went backward in her mind to try to recall her original dream in detail, but it was impossible. She'd dreamed it just once, and she'd wondered if it depicted her mother's death in childbirth. But then, because no one seemed certain that Pauline Kills Quick was dead, she'd forgotten it. Now she realized it might've had nothing to do with her mother at all.

*Maybe I had that dream just so I'd recognize the painting if I saw it.*

Sierra took a gulp of chardonnay, walked to her bed, and sat in front of the painting.

*Arlin Black Thunder, 2002.*

*This is the painting from my dream, but where do I go from here? What does it mean?*

Why would her grandfather have waited until 2002 to paint a picture of his daughter dying in childbirth? That would've happened back in 1974, if it had happened at all. And why would he have painted a warrior astride a war pony, or a white buffalo calf, in the same picture? Pauline Kills Quick was a modern child, educated in a Catholic Indian school. She wouldn't have known anything about war ponies or white buffalo. Arlin Black Thunder himself had seen to that.

"What're you staring at?"

She looked up at Hunter. Even after all this time, he still stopped her heart with his spiky, damp hair and skin glistening from the steaming shower. How in the world had she ever let him go in the first place?

Her gaze slid away from him, and she shrugged. When he sat behind her and pulled her in between his spread legs so she could lean against him, she fought to breathe. How many television shows had they watched in just this position? How many shooting stars had they counted through their bedroom window? When he moved her hair away from the back of her neck so it tumbled like spun silk over one shoulder, she stiffened.

"It's okay, baby girl," he whispered. "I'm not going to do anything you don't want me to do. Your hair is just tickling my nose, that's all."

*I'm not going to do anything you don't want me to do...*

That line was more dangerous to her self-control than any other. For the first time since he'd come back into her life, she allowed little flashes of memory to flit through her mind, like tiny snapshots in time. She hated to admit it, but she felt as if the joy in her life hadn't begun until Hunter Davenport entered it...and it had disappeared once he left.

She remembered the weekend they'd gone camping in Garner State Park and set up their tent in a secluded spot near the Frio River. It was gorgeous and romantic—until a herd of wild pigs crashed through their campsite, scaring the hell out of everyone for miles around.

And then the time they wanted to spend a weekend in a Holiday Inn on the beach down in Corpus Christi, but they didn't have two nickels to rub together. Hunter drove his old clunker to a convenience store on the corner, pulled his radio/CD player out of the dashboard, and sold it for a hundred dollars. Then they threw a few items of clothing into a gym bag, tossed in six peanut butter and jelly sandwiches and a sack of potato chips, and headed for the coast.

They decorated their tiny apartment with beanbag chairs, Parsons tables, and bookshelves made out of bricks. They ate at out-of-the-way restaurants in little towns no one had ever heard of, and bought each other one-of-a-kind presents they dictated couldn't cost more than five dollars. They made love in places where they might get caught just for the thrill of it and watched old movies and ate popcorn until dawn. They played Monopoly by candlelight during thunderstorms, drinking so much wine they had no idea who won. And then there was the night when Hunter had pulled over on the side of the freeway and taught her to waltz in a drainage ditch while a George Strait country song played on his truck radio at full blast...

She slammed the door on her memories. Those days were over. They were different people now.

He tapped the back of her neck. "What're you staring at?" he asked again.

She leaned forward and touched the Indian girl in the painting, grateful for the opportunity to think about something other than the warmth of his body against hers.

"I feel like this girl is from another time. When I had that dream, I thought she was Pauline, but now I don't think so. This girl is pregnant, yes, and I believe she might be dying because the old Indian above the tipi seems to be welcoming her to the afterlife, but it's not Pauline. I don't know what this painting means or why I dreamed about it, but it's not what I thought."

"Didn't Byron say that your great-great-grandmother, Little Hawk, was pregnant when she was killed at Wounded Knee? Maybe that's what Arlin was painting. Maybe he's haunted by that."

"Maybe…"

Then, without another word, Hunter pushed himself away from her and climbed off the bed. He picked up the painting and carried it to the closet.

"What're you doing?"

"You said you didn't want to talk about Indians or visions tonight. Enough already. You can deal with this tomorrow."

She reached for her lukewarm chardonnay in the little paper cup on the table and watched him push the painting to the back of the closet, trying not to admire the way the muscles in his back and shoulders rippled as he moved. The truth was she resented how he'd grown more attractive with each passing year. Every line on his face just added character. Not an extra ounce of flesh marred his physique. And when his hair finally turned silver, he'd look more handsome and distinguished than ever.

He'd ruined her for anyone else. She hadn't been with another man before Hunter Davenport or after him, and she was sure she never would be. She'd closed the door on that part of her life when he left her, and she hadn't been brave enough to open it again. That was why she worked until she was blind, losing herself in someone else's story, living in someone else's love.

In spite of her steely resolve not to submit to the hold he still held over her, her entire body tingled with excitement as she remembered the silky warmth of his flesh against hers. She could never forget the exquisite pleasure they'd once given one another. She'd loved so much about them together: the smoldering expression in his eyes that always told her when he wanted her, the husky desire in his voice when he called out her name, the little pulse in his throat that always throbbed right before he entered, moved, and exploded within her.

But so much more than that had been between them. To her, they'd been real soulmates—the kind of soulmates who recognized one another from a different place or time. That theory had always sounded insane to her, but it felt right. It felt like it made sense. Together, *they* made sense.

She stopped herself right there.

*You were never soulmates. Soulmates don't lie to each other. Soulmates don't keep secrets from each other. He was always honest with you...but you were never honest with him. You made all the decisions and sabotaged your relationship with the only man you'll ever love, and then you blamed him.*

He walked to his bed, pulled down the bedspread, and fluffed his pillows. "You have the blind stares. Are you all right?"

She clasped her hands in front of her and nodded.

He climbed into bed, pulled the covers up to his waist, and continued watching her.

Finally, in desperation, she stood up. "I'm going to take a shower," she announced.

He took the remote control from the table between their beds and waved it absently. "Enjoy yourself."

She didn't answer and headed for the bathroom.

Chapter Twenty-Eight

As Sierra luxuriated in the soft, warm water spraying against her skin, she didn't enjoy her memories as much as she enjoyed her shower. For the first time in years, as tears of guilt and shame flowed down her cheeks, she forced herself to take a good hard look at the truth.

For eight years she'd blamed Hunter for something he knew nothing about. She convinced herself that, had he known the truth, he'd still take the opportunity to leave her the moment she offered him his freedom. He was an ambitious man, creative and competitive, and he never truly wanted to settle down with one woman, in one place…

That's what she told herself the day she broke their engagement, and that's what she'd continued to tell herself for the last eight years.

But she hadn't told him about the baby.

She hadn't told *anyone* about the baby. The day he'd come home to their apartment, flushed with excitement because he was offered a career-establishing opportunity to film a dangerous political story in South Africa, was the day she discovered, to her joy, that she was pregnant. She'd suspected it for a week or so, but her doctor confirmed it just that morning. Even though she was prepared to tell him that evening, his passion for the upcoming assignment halted her romantic plans dead in the water, and she knew she'd never be able to tell him at all.

She'd done the right thing, hadn't she?

Their story was like a lousy, cliché-filled movie about love in the 1990s. They'd both been far too young to commit to a marriage and a child. They were too selfish, too driven, too much alike. She was right to cut him loose when she did, and she was right not to give him a choice. If he'd known she was pregnant, he'd have done the honorable thing and given up what had become a brilliant career. He'd have sacrificed his own happiness and creativity, and he'd have ended up resenting her—and their baby.

Wouldn't he?

As for Sierra, she'd never have written one little book, much less four best-selling novels, and she'd never be as independent as she was now.

She was happy…wasn't she? Of course she was. Everything had turned out just fine, just the way she'd planned it.

Except now he'd come back into her life and told her he wanted her, he'd always wanted her, and he'd never wanted anyone else. When she faced the truth, as she was now, she had to admit those words had filled her with joy—no matter what she said to him afterward.

The truth was she hadn't given him the opportunity to make a decision about whether or not he wanted his own child because…well, she couldn't remember why. No, that wasn't true. She remembered exactly why.

*I just wanted it to be my idea so he couldn't break my heart.*

But he'd broken her heart anyway because he hadn't argued at all. *Not at all.* When she'd told him she didn't want to marry him or anyone else, he'd looked at her for a long time without a word, walked into the bedroom, packed his bags, and strolled out the door as if he hadn't a care in the world. She hadn't heard from him for another four years.

A month later she lost the baby because she hadn't eaten or slept in all that time, and all she could do was cry. Her parents appeared at her apartment one morning and moved her back to the ranch without even asking if she wanted to come. Daddy, like any outraged father, never stopped blaming Hunter and threatened to kill him if he ever saw him again, but Mama always seemed to understand far more than Daddy did.

They never asked any questions, and Sierra never offered any explanations. That wasn't fair of her, either. But the pain of that experience spawned her first novel, *Regina*, and the writing of it—as well as the next three very successful books—set her free.

Or so she'd believed.

She turned off the water, stepped out of the shower, and wrapped her slender body in a thick, oversized bathrobe hanging from a pewter hook on the wall. As she towel-dried her hair, that overwhelming sense of guilt made her sick to her stomach.

Skye's words from a few days earlier rang like a clarion bell in her memory.

"Hunter Davenport adores you, and you're wild about him. Neither of you can hide it. I don't know your story, but whatever it is, it's in the past. Don't waste any more time. Fix whatever's wrong between you and keep it right."

*It's in the past...*

She'd created that past all by herself, but now she

had an opportunity to make it up to him—if he wanted her to. He deserved that much, and so did she. If he turned her down after she told him the truth...well, she'd gotten over one broken heart. She could get over another.

But if he didn't turn her down, if he did truly still want her, no matter what... The image of that possible future was so glorious she was terrified to look at it.

She removed the bathrobe, pulled her nightshirt back over her head, and stepped into an abbreviated pair of lacy panties. But this time she left her slipper socks and thermal underwear lying across the toilet.

If a woman was determined to fight for a dream she'd never stopped dreaming, she couldn't do it looking like West Texas roadkill.

\*\*\*\*

When Sierra returned to the room, Hunter knew from her swollen, red-rimmed eyes that she'd been crying. His heart sank. He hated any woman's tears, but he'd never been a match for hers. Frowning, he clicked off the television, pushed back the covers, swung his long legs over the edge of the bed, and held out his arms.

She walked to him and dropped to her knees, took his hands in hers, and looked up at him. He hadn't seen that vulnerable, open expression on her face in years. The truth was he'd been sure he never would again.

"I have something to tell you," she said softly, her voice trembling.

He tried to help her to her feet, but she shook her head and remained on her knees in front of him.

"No, Hunter. Please. Just listen."

He leaned forward and dropped a light kiss on the

top of her head. "I'm here. I'm listening."

As she began to speak—at first with trepidation, then with more fervor and determination—he listened, stroked her damp hair in encouragement whenever she faltered, murmured reassurance when she needed it. He could see she was wracked with guilt and terrified he couldn't forgive her, but she was wrong. She'd read him like an old book, and she'd read him correctly.

He was the one to blame, not her.

She'd been willing to raise his child alone so he could chase a dream that might or might not have ever included her. And when she lost that child, she'd suffered alone, without even her parents' support. For a woman who wanted to have a baby with the man she loved, that had to have been brutal.

He was swamped with shame, and his own eyes filled with tears. He didn't try to hide them, didn't wipe them away as they slid down his cheeks. If he and Sierra were going to weather this and come out stronger for it, he had to be as honest with her as she was with him.

He drew her up close to him and found her lips with his. She cradled his face in her hands as she returned his kisses softly, then with more urgency and passion, just as she always had so many years ago.

He pulled away and spoke in a voice thick with pain. "Sierra, wait."

"No."

He pushed on. "I shouldn't have left you. I should've known there was some reason. But I was so selfish, so afraid I'd lose my big chance I got out as quick as I could. When you lost our baby, I should've been there with you."

Her entire body trembled. "Do you forgive me?"

He tangled his fingers in her hair and pulled her up to him. His lips covered hers as he tried to drink her in. He needed to absorb her, to somehow lock her into him so he'd never lose her again. "There's nothing to forgive, baby girl."

"Do you love me, Hunter? Do you still love me?"

He groaned and pulled her closer. His heart thundered in his chest. "You know I do."

"No, tell me. Tell me now."

"I love you."

"And I've never stopped loving you. I was so afraid…"

He stopped her words as he kissed her again, parted her lips with his tongue, inhaled her, immersed himself in her heat. He welcomed the passion that surged through his body and surrendered to the desire they'd always shared, trembled with longing as she kissed his throat, stroked his hair, whispered words of love he'd thought he'd never hear again.

*Oh God, it's been so long.*

He couldn't remember the last time he felt so alive. Every other woman he'd ever been with had provided him with nothing more than release—release of tension, boredom, even anger—but not one of them meant anything.

It had always been Sierra.

Now every sense was heightened; every part of his body craved her touch and throbbed with desire as she wrapped her arms around his neck, as if she couldn't get enough of him. When she buried her face in his neck and tangled her fingers in his hair, he moved his head so she was forced to meet his gaze. He needed to look into her eyes. He needed to read her heart.

"Do you want me?" he murmured.

She didn't answer but got to her feet, stepped out of her clothing, and stood before him, shy and trembling. Outlined in a sliver-thin shaft of moonlight streaming through the curtains, her petite form was delicate and slender and gently curving. She seemed to be unaware of the astounding power she still possessed over his body and his soul, but he responded to her just as he always had.

That had never changed, and it never would.

\*\*\*\*

Sleep nestled around Sierra's awareness like a warm cocoon. Somewhere, far in the recesses of her consciousness, she felt the softness of butterfly kisses on her throat, her cheek, her eyelids. She had to be dreaming, yet the gentle stroking of her hair away from her face was so familiar, so intimate, she couldn't be. It was real, as real as the desire flooding her body.

Slowly opening her eyes, she was overwhelmed by a thousand memories of other nights just like this one. She remembered the musky fragrance of desire radiating from flesh and sheets, and how she'd craved it. She remembered sighs of longing and heat and intense desire she'd believed she'd never feel again. And now, as he lightly caressed that sweet and sensitive area just below her naval, she began to tremble.

She whimpered and turned toward him, drew him closer to her, ached to bring him into her and become a part of him. It wasn't a dream this time. It was happening. His every touch scorched her flesh, burned through her body, set it on fire. She cradled his face and found his lips with hers, teased the soft, meaty part of his mouth with her tongue. He shuddered and gave in to an urgency that carried them both to a place beyond all reason.

As he fondled her breasts and teased her nipples until they were taut with desire, his lips were as soft as silk against her abdomen, her buttocks, the delicate inner part of her thighs, and brought her to a fever pitch of excitement. She couldn't breathe. She ached for him. Her longing was exquisite torture. And when he helped her shrug away the blankets so the cool air finally caressed her flesh, she clutched at his body and pulled him close.

She couldn't hold him close enough. She longed to feel him inside her, to fill her, to explode within her. He yielded to her need and groaned, shuddered, entered her at just the right moment. As always, as if they'd never been apart, she began to move with him slowly, easily, reveling in every acute sensation until all her senses focused on that tiny nucleus of intense pleasure she remembered so well. It began to build somewhere deep inside her body and spread until she couldn't breathe. She craved it. She had to reach it. He matched her urgency as she moved faster, harder, bursting with desire. Suddenly, in an explosion of pulsating heat and fluid and excruciating pleasure, she cried out his name, held him close, rode the waves of ecstasy with him.

And then, later, he murmured in her ear, "No more secrets, Sierra, no matter what. Promise me."

She turned in his arms and kissed his neck drowsily. "I promise, my love. No more secrets."

Chapter Twenty-Nine

"All set?"

Sierra closed and locked the motel door behind her. She'd slept so well she didn't even remember falling asleep, and even more important, she hadn't dreamed at all. She felt far more able in this gorgeous morning sunshine to deal with whatever the day offered.

This was a moment she wanted to savor.

The night she spent with Hunter had been breathtaking, the sunrise splendid, and now the morning promised a perfect day. Like so many other times when she and Hunter took off on some unknown adventure, they had a full tank of gas, a few snacks in the backseat, and an overwhelming sense of pleasure just because they were together.

"C'mon, lady! We're burnin' daylight."

She laughed and let herself into the Jeep. He slid in beside her, started the engine, and gave her a long, intimate look.

Her cheeks grew warm. "What?"

"You look great today. I like that new outfit."

She glanced down at her new snug-fitting jeans and simple, long-sleeved white blouse. "Thanks. It only took me twenty minutes to buy it. Are you impressed?"

"I am. That's very adult of you." He backed out of the parking place, drove to the office, and took the key from Sierra. As she waited for him to finalize business at the front desk, she turned in her seat and studied the painting he'd propped up against their gym bags.

This time she tried to be objective about the caliber of her grandfather's work and not question why it might've appeared in her dreams. Arlin Black Thunder was definitely a talented artist, but that had to be a secret from the people around here. From what she could gather, no one knew him at all except through malicious rumors. Surely, if they realized he made his living by painting, someone would've said so.

"What're you staring at now?"

She gasped. He'd opened the door and climbed into the Jeep without making a sound. She placed the painting on the floorboard, turned back around, and buckled herself in.

"Nothing important. I was just wondering why no one told us that Arlin Black Thunder was an artist. Everyone has to know it. He's just too good for them not to."

He pulled out of the parking lot and merged into traffic. "I was wondering the same thing myself, but…I don't know. Doesn't make much sense, huh?"

Hot Springs was small enough that he was able to get out of town quickly and head southeast toward O'Neill's Bison Head Ranch. After about thirty minutes on the main highway leading back toward Pine Ridge, he turned onto a well-maintained county road and drove through some of the most breathtaking landscape she'd ever seen. The granite spires and tall evergreen trees of the Black Hills were visible in the north, while canyons and deep ravines were scattered among grassy meadows and tree-covered hillsides. Not far from the road, about a hundred head of cattle ranged freely.

"How gorgeous," she breathed in awe.

He snorted.

"What's wrong? You don't like this? I love this."

"I love it, too."

"Okay…"

"Pay attention to what we're driving through. This is all Indian land, but you wouldn't know it. It's probably all part of the Bison Head Ranch. I don't know how many acres O'Neill has out here, but I'll bet you at least half of it belongs to some impoverished Indian family living on Pine Ridge. He probably leases it from the feds for about a buck an acre."

"You're sure using the word 'probably' a lot."

He shrugged. "Ask O'Neill. I'm sure he'll tell you."

He slowed the Jeep and turned onto a private drive. A tall iron gate was open, allowing them to pass through, and on the side of the road stood a sign reading *Welcome to Bison Head Ranch, Owner Logan O'Neill.*

"There's the house up ahead. That must be O'Neill on the porch, scanning the horizon for his famous visitor. I just want you to know…I don't like this."

"Oh, stop worrying. I'll be all right."

He pulled into a gravel drive that ran alongside the house and parked. As O'Neill walked down the porch steps toward them, his hand extended in welcome, Sierra was struck once again by how attractive he was for his age. After all, he had to be close to seventy years old, judging by all he'd told her the first time they met, but he didn't look it.

Today he wore faded blue jeans, a white sweatshirt with a picture of Mount Rushmore emblazoned across the front, and an expensive pair of well-polished cowboy boots. His wavy, silver hair was still thick, his body was still straight and strong, and he had only a few lines around his eyes. Logan O'Neill wasn't the picture of corruption everyone had painted. Instead, he personified good health and easy living.

"I'm glad to see you," he said with a wide grin as he came close enough to grip Hunter's hand in his own. "I was getting worried. How are you, Miss Masters?"

"I'm fine, thank you."

"And you, Mr. Davenport? Did you have a nice trip down?"

"We did."

O'Neill waved toward the house. "Well, come on in. Miss Masters, my Valentina is in the sunroom, and she can't wait to meet you. Shall we go there first?"

"I'd love to."

As she followed O'Neill up the steps and into the house, she noticed how light and airy the rooms were. The ranch itself might have been old, but the house had been remodeled with an eye toward bringing the spectacular view indoors through every large window, blending the earth tones of the walls and tile floors with the colors of the canyons and rolling hills outside. It created a rich, warm atmosphere in every room.

"Did your wife decorate your home, Mr. O'Neill?" she asked, giving the sparkling chrome and white kitchen an admiring glance as they walked down a wide hallway. "It's truly beautiful."

O'Neill shook his head. "No, unfortunately. There was a time when Tina would've been right in the middle of a remodeling job as big as this one was, but that was a long time ago. She seldom leaves her rooms now. The sunroom, where she is this afternoon, was only completed a month ago."

"Oh, that's right. You said she wasn't well. I'm sorry."

"That's true, but she sure did perk up when I told her you were coming."

"I'm so glad."

As the stilted conversation ran out, Hunter cupped his hand around her elbow and guided her down two tiled steps into an enormous room with three large picture windows. The view was so magnificent she caught her breath.

Far below them, a river snaked through a thick line of pine trees, and horses grazed among granite boulders scattered over a grassy hillside. Beyond that were the red-and-gray ridges of a deep and ancient canyon. Each picture window opened onto an enormous wooden deck. A small bathroom was just off the entrance.

"How spectacular," she breathed, clasping her hands beneath her chin. "How truly spectacular."

O'Neill moved past her and walked to a bird-thin woman sitting in a rocking chair near a window, a book in her lap that Sierra recognized as an early hardback copy of *Regina*. But the woman didn't seem interested in the book at all.

Instead, she stared straight ahead, eyes blank and mouth slack. Although she was impeccably groomed, from the snow-white bun braided at the nape of her neck to her dusky-rose nail polish, Sierra guessed the woman could no longer take care of herself.

*The lights are on, but nobody's home...how sad. I wonder what happened.*

Gideon's words played through her memory. "He's nearly killed my mother..."

O'Neill knelt in front of the woman he'd called Tina. "Miss Masters is here to see you, Mama. Isn't that nice?"

When she didn't respond, he gestured for Sierra to join him beside the rocking chair. As she moved closer, she noticed Valentina's frail hands were clasped together so tightly on top of the book that her knuckles were white. She frowned and glanced at Hunter, then knelt beside O'Neill to look into the woman's vacant yet still-lovely blue eyes.

"I'm Sierra Masters, Mrs. O'Neill, and this is my friend Hunter Davenport. It's very kind of you to invite us into your beautiful home."

Again, the woman didn't respond, and O'Neill shook his head in obvious disappointment. "She was so happy this morning when I told her you were coming. I don't know what happened. I just can't predict—"

An unmistakable spark of icy fire flashed in Valentina's eyes, and she held up her hand, stopping O'Neill's apology in its tracks. "Get out."

"Now, Mama—"

Sierra panicked, but Hunter just chuckled. He spoke as if the two men were old friends. "Come on, Logan. Why don't you show me around while these two ladies get to know each other? I think we might be in the way here."

When O'Neill stood up, clenched fists at his sides showed how humiliated and angry he was. "I don't think that's such a good idea…"

Once again Hunter cut him off. "I can see by the pottery and artwork you have around the house that you've got a terrific collection. Would you mind showing it to me? We can come back and check on the ladies in a few minutes if you like."

"Well…" O'Neill's voice trailed away.

Sierra's mind raced. *We can still do it. We're still a great team.*

She remained on her knees in front of Valentina, took her hand, and patted it. "We'll be fine here, just the two of us, won't we, Mrs. O'Neill?"

To Sierra's astonishment, Valentina met her eyes and nodded. Her lips twitched in a tiny smile.

The moment Hunter and O'Neill were out of the room, Valentina grabbed both Sierra's hands with a fierce, urgent grip. In an instant the light in the room changed and exploded with brilliance, as if the sun itself had erupted and showered the world in dazzling color.

Sierra found herself in the corner of a windowless space.

Valentina O'Neill, white-haired and bent, shoved a large wadded-up piece of material into an old trunk. At first Sierra couldn't see what the item was, but then, as if she had a powerful zoom lens in her eyes, she saw the material up close and in detail.

It was heavy, brown, fringed, old…and stained with blood.

In the distance a dog barked, and somewhere in the house a man laughed. She jet-propelled back into the room and found herself still on her knees beside Valentina.

Valentina tilted Sierra's chin so she was forced to meet the elderly woman's eyes. After a moment she touched Sierra's cheek and stroked a strand of hair away from her face. But when she spoke, Sierra didn't understand.

"I knew you'd come here," she said softly. "I always knew you'd come."

The brief moment of lucidity was gone. Valentina had no clue what she'd said or who she'd said it to.

Sierra needed a moment alone and spoke in a whisper. "I have to use the restroom. May I use the one over there?"

Valentina gave a furtive look around the sunroom and placed a finger against her pursed lips. "Be careful."

"I will. I'll be right back."

Once in the bathroom, she closed the door and leaned against it, fighting panic. This woman was so tragic, and it was much more than her mental confusion. It was the condescension in O'Neill's voice when he called her Mama. It was the clear hatred in her eyes when she looked at him. This was a woman who'd chosen, for some reason, to stop living. Oh, her heart was still beating, and she was still breathing, but she was just passing time, waiting…for something.

Sierra's attention was captured by several small silver-framed photographs on a white-skirted dressing table beside the commode. As she picked them up, one after the other, she smiled.

The O'Neills had once been a normal family.

A towheaded toddler about two years old, maybe Gideon, played naked in a small plastic swimming pool.

The same toddler and an unknown man in a cowboy hat sat astride a pony.

Logan O'Neill stood overlooking a canyon, holding on his hip a young child wearing only boots and a diaper.

Sierra looked more closely at the last photograph

and caught her breath. Her heart began to thunder in her ears. She couldn't breathe.

The family stood in front of a baby grand piano in somebody's living room. The towheaded youngster appeared to be about six years old, and a young couple, clearly Logan and Valentina O'Neill, knelt behind him. Standing behind them, her hands on their shoulders, was a smiling Indian girl dressed in a Catholic school uniform, her long black hair pulled into a ponytail. She was no more than twelve years old.

A wave of nausea washed over Sierra as she carefully placed the photograph back on the dressing table. She couldn't believe her eyes, yet she knew it was true. She'd never forget that beautiful face.

The young Indian girl in the photograph was her mother, Pauline Kills Quick.

Valentina's words whispered through Sierra's memory. *I knew you'd come here...*

Perhaps time had stopped for Valentina, and she believed that Sierra was Pauline. But if she did, that was only confusion. It wasn't insanity.

All that she'd heard about Logan O'Neill slammed into her memory with the force of an F5 tornado.

"The O'Neill family is very powerful here," Hunter had told her. "They do what they want, and no one stops them."

And Byron had recalled, "There were some rednecks in the holding cell next to me, and they were laughing about a little Indian girl that 'got hers' from some high-powered White guy out in the Badlands. Seems no one ever pressed any charges that stuck, even though he seemed to make a habit of getting little girls from the Indian boarding schools around South Dakota.

They were laughing about one up in Sisseton and another one over in Marty—"

And, just yesterday, Gideon had begged her not to visit this ranch. The fear in his voice had been unmistakable. "He's dangerous. He's nearly killed my mother. You have no idea what he's capable of."

*Does Gideon know his father is a rapist...maybe even a serial rapist?*

*Oh, sweet Jesus, does Valentina?*

*Calm down, you idiot. You can't let on, especially to O'Neill. God only knows what he'll do if he figures out you may be his daughter...*

*If you really look so much like Pauline, he might have figured it out already.*

She had to get out of this house.

A knock sounded on the bathroom door, and she went weak with relief when she heard Hunter's concerned voice.

"Are you all right in there?"

She opened the door, trying to catch her breath, and managed a chuckle. "I'm sorry. I had to...you might want to...well...we'll be leaving soon and—"

He seemed to understand. "Right. I'll be out in a minute."

She stood aside to let him pass.

*He'll see the picture, and he'll know what it means.*

She walked toward Valentina, who remained very still and blank in her rocking chair, and knelt beside her once again. "Shall I sign your book, Mrs. O'Neill?"

Valentina nodded and handed it to her, but her eyes never left the far horizon outside the picture window. Even before Sierra's fingers closed over the book, she felt Logan O'Neill's presence somewhere in the room.

Bile burned the back of her throat.

"Mr. O'Neill, my bag is on the sofa," she said without looking around, her voice calm. "If you'll look in the zippered front pouch, you'll find a pen. I'd like to sign this book for Mrs. O'Neill before I forget."

"Sure." His footsteps sounded heavy against the tiled floor as he walked to her side. "I appreciate you doing this. Thank you very much."

"You're more than welcome." She wrote her message on the first page beneath her name and placed the book in Valentina's lap. "There you are, Mrs. O'Neill. I'm glad you enjoyed *Regina*. It's my favorite, too." She got to her feet, straightening her blouse as she stood up, and tried to discreetly wipe the perspiration from her palms.

"Where's your friend?" O'Neill asked quietly.

"Right here," Hunter answered, adjusting his jeans as he walked out of the bathroom. "I had to make a pit stop. Sorry."

"I want to take you two out to my warehouse."

Sierra frowned. "Your warehouse?"

"Yes. It's where I keep all the O'Neill history. You mentioned you'd like to see it."

"Of course. Thank you." Then she squeezed Valentina's shoulder and leaned in to speak in her ear. "It was a pleasure, ma'am. Thank you for having us in your home."

At that instant, Valentina O'Neill met her eyes and nodded. It was a lucid and private moment between two women who'd been strangers an hour before, but Sierra understood her now.

Now they shared an unspeakable bond based on secrets, heartbreak…and hatred.

Chapter Thirty

The sky had grown overcast during the short time they were indoors, and a definite chill nipped the air that hadn't been there before. Sierra shivered as she walked with Hunter and O'Neill down the gravel drive to a warehouse encircled by tall pine trees. Built almost entirely of concrete, it had a steep metal roof and was large enough to house a small family.

Her lip curled. *If this place was on Pine Ridge, the government would see to it that thirty people lived in it.*

O'Neill used a key to open the door, then flipped on an overhead light and stood aside so they could pass. "This building is climate controlled. It won't take you long to warm up."

She looked around, stunned. She'd never seen a private collection of any kind as extensive as this one. Hunter gave her a firm but subtle nudge forward so O'Neill could close the door. When she heard the ominous sound of a lock sliding back into place, she fought apprehension.

Several beaded cradleboards, bows, spears, and even a pair of suede leggings hung from rafters in the ceiling. Drums, dancing sticks, and pipe bags seemed scattered throughout without rhyme or reason. Tall display cases containing enormous feathered headdresses and colorful war bonnets lined one wall, and wider glass cases, lower to the ground, were set in rows throughout the room. Some containers held jewelry and sacred medicine items while others revealed laminated magazine and newspaper articles. Attached to another wall were cattle skulls, a fully furred buffalo head, and even a moose antler rack. Crates and boxes, all neatly labeled, were stacked beside what appeared to be a back door.

She turned in a slow circle, trying to take it all in. "My goodness."

This seemed to be the reaction O'Neill wanted—and expected. He grinned. "I know this looks like a hoarder's paradise, but the truth is every item in here is catalogued. I know where it came from and what it's worth."

"I can see that," Hunter said. "Thank you for showing us."

O'Neill shrugged. "Well, of course. A lot of it has been in my family for generations. I've loaned out much of it to various museums and universities over the years—part of my collection is showing in a Denver museum right now. I've got another one starting in Fort Collins in a couple of months."

"Well, like I said, we appreciate it."

O'Neill looked uncertain. "You're not pulling my leg, are you?"

"Excuse me?"

"I checked you out online the other night. You have quite a list of left-leaning documentaries to your credit. I find it hard to believe you'd be interested in anything I have to say."

Hunter chuckled. "To the contrary, Mr. O'Neill. I go where the money is. I film the documentary I'm paid to film. It's just business."

"And what documentary are you being paid to film here?"

Sierra held her breath. He needed to be careful now.

She needn't have worried.

His voice was respectful. "Our sponsors want an hour-long special about the changes being attempted on Pine Ridge and how we might help them be more successful than they've been in the past. I'm sure your opinion would carry a lot of weight with many of our viewers because your family has been here for so long."

She'd forgotten how smoothly he operated when he was working his way into an enemy camp, but this time she couldn't listen to it. She moved away from the two men and walked toward a tall glass display case set in a corner against the far wall. Suddenly the air felt heavy around her, as if a storm were brewing inside the warehouse. A whistling, whispering sound reached out to her.

Her eyes began to burn.

She felt an irresistible pull toward the display case; she couldn't have halted if she wanted to. She didn't look at any of the other exhibited items as she moved forward, single-minded and focused on an unknown destination. The men's voices receded into the background until they rang deep and hollow, like a misdirected sound system.

But that didn't matter. She wasn't listening anyway.

When she reached the display case, she gripped the wooden edges and stared through the polished glass at the items inside: misshapen bullet casings and old coins, a corncob pipe and a tobacco pouch, a pair of water-stained boots and a tattered cavalry cap—but nothing remarkable or compelling. She relaxed her hold on the display case.

"Ah," O'Neill said behind her. "I see you've found some of my Wounded Knee artifacts. These are particularly interesting."

"Why is that?"

"Well, back in 1891 when Wounded Knee relics started showing up all over the country, especially back east, no one was interested in this kind of White-man stuff—which is why I wanted to find some. It's always been about Indians. And before you knew it, supposedly authentic Ghost Shirts belonging to real Ghost Dancers were being sold to the highest bidder. Toys from the battlefield, beaded dresses…stuff like that. Chief Big Foot could've opened his own shoe store with all the bloody moccasins people claim to have found on his body. In other words, it was impossible for all that garbage to have come from Wounded Knee, yet it still shows up today. I used to have a genuine bloody Ghost Shirt myself, but it disappeared some time ago. I don't know where it went."

Sierra managed to sound unmoved. "Really? How did you manage to lose something so valuable?"

He shrugged. "I have no idea. But most all of the Wounded Knee stuff in this warehouse—I know exactly where it came from."

Hunter joined them at the display case and leaned forward to get a closer look. "And how do you know that?"

"My grandfather, Paul O'Neill, picked it up on the battlefield himself. He was a volunteer with the home guard, and he went out with a group of men in early January 1891 to bury all the combatants. It took a few days."

*Combatants? Starving women. Babies and children. Old folks singing their death songs.*

She felt sick.

"Grand-Pop told my dad the area was pretty well picked over by the soldiers, who either sold stuff for cash or kept it for themselves. And many Indians came back later and took stuff as well, then sold it at the agency for a dozen times more than it was worth. They knew how to play the White man, that's for sure, and they didn't hesitate to do it. They still do. So much for hating capitalism."

She choked on fury. *Stuff. How much disdain can you put into a single word like stuff?*

"Your grandfather wasn't involved in the actual fighting at Wounded Knee, was he?" Hunter asked.

O'Neill didn't respond for several moments. To Sierra, the silence seemed to stretch for eons. Even her breathing sounded too loud in her ears.

Finally, he seemed to reach a decision and nodded.

"He was, but my dad said he didn't talk about it much. Grand-Pop died several years after I was born, and we were pretty close, but I don't remember him ever mentioning it. My mother told me he used to say Wounded Knee was in the past and we all needed to move forward. Not forget about it, but just move on."

Sierra didn't miss the flash of anger in Hunter's eyes, yet he managed to keep his voice even. "Some people might find that difficult."

O'Neill surprised Sierra with his response. "You're right, Davenport. It's not like we beat them fair and square. We just outmaneuvered them. They were the greatest warriors, the greatest horsemen, the greatest hunters the world has ever seen, but they couldn't beat the diabolical determination of the White man to rule every inch of land he laid his eyes on."

"Well said," Hunter replied with a nod, "and I agree with you. I guess they're just going to have to accept the world they find themselves in now and manage to live in it."

"Well, that's how my father felt, too. He tried to help the Indians when he became senator. He was one of the first conservationists to set his sights on restoring the bison to Indian land. That's where the name Bison Head Ranch came from. He also believed in assimilating the natives into White society by sending them to Indian boarding schools, but they didn't appreciate that too much, either."

Sierra edged away from the two men. As she walked toward the door at the back of the warehouse, she tried to focus on the various items in the glass cases as she passed.

*Canteens, shoes, keys...*

*Medicine bags, sage and sweetgrass, baby moccasins...*

The heavy pounding in her ears returned as she drew nearer to the back door.

Once more that nauseating sense of dread threatened to overwhelm her, but this time she recognized it. It was the same feeling that had washed over her when she walked through Sloan Turner's dark and musty museum.

Now a closed door beckoned to her. No, it was more than that. Whatever was locked behind that door all but screamed her name. As crazy as it sounded, even in her own mind, Sierra *needed* to get into that room.

But she couldn't do that. She didn't even have the nerve to touch the doorknob. Somehow, she had to charm Logan O'Neill into letting her in himself.

She turned her back to the door and tried to hear the conversation of the two men as they neared her.

"I met your son yesterday," Hunter was saying, "and he tells me that he's an anthropologist with a special interest in Native American studies. That's impressive."

"Yeah, I saw you with him. Gideon is an archaeologist as well, but don't be too impressed. We're...estranged. He blames me for his mother's breakdown."

*Estranged...a quaint word for such a sad situation.*

"I'm sorry to hear that," Hunter replied. "He didn't mention it. Has she been ill for a long time?"

O'Neill appeared uncomfortable with the turn this conversation was taking. "Since Gideon was about ten. Do you like Indian jewelry, Davenport? There's some beautiful silverwork in this cabinet."

Sierra stepped over to a case beside the door and stared down at a display of old letters and a couple of magazine articles about the Sioux Indians published by a university in Nebraska. Pretending to be engrossed in the laminated relics, she did some rapid math in her head.

*Tina had her breakdown when Gideon was about ten. Gideon is now about forty, and he blames his father for what happened to his mother. Thirty years ago was...1974. Pauline Kills Quick was raped by a powerful White man in 1973...*

295

*And I was born in 1974.*

If the photo of Pauline with the O'Neill family hadn't been enough circumstantial evidence to convince her that O'Neill might have been the White man who raped her mother, the math was. Numbers didn't lie.

From a legal standpoint, it didn't matter. The statute of limitations had long since run out. And no one would ever prosecute Logan O'Neill, anyway.

Feeling someone's intense gaze on her, she glanced up to meet Hunter's eyes and guessed he'd just reached the same conclusions. He gave a quick shake of his head in a warning to keep still, then resumed his quiet conversation with O'Neill.

She took a deep breath and moved closer to the door, stopping at a set of glassed-in shelves on the way.

*Must be his come-to-Jesus section.*

These shelves contained old Bibles, prayer books, exquisite rosaries made of onyx and mother-of-pearl, and several large crucifixes. One was an antique, made of silver and bronze, and hung from a rope. Sierra caught her breath and leaned in to study it more closely.

"What'd you find?" O'Neill asked behind her.

Her heart raced, but she kept her voice steady as she pointed at the antique crucifix. "This is beautiful. I have a friend who collects them, but I've never seen one like this."

O'Neill opened the door, removed the crucifix, and handed it to her. "This one apparently belonged to a priest who came to the St. Paul Mission on the Rosebud Reservation sometime in the 1880s. I guess he lost it. Someone found it near the Wounded Knee Creek about fifty years ago and gave it to a Jesuit priest who still taught at the school. A good friend of mine, Father

Michael O'Hanlon, somehow came to have it and gave it to me."

Sierra's hand shook as she held the crucifix. She'd seen the priest rip it away from the rope around his waist and throw it as hard and as far as he could toward the ravine by the creek. She'd experienced the internal battle that raged through his soul that day. And now his pain flooded through her. She fought back tears.

"Please take this, Mr. O'Neill."

"No, I'd like you to have it. You could give it to your friend."

She shook her head.

O'Neill shrugged and placed the crucifix back in the case. When Hunter's fingers closed around her shoulder, she was so relieved her legs all but gave out.

"I think I'd like to go now—"

Hunter's cell phone rang. He jerked it from the small leather holster he'd attached to his belt and turned away. He spoke in a low voice. "Hello?"

Walking away to give him privacy, she didn't even notice she'd reached the back door and now stood staring at the photograph-covered wall beside it. O'Neill remained behind her, so close she could smell his aftershave. Her stomach churned.

She struggled to focus on the collage of pictures, most of them so faded she couldn't distinguish much of anything. When she spotted a larger photograph of an older man, framed in cedar and glass and placed at the center of the wall, she narrowed her eyes to study it. The man's features weren't easy to discern—he wore a wide-brimmed hat and was heavily bearded—but she knew who he was.

She'd seen him in her vision. He was the soldier

who'd handed a fresh Indian scalp to someone who resembled Sloan Turner, and received a blood-stained Ghost Shirt in return.

Once again, those eerie whispers floated through the air.

*Good trade… Good trade…*

She stepped away and pointed to the photograph. "Who is this?"

"That was my Grand-Pop."

"He looks a little sad, don't you think?"

O'Neill chuckled. "Must be your writer's imagination. He was too mean to be sad."

"Well, you would know, I guess. He just looks sad to me."

"Where'd your boyfriend get off to? Is he still on the phone?"

She pretended casual interest in the photos covering the wall as she shrugged, then looked around the warehouse. Hunter was nowhere to be seen. Her heart began to thud.

"He's been trying to reach a colleague in Austin most of the day. I guess they finally hooked up."

O'Neill cupped his hand around Sierra's elbow and pushed open the door to the room she'd wanted so badly to enter just a few moments earlier.

"Let's go in here, Miss Masters. This room is filled with uncatalogued items, so it's a treasure trove of interesting history. More like a scavenger hunt than anything else. I think you'll enjoy it."

She allowed O'Neill to guide her—she didn't have much choice. He flipped a wall switch, illuminating the room in an almost blinding fluorescent light.

"Watch your step."

His voice was too loud and high pitched, like a child's. But somewhere in the distance, far beyond the tinny sound of his voice, she heard the deep rhythmic beat of long drums, thudding and throbbing as if reverberating off canyon walls and echoing through time.

She didn't try to run. Somehow, concealed by relics seized from sacred resting places and hidden burial grounds, the drums reached out to her from beyond the chaos in this room.

She waited, held her breath, stood still.

Logan O'Neill hadn't exaggerated when he said this room wasn't well organized. Dusty boxes were piled against the walls, old books heaped into corners, and display cases were stacked almost to the ceiling. Several small paintings had been tossed without care on top of an old table nearby.

"Follow me," O'Neill said as he made his way toward the table. "Watch your step."

Helpless, she obeyed. The drumbeats grew louder, deeper, more insistent.

"Shoot," O'Neill said with disgust, "someone's pounding on the front door. Just wait here and don't touch anything. I'll be right back."

Chapter Thirty-One

Hunter flipped his cell phone closed and watched O'Neill as he strode out of the back room, Sierra right behind him. The banging on the door reverberated throughout the warehouse, like throbbing kettle drums.

"Keep your shorts on!" O'Neill bellowed. "Who is it?"

"It's me, Pop! It's Gideon!"

As O'Neill stormed by, Hunter stepped out of the shadows and grabbed Sierra's arm. When she gasped, he grinned and put a finger to his lips, then tucked his hand in the crook of her arm.

O'Neill stopped in front of the door and didn't move. Silence stretched.

Gideon's soothing voice came from the other side, like he was placating a small child. "I just want to talk, Pop. That's all. We need to talk."

"Nothing to say. Get the hell out of here."

"I'm not leaving, Pop. You might as well let me in."

His face contorted in disgust, he unlocked the door and threw it open.

As Gideon stood in the late afternoon shadows, his tall figure was outlined by golden beams of fading sunlight. His voice was casual. He might have been passing the time of day with a stranger. "Hey, Pop."

"What do you want?"

Gideon stood aside as a well-dressed man walked into the warehouse, a clipboard in his hand.

"I think you know Breeden Jones," Gideon said.

Hunter gave a low whistle of incredulity and squeezed Sierra's arm.

O'Neill's voice dripped venom. "What the hell are you doing here?"

Breeden Jones removed a legal-sized document from his clipboard and handed it to O'Neill. "Someone in this area's been selling illegal artifacts on the black market. I immediately thought of you."

O'Neill glanced at the document. "What's this?"

"A search warrant. I've been working undercover for the last fourteen months with the Bureau of Land Management, the National Park Service, and the Fish and Wildlife folks. I've even made some friends in the FBI. Imagine that. Anyway, the evidence trail has led us right here—and to Sloan Turner's truck stop up on I-90, which we started tossing last night."

"What evidence trail?"

Now Hunter chuckled softly, enjoying the drama even more than he'd thought he would. His grin widened as Gideon stepped aside to allow two uniformed state troopers carrying empty boxes to enter the warehouse.

Gideon spoke to his father carelessly, as if they were no relation at all. "Mr. Jones is a jack-of-all-trades, Pop. Today he's operating as a special tribal liaison with all those agencies as well as the state police and the FBI—who are outside in case you get some crazy idea about trying to hurt somebody. What you're holding in your hand is a warrant to tear this hellhole apart."

O'Neill snorted. "I'll ask again. What evidence?"

"Well, let's start with an authentic Ghost Shirt, Pop. It has a century-old bloodstain as big as your ego." Gideon paused, then shook his head. "Look, you just be a good boy, and nobody'll get hurt. I've spent the better part of my life waiting for the opportunity to do this, and you're not going to get in my way."

O'Neill gave a mocking chuckle. "I'm a lawyer, son, and there's no way you can prove that old Ghost Shirt belongs to me. It might've gotten you a warrant from some senile judge that doesn't recognize the O'Neill name, but it'll never get you a conviction."

Gideon held up his hand. "Number one, I'm not your son. Number two, you were a lousy lawyer. The power of your name is all that ever kept you in a courtroom, and you know it. Number three, Mom and I both can testify that Ghost Shirt is yours—"

"Your mother can't testify to anything."

The silence was long and tense. Then Hunter was shocked to hear Sierra's small but firm voice coming unexpectedly from beside him.

"I wouldn't bank on that, Mr. O'Neill."

\*\*\*\*

As Sierra watched the blood drain from O'Neill's face, a sense of satisfaction stole through her. She took a deep breath, remembering Gideon's words from yesterday.

*Nothing would make me happier than to bring down my father.*

He meant it. He was doing it now. And she was going to help him.

Pallid and sweating beneath the glare of fluorescent lights, O'Neill dropped the search warrant on the floor.

He pulled his cell phone out of his back jeans pocket and began punching keys on the dial pad. "Nobody move. I'm calling my lawyers."

"Go right ahead," Breeden Jones said, picking the paperwork up off the floor, "but our warrants are airtight. We got two of them from Federal Judge Ralph Homer in Custer late yesterday afternoon. We've already hit pay dirt at Sloan Turner's, and I imagine we're going to hit pay dirt here."

O'Neill put his cell phone up to his ear and spoke rapidly. "Hey, Judy, it's Logan. I need to speak to Carter. It's urgent. What? Okay, I'll hold." He looked at Breeden and spat out his words. "Listen, I don't care what your title is—it doesn't change what you are. Warrant or no warrant, I'll have your job."

Breeden shrugged. "Take your time talking to your attorney, O'Neill. Far be it from me to stop you from getting every constitutional right you're entitled to. That's the White road, not mine."

With that, Breeden walked toward Sierra and Hunter, his hand outstretched, once more smiling and affable. "I'm glad to see you both again. I'm sorry I couldn't tell you why I was at Nathan's gathering, but I was working that day. I hope you understand."

After Hunter shook Breeden's hand, he asked curiously, "What were you doing, Mr. Jones?"

"Please, call me Breed. Well, we had several reports that there was suspicious activity down at Wounded Knee Creek on and off, late at night. I was checking it out. I'd forgotten that Nathan's gathering was that day, even though everyone on Pine Ridge was going and that's all anyone was talking about. And you guys were sort of local celebrities—at least for the moment. So I thought, if nothing else, I could use you as my excuse for being there in case I didn't get out quick enough—which I didn't."

Sierra couldn't help but recall with some embarrassment her initial opinion of Breeden Jones. As she studied him now, she realized his ability to pass as an affluent White rancher worked in his favor for the profession he'd chosen. But, in truth, he was a long way from the "arrogant, swaggering, drugstore cowboy" she'd originally thought him. Aloud, she said only, "Did you find anything?"

"Nope."

"You could ask O'Neill about local ghost-hunting if you want," Hunter suggested without missing a beat. "He was over there yesterday taking pictures. He said that land was for sale."

Breed chuckled. "Oh, we know about that. Gideon called and told me. I know that an old White guy owns a lot of that land, but I checked, and it's not for sale—at least not right now. A couple of Winterhawk allotments are in that area, too, but they're leased out by the BIA to some rancher we can't even track down. You want to help us out and tell us why you were there, O'Neill?"

"It's no crime to take pictures."

Breed shrugged. "Your choice."

"Does Nathan Winterhawk know about you?" Hunter asked suddenly. "About what you do, I mean?"

"No. Nathan hasn't spoken to me in years—and I don't blame him." He turned back to O'Neill. "I have a friend of yours outside. He might jog your memory. Mike, do me a favor and get Turner, would you?"

"Sure," a young police officer answered. "I'll be right back."

For the first time, O'Neill's mask of nonchalance slipped, giving Sierra a perverse sense of satisfaction. When the officer returned with Turner, whose hands were cuffed in front of him, O'Neill's face was shiny with sweat. But even more interesting was the change in Sloan Turner's demeanor. The frightened little man from just a few days ago had disappeared. Now he seemed confident and relaxed, as if relieved to be taking his life back.

Sloan Turner strolled toward Logan O'Neill and stopped in front of him for a moment. Suddenly, without warning, he shoved his cuffed fists into the older man's chest. O'Neill stumbled backward into a glass case containing a dizzying array of arrowheads and beadwork. Still clutching his phone, he swore and looked to Breeden Jones for assistance, but Breed didn't move.

Turner jabbed his fists into O'Neill's chest again. "He's not going to help you. No one's going to help you. You don't scare me anymore. I know I'm going to prison, but that's all right with me. You will, too."

O'Neill's face was paste white, but he stood up straight. Proud. Arrogant. "Don't count on it. They'll lock you up and throw away the key. Then I'll drive myself home."

Turner grinned. "I'm not an idiot. Do you really think I haven't protected myself? I've recorded phone calls, photographs, emails... I've even got copies of every shipping slip and purchasing order that ever came and went out of your warehouse and mine. I gave everything I have to the cops. I learned from the best."

Logan O'Neill looked sick to his stomach. Suddenly he closed his cell phone with a foul expletive and muttered, "I got disconnected."

Breed chuckled. "Yeah, well...you might want to get used to that."

For a moment Sierra almost felt sorry for Logan O'Neill. Now he looked old and confused. All the fight had gone out of him. Everything he'd come to expect in his privileged life had disappeared.

She slammed the door on her pity before it got the better of her, and remembered who and what he was. He was a rapist, a thief, and a self-righteous bigot who believed he was entitled to everything he'd stolen from an entire people, as well as from a young girl.

*And...the fight will resume soon enough.*

Breed turned his attention back to Sierra. "Forgive me if I'm speaking out of line, but Gideon tells me you have a nose for genuine artifacts and where they might be located. This is a mighty big warehouse, and I don't want to waste any time. Where do you think we should start?"

She didn't hesitate. "In that back room."

O'Neill scowled. "Why the hell are you asking her? She's never been here before. There's nothing in that room but a bunch of junk—"

Breed spoke over him. "Gideon, would you take Mike back there with you and start looking? You know how to do it, so be sure he doesn't hurt anything. I'll be there in a minute."

"My pleasure." Gideon looked at Sierra, one eyebrow lifted. "Care to join us?"

"What's going on?" O'Neill demanded. "She's got no business going back there! She's not part of any agency listed on this paperwork—"

Gideon stifled a yawn. "Oh, shut up, Pop. Your

days of giving orders are over. You might as well sit down and stay out of the way. Come on, Sierra."

At that moment, the door to the warehouse swung open, and Byron Little Hand's enormous figure blocked the setting sun. When the door closed behind him, Byron stared at Logan O'Neill as if he were something repulsive left on the side of the road. "Is this gathering by invitation only, or can anyone join?"

"Hey, there," Breed said. "I didn't know if you were going to make it or not. I couldn't stall much longer."

"Thanks for waiting."

O'Neill took a step forward, but Gideon grabbed his arm and jerked him back. No one else moved.

"You don't mind if I speak to your father, do you, Gideon?" Byron strode toward O'Neill without waiting for an answer. "I've got a couple of questions."

"Ask away. Pop's got all the answers—always has."

"I'm not talking to anyone without my lawyer," O'Neill stated. "You might as well relax."

Byron dwarfed O'Neill as he loomed over him. "I just wanted to ask you a question based on something Mr. Turner here mentioned at his place last night. But if you don't want to talk to us, that's fine. The feds can deal with you later."

"Whatever he said, it's a lie."

"Well, it might be—or not. Turner mentioned that your grandfather leased about a hundred acres of property in the vicinity of Wounded Knee from the BIA back in 1898 and that you automatically renew that lease every time it comes up—so that nobody else can, including Nathan Winterhawk. We knew someone was trying to keep him from getting that land to grow his bison ranch, but we didn't know who it was...until Turner mentioned it last night. You hid your tracks real well."

"It's all legal."

"I'll leave that up to the experts. I just want to know why you care. You own and lease more land on the rez than anyone else around here. Hell, us Indians talk about that all the time—how this is Indian land, and you White folks have it all. Good setup if you can get it. I'd do the same thing if I could."

O'Neill looked at him, eyes narrowed.

Byron rubbed his chin. "Of course, if I thought there was something of value around the Wounded Knee area and Nathan Winterhawk's *tiyospaye* actually leased or owned the land it was on, *that* might make a difference to me...especially if I was a rich, White collector used to getting what I wanted. I mean, I'd rather *me* have it than Winterhawk."

"You're not making sense."

Byron ignored him. "Oh, I think I am. For some reason, you don't want Winterhawk—or any other Lakota—to have access to land that belongs to this tribe. Wounded Knee land. *Sacred land.* Land that doesn't mean a damn thing to you and everything to the Lakota. But that's land *you* want for some reason, and you're willing to do just about anything to get it, including seeing to it that the BIA just keeps losing all Nathan's paperwork. I figure the way this thing is going, you could keep it tied up for the next two hundred years."

O'Neill scoffed. "How would I have all that power?"

Sloan Turner answered, and his voice shook with rage. "Because of your family's money. By blackmail and payback. Collecting chips from anyone you've ever done anything for—"

"Yeah, that would work," Byron interjected, his words dripping with sarcasm. "After all, if you've got that skill, why not use it?"

"I'm not that important."

"Humility doesn't become you, O'Neill. I figure it like this. If you keep that land out of Winterhawk's hands, he can't get in the way of whatever it is you want to do down around Wounded Knee. Everything was going along pretty well, too—until Hunter Davenport and his crew showed up on the rez and started filming a documentary that builds up Winterhawk's bison ranch. That's going to encourage other businesses to start up and spread the wealth, so to speak, which would make things very hard on you. You've had your way for years, but you've always had to work in the dark—like a cockroach. But new businesses, new residents, educated Indians coming back to the rez—all that sheds light on a troubled place like Pine Ridge. You can't afford that."

O'Neill smirked. "And what is it I want to do so bad?"

Byron's expression darkened, but he didn't skip a beat. His voice was casual. "How much do you get for an Indian baby's skull?"

Now O'Neill shot up from his casual lounging position against the cabinet as if someone had shoved a steel rod up his spine.

Gideon grabbed him. "Oh, come on, Pop. You know the answer to that better than anyone."

Sierra's head spun. A wave of nausea crashed over her, and her entire body felt bathed in sweat. Then, as quickly as it had come, the queasiness began to pass. After a few more moments, it disappeared. Closing her eyes, she took a deep breath.

After a moment, she managed to whisper, "Is that what's at Turner's place? A baby's skull?"

Byron nodded.

"In that back room?"

He nodded again. "Among other things I hear are guaranteed to bring a small fortune."

She closed her eyes and pictured two men standing together on the killing field of Wounded Knee, exchanging a fresh Indian scalp for a bloody Ghost Shirt.

*Good trade…*

Her eyes flew open. "You didn't happen to find a very old Indian scalp there, did you?"

"I don't know. Maybe." Byron looked away from her and spoke to Gideon. "Keep a grip on your old man there, okay? He's not going to like this."

As Byron strolled to the door, the tension in the room grew until it was almost unbearable. He opened the door and spoke to someone, then stood aside as a young woman entered the warehouse.

Dressed in expensive khaki slacks and a matching blazer, her dark hair cut in a stylish, shoulder-length bob, and sunglasses perched on top of her head, she might have been one of a million college students. Byron took her hand and tucked it into the crook of his arm, patting it as he walked with her toward Logan O'Neill. She didn't even reach Byron's massive shoulder, but her stride was confident, her lovely face set and determined.

Sierra couldn't pull her gaze away.

When Byron and the young woman stopped in front of O'Neill, she didn't let go of Byron's arm. Her voice was low, husky. "Hello, Mr. O'Neill...Gideon."

Both men stared at her with blank expressions.

"My God," she whispered, "you don't even know who I am, do you?"

"No, I'm sorry," O'Neill answered. "I don't."

But Gideon's eyes widened, and Sierra thought she saw a spark of recognition.

Now the young woman removed her hand from Byron's arm and stepped closer to Logan O'Neill. She pushed her silky hair back and lifted her chin.

"Come on, Mr. O'Neill, look at me. You're an old man, but your memory can't be that bad. My bruises are long gone now, and I washed the blood away years ago, but other than that, I look pretty much the same." She paused. "On the other hand, what lives inside of me is a different story."

Silence lengthened. Eons passed. Nobody moved.

Gideon broke the stillness in a choked voice. "Pauline...?"

She didn't answer.

"Pauline...?"

Finally, the young woman turned toward Gideon, and Sierra was able to see her face.

Time stopped. Her world tilted, then slipped completely off its axis.

Chapter Thirty-Two

To Sierra's shock, Logan O'Neill began to chuckle. It wasn't a nervous laugh but one of pure enjoyment. Her thoughts whirled around in her head as loose and disconnected as marbles spinning inside a pinball machine.

*Pauline Kills Quick. She's here. In this room. My mother.*

*My father. A sociopath, a narcissistic sociopath.*

*Why the hell is he laughing?*

She struggled to pull her thoughts back to the present and arrange them into some kind of order. Logan O'Neill might be amused by what he saw as a situation he could control, but she knew better. The next moments could well be the most important of her entire life.

Pauline Kills Quick seemed to realize that, too. She held out her hands to Gideon and gave him a warm smile. "Gideon! I can't tell you how happy I was when Byron told me I'd see you today."

He blushed crimson and seemed unable to speak. He grasped her hand without removing his grip from his father's arm, and his eyes glistened with unshed tears. "Where have you been?" he managed.

She withdrew her hand from his and touched his cheek before she turned back to O'Neill. "Have *you* ever wondered that, Mr. O'Neill? Even once?"

"Nope, can't say that I have."

Her lips twitched in a small, mocking smile. "Well, here's how I understand it, Mr. O'Neill. There's a statute of limitations on rape. Poor me, lucky you. But there's no statute of limitations on murder."

"What're you talking about?"

Her dark eyes flashed. "Does the name Julia Farewell mean anything to you?"

Sierra caught her breath.

"No," O'Neill answered.

Pauline took a step closer to him. "Of course it does. Julia Farewell was my aunt. You know that. Her body was dumped on Whisper Butte out in the Badlands in 1974—just a few months after my baby was born. You know that, too. And why was she murdered? Because she knew everything. How you raped me. How you had my insides taken out so I could never have any more children. How you blackmailed people so no one could ever turn on you—people like Sloan Turner and dear old Father O'Hanlon, who just didn't want to live anymore because of all he knew and couldn't tell."

Sierra's stomach twisted as Pauline's accusations echoed in her ears.

*How you had my insides taken out so I could never have any more children... Oh, sweet Jesus. What kind of man would do that?*

O'Neill was unmoved. "Young lady, I'm a lawyer, and I know what you're doing. You're throwing allegations out there just to see what sticks. Nothing's sticking. You have to have proof—and you don't have any."

Byron spoke up. "I wouldn't be too sure about that.

Do you remember a lady named Cecilia Long Soldier? She was a counselor at the St. Paul Indian School back in the early 1970s."

"No. I don't know anybody from that school."

Hunter cleared his throat. "You might want to rethink that statement."

"Why?"

"Well, you said you were a legal services attorney on the Rosebud for many years, and we all know how bad the Indian boarding schools were. I figure you probably dealt with *someone* at St. Paul, at least at some point—"

"You figure wrong."

Hunter shrugged. "Oh. I'm sorry. My mistake." He reached into his back jeans pocket, pulled out a folded photograph, and handed it over to Byron Little Hand. "I removed this from Mrs. O'Neill's bathroom this afternoon."

Nauseated, Sierra closed her eyes as she pictured the photograph that had changed her world in a single instant. In appearance, the perfect family… yet so sick, so twisted.

Byron opened the photograph and gazed at it without a word. Finally, he passed it over to Pauline, who studied it in silence. She handed it to O'Neill. "That's me in a St. Paul uniform. That's you with your sweet little family. Remember now?"

O'Neill didn't even look at it. He dropped it and pulled out his phone. "I'm going to call my lawyers again."

Gideon picked the photo up off the floor and handed it back to Byron. "That might be a good idea, Pop."

But Byron shook his head and grinned. "You should wait. Might as well have all the facts before you try to talk to them—especially since they'll probably leave you on hold for an hour or so."

Now O'Neill's voice cracked. "What facts?"

"Well, I spoke with Cecilia Long Soldier yesterday, and she recalled Pauline Kills Quick real clear. But before she told me what she knew, she said she'd managed to run down some documents that would back up her story. She faxed those documents to my place last night, and I have them with me now—just in case you want to say none of this is true. Are you interested?"

"No."

"Well, I sure as hell am," Gideon growled.

"Good. I'm dying to tell *somebody*. O'Neill, I promise not to take much of your precious time, but let's walk down memory lane. Back when you were such good friends with Dickie Wilson, pouring your money into arming his GOONs and using your family name to weasel your way into and out of whatever evil you could find, it probably never occurred to you that one day it would end and someone would call you on it. Am I right?"

"That's ridiculous. You can't prove that."

"I wouldn't be so sure. You thought you could rape Pauline Kills Quick and she'd never tell anyone, but you were wrong. That very night, when she got back to the boarding school, she told her counselor, Cecilia Long Soldier, who then told Father Michael O'Hanlon. But since you donated a lot of money to the St. Paul Mission, Father O'Hanlon knew better than to bite the hand that fed him. He told the ladies not to say anything because nobody was ever going to believe them, anyway. After all, they were both Indians. But he did help Julia Farewell get Pauline off the rez, and Pauline stayed with friends of Julia's up in Rapid until her baby was born."

Sierra gave an admiring glance toward Pauline and felt a tiny quiver of pride. Her father might be a monster, but her mother was courageous and strong.

"That's not proof. That's hearsay."

"Shut up. Father O'Hanlon tried to do the right thing. He wrote a letter to be opened in the event of his death and mailed it to Cecilia Long Soldier. When he died a few years ago, Cecilia read it. That letter tells all about what you did to Pauline and what Father O'Hanlon did to protect you—but Cecilia didn't know what to do with it until I called her about a week ago and started asking questions. You've been one lucky pervert all these years because everyone did as they were told, and your life just kept sailing right on along."

"I'm not a pervert—"

"Oh yeah…you are. I heard about you when I was in jail in Nebraska back in '73 and some drunk rednecks in the holding tank next to me were laughing about how you got your little girls from Indian schools all over the place. 'Course, I didn't remember all the details 'til a few days ago on account of I got coldcocked while I was there. But when I did remember, I called Cecilia up in Rapid and asked her to do some snooping for me. I don't need to tell you how happy she was to help me. Thirty years is a long time to carry a secret as dirty as this one—at least, if you're a human being with a conscience, which you're not."

O'Neill's objection was feeble. "You're just

fishing—"

Byron held up his enormous hand and shook his head warningly. "Anyway, Pauline gave birth by C-Section to a baby girl up in the Indian Hospital in Rapid City on March 28, 1974, and Julia Farewell, who worked in that hospital, gave the baby girl to a waiting White couple from Texas just four days later. After Pauline healed up, she went to a girls' boarding school in Denver. Not an Indian school, O'Neill, but a nice, private, expensive boarding school for well-to-do young ladies—*White* young ladies. But Indian or not, she was their valedictorian in 1978 and went on to the University of Colorado. She graduated from there in 1983 and now oversees Native American art and history exhibitions at a very well-known museum in Fort Collins."

O'Neill looked sick, and Sierra loved it. He'd walked into a trap of his own making, and it was clear he was beginning to realize it.

Now Byron's eyes danced. "You sent your collection straight to the museum where Pauline Kills Quick works. You can imagine how thrilled she was to come across a collection with your name on it—not to mention an illegal Ghost Shirt you didn't even know was in there."

"Just a minute, Byron," Pauline interrupted. "I need to say something."

She walked to O'Neill and jabbed his chest with a pointed finger. "But raping a fourteen-year-old girl wasn't enough for you, was it? You had to destroy my entire life and any chance I ever had of forgetting you and starting over. I got a bad infection after my baby was born and ended up back in the hospital. That's

Rosetta Diane Hoessli

when I discovered they'd taken my insides out at the same time they did my C-section and left me so empty nothing will ever grow inside of me again. I have paperwork to prove it."

"I don't know what you're talking about. You can't prove I had anything to do with that—although I'm sorry it happened."

"Shut up. My father, Arlin Black Thunder, trusted you. I don't know how you forced him to do it, but he made you my legal guardian back when I first went to the Indian school. Maybe it was because you were a rich and powerful man, and he thought I'd do better in the White world if you took care of me. That had been important to his father, so it was important to him.

"Regardless, *you* signed the hospital forms giving them permission to sterilize me, which it seems was an actual government program back in those days. Auntie Julia wrote everything she knew in her diary, and she gave it to my grandma Madonna for safekeeping. After Auntie Julia was murdered, I was sent up to that girls' school in Denver, and I tried to start over. I never contacted anybody in my family because Auntie Julia told me not to, but I always knew that one day I'd see you again." She paused to take a breath, finished, "And here I am."

A single bead of sweat rolled down O'Neill's cheek. "I didn't kill your auntie," he muttered.

She shrugged. "I'll leave that up to the authorities."

Byron spoke up again. "Oh, here's something else, O'Neill. Do you know who paid for all that excellent education?"

"No. How would I know that?"

Byron chuckled. "You paid for it. Well, your wife

did. Your wife *is* Valentina O'Neill, right?"

O'Neill took a deep breath, released it in an explosive sigh, and threw up his hands. "Okay, what can I say? Pauline was young, beautiful, and sexy as hell. She came on to me, and I was a middle-aged man with a wife and a kid—how was I going to turn that down? I couldn't. I didn't even want to. But it only happened once. Later I heard she was pregnant, but I didn't know whose baby it was. It could have been anyone's."

Pauline shrieked and lunged for him with fingers curled into talons of rage as she aimed straight for his eyes. O'Neill seized her hands and hauled her up in front of him, his face a mask of blind hatred and fury. She drew up her legs and shoved both feet into his groin with so much force that he yelled, staggered, flung her to the floor. She sprawled out, silent and motionless.

Gideon grabbed a handful of shirt collar and jerked his father so close they were nose to nose, his face beet red in fury.

Breed seized Gideon's arm. "Don't do it, man! You touch him, he walks."

Using a coarse expletive, he released him with so much force that O'Neill staggered backward.

"You're not worth it," Gideon muttered.

Breed stepped between the two men, the warning expression still on his face, and let go of Gideon's arm. Gideon walked toward the motionless figure on the floor and knelt beside her. He stroked her hair away from her face until she moaned and opened her eyes. She appeared confused—until her gaze fell on him. She smiled and reached for his hand.

Sierra took a step closer to them, hoping to hear their words. She knew their conversation was meant to be private, but she had to hear it. She had to wrap her mind around this evil, and she just couldn't do it.

With Gideon's help, Pauline managed to push herself into a sitting position and leaned against a glass case, pressing her fingers against her right temple.

His face was pale. "Are you all right?"

She nodded. "I think so."

"I'm so sorry. This shouldn't have happened."

She chuckled. "I did it, silly, you didn't."

He looked miserable. "No, I mean, I'm sorry about all of this...my father... If I'd known, I could've stopped him—"

She touched his cheek. "Don't be silly. You were just a child."

"I wasn't that much younger than you. We were both just children." He shook his head. "But my mother knew, and she had to live with it. That's why I couldn't save her."

"What do you mean? What's wrong with your mother?"

Sierra couldn't keep silent any longer. She walked to Gideon and Pauline, knelt beside them, and put her hand on Gideon's shoulder. "Excuse me," she said softly. "I'm not a doctor, but I don't think there's anything wrong with your mother that a month in a lovely place away from your father wouldn't cure. Minus the sedatives, that is."

He frowned. "I don't understand."

"I went to your ranch this afternoon, remember? I met your mother. As soon as she was alone with me, she said, 'I knew you'd come here.' She knew me."

"That's crazy. She's never seen you before in her life."

Sierra's gaze slid to Pauline's face before she nodded. "I know, but that's what she said. And there's more. Your mother put that Ghost Shirt into one of your father's boxes before it was shipped down to Fort Collins. She's had it hidden for years. She knew exactly what she was doing."

"How do you know that?"

She dropped her gaze. "When she touched me...I saw her do it."

His frown deepened.

*Oh God, please don't ask me any more questions.*

His face cleared, and she could see he somehow understood. She went weak with relief. He wasn't going to give her away.

Pauline's voice, shaky and small, broke the stillness. "Who *are* you?"

Desperate and terrified, Sierra looked pleadingly at Byron, but he only smiled with encouragement and gave her a thumbs-up.

She turned to Pauline and held out her hands. "I'm Sierra Masters."

"Masters?"

She nodded.

"Masters," Pauline repeated in bewilderment. "I'm sorry. I feel like I should know you. Do I know you?"

"No, ma'am."

Pauline began to tremble. She leaned forward and gripped Sierra's hands. "Wait. Look at me."

Overcome with inexplicable shyness, she obeyed.

Pauline's voice was choked with emotion. "My grandmother's eyes have those little gold flecks in them, like yours, and you look like my auntie Julia."

Sierra held her breath.

And then Pauline's grip tightened on her hands. "Are *you* my daughter?"

Sierra's eyes filled with tears, but she didn't look away. "I think so."

Without warning, two words wafted through the stillness and filled her spirit with a joy she hadn't even known she was missing.

*My tiyospaye...*

*It begins here.*

Chapter Thirty-Three

Hunter saw O'Neill move before anyone else did. He yelled and sprinted toward him, but Sloan Turner thrust his foot out and sent the older man sprawling to the floor. Without a word, Byron hauled him up and held him away from his body, as if O'Neill were a weightless old rag doll that smelled bad.

"Cuff him and get him out of here!" Breed snapped at no one in particular. Mike, the young police officer, hastened to obey.

But Pauline scrambled to her feet, still holding Sierra's hand. "Just a minute, Mr. Jones," she interrupted. "Can you just keep him cuffed and close by you? I may need his help."

Hunter frowned. What kind of help could that lousy excuse for a man give to Pauline Kills Quick? But then, at just that moment, he caught an expression of instant recognition passing between the two women, and he understood.

"Sure," Gideon answered quickly. "Should we take him with us into the back room, Pauline?"

She looked at Sierra, a question in her eyes.

"That's a great idea."

*Gideon must know all about the strange gift these two women share.* Hunter stifled a grin and almost felt sorry for Logan O'Neill.

*This is going to be very, very interesting.*

He ignored his instinct to move to Sierra's side in case she needed him, and walked instead behind the group as they made their way to the back room. Sierra and Pauline seemed to have reached some sort of unspoken agreement, and he'd be in the way. Besides, he was an investigative reporter with a sixth sense of his own.

That sixth sense was in active mode now.

As he followed the group, he focused on the two crimes O'Neill could be prosecuted for—if proof could be found. One was the possible murder of Julia Farewell. The other was illegal trafficking in American Indian artifacts, especially if the FBI had truly found an identifiable Indian baby's skull on Sloan Turner's premises. The rapes had occurred too many years before, and no one would care anyway. Pauline's sterilization was part of a government program that had begun in the late 1960s and fizzled out in the late 1970s, so nothing illegal there. And the fact O'Neill wanted land around Wounded Knee didn't matter, either. In fact, lots of people probably did.

No, if he was going to earn his keep, he had to focus either on a long-ago murder no one cared about or the concealed bones of dead Indian babies.

Before he could pursue this line of thinking, the group came to a sudden halt in front of a large, cedar-framed photo of an elderly man. As he watched Sierra and Pauline move closer to the picture, he couldn't help but remember how he'd felt a few days before, when Sierra had her first real vision and he'd been so sorry he'd brought her to this troubled place.

*But I was wrong, so wrong.*

If Sierra had ever been afraid—and he was sure she

had been—she wasn't now. She touched the wall below the photo, then the frame, then the picture itself, and he was awed by how certain her actions were. She was working now, using what the people called "the power." Even Pauline stood back and watched her respectfully, as if she recognized her daughter's gift was strong.

After a few moments, Sierra shook her head and pointed to the door. Byron gave O'Neill a little shove toward it and stood to the side, waiting. For one long, tense moment, O'Neill tried to stare the enormous Indian down, but it didn't work. The man couldn't be intimidated.

He shrugged and opened the door.

For the first time since Hunter had walked back into Sierra's life bearing the photographs that turned both their worlds upside down, he was more than uneasy. He was filled with foreboding as he followed the group into the room.

He didn't have to have any psychic power to know something wretched and broken was inside.

****

Sierra glanced around the room, taking inventory of her friends' positions. Against the back wall, next to a long table covered with unframed canvases and posters, Byron and Breed stood like guardian bookends on either side of O'Neill, whose hands were now cuffed in front of him. Their faces were tense and expectant as they watched her, waiting…for something…she didn't know what. Followed by Sloan Turner who seemed determined to explain the history of every item he saw, Hunter prowled through the room with the slinky grace of a feline predator, stopping here to examine a painting on the wall, halting there to touch a box, a book, or a piece of memorabilia. Pauline and Gideon stood right behind her, silent and watchful. She was grateful for their close presence.

The room seemed darker than before, even with the overhead light on, but it wasn't the kind of darkness that accompanied the setting sun. It felt different, thicker, as if the atmosphere itself had changed. As she looked around the room, she realized even though he was restrained, O'Neill was guarding that table pushed against the back wall.

That was all the information she needed. She made her way toward it.

When she reached the table, she began to move the paintings from one side of the surface to the other, careful not to damage canvases. Some were quite old, others much more recent, but all contained an American Indian theme. She didn't waste time admiring the work or studying the style.

She waited for a signal, a mental flash, a feeling.

At the bottom of the pile, she touched a wooden frame. She moved the last few canvases away from the painting, which was bordered by wide matting, and gazed down at it.

A processional of Indians led a painted pony into a row of cottonwood trees. On the pony's back was an unwieldy burden covered by a buffalo robe. A deep ravine was visible beyond the vegetation, and beyond that was a winding creek.

She remembered this vision well.

She lifted the painting and looked at it more closely. If the artist had signed his work, the matting hid his name from view, but she didn't know why that would matter. Then, strangely, the longer she gazed at the painting, tiny dots of red paint blurred into splotches of blood running down the canvas.

She turned to Gideon, who remained close behind her, and handed the painting to him. "I need to know who painted this."

He just nodded. He took a small pen knife from his jeans pocket and pried the thick backing from behind the painting, then removed the matting so the entire canvas was visible. Sierra stared at the artist's name.

*Arlin Black Thunder, 1970.*

Pauline seized Sierra's arm in a vise-like grip, and her voice was shaky. "My father?"

She nodded. She couldn't speak.

"Why is blood splattered on it?"

Sierra caught her breath. "You can see that?"

"Of course. What does it mean?"

"Do you see blood on this painting, Gideon?" she asked.

He stared at it for a while before he shook his head. "No, I'm sorry, I don't." He paused, then added, "But I do know where this is."

"Isn't it Wounded Knee?"

"Yes, but it's more than that. This processional of Indians going into that patch of cottonwood trees... See the bulky buffalo robe covering something on the back of the painted pony they're leading? I think that's supposed to be the body of Crazy Horse, and the processional with him is his family and friends. They spirited him out of Fort Robinson after they brought in a black-tailed deer to use as a decoy, and they buried him out in the Badlands—at least that's one of the legends. But many stories tell of later years when his

327

bones were moved from one resting place to another because the army wanted his head—literally. There was a big reward out for it." He pointed at the row of cottonwoods in the painting. "Anyway, one of those burial places is said to be in this area near Wounded Knee. Of course, no one knows for sure."

Sierra's voice trembled with excitement. "I saw that processional in my vision at Wounded Knee yesterday. They appeared, went into the trees, and disappeared. Like smoke."

Byron joined them. "Excuse me. May I see that?"

Gideon handed him the canvas.

Byron stared intently at the painting. As she waited, Sierra's gaze wandered around the room and settled on O'Neill's face.

The man was pale, sweaty, visibly shaking. He was terrified.

*Why?*

O'Neill hadn't shown any reaction when he'd been accused of Julia's murder or Pauline's rape or even when he heard Byron's statements about the remains of Indian babies being found on Sloan Turner's property. But something about this painting had him scared to death.

A name whispered through the room. *Tasunke Witko…Tasunke Witko…*

Byron held the canvas toward Sierra. "I think Gideon is right. I think this is supposed to be Crazy Horse's burial party. But what interests me is that Arlin Black Thunder painted it. Sierra, do you remember what I told you about Arlin's great-grandfather, Black Rolling Thunder?"

She pulled herself away from the background

whispers and frowned. "You told me that one legend says Black Rolling Thunder was a close friend of Crazy Horse's, and he went with the family to bury him, right?"

"Do you know anything about that, Pauline?" Byron asked.

She shook her head. "I don't know anything about my family. I probably know less than Sierra."

"Well, I think that your father's been trying to paint stories about his family because he has no one he can tell them to. I doubt this is the only painting he's ever done. He's far too good."

"You're right," Sierra murmured. "We have another one in the Jeep. I'll show it to you later."

"I'd like to see it." Byron walked back to O'Neill, head cocked, and asked curiously, "How much would that Wounded Knee land be worth if Crazy Horse's bones were actually buried there? Or…better yet…his head?"

O'Neill shrugged.

"Well, you can put this in granite, my friend. You can lease that land, and you may even be able to keep Winterhawk from getting his hands on it, but—and here's the granite part—you'll never dig it up. Never. There's not an Indian within a million miles of here, or any tribe, that would allow it. You'd be a dead man."

"Are you threatening me?"

"I'm promising. The crowning achievement of your pitiful career would be to dig up Chief Crazy Horse's bones and sell them to the highest bidder. Don't think we don't know that. You might believe you can find them on that property down by Wounded Knee, but I'm here to tell you it'll never happen. I'll kill

329

you myself."

She stifled a grin as Byron Little Hand took a step closer to O'Neill, who shriveled like a salt-covered slug right before her eyes. If she lived to be a hundred years old, she'd never enjoy a sense of vengeance as sweet as she felt right now. He'd get away with everything, she was certain, but at this moment he was afraid, and that made it all worthwhile.

"Excuse me. Miss Masters?" Sloan Turner's reed-thin voice quavered slightly as he touched her shoulder.

She turned to him. "Yes?"

"I want to give you something. It's my way of apologizing for the way I acted the day we met."

"Mr. Turner, this really isn't the time. I—"

He colored and held up his hand. "Please, don't say anything yet. Just follow me. Miss Kills Quick, you come along, too."

They followed him down the narrow aisle to a large metal armoire at the end. From the corner of her eye, she saw Byron grab O'Neill's arm as the elderly man took a step forward.

O'Neill hissed desperately, "Don't be a fool, Turner!"

Sloan Turner kept walking. Halting in front of the armoire, he pulled a set of keys out of his back jeans pocket and selected one. Her throat went dry as she waited for him to open the door.

He looked over his shoulder. "Come up here, Miss Kills Quick."

Pauline moved to the other side of Sierra and gripped her hand. Sierra gave her a little smile of encouragement.

Turner looked at both women squarely, his face

shiny with perspiration, but he seemed determined to accomplish what he'd set out to do. "I want you to know how sorry I am and how wrong I've been. That's why I'm giving this to you."

Now O'Neill's voice was actually shaking. "Turner, don't be an idiot!"

Sloan Turner stopped to give O'Neill a long look before he opened the armoire and removed a small metal safe. He moved the combination lock back and forth until it unlocked with a faint click. He lifted the lid, then handed the safe to Pauline. "Be careful."

She stared down at the contents and shook her head, clearly baffled. She carried the safe to a nearby table, set it down, and began removing what appeared to be nondescript items tossed inside without care: two old beaded keychains, a small inexpensive dreamcatcher made in China, a tiny crucifix on a long leather strap, and several folded flyers concerning lawn care and ordering Italian food online.

Finally, only one article was left in the safe.

"Oh my God."

Sierra was silent. *What on earth...?*

Pauline picked up the item—a beautifully beaded, very old medicine bag—and held it aloft. It was stained with blood.

"I don't understand," Sierra whispered.

Pauline's face crumpled, and tears streamed down her cheeks. "Auntie Julia always wore this medicine bag. It was passed down in our family from my grandmother's grandfather, Kills Buffalo Quick. My grandmother gave it to Auntie Julia because she had no sons and she wanted Auntie Julia to receive its power."

"I don't understand," Sierra repeated. "Why is it

here?"

Turner joined Pauline at the table and began to shove the items back in the safe. When he spoke, he looked directly at Logan O'Neill. "It's here because I put it here. We'd been watching Julia Farewell for months because we knew she was making strides against us in AIM. We even got one of Wilson's GOONs to beat the crap out of her one night just to warn her, but she didn't seem to understand. I was all for just letting it be and seeing what was going to happen, but O'Neill couldn't keep his pants zipped.

"He raped Pauline sometime in 1973, right after the Wounded Knee occupation was over. She had her kid sometime in '74, and we heard through the rez grapevine that Julia was nosing around the hospital about sterilizations going on without permission. That wasn't good because O'Neill had approved Pauline's sterilization, and he knew it was just a matter of time before Julia found out. We also knew she was working directly with AIM to find out about funds O'Neill was funneling to Dickie Wilson in exchange for...well...for whatever he happened to want at the time. Anyway, she had to go. She knew way too much.

"I did it. I was driving the car. And I was alone. She came out of an AIM meeting in Wanblee one night, and I hit her. That's all. She died instantly. I put her in the car, took her out to Whisper Butte, and dumped her body there. I took the medicine bag because I liked it, that's all. No other reason. I put it in this safe because it was the best place to keep it—right here on O'Neill's property. I knew no one would ever go after him."

O'Neill seemed to have gathered his wits during Turner's confession. He no longer seemed afraid. His voice was soft, menacing. "You're an idiot. Where's your attorney?"

Turner gave a bitter smile. "*You're* my attorney, remember?" He closed the safe and touched Pauline's shoulder. "This medicine bag has been in this room since the night your auntie died in 1974, and I want to make it right. I think it's time you took it home."

Chapter Thirty-Four

Sierra yawned, stretched, and threw her arm over her eyes to shield them from the golden rays of early morning sunlight streaming through the cabin window. When she moved one leg to feel for Hunter and realized his side of the bed was vacant, she propped herself up on one elbow and looked around the room.

"Hunter?"

Towel-drying his hair and wearing only a pair of faded blue jeans, he came out of the bathroom, his skin rosy and glistening from a steaming hot shower. He grinned and tossed his towel on the kitchen counter. "Get up, sleepyhead. We have a busy day ahead of us."

She groaned and snuggled back beneath the blankets. "I'm tired of busy days." She pouted. "Come back to bed. I want you."

He chuckled and pulled a deep crimson hoodie over his head. "Not fair. And not happening. We have orders from Melanie. Get dressed. It's cold outside."

"Since when do you do what a woman tells you?"

"Since it's Melanie. She scares me to death. Get up."

"Slave driver," Sierra muttered and crawled out of bed.

With a whoop, Hunter grabbed the curtains and jerked them shut. "Sweet Lord, lady, you're buck naked."

She ignored him and headed for the bathroom. "I told you to come back to bed. You didn't listen."

Later, as she stood half asleep beneath the strong stream of hot water, she didn't even try to battle the unfamiliar euphoria that very nearly overwhelmed her.

*It has to be a sin to be this happy.*

She'd moved her belongings out of the motor home and into Hunter's cabin only a week earlier, but they'd settled back into their easy relationship as if they'd never been apart. She wasn't naïve. This little vacation would end, and they would each go back to their own corner of the world, but in the meantime, she intended to relish every second they could spend together.

Nothing was permanent, especially joy as rich and intense as this.

*It's probably just as well, anyway.*

She stepped out of the shower and wrapped her slender body in a thick towel. If her father knew she and Hunter were together again, he would have a coronary, and she didn't want that. She removed her shower cap, shook her hair loose, and headed for the closet.

Once she dressed in what had practically become a uniform—her favorite black jeans, a turquoise turtleneck sweater, and a pair of black cowboy boots—she rapidly plaited her waist-length hair into a single braid that hung from the nape of her neck. Living as she was in a cabin out here in the South Dakota Badlands, she didn't need to do much more. Finished with the braid, she slathered on some moisturizer, applied a little lip gloss, and walked to the window.

She stood there for a moment, a small, bittersweet smile playing around her lips as she watched Hunter straighten up the inside of the Jeep. She was going home in just three days, he was flying back to Dallas, and that would be it.

She shrugged off the thought, planted a bright smile on her lips, and walked outside, locking the door behind her. Three days was a long time.

"Oh, good, there you are." Hunter waved from the back of the Jeep. "I've got bottled water and sodas in the ice chest back here and some snacks in a sack under your feet. Are you ready to go?"

She glanced down a long road that led from the cabin to her motor home campsite and frowned. Her tow vehicle was missing. "Did you see Colt or Skye leave this morning?"

"Nope." He walked around the Jeep, opened Sierra's door, and bowed from the waist. "Your chariot awaits, my lady. Climb in."

She curtseyed and scrambled into the Jeep, pushing the sack of snacks under the seat. "If you're supposed to be my knight in shining armor, this white steed of yours leaves a lot to be desired."

He clutched at his chest in feigned pain and staggered backward. She laughed out loud and watched him as he walked around the Jeep to the driver's side, admiring the way his hair shone like burnished gold in the morning sunlight.

*Lord, I'm going to miss him.*

He slid into the seat, started the engine, and backed away from the cabin. He glanced at her with a little frown. "You look like you've lost your best friend. What's going on?"

She gave him a quick smile. "I was thinking about Pauline. I wish I could've spent some time with her before she went back to Fort Collins."

He nodded. "I know, but Byron said she had a couple of important meetings with the museum this week and just couldn't stay. I'm sorry."

"It's all right. At least now I know where she lives. Have you heard anything about O'Neill and Turner?"

"Well, they're both in jail up in Rapid, but that's all I know. I'm sure O'Neill will get out before much more time passes. Turner...maybe not so much."

"Unfair," she muttered. "What about Valentina? Did Byron say anything about her?"

"Just that Gideon had put her in a really great hospital in Omaha, and she was already improving. My guess is he'll take her back to the Bison Head Ranch later and stay with her until she's well. It's her home."

"Is it safe for her there? I mean, if O'Neill gets out—"

"How about we not worry about that today, okay?"

"You're right. Where are we going?"

"Down to Wounded Knee."

"Of course, we are. Why?"

He turned south out of the campground and mumbled, "I have no idea."

"Is this another order of Melanie's?"

"Yep."

"Wow. You know she's barely five feet, right?"

"That's why I'm so scared of her. She reminds me of someone else I know."

"No, you're scared of her because Nathan is."

He chuckled as he rolled to a stop and turned onto the BIA highway that led toward Wounded Knee. He glanced at her. "Quit changing the subject. Why do you look so sad? It's a gorgeous day, and you're with me.

What more do you need?"

She stuck her tongue out at him. "I'm going to miss you. You've grown on me already...like a fungus."

"Really?"

Now she stared at him, dumbfounded. "Are you serious?"

He didn't answer but pulled over to the side of the road. He flipped on his hazards and turned in his seat, then reached for her hand and cradled it in his. "I've been thinking about something, and I want to talk to you about it."

Her heart skipped a beat, but she linked her fingers with his and tried to sound noncommittal. "Sure."

She couldn't look at him. She stared down at their clasped hands in desperation, praying she could take whatever he was going to dish out this time like the strong woman she believed she was. She had survived his leaving before, and she could survive it again.

He cleared his throat. "Okay, here goes. I was thinking you might want me to travel back to Texas with you in your motor home, instead of me flying home by myself. Also, the lease to my apartment in Dallas is up soon, and I was wondering about moving closer to you. Maybe Alpine. It's a good-sized little town, and they have an excellent university there, so I could find interns without any problem. The truth is I can work from anywhere."

Her fingers tightened on his, and her heart began to thud. "Alpine? That's only an hour or so from me."

He nodded.

"But what about your crew? Don't you usually work with the same people? Aren't they all in Dallas?"

He laughed and squeezed her hand. "You let me

worry about that. I just wanted to be sure it was all right with you. I didn't want to move…you know…if you didn't want me that close."

She didn't know what to say, how to act. All she could do was press his hand against her cheek.

He cleared his throat again. "I guess this means…you like my idea?"

She nodded.

"Good. Because I just thought…well, you know…if we're going to work on the documentary—"

She pulled herself together and gave him a wink. "Just stop. You want to be with me. Admit it."

He pulled his hand away. "You're right. I admit it. There's nothing in this world I want more."

"Me, neither," she whispered.

"I just wanted to be sure we were on the same page." Relief throbbed in his voice. "The last time, you made the decision for me, and I understand that. You might've even made the right decision. But I'm not the same man anymore, and you're not the same woman. I want us to take it slow—but I want us to take it as far as we can."

She gazed at him, committing to her memory his chiseled jawline and the deep cleft in his chin, his intense, thickly lashed, icy-blue eyes, and the gleaming, gold highlights in his hair. She touched his cheek. "I want that, too."

He took her face in his hands and kissed her. As his lips moved gently against hers, she didn't even try to fight her tears of joy. She just reveled in the moment and prayed it would last.

**\*\*\*\***

When Hunter pulled into the makeshift parking

area in front of the Wounded Knee cemetery, Sierra noticed a lone black Ford truck parked near the arched entrance and no sign of the occupants. He pulled in beside it and turned off the engine.

"Why are we here?" she asked.

He shook his head. "I have no idea."

"Melanie again?"

He nodded.

She smiled and unclasped her seat belt, opened the door, and stepped outside. Once more the reverent silence closed in around her, only to be broken by the chirping of unseen birds and the caressing murmurs of an autumn breeze. She stood still for a moment and gloried in the rich golden tones of tall prairie grasses carpeting the rolling hills stretching out far ahead of her, marveling once again that the violence that had occurred here so many years before could now be blanketed by such beauty and serenity.

To Sierra, Wounded Knee itself had a soul and a memory, as if it wanted nothing more than to embrace and heal all who came here.

She walked through the arched entrance into the old cemetery and stopped at the wind-bowed fence that enclosed the mass grave. She rested her hand on the gate and admired the prayer ties, feathers, and personal mementos attached to the chain links, blowing in the breeze. As strange as it sounded, she was really going to miss this place.

"Miss Masters?"

She stifled a shriek and whirled around to face an elderly man she'd never seen before. Standing beside him was Breeden Jones.

"Oh my God," she gasped. "You scared me to

death!"

Breed gave a slow grin and removed his cowboy hat. "I'm very sorry." He nodded toward his companion. "Miss Masters, I have someone here who'd like to meet you."

She turned her gaze to the older man and caught her breath. She knew him, she knew him well, yet she'd never seen him before, at least, not in person. He was dressed more like a well-to-do South Dakota rancher than a reservation Indian, yet he was clearly a full-blood Lakota Sioux. His salt-and-pepper hair, while still thick, was cut short, and his wide, dark eyes snapped with intelligence. His smile was shy, a little uncertain, but infectious. She smiled back.

"Miss Masters," Breed said quietly, "I'd like you to meet your grandfather, Arlin Black Thunder."

The world went silent. This was the man she'd wanted to meet almost as badly as she'd wanted to meet her birth mother, but now she couldn't think of one single coherent thing to say.

His eyes softened, and he took a step backward, as if he felt he was intruding on her space. She could read the deep sadness on his face and understood what it had cost him to come here. In his mind, he'd sacrificed his own daughter as well as her child on the altar of one White man's greed, even though he'd done it with the purest of intentions.

On impulse, she thrust out both her hands. When he took them in his, his touch was warm and comforting. She felt as if she'd come home, and she knew what he needed to hear.

"Grandfather, please don't feel bad," she said, praying he didn't doubt her sincerity. "You've done nothing wrong. You did what you thought was best for your child. My life has been good. I've been blessed. I'd be so happy if you could meet my parents so you'd know I'm telling you the truth."

His smile widened. "I'd like that."

"Really? You would?"

He released her hands. "It would make me very happy."

"Excuse me, Miss Masters," Breed interrupted politely. "I have something I'd like to tell you about your grandfather."

Arlin Black Thunder's dark eyes narrowed as he shot a warning glance in Breed's direction, but Breed seemed oblivious.

She felt the need to protect him. "Only if my grandfather would like for me to know it."

Breed nodded, but he continued, anyway. "I want you to know your grandfather was the man who originally tipped us off to O'Neill and Turner selling illegal artifacts over the internet about a year ago. We'd never have known about any of it if not for Arlin Black Thunder. Whatever mistakes he made in the past, he's more than paid for."

She was puzzled by the miserable expression on her grandfather's face. For whatever reason, this was a tidbit of information he didn't want anyone to know.

She moved closer to him. "Your secret is safe with me," she whispered.

He grimaced in embarrassment. "Thank you."

"Grandfather, can I tell you something?"

"Of course."

"I bought a painting of yours at a little place in Hot Springs. I saw it in a dream back in Texas."

"Hot Springs?" He frowned. "Oh, yes! I have a painting in the White Buffalo. It has been there quite a long time."

She touched his arm. "You *had* a painting. I have it now."

He met her eyes. "And you saw it in a dream?"

She nodded.

He didn't speak for a long moment, and he didn't remove his gaze from her face. She felt as if he was trying to decide whether or not to take her into his confidence, and all she could do was hope she passed the test.

"My Angel did that, too," he said at last, "and so did her mother, Madonna. I believe most of the women in the Kills Quick family have had that power."

"Pauline does as well."

"Excuse me," Breed interrupted with a grin, "but you can talk about your genetics later. We've all been invited to Red Tail Park where Nathan's giving one of his famous gatherings. I can smell the fry bread from here."

She cocked an eyebrow. "You're coming, too?"

Breed nodded, clearly pleased. "Nathan and I spoke for the first time in years just a few days ago, and we were able to clear the air between us. So today is a great day—even greater than you know."

"And why is that?"

"Aha!" He gave her a conspiratorial wink and spoke in silly Indian lingo. "That is not for me to tell you, my child. It is for you to find out."

She laughed out loud. "That sounds wonderful and very dramatic—especially the fry bread part—but there's something I need to do first."

343

"Of course," Breed said. "We'll see you there."

Sierra walked through the gate and down the hill toward the Wounded Knee Creek. She waved as Hunter backed the Jeep away from the old cemetery and followed her slowly, the black truck close behind him. She smiled.

*I have my own cavalry.*

She crossed the road and headed toward the cottonwood trees lining the rim of the deep ravine. Although she didn't want to encourage another vision based on memories, she couldn't help but recall the young priest who had appeared to her just a week earlier. She looked around to see if perhaps he had returned. Drawing closer to the line of trees, she continued scanning the area.

Like any history lover, she could easily visualize the ragged Indian camp and the Hotchkiss guns set up by the 7th Cavalry on that cold winter's day in 1890. She could even hear the horses and the drums and the singing in the faraway distance. But she couldn't *feel* it. She couldn't enter it. She couldn't be a part of it.

Perhaps they didn't need her anymore.

She stopped at the tree line and looked down into the ravine. Although several of her ancestors had been murdered here, and the rocks and dirt and buffalo grass had been stained with their blood for over one hundred years, the expansive landscape was peaceful and beautiful now as it flowed along in the natural continuity of life.

Even so, she felt empty.

*Why had it all happened?*

*What did it all mean?*

She didn't know the answers, at least not yet, but

she did feel that everything would soon become clear to her. In the meantime, she was grateful for the experience—and the new family that had come with it.

Chapter Thirty-Five

As Hunter and Sierra walked arm in arm toward the open-air pavilion crowded with people filling their paper plates from large, steaming containers set out on long tables, she remembered the first Winterhawk gathering they'd attended a little more than a week earlier. So much had happened in that brief period she didn't know what to think now.

"Here you are. Thank goodness. I was going to send out a search party."

Sierra laughed out loud as Skye swooped down on her and engulfed her in a rib-crushing bear hug. "Good grief, girlfriend! Let me go. I can't breathe."

Skye released her and stood back to appraise her friend. "You look wonderful," she announced. She winked at Hunter and hugged Sierra again. "I don't know what you've been doing, sweet pea, but it suits you."

The hot blood rushed to Sierra's cheeks, and she pulled away. She looked around the crowded park. "What on earth is going on?"

"A powwow, silly. No competitions today, though—just exhibition dancing."

"Is Nathan here?" Hunter asked, shading his eyes from the sun as he searched the crowd. "I need to talk to him."

"He's somewhere, with Melanie. This is his

shindig."

"Yes, but why?" Sierra persisted.

"I'm not sure, but they insisted we all come. So…here we are. No one ever argues with Melanie. Let's eat." Skye gave a mischievous grin. "Something tells me you haven't had much nourishment in the last seven days."

Even though she longed to crawl beneath a table and hide from her friend's dancing eyes, she managed to grab Hunter's hand and follow Skye into the pavilion. "Gosh, it smells like heaven in here. I didn't realize I was so hungry."

"There's a big pot of *wohanpi* on the table in that far corner," Skye said. "That's a traditional Lakota stew using bison and fresh vegetables—Melanie made it. Then there's a big pot of *wojapi*, a traditional berry soup. There's always Indian fry bread, Americanized with some powdered sugar if you want it. My poor White man's potato salad and cherry cobbler is on that table by the loudspeaker."

"When did you become such a traditional food expert?" Hunter asked.

She arched one eyebrow and grinned. "Well, I love to cook, and I've been helping Melanie and Cecilia Long Soldier all week. I'm an honorary Lakota now."

"Cecilia Long Soldier?" Sierra echoed. "She's here?"

"Well, not anymore. She had to go back up to Rapid to give Julia Farewell's diary to the FBI. I'm sorry you missed her. You would've liked her. Maybe another time."

"I thought Pauline said Julia gave the diary to her grandmother."

347

Skye nodded. "She did. But Grandma Madonna was more than happy to turn it over to Melanie."

A smiling elderly woman held up a ladle of steaming stew with a questioning expression on her heavily lined face, and Sierra nodded, holding out a deep soup dish for her to fill.

Her mouth watered. "Thank you. This looks wonderful."

The woman's smile widened, displaying three missing front teeth. "You're welcome. Would you like some *wojapi*?"

"Yes, please. And some fry bread. Oh Lord, that smells good. I don't know why I'm so hungry—it must be because it's chilly. Thank you very much."

"You're welcome, Miss Masters."

Sierra glanced at her in surprise, but the woman had turned away. She followed Skye and Hunter to a picnic table placed near what appeared to be a speaker's area at the edge of the pavilion, sat down, and began eating.

She was so engrossed in relishing the smooth, rich flavors of the bison meat and fresh vegetables in the *wohanpi* that Nathan's voice over a loudspeaker didn't even register until Hunter nudged her.

She looked at him, surprised. "What did he say?"

"He said for us to come to the tipi on the other side of the dance arena when we're finished eating. Do you know what that's about, Skye?"

Skye shook her head and took a big bite of fry bread. "No idea," she mumbled, mouth full, "but you go on. I'll catch up in a little while."

Sierra grinned. "Lord, you're a lousy liar, Sunshine." She finished off her meal and wiped her lips with a paper towel. "Hurry, Hunter. I want to see what's happening. I've never been invited to someone's tipi before."

**** 

Sierra and Hunter walked hand in hand toward a tall tipi nestled into a clump of trees, far beyond a round field—the dance arena, she presumed. Beneath a circular branch-covered arbor off to the side, several men sat around a massive drum, laughing and talking together. She admired the Indians dressed in beautiful regalia as they milled around the park, some lounging near a roped-off area containing a microphone and tall speakers while others posed for photographs and played with young children. The powwow would soon be in full swing.

*Those must have been the singers and drums I heard at the cemetery.*

For some reason, that realization comforted Sierra. But when she felt the musicians' collective gazes turn and follow her as she walked past them, her fingers tightened on Hunter's hand.

By the time they reached the tipi, Sierra's palms were cold and damp with perspiration. "You go check, okay?"

Nodding, Hunter released her hand and moved the tipi flap slightly. "Hello?"

"Come in."

Hunter held out his hand, and Sierra latched on to it once again, following him inside the cavernous tipi. After a moment, her eyes adjusted to the late afternoon shadows, and her mouth dropped in disbelief.

"Mama? Daddy? Good Lord, what're you doing here?"

Laughing, Mama scrambled to her feet and held out her hand to help up her husband, who arose with a little more caution. She gathered Sierra in her arms and held her for several silent minutes. Sierra clung to her mother with all her strength. These two people, birth parents or not, had always been the solid foundation of her world, and she'd never been so happy to see them both.

"How long have you been here?"

Daddy chuckled and glanced at Hunter. "A few days. We were told not to disturb you guys, which was fine with us. We've had a wonderful time with folks we haven't seen in years and did some sightseeing we never got to do before."

She punched her father's beefy arm. "Who told you not to disturb us, for crying out loud?"

"I did." Nathan's teasing voice came from the other side of the tipi. "Since your parents saw to it that Melanie and I were able to be together for a long weekend thirty years ago, I thought that was the least we could do to help you and Hunter out."

She closed her eyes. "Oh sweet Lord," she whispered, praying the ground would open and swallow her whole. "Nathan, I'm going to kill you…"

"Oh, come on now, little one." Nathan laughed, getting to his feet with a grunt. "Indians don't have the same inhibitions about these things as you White folks do. You've had a wonderful week, haven't you?"

She sighed and gazed at Hunter, a soft smile playing over her lips. "Yes, we have."

"All right, then. You're welcome."

Hunter dropped Sierra's hand. "I should leave you guys alone—"

Daddy spoke up. "No, wait. Don't go."

"Sir?"

He turned to Hunter with his hand outstretched. "Nathan told us what you've done for the people, and I want to thank you for that. My wife also hasn't stopped telling me what a horse's butt I've been, and I want to apologize for that, too. It's clear you've made our Sierra a very happy woman. So…welcome back. It's good to see you."

Hunter gripped Noah's hand, a faint flush staining his face. "Thank you, sir."

Sierra swallowed a huge lump in her throat and turned to her mother to try to conceal her emotion. "Have you eaten yet? They're serving a stew that's—"

"*Wohanpi*, I know. I've had some."

"Wait, ladies." Nathan's hand closed over Sierra's arm. "We can't go anywhere."

"Why not?"

At that moment the tipi flap moved, and Melanie stepped inside. "Because I have something for you." She turned and pushed the flap back farther. "Come in, Grandma."

An old woman stepped into the tipi, leaning on a thick tree branch doubling as a walking stick. She was so bent she resembled a corkscrew. Her shapeless gray dress couldn't hide her heavy breasts and a large hump on her back. Her long hair was white and plaited into two thin braids that hung over her shoulders and fell past her waist. But her face, while lined and leathered by years in the treacherous South Dakota sun, was still beautiful.

Grandma Madonna made her way to stand in front of Sierra. She was a good two inches shorter than Sierra because of her humped back, but she was alert, aware, and attentive to everything going on around her.

But that wasn't what caught Sierra's attention.

It was her eyes. They were slanted and a unique shade of light brown with topaz flecks, just like Sierra's own.

She didn't move. One thought, one refrain, ran through her mind.

*This is my great-grandmother...my great-grandmother...*

It was all too much for her. Tears filled her eyes, and she tried to keep them from falling down her cheeks, but she failed. Grandma Madonna touched a single tear with an arthritic finger and spoke in a quavering voice, in Lakota.

Sierra shrugged in confusion and looked at Melanie.

"She says she knew you were coming," Melanie explained. "You and Pauline. She says she's been waiting for you both."

"That's not possible."

Melanie grinned. "I told you. She has the power, too. I'm sure she saw you."

Grandma Madonna took Sierra's hand and gave a sweet smile. In a flash of lucidity, Sierra realized this old woman, if she'd played her rightful role in Sierra's life, would've raised her in the old ways. Her first language would've been Lakota, and she would've learned to cook traditional Lakota foods. Sun dances, sweat lodges, and medicinal herbs would've been second nature to her.

But that hadn't happened. Instead, she'd been given a privileged American upbringing like everyone else she knew. Hunter used to call her a princess, infuriating her at the time, but now she had to admit he was right. Life had been so easy for her—all because she'd been spirited off this reservation in the middle of the night thirty years ago.

Grandma Madonna released her hand and turned to Mama, dropping her walking stick and holding out her arms. She spoke in Lakota once again, and Mama moved into the old woman's embrace, tears streaming down her own cheeks. Daddy joined them and held them both in a sort of group hug. When Mama responded to Grandma Madonna, Sierra was amazed to hear her mother speak what sounded like fluent Lakota.

Sierra whispered to Melanie, "Doesn't my great-grandmother speak English?"

Melanie chuckled. "Of course, she does—very well. But she doesn't like it. She calls it 'the serpent's tongue.' "

Before Sierra could answer, she heard Gideon O'Neill shout from outside the tipi, his voice cracking with excitement, "Hey, you guys, come on! You've got to see this!"

Nathan muttered something about a lunatic under his breath and stalked to the entrance. "We're busy in here."

"I know, I know, but everyone…come on!"

Nathan turned to Sierra and shrugged. "I'm sorry, but we'd all better go. Gideon never gets excited about anything."

Hunter took her hand and led the way out of the tipi. Once outside, she stopped, stock-still and rooted to the ground, gaping in amazement.

The entire Oglala Lakota tribe seemed to be

surging away from the park and moving toward the rolling hills beyond like a multicolored tsunami. Some were on horseback, shrieking in a terrifying way that hurtled Sierra back to the days of the old westerns, while others in full regalia walked more sedately. Still others trotted along in their contemporary blue jeans and tribe-affiliated T-shirts.

Yet everyone in the crowd seemed to know where they were going.

"Sierra?"

The soft female voice broke through her astonishment, and a small hand gripped her arm. The woman's identity didn't register until Sierra recognized Julia Farewell's small, beaded medicine bag hanging around her neck.

"Pauline!"

Pauline gave a shy smile. "Hi."

Sierra drew her into a warm embrace and gave her a little extra squeeze. "How wonderful to see you. I thought you were in Fort Collins."

"I flew back here a couple of nights ago. Melanie said I had to come."

Sierra laughed out loud. "Melanie again. Hey, do you know where everyone's going?"

"No, but Gideon looks like he's going to bust a gut, so I guess we'd better tag along."

She put out her hand. "You might want to wait. There's someone in that tipi I'm sure you're going to want to see—"

A squeal of ecstatic disbelief erupted from Pauline before Sierra was even able to finish her sentence. She smiled and stood aside as Pauline rushed to the old woman who made her way through the tipi entrance. As she watched them embrace, both weeping with happiness, Sierra realized with deep gratitude how hard Melanie had worked to pull this off.

*No wonder Nathan loves her so much. No wonder everybody does.*

Grandma Madonna straightened as much as her humped back would allow, stepped away from Pauline, and held up her hand to halt two men walking toward them. Sierra looked over her shoulder and swallowed, hard. Her heart began to hammer in panic, but she turned around anyway and managed to plant what she hoped was a welcoming smile on her face.

*So much for our tiyospaye...*

Breeden Jones didn't seem to notice Sierra but removed his cowboy hat and walked toward Grandma Madonna. She noted that he didn't look at the elderly woman head-on, which would have been an insult to her status, but kept his eyes lowered, even when he began speaking. He handed a buckskin pouch to her.

"I have given you tobacco, Grandmother, although I know I am not deserving of your forgiveness. I know you can never forgive me for destroying Nathan's cousin's home in Wanblee so many years ago, but I still must ask. Please forgive me."

"It was not my family you hurt. You hurt my people."

Her voice was strong, unwavering, resolute. Sierra could *feel* the physical strength and power return to the old woman's bent and withered body, and had no doubt she was in the presence of great courage.

"I understand I hurt all the people, but Julia might not have been murdered if I hadn't worked with Dickie Wilson. Julia was *your* family."

Grandma Madonna lifted her chin in that stubborn gesture so familiar to Sierra. "It is not me you should apologize to. You should apologize to Nathan and Melanie."

Nathan stepped forward. "He has done this, Grandma."

"And you are pleased?"

"I am."

When she smiled, her topaz-flecked eyes nearly disappeared into a walnut-colored roadmap of wrinkles. "This is good."

Sierra spotted Arlin Black Thunder making his way toward them, twisting his cowboy hat in his hands, and her heart went out to him. This had to be the most difficult walk he'd ever taken. It wouldn't end well, but he had to take it.

*Please, Grandma, hear him out.*

When Arlin reached the old woman, he shoved the cowboy hat back on his head, took a small pouch of tobacco from his jacket pocket, and offered it to her. But she made no move to accept it. She glared at him, her body rigid with hatred.

Sierra closed her eyes. Grandma Madonna had every right to hate him. This was the man who had taken her precious granddaughter and handed her over to a dominant society the old woman despised with every fiber of her being. Nathan claimed Arlin Black Thunder had so crushed her spirit that day she sang her death song in her yard and never recovered. This same child had been raped by a powerful White man who was given easy access to her by a cruel and insensitive church that saw her as less than human.

All this had happened because of Arlin Black

Thunder's unfortunate decision to hand his child over and walk away.

If that was true, how could Grandma Madonna forgive him now?

Then, like all the pieces of a puzzle falling into place, the answers came to her. She caught her breath. Grandma Madonna was a traditional Lakota Indian, and she valued the Old Ones. Did she know about Arlin Black Thunder's family? She had a gift, but had the Old Ones ever visited her the way they'd visited Sierra? Could she even begin to understand how Arlin had reached his fateful decisions?

Sierra tried to contain her excitement. The more she thought about it, the more certain she was that she was right.

*This has to be why I was shown the past in this way...so I could try to help heal this family...my tiyospaye.*

Arlin Black Thunder sagged as if the wind had just been kicked out of him. He put the pouch of tobacco back into his jacket pocket, removed his hat again, and bowed his head. He stood so still in front of the old woman, so penitent, Sierra was positive Grandma Madonna could do whatever she wanted with him and he wouldn't object. He just waited for her to make the next move.

"Why are you here?" the old woman spat finally. "You do not belong here."

Arlin lifted his head. "You hate me. I understand. I *deserve* that. But you're wrong. I do belong here."

Sierra had to act now. She moved closer to Grandma Madonna and touched her arm. She opened her mouth to speak, but no words came out. She cleared her throat and tried again. "Grandma, you said you saw me and Pauline in a vision and knew we were coming. Is that right?"

She smiled, covered Sierra's hand with her own, and nodded.

"Do you know why that might've happened?"

She frowned. "It was time."

"Yes, Grandma, it was. But maybe it was more than that."

"How?"

Sierra took a deep breath and prayed for words. "I'm not sure, Grandma, but I do know my Black Thunder ancestors came to me at Wounded Knee. I saw everything that happened to them. I saw them running from the soldiers, Grandma, and I saw them die. And before that, I saw them in a funeral procession that some say carried Crazy Horse to his final resting place near Wounded Knee Creek. This man you hate so much, who hurt you, is from strong blood—and all he wanted was to do right by his daughter. He did what his father had done. He never, ever meant to hurt her, Grandma. He never meant to hurt your people. You must know that. I believe the Old Ones *need* you to know that."

Grandma Madonna didn't respond, but Pauline moved closer to Arlin Black Thunder. When she spoke, her voice was little more than a whisper. "Wait... Are you my father?"

He bowed his head.

Pauline took Arlin Black Thunder's face in her hands. The silence was heavy and thick, but no one broke it.

Finally, she nodded. "Yes," she whispered. "I see it

now. I think I remember you."

Arlin took her hands in his with urgent intensity. "I need you to know how sorry I am that I ever left you at that school, Pauline. Your mother died when you were born, and I should have let you stay with your grandmother, but I thought I was doing the best thing for you. I did what my father did—"

Pauline put her finger against his lips. "I understand. My intention was always to return to this reservation when it was safe for me, and I'm going to do that now. I can help here. I *want* to help here. Perhaps Grandma blames you and is angry with you, but I'm not. You're my father. I've been without my family for far too long."

The old woman's face darkened, but she said nothing. She turned and walked away from the tipi, leaning heavily on her walking stick as she followed the crowd. Melanie flashed a startled look at Sierra, then rushed to stop the old woman. Catching up with her, Melanie put a soothing arm around her shoulders and whispered something in her ear. After a few minutes of conversation, Grandma Madonna shrugged away from Melanie's arm and made her way back to the group. She stood in front of Arlin Black Thunder and stared up at him without a word.

After a while, she seemed to come to a decision and began to speak. "Melanie tells me you were the person who reported the artifacts being sold, and that is a good thing. They have found many items that should be returned to our people, and you did that for us. I think Pauline is right. Our *tiyospaye* will come back together. I welcome you. This is all I will say about that."

As Pauline took the old woman in her arms once again, Hunter tugged on Sierra's hand.

"Come with me."

Hunter strode toward a slight hill, fixated on something beyond that gentle incline. Once they'd reached the top, Sierra looked out over acres of tall green and gold grasses waving across the prairie. Family units of bison grazed on the grassland, just as they had two hundred years earlier.

Moving to the front of the large crowd, Hunter pointed toward a clump of pine trees, where a mama bison and her baby hovered in its protection. The people were hushed and respectful as they stood watching. Even the riders on horseback were silent. Sierra caught her breath and tightened her fingers on Hunter's hand.

The baby buffalo was white.

Chapter Thirty-Six

"Nathan called me about her birth a few days ago," Hunter said, taking a small camera from his jacket pocket. "He said she was born about the same time that Pauline returned to Rapid City. They've named her Spirit Heart. She will be the core of Nathan's Buffalo Spirit Ranch."

Sierra couldn't speak.

Hunter took a picture of the two bison and turned back to her. "It's rare for a baby buffalo to be born white, but it happens. The key is to see how long she stays white. But whether she stays white or not, this baby buffalo will be seen as a sign of hope, unity, and prosperity to the Lakota of Pine Ridge. Nathan believes you brought this promise."

"Me?"

"Yes. Nathan wants us to return in about six months. Will you come with me?"

"Of course. But why in six months?"

He put the camera back into his pocket and took her hand once more. "Gideon thinks the Indian baby's bones will be released to the tribe by then, and there will be a freeing-of-the-spirit ceremony when they receive them. The Ghost Shirt will also be turned over to the Heritage Center at the Red Cloud Indian School on Pine Ridge around that time. Nathan wants us to come." He paused and motioned at the magnificent sunset bathing the prairie in an otherworldly golden light. "By the way, did this place help you with your writer's block like I promised you it would?"

She looked up at him in amazement. "I haven't even thought about that."

"Are you serious?"

She squeezed his hand. "It must be the company I'm keeping these days. But I promise you it'll pass."

He looked down at her and chuckled. "I'm sure it will."

Then, from the Red Tail Park dance arena, came the rhythmic thudding of the drum; the trilling, high-pitched singing began just a few beats after. Sierra's heart gave a slight leap in response.

*The heartbeat of a nation.*

"We should probably go back," he said.

As she followed him down the hill, she heard Nathan's voice over a microphone encouraging everyone to come to the dance arena.

He stopped in front of the tipi. "I think I hear your dad in there."

"Don't you want to go in?" She winked. "You aren't still afraid of him, are you?"

He grinned. "I've never been afraid of him. He just wanted to take care of you. If I ever have a daughter, I want to be a father exactly like him. You go on in. I'm going to be sure Nathan doesn't need anything."

She lifted the tipi flap, stepped inside, and took a moment to allow her eyes to adjust to the gathering evening shadows within. "Hi, everyone. May I join you?"

Turning around from the far side of the tipi and holding a lit lantern aloft, Daddy motioned toward the small group—Mama, Arlin Black Thunder, Grandma Madonna, and Pauline—sitting on the earth around stacked pieces of charred wood and the ashes of a cold campfire.

Mama patted the ground next to her. "You're just the person we need," she said as Sierra sat down beside her.

"How can I help?"

"I'm trying to talk your grandfather into letting Skye and me take a few of his paintings back to Texas. Skye knows a lot of art gallery owners, and I'm sure someone would love to show his work, either in the Bandera area where I live or in the Big Bend region you call home. But I don't think he wants to sell anything."

Sierra nodded and leaned toward her grandfather, who sat across from her. "Grandpa, is there a reason you don't want others to see your paintings?"

He shook his head. "Not that you would understand."

"I might surprise you."

He smiled. "You're right. Here it is, then. I've had many opportunities to make a great deal of money with my paintings, but my work is all I have left that the White world hasn't infected. I've sold out every other part of my life. My paintings are the stories of my ancestors, so I keep them to myself. I've only sold one or two of them."

Before she could respond, Grandma Madonna pointed a gnarled finger at him and spoke as if he were a young, not-too-intelligent child. "The Creator gives us all a gift, my friend, and we must share it with the rest of the world—White and Indian alike. If you don't want to make money with your gift, that's your choice, and it's an honorable one. But that doesn't mean you can't show your work and perhaps tell your stories. Your own granddaughter is a writer in the White world. Surely the two of you can think of some way you could both use your gifts—your art, her words."

Daddy grunted as he eased his long and muscular frame into a space between his wife and Pauline. He placed a lantern in the center of the circle. "I think I have a solution. Tell me what you think about this."

Sierra could feel the group's respect as they waited for him to continue. Even though he was a White man, her father had walked the talk back in the day of the Wounded Knee Occupation. The Lakota people would never forget that.

"Mr. Black Thunder, why don't you let Sierra take a painting or two down to her place in Texas? She knows many people, and so do Hunter and Skye. As Grandma says, you don't have to sell your work for it to have an impact. And you know Sierra will protect whatever you give her."

Arlin Black Thunder's face was solemn as he sat still for several minutes, saying nothing. Sierra guessed he was trying to determine whether or not these White people were trustworthy.

"I will give you two of my favorite paintings," he told her finally, "but not to sell. I'd like for you to find a place to exhibit them. We can see what happens after that if you like."

"Well, there's a wonderful college in Alpine I believe would love to have them, Grandpa. It's about an hour or so away from me, and I know several people there, so that's where I'll take them first."

Daddy's enthusiasm was contagious. "Excellent.

And in just a few months, the Triple M Ranch—our working dude ranch—starts a new season. Lexy and I would love it if all of you would come down to Texas and spend a little time with us. We've already invited Nathan and Melanie, and they're planning to come."

Sierra gave a little bounce of excitement and smiled at Pauline. "What a wonderful idea. After that you could all come out to Big Bend country and stay with me. What do you think?"

Pauline took Grandma Madonna's hand. "We'd love that, wouldn't we, Grandma?"

"Well, then it's settled," Daddy said with an air of finality. He got to his feet and held his hand down to his wife. "Come on, my love. Nathan's giving the final call before the dancing begins."

\*\*\*\*

As Sierra stood beside the dance arena, watching the final crimson and pink fingers of a magnificent sunset, a gentle hand rested on her shoulder. Startled, she whirled around to see Byron Little Hand. He wore fringed leggings, a loincloth made of tanned deer hide, and beaded, knee-high moccasins. A horn-and-bone breastplate covered his chest and belly. His long silver hair hung straight and loose to his waist, and he carried a tall staff decorated with eagle feathers and animal fur. With his immense height and still-muscular body, he made a formidable figure. Eli Winterhawk stood beside him, dressed in the same regalia, the only difference being a hawk feather hanging from a beaded headband holding back his glossy black hair.

She tried to ask her question without sounding too ignorant. "What are you performing?"

"The Lakota war dance," Eli answered with a grin.

She smiled back. "Oh. Of course you are. I knew that."

"Where have you been?" Byron asked. "We've been looking all over for you."

"Hunter took me up to see the little white buffalo, and then I visited with my family for a while."

Byron smiled. "I like the sound of that. You were visiting with your family."

Sierra touched his hand impulsively. "Oh, I'm so sorry, Mr. Little Hand. I haven't thanked you for all you've done for us—and I appreciate it more than I can tell you."

Before he could respond, several tall floodlights came on, illuminating the dance arena as if it were still mid-afternoon. Byron gave her a small salute and a wink. "It was my pleasure, Miss Sierra. We could never have done it without you. Now if you'll excuse us, we have to join the other dancers."

She smiled and nodded. "Of course. Have fun."

As they walked away, she looked around for Hunter and spotted him standing beside the circle of drummers. She walked quickly toward them, pulling her jacket closer to her body. Somehow it had grown much colder without her realizing it. When she reached the drummers, she couldn't help but grin. Nathan was seated with them, drumming and singing with gusto. Standing behind him was Breeden Jones, looking like the proverbial fish out of water.

"Every time I see Nathan sing and drum like that, I feel like I've been thrown back a couple of hundred years," Melanie said into Sierra's ear, her throaty voice warm with affection. "It's the only time he ever seems truly at peace with himself."

"I know. He fights hard, doesn't he?"

"He does. It's his mission." She put her arm around Sierra's shoulders. "I wanted to thank you for what you want to do for the people. Hunter told us about your ideas the other day, and I can't even begin to tell you how grateful we are."

Sierra looked away, uncomfortable with Melanie's gratitude. "You're welcome, but please don't tell anyone. I want it to be secret. We'll talk about it more when you come down to visit, okay? In fact, that'll be a perfect time to get everything set up."

"That sounds great. Oh, look, here comes Pauline and Grandma." Melanie waved at the two women as they made their way carefully toward the drum circle. "Don't they look wonderful together?"

As Sierra rested her gaze on them, she was nearly overwhelmed with a warm sense of satisfaction. Her great-grandmother, bent and aged as she was, held tightly to her walking stick while Pauline, looking little older than a well-groomed college student, kept a firm hand on the elderly woman's elbow. Behind them both walked Gideon O'Neill, his gaze glued to Pauline. The look of tenderness on his face told Sierra where his heart lay.

"Do you see what I see?" Melanie asked softly.

She grinned. "I do."

"Well…and why not? She's only a few years older than he is."

"I think they look great together. I just hope she can forget who his father is."

Melanie shrugged. "It may be harder for Gideon to forget than her. But you're his half sister. You can help him. We'll just have to see what happens, won't we?"

"Hello, ladies," Gideon called as he approached with his two companions. "Can we get Grandma a chair?"

"Come on," Melanie answered. "We have a place of honor set up for all of you."

As Sierra followed the group toward the small arbor set slightly apart from the drum circle and the dance arena, all sound ceased. She halted and took in what appeared to be a painting in which everyone had stopped, holding their dance positions—even the drummers, whose arms were poised in the air, immobile. In the center of the arena stood a single figure—a young woman, tall and erect, bathed in a circle of golden light.

Pauline's voice in Sierra's ear was soft and shaky. "Do you see her?"

She nodded, speechless.

"She came—" Pauline whispered.

"Who? Who is she?"

"She's Julia Farewell. My auntie. She came…"

As soon as the words left Pauline's lips, the figure disappeared. The drumming began again. The dancing resumed.

Pauline turned and gripped Sierra's shoulders. "She's telling us we're all together again, our *tiyospaye*, and she's pleased. All I've ever wished for has happened. They took everything from me, but they could never take you. This is the day I've lived for."

Sierra pulled her mother into her arms and held her close, breathing in the fragrance of her freshly washed hair. Finally, releasing her, she noticed Hunter nearby, taking a photograph of this very special moment.

*Six photographs had started all this.*

Life had come full circle—just as it should. After all, it was the Lakota way.

Afterward

When my husband and I first took our motor home to that magical place called South Dakota in the autumn of 2000, we visited like the typical tourists we were— non-Indian products of the United States public school system.

For instance, we were unaware that the Battle of Wounded Knee, which occurred on December 29, 1890, was primarily the slaughter of women, children, and the elderly by a detachment of the US 7th Cavalry Regiment and is actually called the *Massacre* of Wounded Knee by American Indians. We didn't realize that the sacred Black Hills belonged to the Sioux Indians by virtue of the Fort Laramie Treaty of 1851 and 1868 and that, as such, many Indians believe the heads of our beloved presidents should never have been carved into Mount Rushmore. While we barely remembered televised news flashes covering the Occupation of Wounded Knee by members of the American Indian Movement (AIM) in 1973, we learned it was a highly significant event to the Indians for a variety of reasons.

While we were in South Dakota, I discovered for myself why some people call this state (as Hunter Davenport did) a "thin place." Although I'm no visionary, as I stood beside Wounded Knee Creek where the actual massacre occurred, it was all I could do to breathe because the air was so thick with smoke and the acrid odor of gunpowder. Since then, many people have shared with me their own experiences at Wounded Knee Creek, so I know I'm not alone. This event was so eerie and disturbing to me that my initial idea for the plot of *Whispers Through Time* came from it. Many more similar events were to follow as we roamed around the mystical countryside of South Dakota.

However, reality was when we witnessed an irate Indian woman shouting at a group of respectful White students and chasing them away from the cemetery at Wounded Knee. Shaken, we later learned from an Indian tour guide the many reasons the woman felt so passionately that Whites had no right to step foot on that hallowed ground.

We spent several days on the Pine Ridge Indian Reservation and discovered the impoverished area is indeed a third world country right in our own backyard. We also learned American history from the perspective of Whites and Indians is diametrically opposed, and there is little room for compromise. However, I chose not to dwell on that aspect of reservation life in *Whispers Through Time* simply because I feel there is so much more to these people than their poverty and social ills, which are well documented. I found them to be generous of spirit, open, and tolerant, a people who love to laugh and be together. I wanted the characters of Nathan Winterhawk and Byron Little Hand to personify how in Lakota culture the elders are all about family— and they are fighting desperately to pass that down to the next generations. I pray they are successful.

The characters of Nathan and Melanie Winterhawk

are loosely based on aging AIM members and young entrepreneurs who now reside on or near the Pine Ridge Indian Reservation. While one such individual, now a highly respected elder, understands business in the twenty-first century, he is also a fervent believer in the Old Ways and their importance to the strength and health of his people. There's a great deal of information about this movement online and in print.

We learned much of the history behind the American Indian Movement from the AIM Museum (which had just opened and wasn't complete in 2000) near the Wounded Knee cemetery on the Pine Ridge Indian Reservation. The character of Eli Winterhawk, that handsome, long-haired, outspoken Indian activist, is loosely based on several AIM leaders of the 1960s. If you're interested in discovering more about that very important organization, there are several excellent websites you can visit to get you started.

The Reign of Terror on the Pine Ridge Indian Reservation did indeed take place between February 27, 1973, when the Occupation of Wounded Knee by AIM and AIM sympathizers began, and continued through May 1, 1976. The progressive tribal president Richard (Dickie) Wilson and his squad of GOONs (Guardians of the Oglala Nation) ruled the reservation with an iron fist even before the occupation, but their brutality against Traditional Indians afterward was breathtaking. During this time more than sixty AIM members and supporters died violently on the reservation or in areas immediately adjacent to it. At least 342 others were injured in violent physical assaults. (The United States Department of Justice finally opened an investigation into the Reign of Terror in 2012, but the results are still pending.)

In my research to create Pauline Kills Quick's backstory, I discovered and verified that the US government (through funding the Indian Health Service and the Bureau of Indian Affairs) did indeed participate for a limited time in the forced sterilization of American Indian women, some in South Dakota. This policy was exposed by AIM members in 1972 when they discovered pertinent documentation during their week-long occupation of the Washington headquarters of the Bureau of Indian Affairs (BIA). A great deal of information about this horrific policy can be found online.

Also, over many years, young Indian women have been violated by powerful White men without repercussion, and the character of Logan O'Neill is based on one such political giant. In addition, many Indian children were removed from reservations around the country and given to White families. Sierra Masters' discovery she was one of these children isn't novel, and the fact her adoptive parents were liberal White activists involved at the Occupation of Wounded Knee wouldn't be, either. In fact, as I write this, American Indians across the US and Canada are making similar discoveries and returning to their reservations, hoping to find their families.

If you're interested in the individuals who developed the American Indian Movement, you might enjoy reading the angry but fascinating *Where White Men Fear To Tread*, by Russell Means (who died in 2013), *My Life is My Sun Dance*, by Leonard Peltier (who remains in prison for his alleged shooting of two FBI agents on the Pine Ridge Indian Reservation in

1975), and *Like a Hurricane: The Indian Movement from Alcatraz to Wounded Knee*, by Paul Chaat Smith and Robert Allen Warrior.

Although the Native American Graves Protection and Repatriation Act (NAGPRA) was signed into law on November 16, 1990 by President George H. W. Bush—ten years before our visit—we knew nothing about it until we arrived in the Badlands of South Dakota and discovered it wasn't unusual for people to dig for fossils or artifacts on or near ground the Indians considered sacred. We also found that even after NAGPRA was passed, many people still feel they should be able to keep, sell, or trade Indian artifacts they find anywhere—in their own backyards, in deserted villages, or in known Indian burial grounds. The term "Finders Keepers" took on a whole new meaning for me.

The painful truth about the church-run Indian boarding schools has come to light in the last several years, especially in terms of how forced assimilation into White society so devastated the American Indians—which is why I chose that issue for the Black Thunder leg of Sierra's family. One of the finest documentaries I've seen on that subject is entitled *A Good Day to Die* (2010), narrated by AIM leader Dennis Banks as he eloquently shares his own experiences. If you prefer your historical drama about Indian boarding schools with a paranormal twist, check out Georgina Lightning's terrific movie *Older than America.*

Hollywood can take a great deal of the blame for the way we have seen American Indians in the past, but a few excellent films have appeared in the last couple of decades, beginning, of course, with the now-classic *Dances with Wolves*. If you're interested in furthering your knowledge of American Indian history from the perspective of American Indians, check out the films *Thunderheart, Smoke Signals, Powwow Highway, Dreamkeeper, Imprint, Skins*, and the documentary *Reel Injun*. *Bury My Heart at Wounded Knee* (based on the classic book of the same title by Dee Brown) and *Into the West* are also ambitious television mini-series that attempt to show the American Indian in a more truthful light. Most of these movies were written, acted in, and directed by indigenous people.

The aforementioned *Bury My Heart at Wounded Knee* chronicles very well, in part, how the Dawes Act of 1887 carved up and stole Indian land so that even now families have no idea how much land they have, where it's located, or how much it's worth. With the theft of this land, *tiyospayes* were shattered and family members forced to live many miles apart—the ramifications of which are still being felt today. Nathan Winterhawk's battle to locate and consolidate all his family's allotted land isn't unique.

If you'd like more information about the many legends surrounding the burial location of Chief Crazy Horse (one of which is depicted when Sierra "sees" a funeral procession carrying his body into the trees near Wounded Knee Creek), I suggest you begin by reading a fascinating book on the subject, *To Kill An Eagle: Indian Views on the Last Days of Crazy Horse*. The American Indians never wrote their history down, so this book is an oral compilation of stories told (and notarized) by those who knew him.

In closing, I'd like to stress that I'm only a writer

with a story I wanted to tell, one I hope you enjoy. It's not my place to interpret the way Indians see the world, and I would never presume to try to describe their traditions, culture, or spiritual practices except from the vantage point of a confused and disoriented major character like Sierra Masters. While much of this story is based in history and on my own experience, all the characters are the products of my imagination.

### A word about the author...

Rosetta Diane Hoessli has been a freelance writer since 1985, publishing articles in McCall's, Christian Herald, and many other smaller forums. A winner of national and state-wide writing contests, she has served as senior feature writer, columnist, and executive editor for three (3) regional publications—two in San Antonio and one in Houston, Texas.

Ms. Hoessli also collaborated with New York socialite Jeanette Longoria in Longoria's self-published book entitled *Aphrodite and Me: Discovering Sensuality and Romance at Any Age*, co-authored biographical novel *Falling Through Ice* with Carolyn Huebner Rankin, and edited a book of short stories, *Working on the Wild Side*, compiled by Florida Fish and Wildlife officer Jeff Gager.

Today Ms. Hoessli focuses most of her attention on writing historical fiction and traveling with her husband, Kevin, in their RV to discover new plotlines, locations, and characters. They reside in San Antonio, Texas, with their two fur-kids, near their daughter and two grandchildren.

*Whispers Through Time* is Ms. Hoessli's first novel.

~\*~

Find Ms. Hoessli online at:
http://facebook.com/RosettaDianeAuthor

* 9 7 8 1 5 0 9 2 3 8 1 5 6 *